THE BACKUPS

[Imprint]
MAKE YOUR MARK

A part of Macmillan Publishing Group, LLC

120 Broadway, New York, NY 10271

Library of Congress Cataloging-in-Publication Data is available.

Our books may be purchased in bulk for promotional, educational,
or business use. Please contact your local bookseller
or the Macmillan Corporate and Premium Sales Department
at (800) 221-7945 ext. 5442 or by email at
MacmillanSpecialMarkets@macmillan.com.

Inking by Ted Brandt

Coloring by Dee Cunniffe

Paper doll artwork by Ashe Samuels

Imprint logo designed by Amanda Spielman

First edition, 2021

Paperback ISBN 978-1-250-21259-7
10 9 8 7 6 5 4 3 2 1

Hardcover ISBN 978-1-250-15394-4
10 9 8 7 6 5 4 3 2 1

fiercereads.com

Why would you steal
what you can borrow for free
from the magical shelves
of your neighborhood library?

THIS BOOK IS FOR EVERYONE
WHO HAS A DREAM.
—ADC

FOR MY MOTHER,
WITHOUT WHOSE SUPPORT I WOULDN'T BE DOING THIS.
AND FOR RO, WITHOUT WHOM I'D BE LOST.
—TB

FOR MY BACKUPS—
CIARA, CONOR, TARA, AND FIONN
—DC

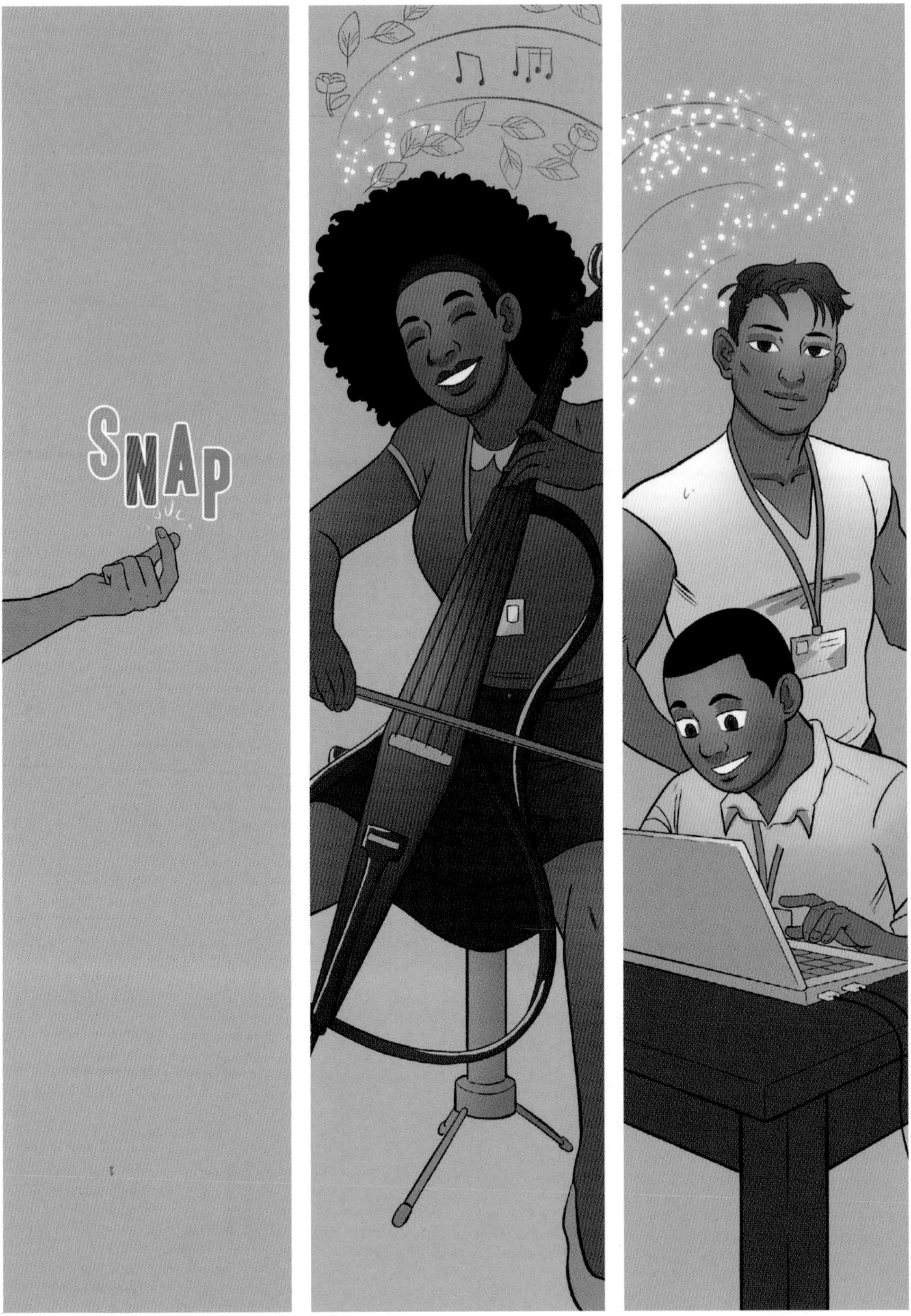
SNAP

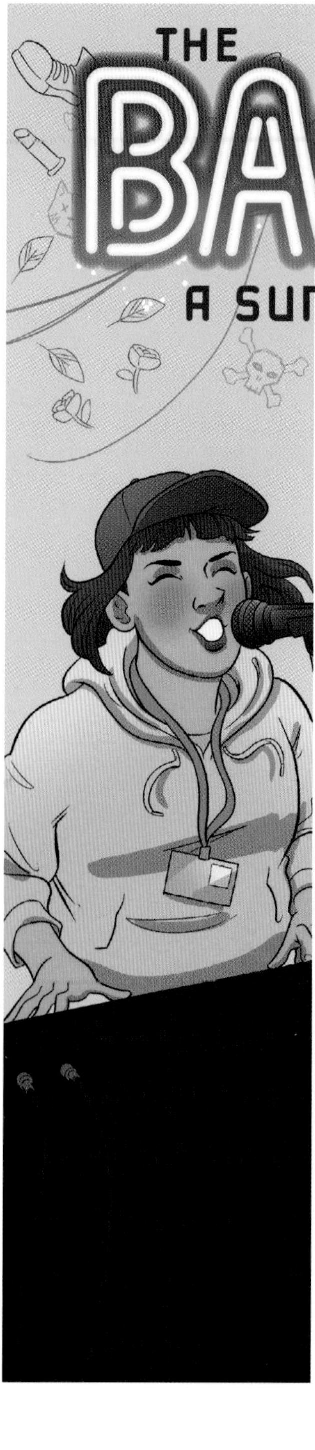

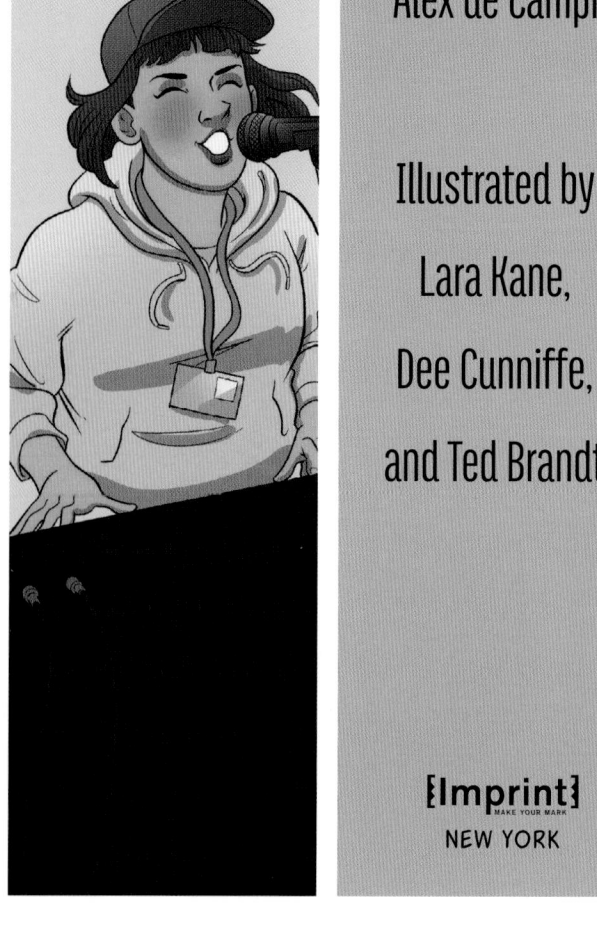

THE BACKUPS

A SUMMER OF STARDOM

Alex de Campi

Illustrated by
Lara Kane,
Dee Cunniffe,
and Ted Brandt

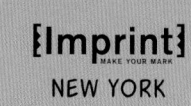

[Imprint] MAKE YOUR MARK
NEW YORK

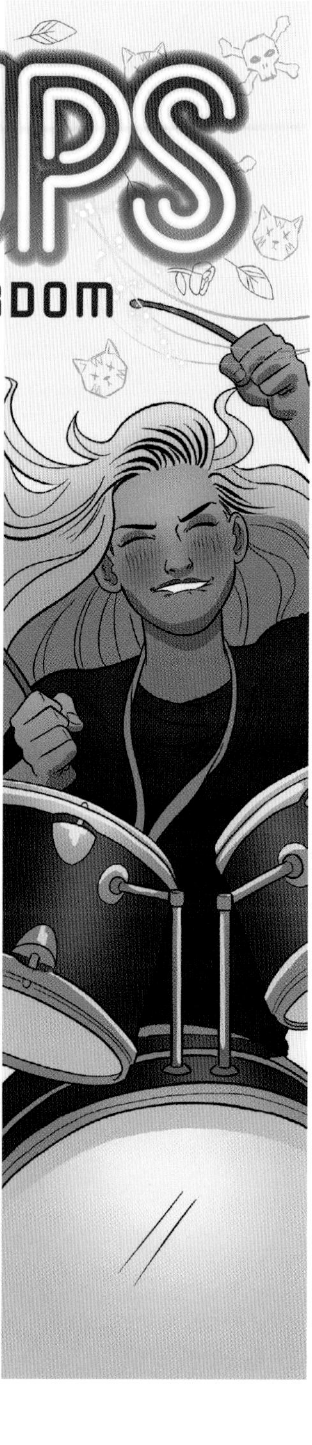

PROLOGUE

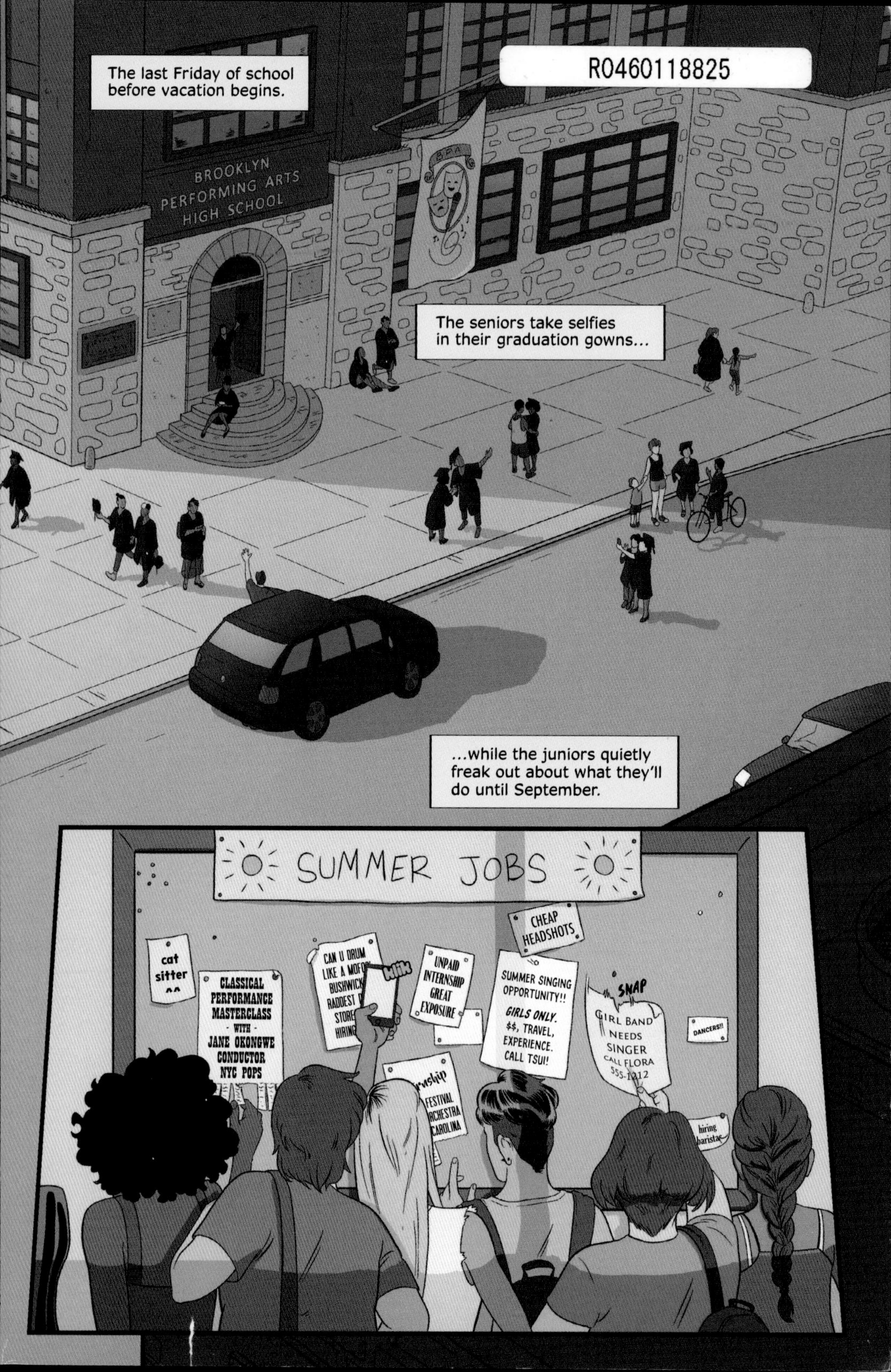
The last Friday of school before vacation begins.
BROOKLYN PERFORMING ARTS HIGH SCHOOL
BPA
The seniors take selfies in their graduation gowns...
...while the juniors quietly freak out about what they'll do until September.
SUMMER JOBS
CHEAP HEADSHOTS
cat sitter ^^
CLASSICAL PERFORMANCE MASTERCLASS - WITH - JANE OKONGWE CONDUCTOR NYC POPS
CAN U DRUM LIKE A MOFO
klik
UNPAID INTERNSHIP GREAT EXPOSURE
SUMMER SINGING OPPORTUNITY!! GIRLS ONLY. $$, TRAVEL, EXPERIENCE. CALL TSUI!
SNAP
GIRL BAND NEEDS SINGER CALL FLORA 555-1212
DANCERS!!
FESTIVAL ORCHESTRA CAROLINA
hiring baristas

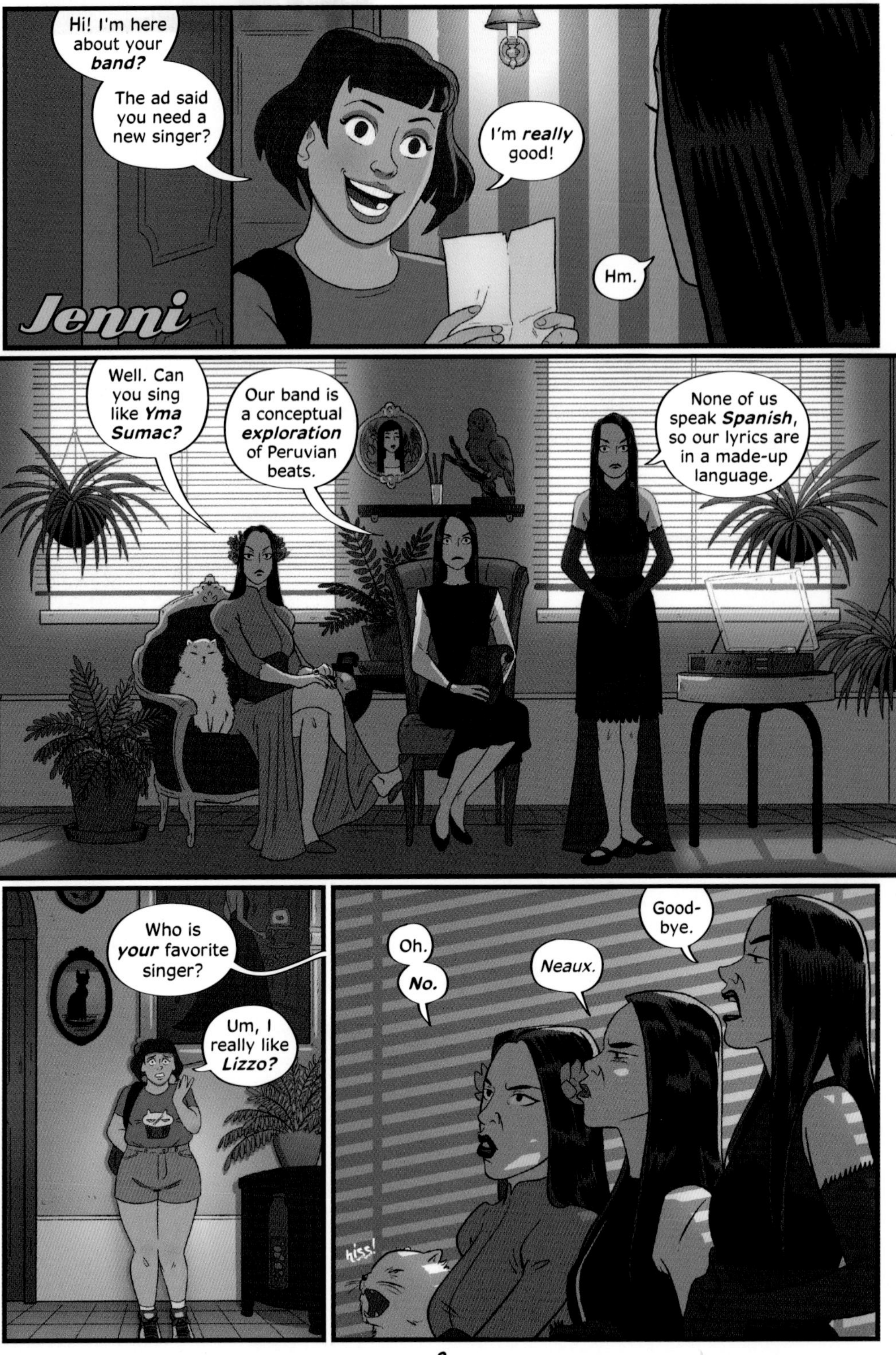
Hi! I'm here about your *band?*
The ad said you need a new singer?
I'm *really* good!
Hm.
Jenni
Well. Can you sing like *Yma Sumac?*
Our band is a conceptual *exploration* of Peruvian beats.
None of us speak *Spanish*, so our lyrics are in a made-up language.
Who is *your* favorite singer?
Um, I really like *Lizzo?*
Oh.
No.
Neaux.
Good-bye.
hiss!

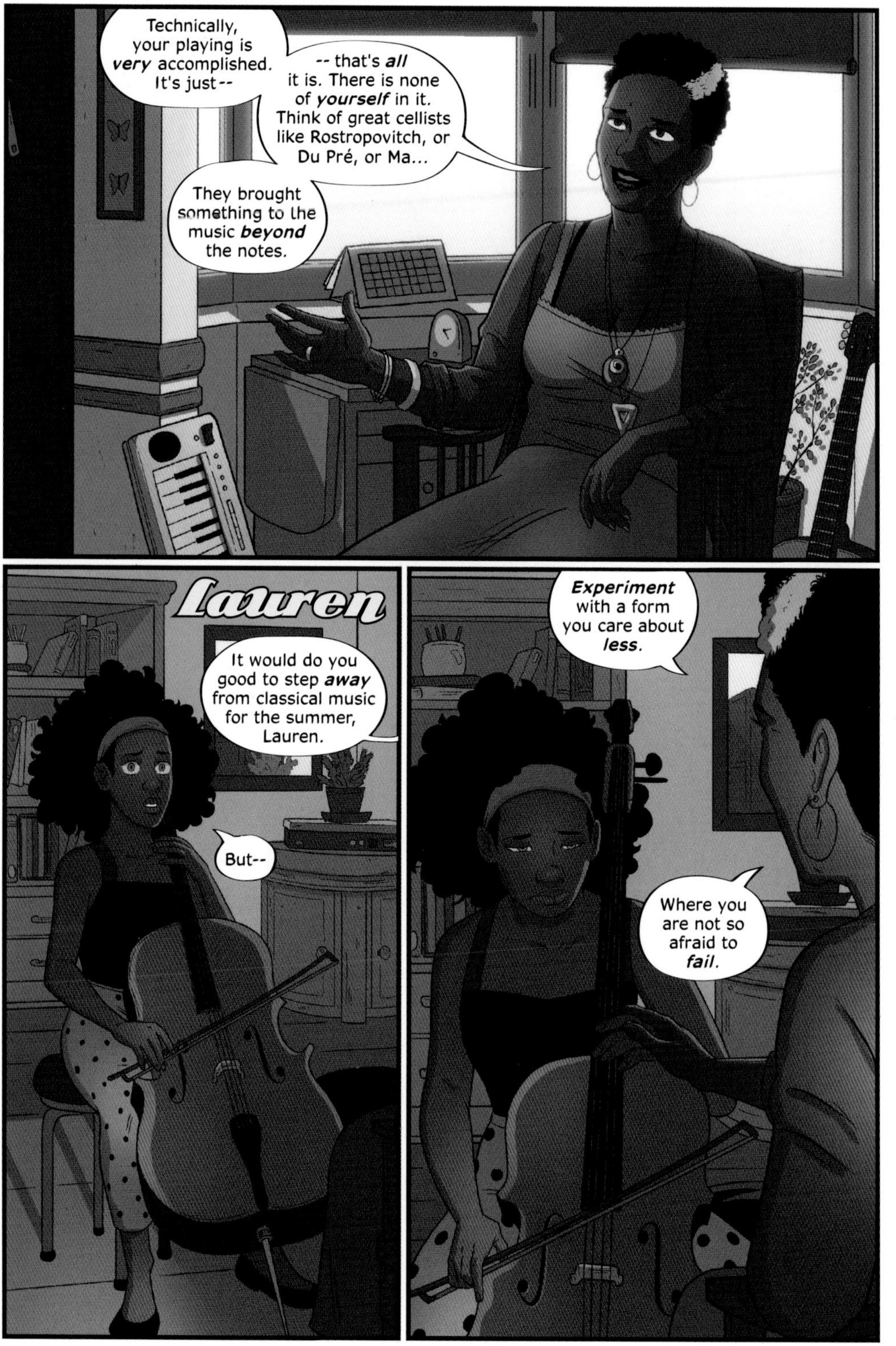
Technically, your playing is *very* accomplished. It's just--
-- that's *all* it is. There is none of *yourself* in it. Think of great cellists like Rostropovitch, or Du Pré, or Ma...
They brought something to the music *beyond* the notes.
Lauren
It would do you good to step *away* from classical music for the summer, Lauren.
But--
Experiment with a form you care about *less*.
Where you are not so afraid to *fail*.

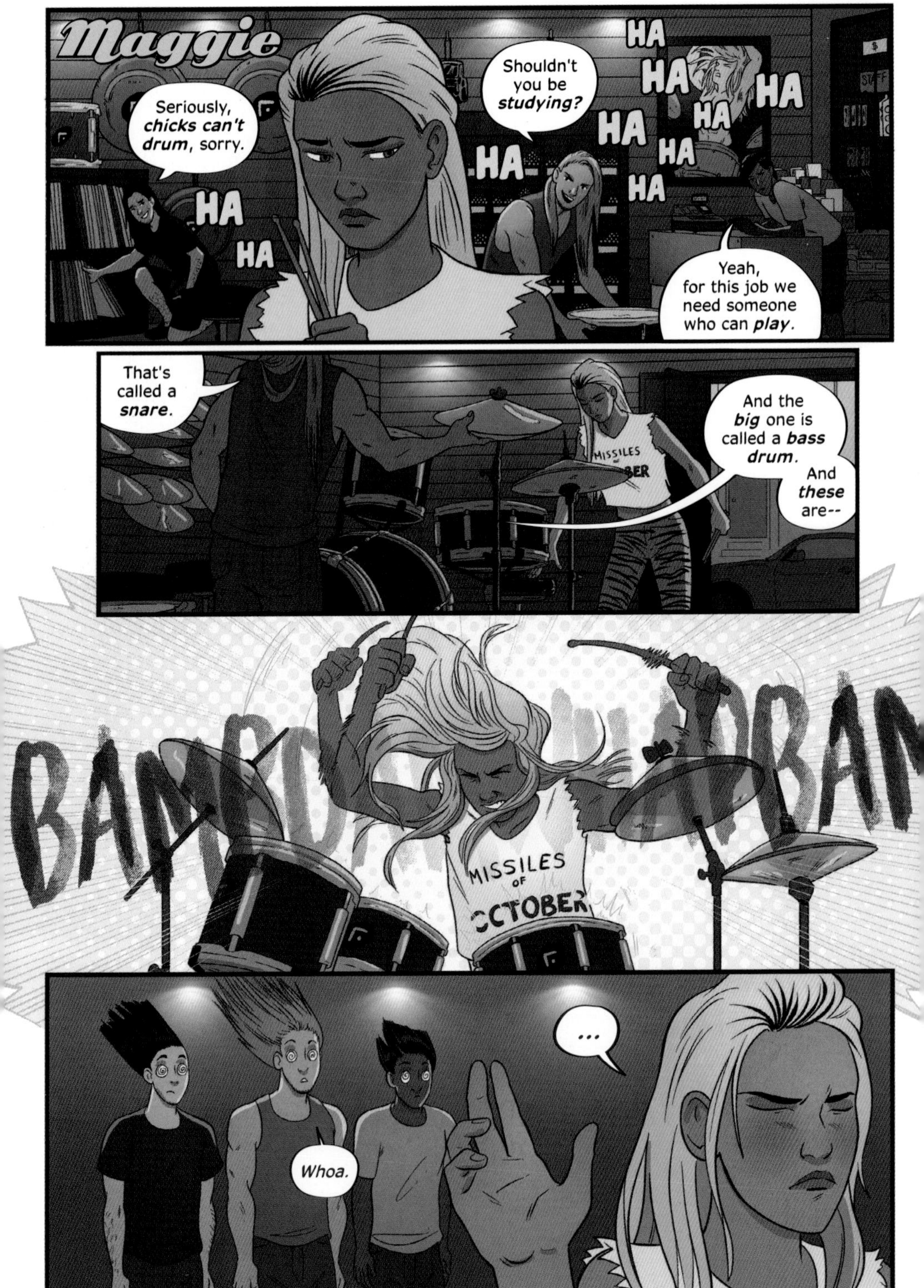
Maggie
Seriously, *chicks can't drum*, sorry.
HA
HA
Shouldn't you be *studying?*
HA
HA HA HA HA HA HA HA HA
Yeah, for this job we need someone who can *play*.
That's called a *snare*.
And the *big* one is called a *bass drum*.
And *these* are--
MISSILES OF
MISSILES OF CTOBER
Whoa.
...

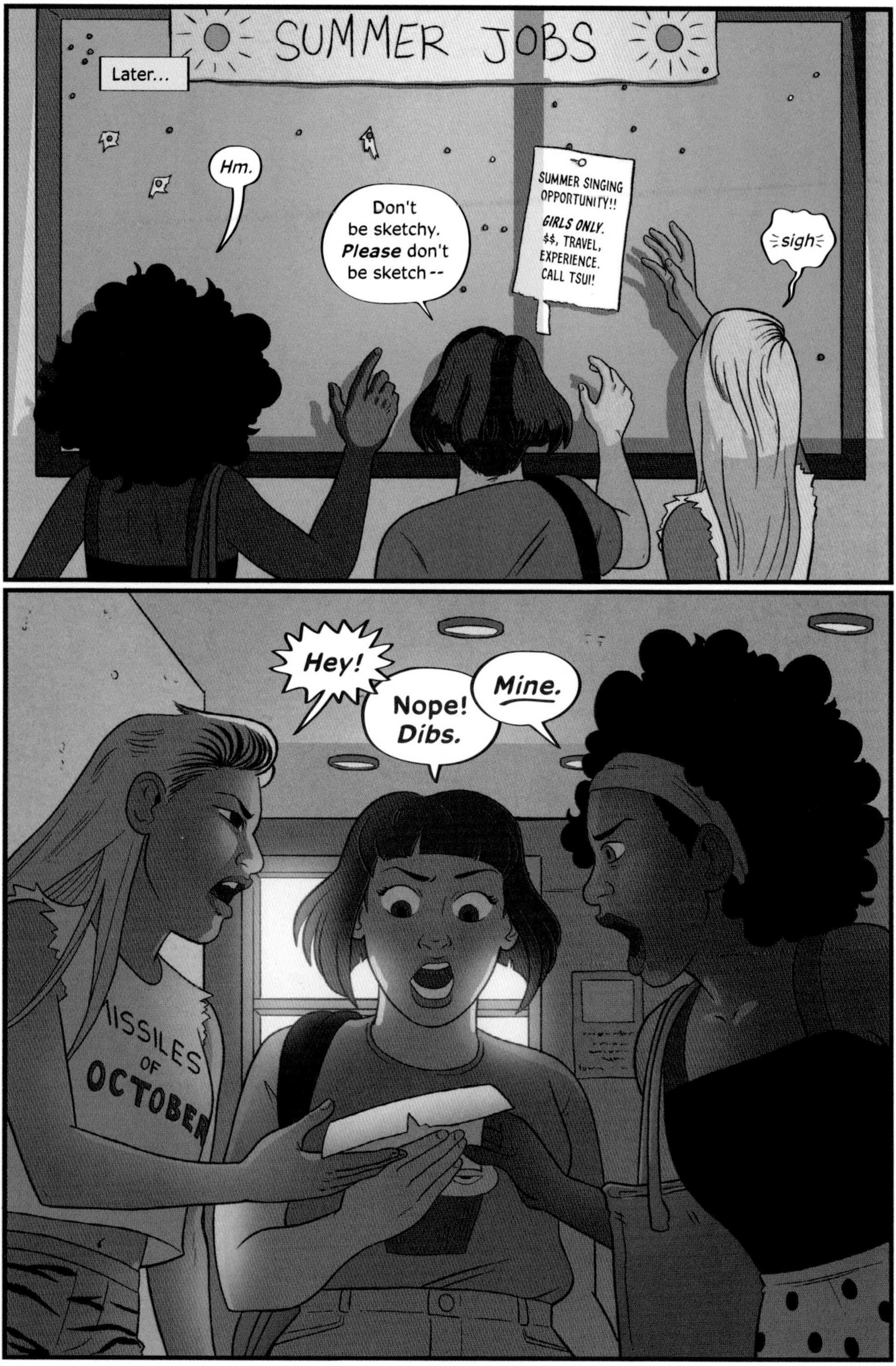
SUMMER JOBS
Later...
Hm.
Don't be sketchy. *Please* don't be sketch--
SUMMER SINGING OPPORTUNITY!! *GIRLS ONLY.* $$, TRAVEL, EXPERIENCE. CALL TSUI!
sigh
MISSILES OF OCTOBER
Hey!
Nope! Dibs.
Mine.

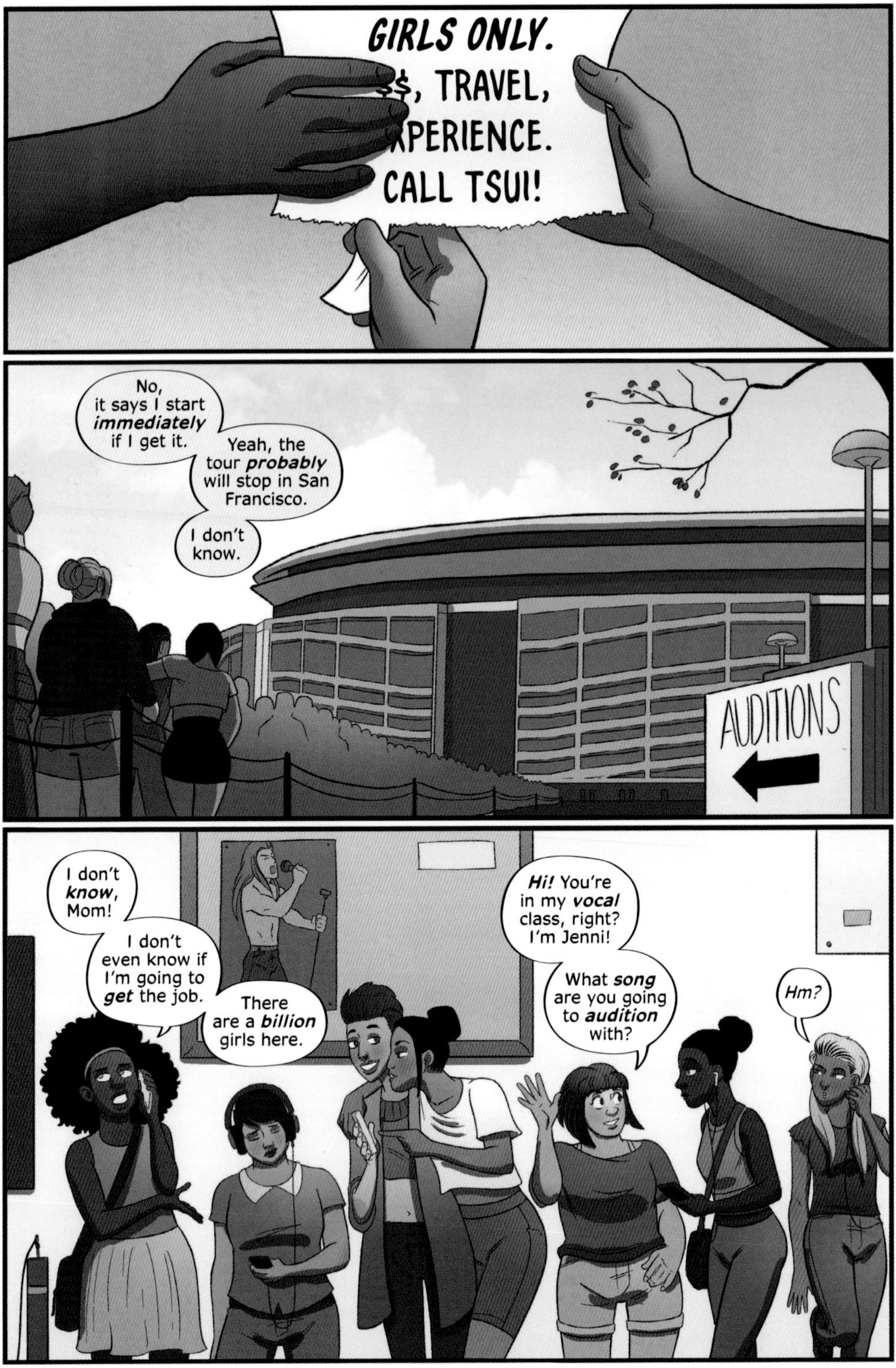
GIRLS ONLY.
$$, TRAVEL,
XPERIENCE.
CALL TSUI!
No, it says I start *immediately* if I get it.
Yeah, the tour *probably* will stop in San Francisco.
I don't know.
AUDITIONS
I don't *know*, Mom!
I don't even know if I'm going to *get* the job.
There are a *billion* girls here.
Hi! You're in my *vocal* class, right? I'm Jenni!
What *song* are you going to *audition* with?
Hm?

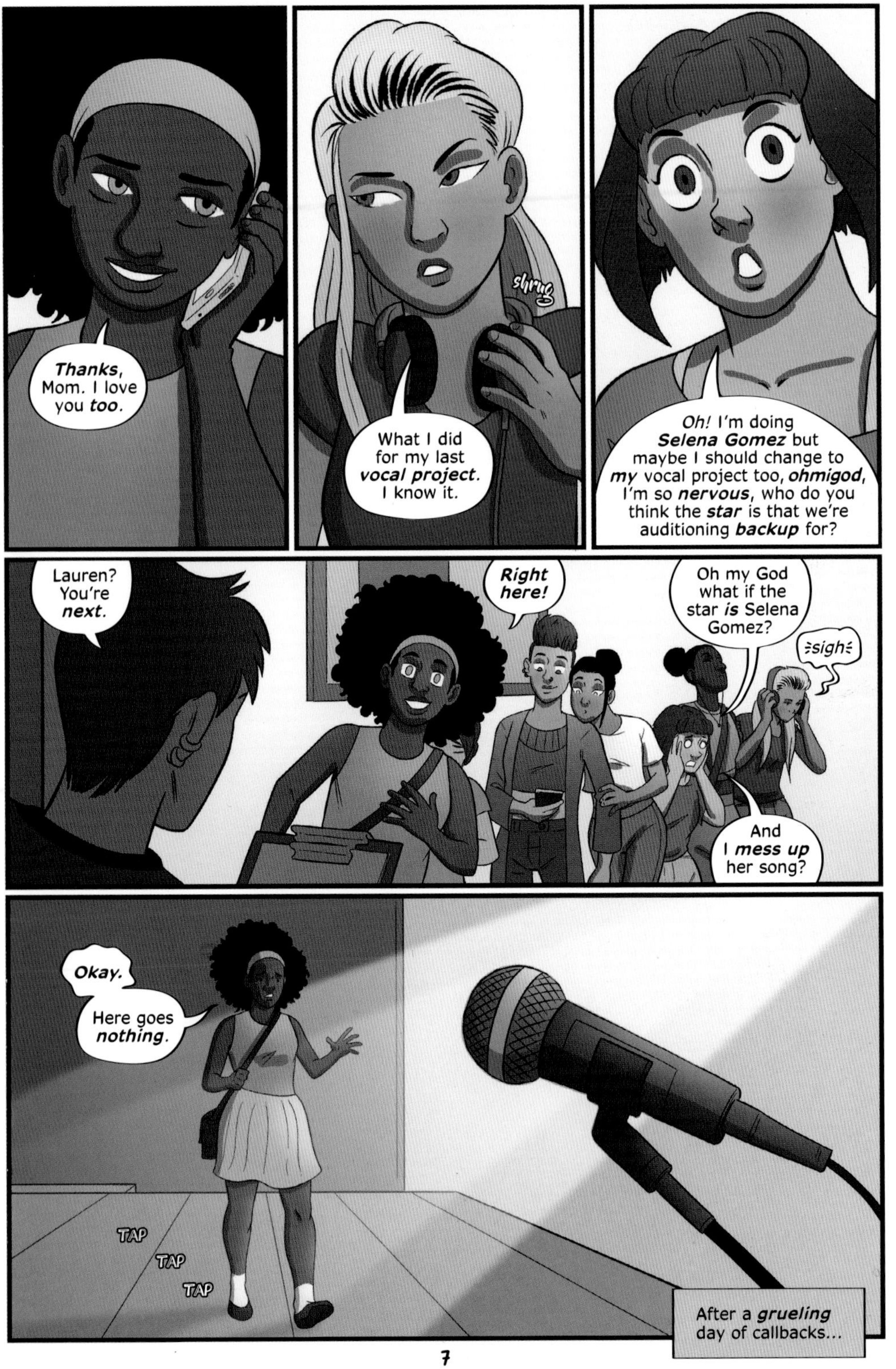
Thanks, Mom. I love you *too*.
shrug
What I did for my last *vocal project*. I know it.
Oh! I'm doing ***Selena Gomez*** but maybe I should change to ***my*** vocal project too, ***ohmigod***, I'm so ***nervous***, who do you think the ***star*** is that we're auditioning ***backup*** for?
Lauren? You're ***next***.
Right here!
Oh my God what if the star ***is*** Selena Gomez?
≶sigh≷
And I ***mess up*** her song?
Okay.
Here goes ***nothing***.
TAP
TAP
TAP
After a ***grueling*** day of callbacks...

CHAPTER

1

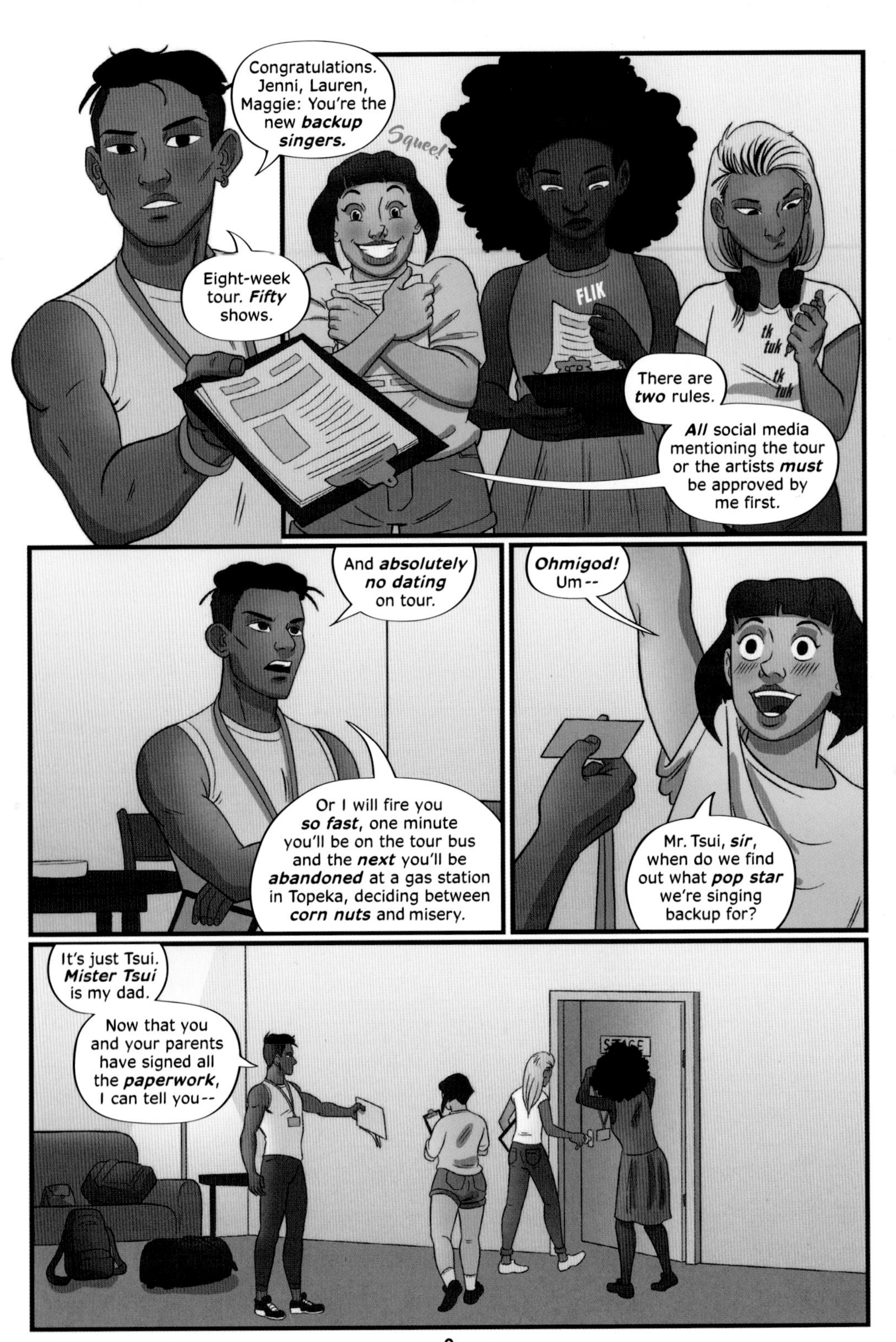
Congratulations. Jenni, Lauren, Maggie: You're the new **backup singers.**
Squee!
Eight-week tour. *Fifty* shows.
FLIK
tk tuk
tk tuk
There are **two** rules.
All social media mentioning the tour or the artists ***must*** be approved by me first.
And ***absolutely no dating*** on tour.
Or I will fire you ***so fast***, one minute you'll be on the tour bus and the ***next*** you'll be ***abandoned*** at a gas station in Topeka, deciding between ***corn nuts*** and misery.
Ohmigod! Um--
Mr. Tsui, ***sir***, when do we find out what ***pop star*** we're singing backup for?
It's just Tsui. ***Mister Tsui*** is my dad.
Now that you and your parents have signed all the ***paperwork***, I can tell you--

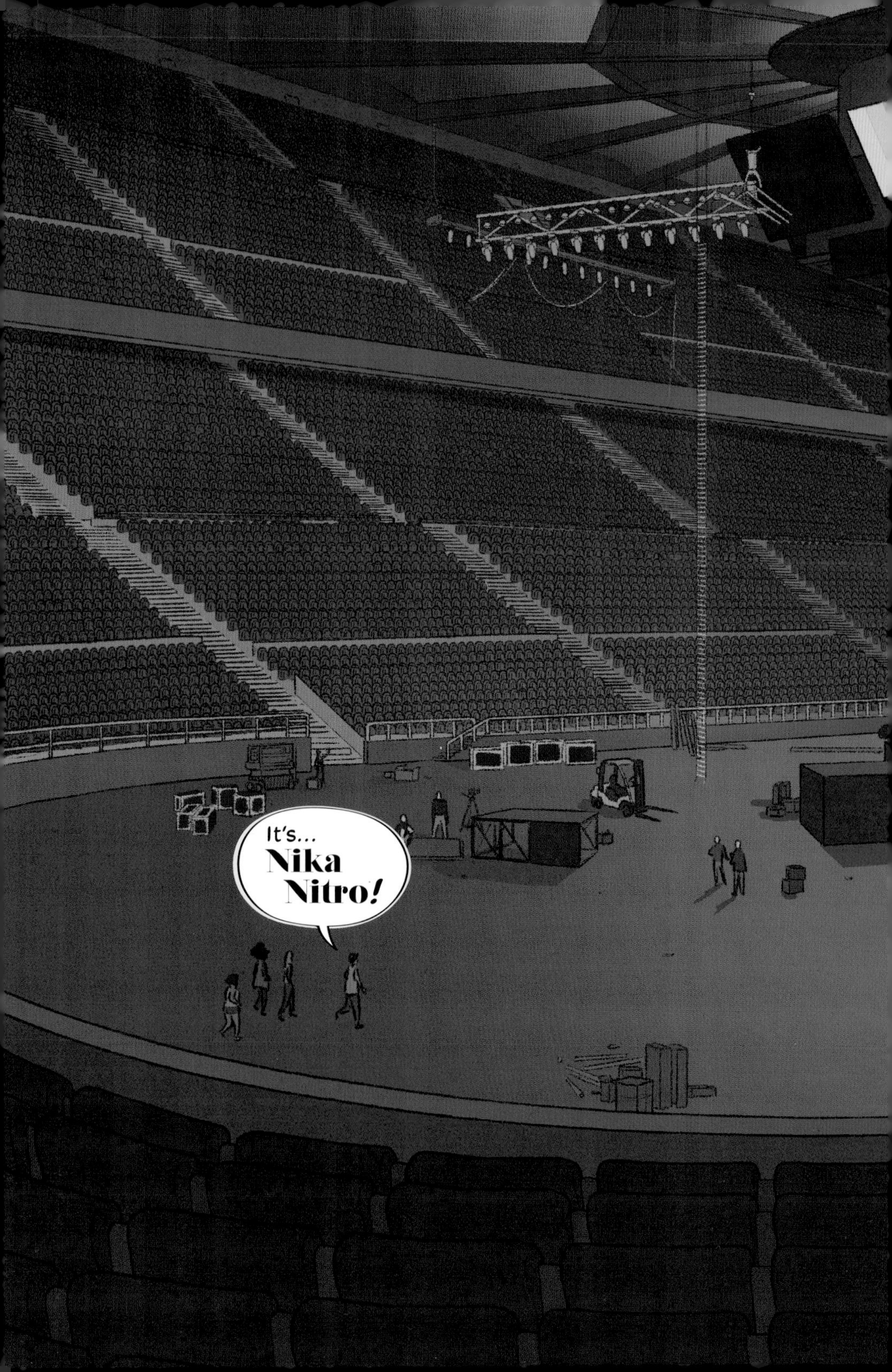
It's... Nika Nitro!

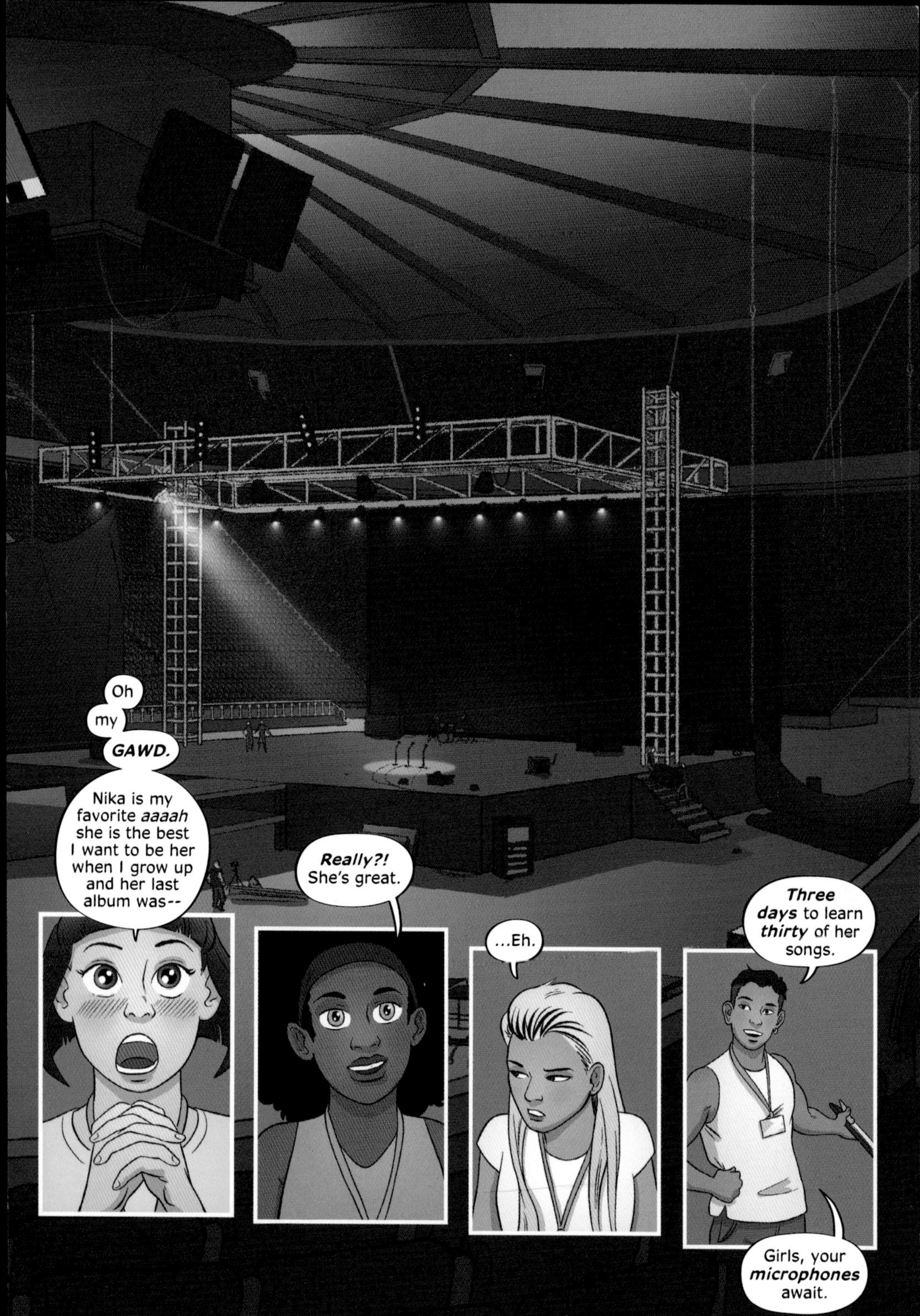
Oh
my
GAWD.
Nika is my favorite *aaaah* she is the best I want to be her when I grow up and her last album was--
Really?! She's great.
...Eh.
Three days to learn ***thirty*** of her songs.
Girls, your ***microphones*** await.

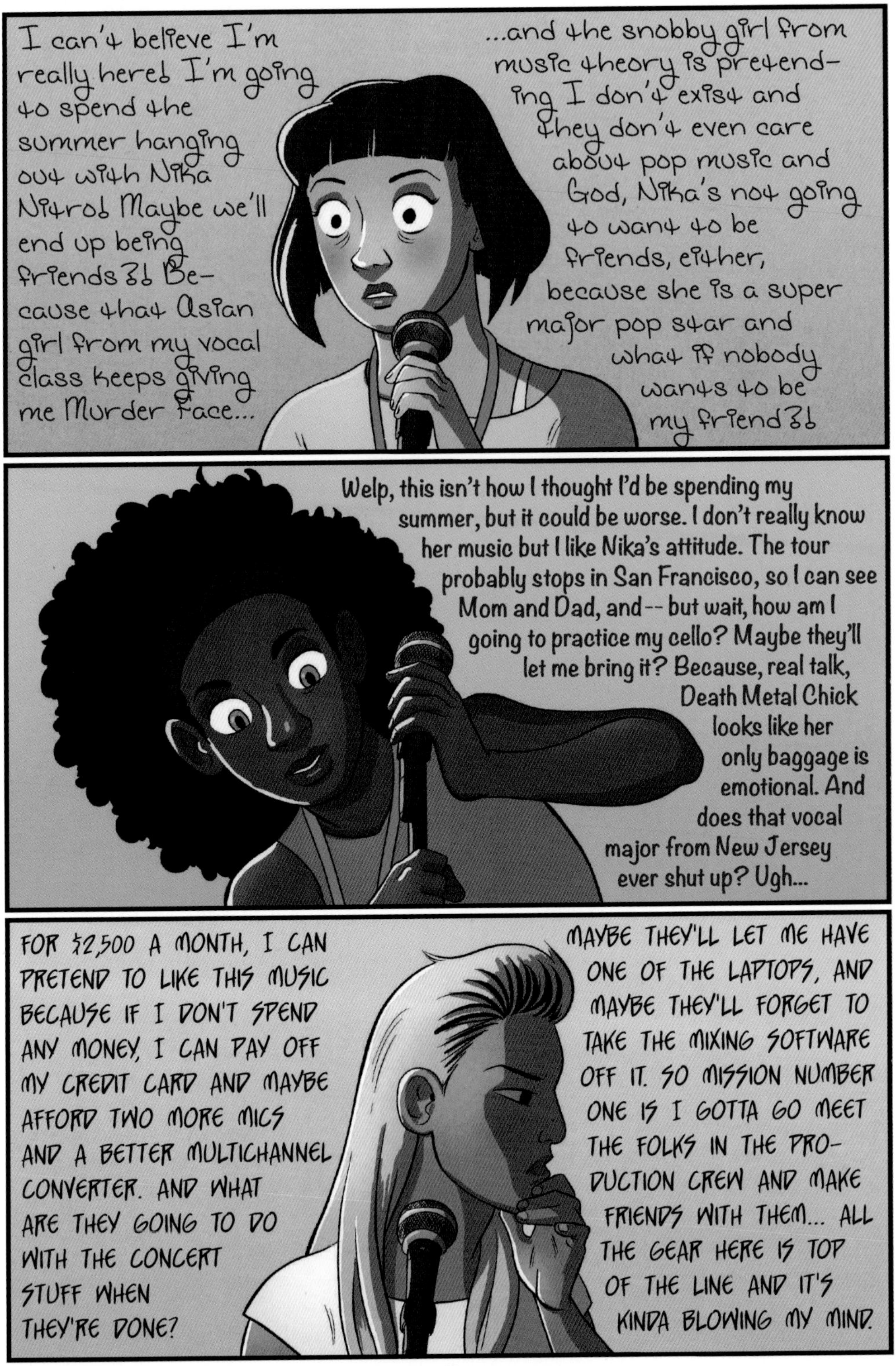
I can't believe I'm really here! I'm going to spend the summer hanging out with Nika Nitro! Maybe we'll end up being friends?! Because that Asian girl from my vocal class keeps giving me Murder Face...
...and the snobby girl from music theory is pretending I don't exist and they don't even care about pop music and God, Nika's not going to want to be friends, either, because she is a super major pop star and what if nobody wants to be my friend?!
Welp, this isn't how I thought I'd be spending my summer, but it could be worse. I don't really know her music but I like Nika's attitude. The tour probably stops in San Francisco, so I can see Mom and Dad, and-- but wait, how am I going to practice my cello? Maybe they'll let me bring it? Because, real talk, Death Metal Chick looks like her only baggage is emotional. And does that vocal major from New Jersey ever shut up? Ugh...
FOR $2,500 A MONTH, I CAN PRETEND TO LIKE THIS MUSIC BECAUSE IF I DON'T SPEND ANY MONEY, I CAN PAY OFF MY CREDIT CARD AND MAYBE AFFORD TWO MORE MICS AND A BETTER MULTICHANNEL CONVERTER. AND WHAT ARE THEY GOING TO DO WITH THE CONCERT STUFF WHEN THEY'RE DONE?
MAYBE THEY'LL LET ME HAVE ONE OF THE LAPTOPS, AND MAYBE THEY'LL FORGET TO TAKE THE MIXING SOFTWARE OFF IT. SO MISSION NUMBER ONE IS I GOTTA GO MEET THE FOLKS IN THE PRODUCTION CREW AND MAKE FRIENDS WITH THEM... ALL THE GEAR HERE IS TOP OF THE LINE AND IT'S KINDA BLOWING MY MIND.

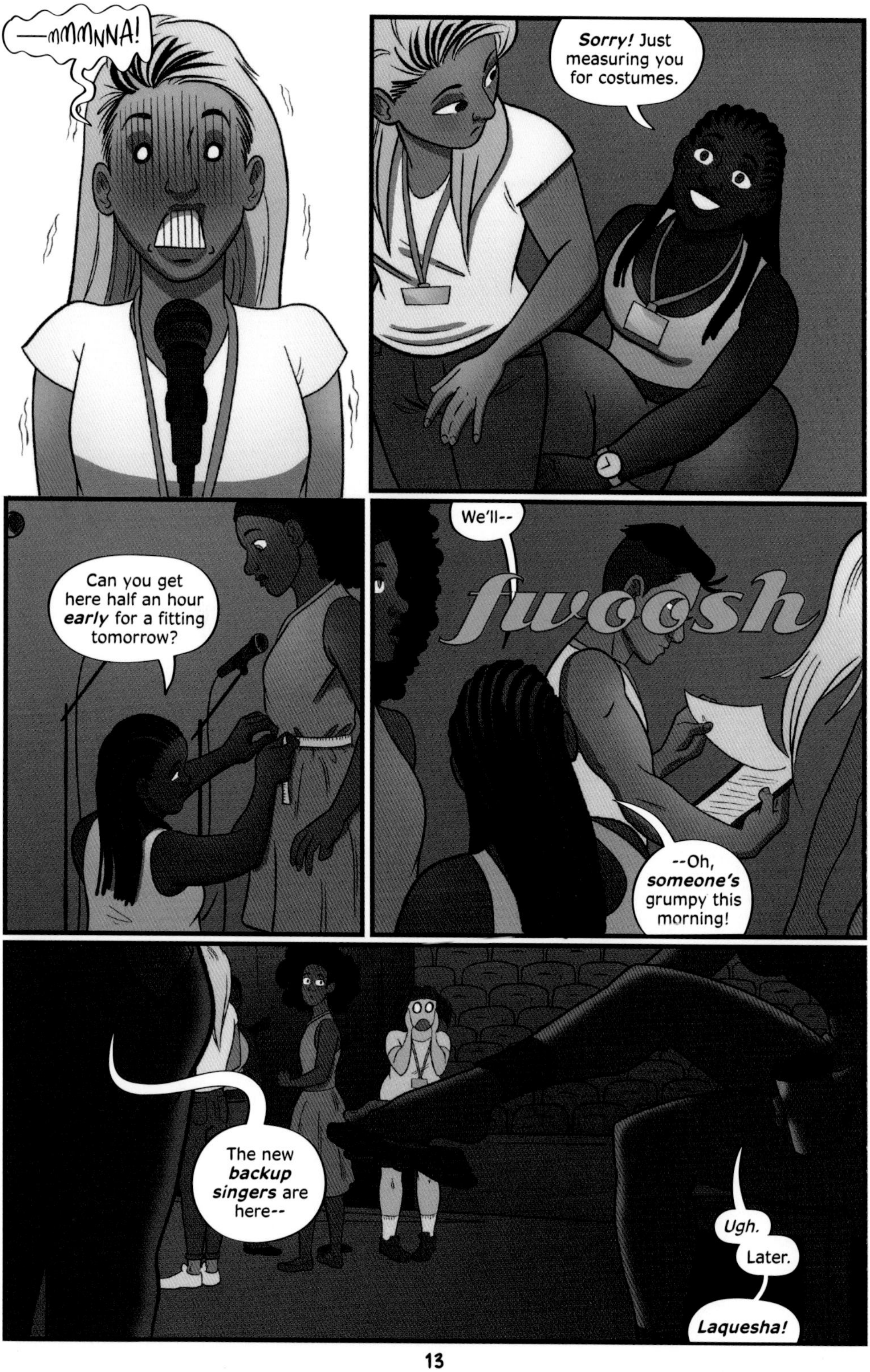
—mmmNNA!
Sorry! Just measuring you for costumes.
Can you get here half an hour *early* for a fitting tomorrow?
We'll--
fwoosh
--Oh, *someone's* grumpy this morning!
The new *backup singers* are here--
Ugh.
Later.
Laquesha!

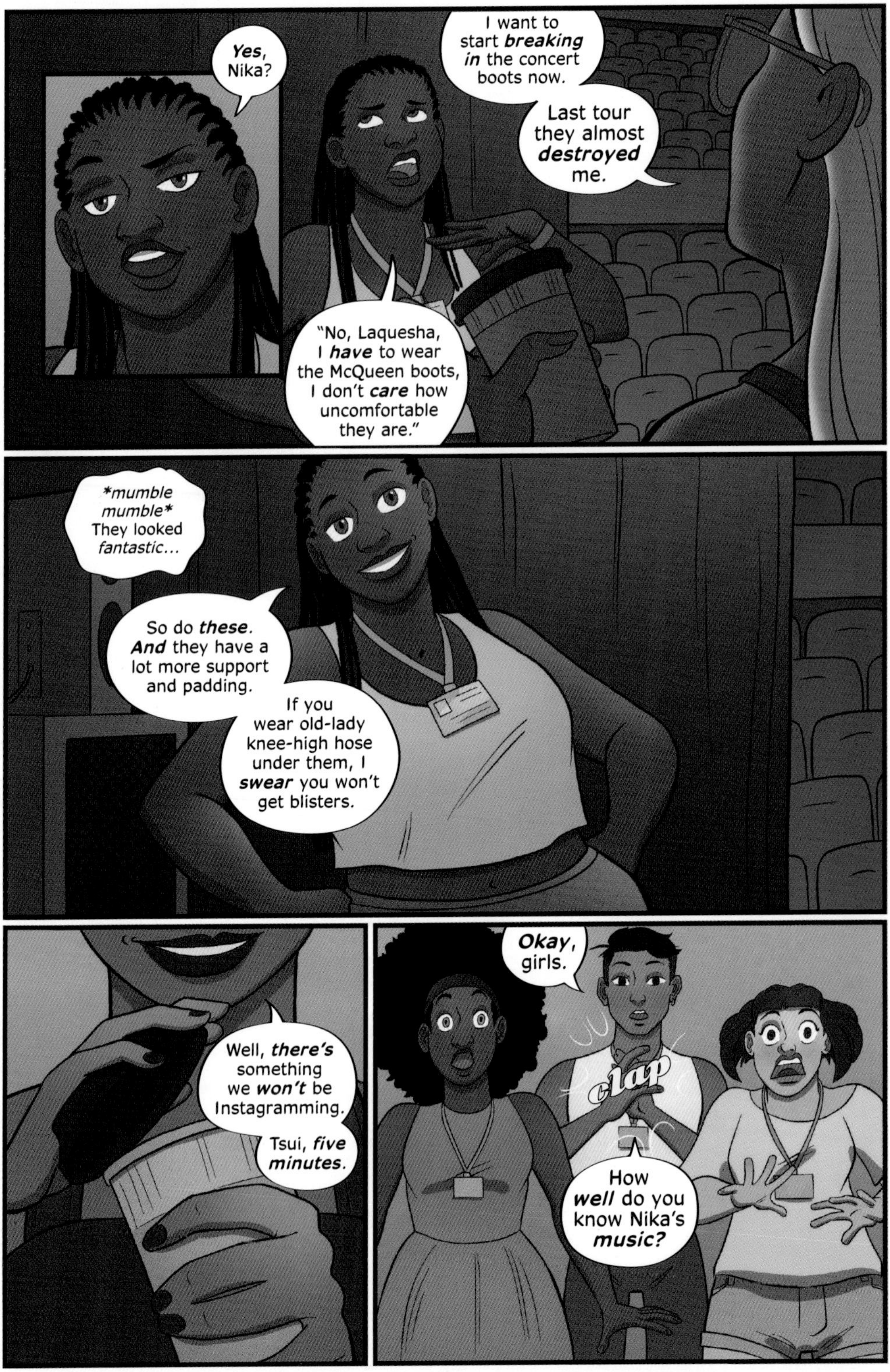

Yes, Nika?
I want to start ***breaking in*** the concert boots now.
Last tour they almost ***destroyed*** me.
"No, Laquesha, I ***have*** to wear the McQueen boots, I don't ***care*** how uncomfortable they are."
mumble mumble They looked *fantastic*...
So do ***these***. ***And*** they have a lot more support and padding.
If you wear old-lady knee-high hose under them, I ***swear*** you won't get blisters.
Well, ***there's*** something we ***won't*** be Instagramming.
Tsui, ***five minutes***.
Okay, girls.
clap
How ***well*** do you know Nika's ***music?***

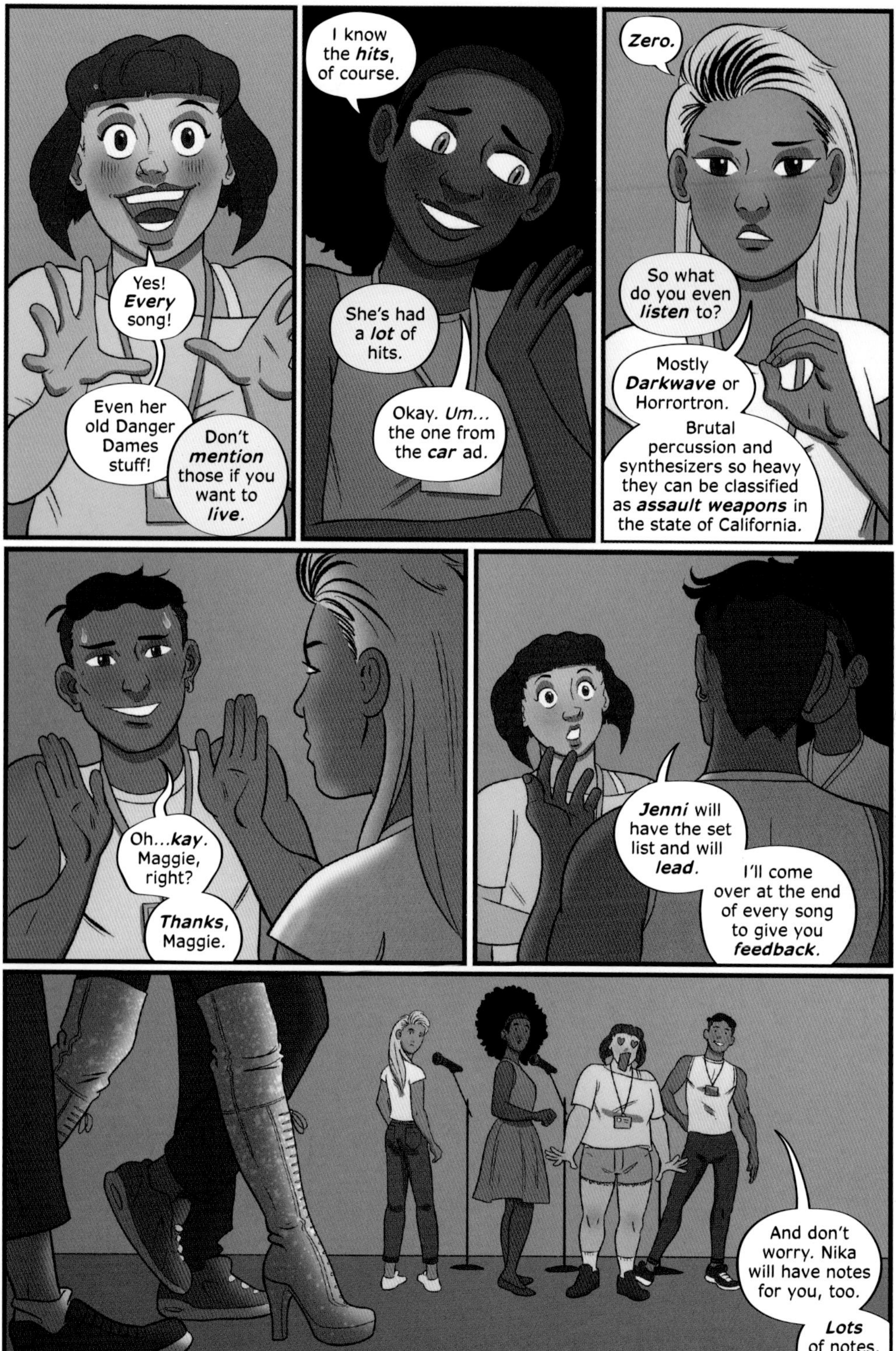
Yes! *Every* song!
Even her old Danger Dames stuff!
Don't *mention* those if you want to *live*.
I know the *hits*, of course.
She's had a *lot* of hits.
Okay. *Um*... the one from the *car* ad.
Zero.
So what do you even *listen* to?
Mostly *Darkwave* or Horrortron.
Brutal percussion and synthesizers so heavy they can be classified as *assault weapons* in the state of California.
Oh...*kay*. Maggie, right?
Thanks, Maggie.
Jenni will have the set list and will *lead*.
I'll come over at the end of every song to give you *feedback*.
And don't worry. Nika will have notes for you, too.
Lots of notes.

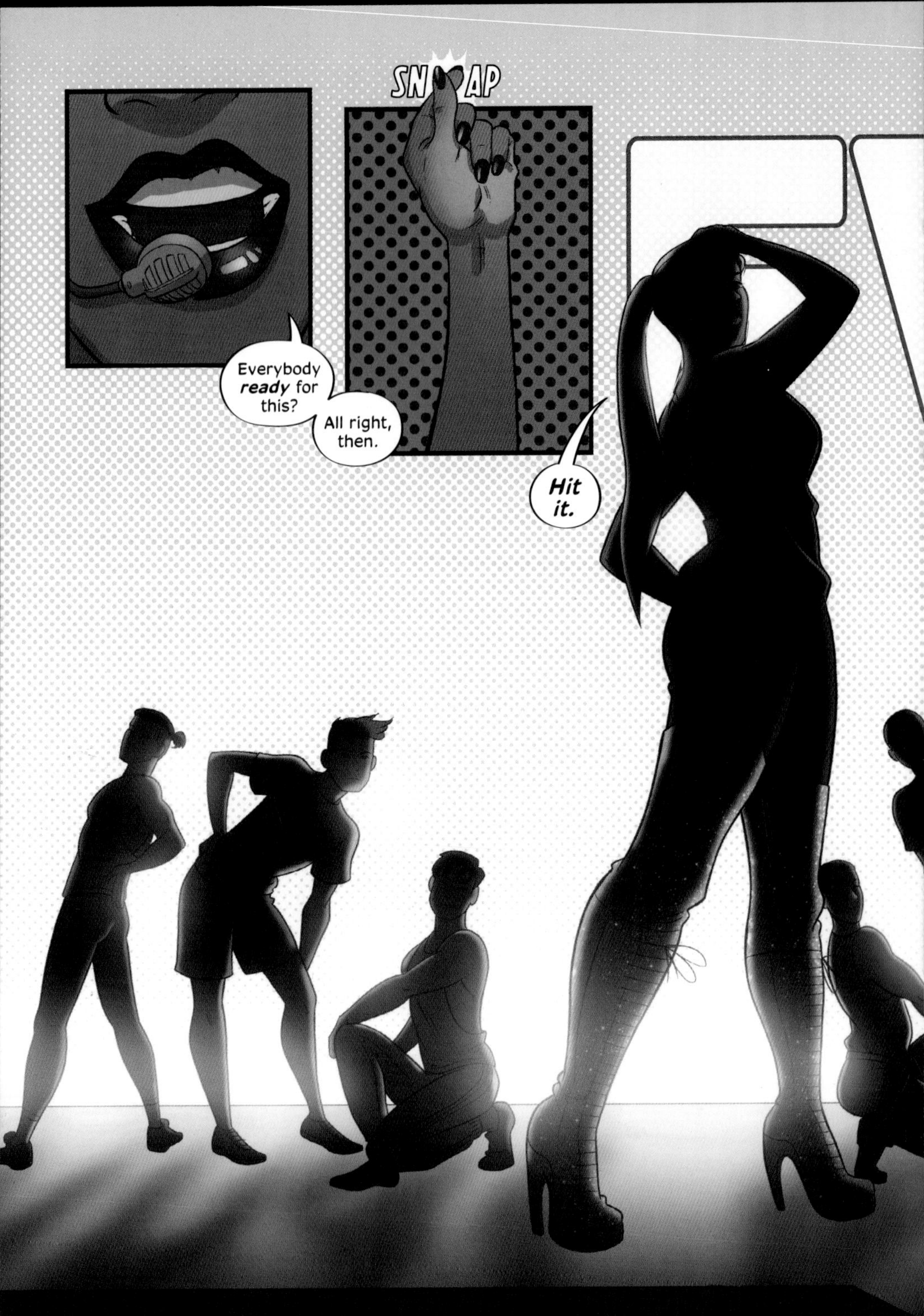
SNAP
Everybody *ready* for this?
All right, then.
Hit it.

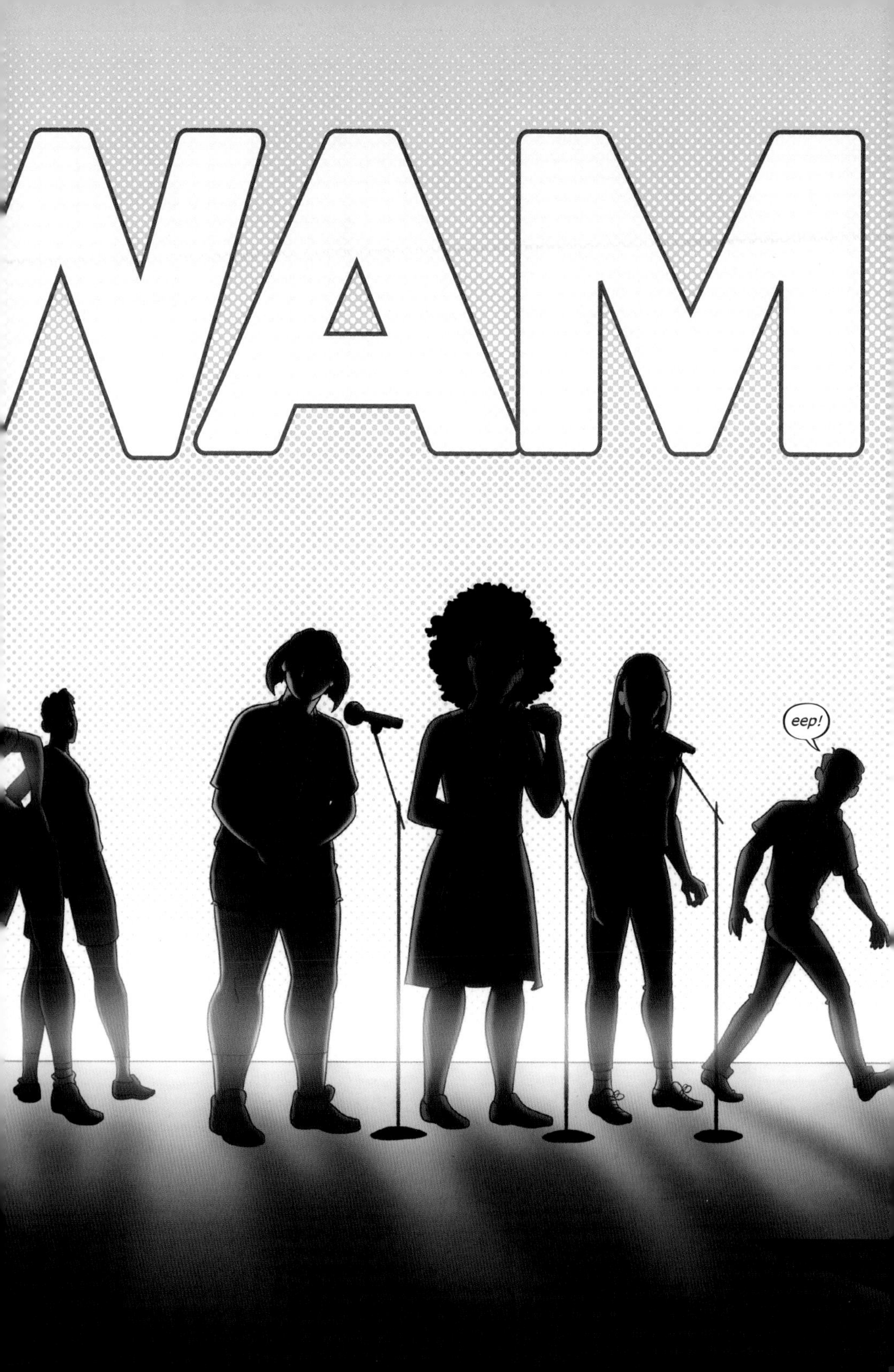
WAM
eep!

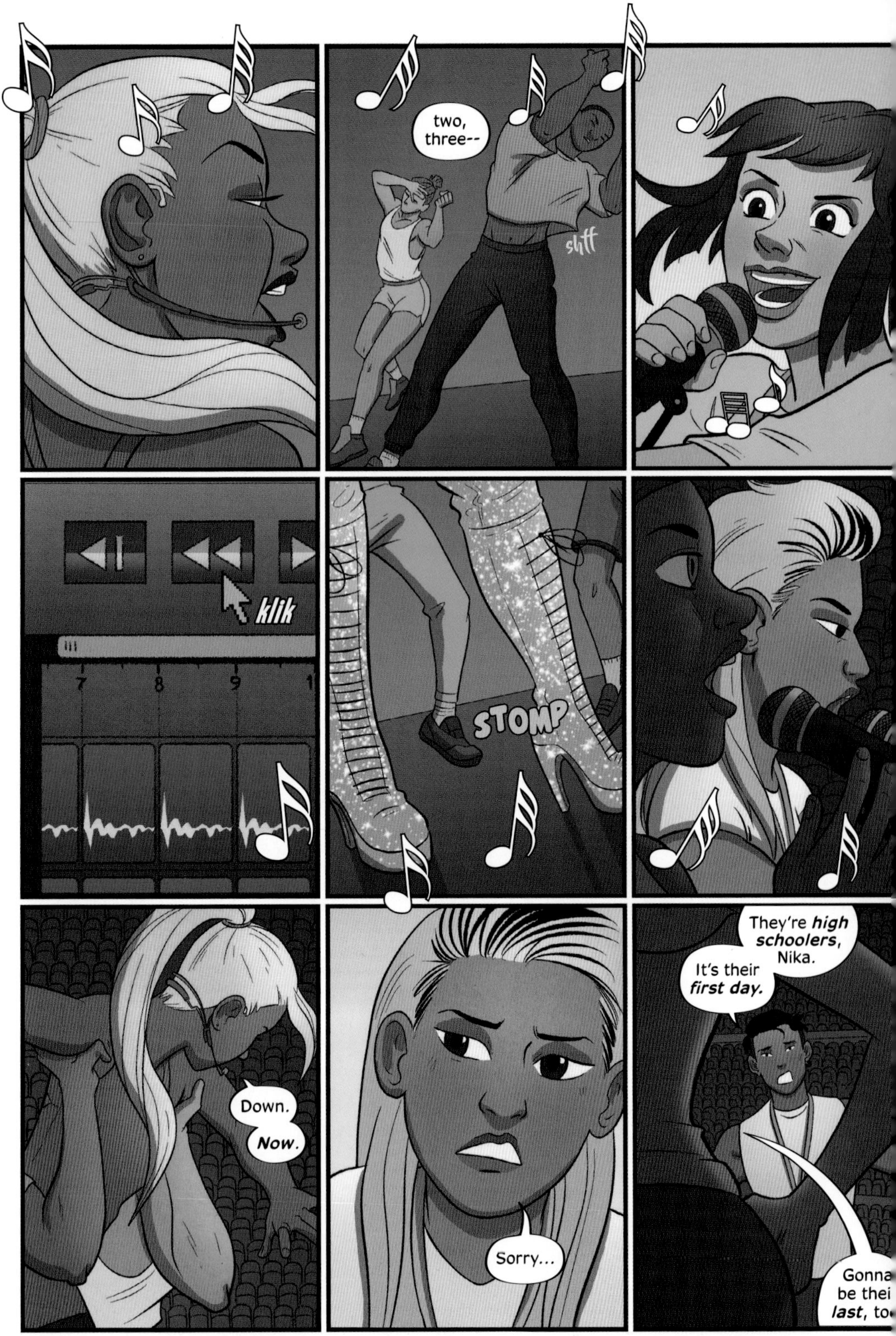
two,
three--
shff
klik
STOMP
Down.
Now.
Sorry...
They're *high schoolers*, Nika.
It's their *first day.*
Gonna
be thei
last, to

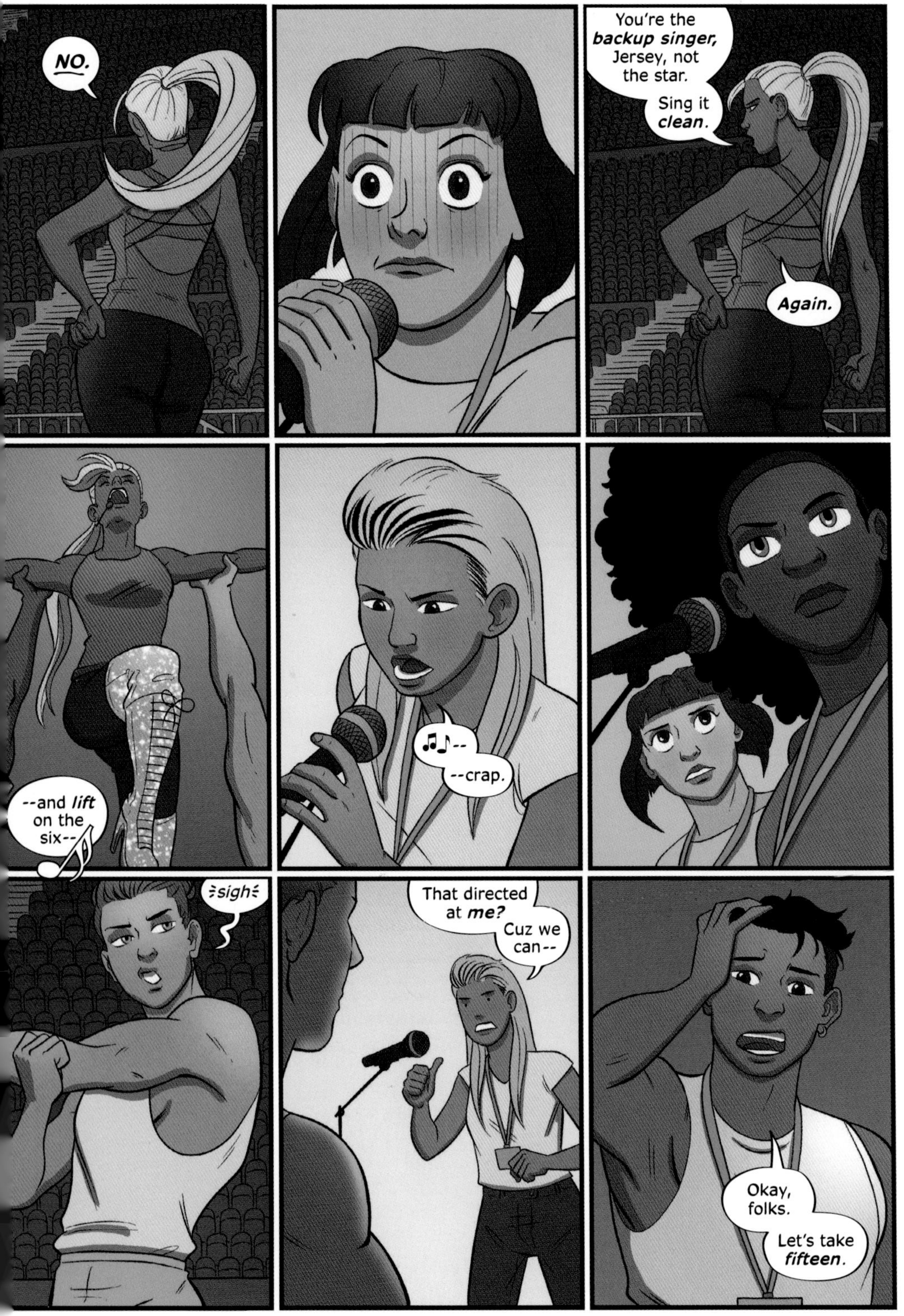
NO.
You're the *backup singer,* Jersey, not the star.
Sing it *clean*.
Again.
--and *lift* on the six--
♫♪--
--crap.
≷sigh≶
That directed at *me?*
Cuz we can--
Okay, folks.
Let's take *fifteen*.

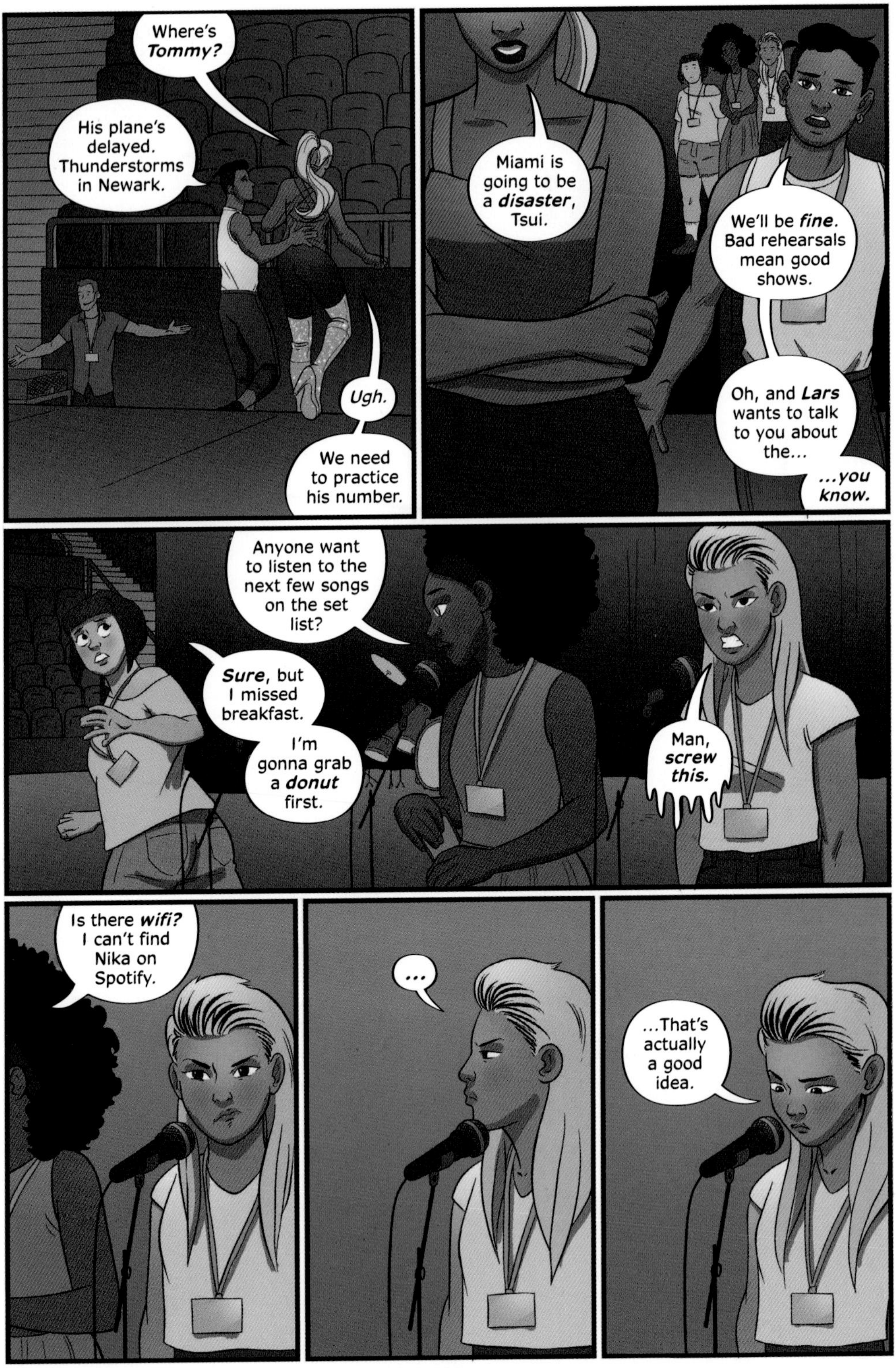
Where's *Tommy?*
His plane's delayed. Thunderstorms in Newark.
Ugh.
We need to practice his number.
Miami is going to be a ***disaster***, Tsui.
We'll be ***fine***. Bad rehearsals mean good shows.
Oh, and ***Lars*** wants to talk to you about the...
...you know.
Anyone want to listen to the next few songs on the set list?
Sure, but I missed breakfast.
I'm gonna grab a ***donut*** first.
Man, ***screw this.***
Is there ***wifi?*** I can't find Nika on Spotify.
...
...That's actually a good idea.

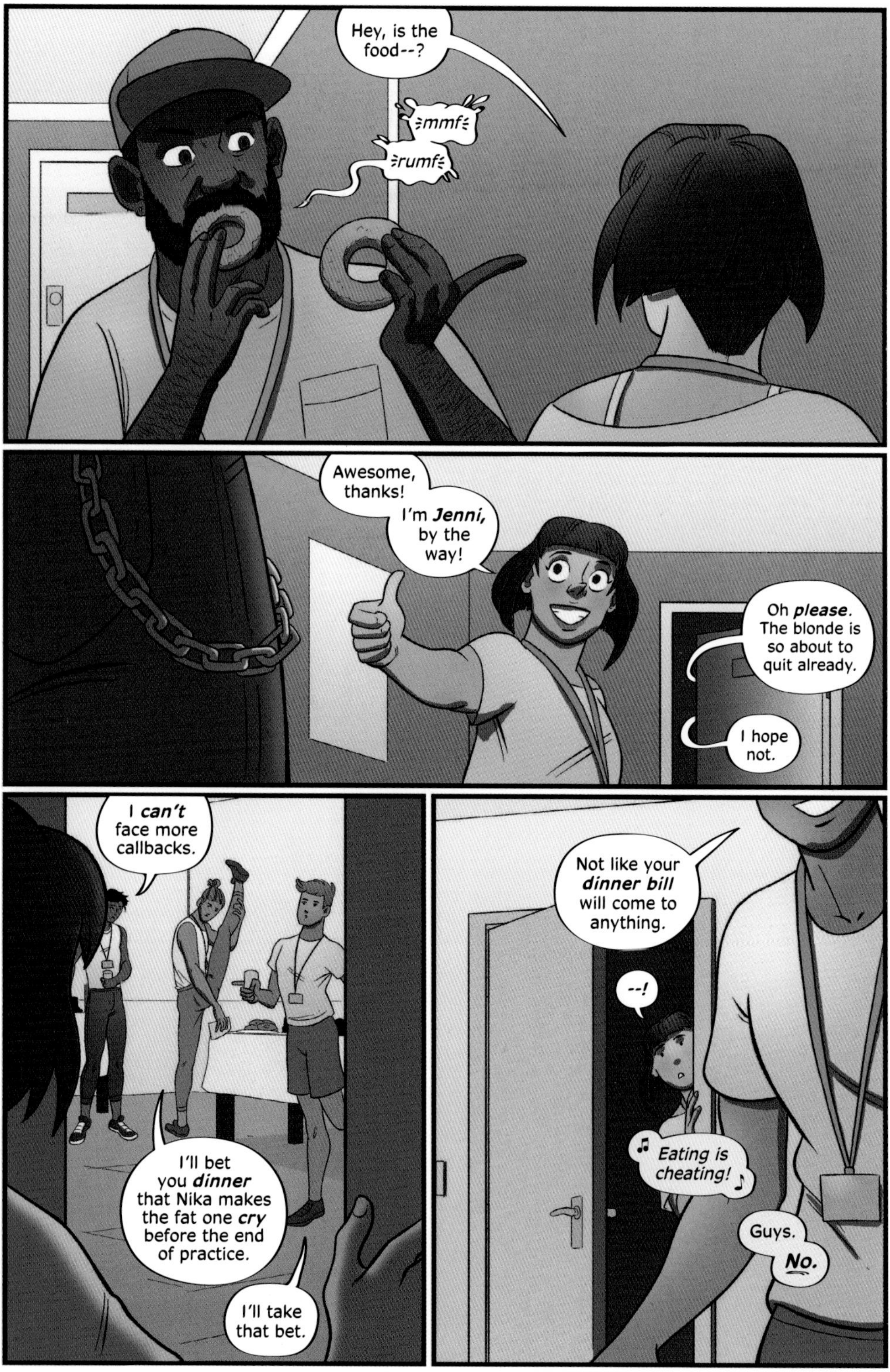
Hey, is the food--?
mmf
rumf
Awesome, thanks!
I'm *Jenni,* by the way!
Oh *please*. The blonde is so about to quit already.
I hope not.
I *can't* face more callbacks.
I'll bet you *dinner* that Nika makes the fat one *cry* before the end of practice.
I'll take that bet.
Not like your *dinner bill* will come to anything.
--!
Eating is cheating!
Guys.
No.

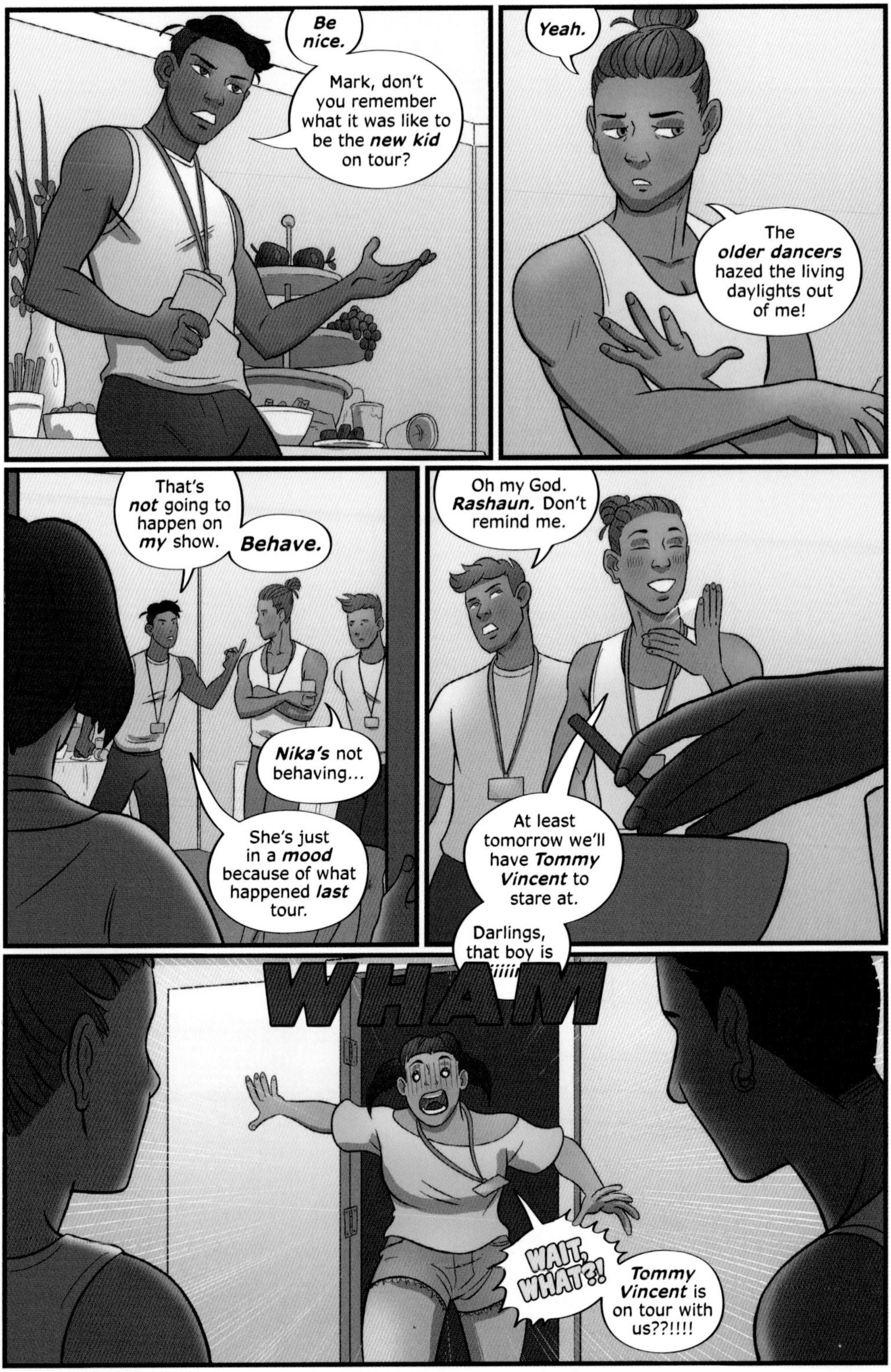
Be nice.
Mark, don't you remember what it was like to be the *new kid* on tour?
Yeah.
The *older dancers* hazed the living daylights out of me!
That's *not* going to happen on *my* show.
Behave.
Nika's not behaving...
She's just in a *mood* because of what happened *last* tour.
Oh my God. ***Rashaun.*** Don't remind me.
At least tomorrow we'll have ***Tommy Vincent*** to stare at.
Darlings, that boy is
WHAM
WAIT, WHAT?!
Tommy Vincent is on tour with us??!!!!

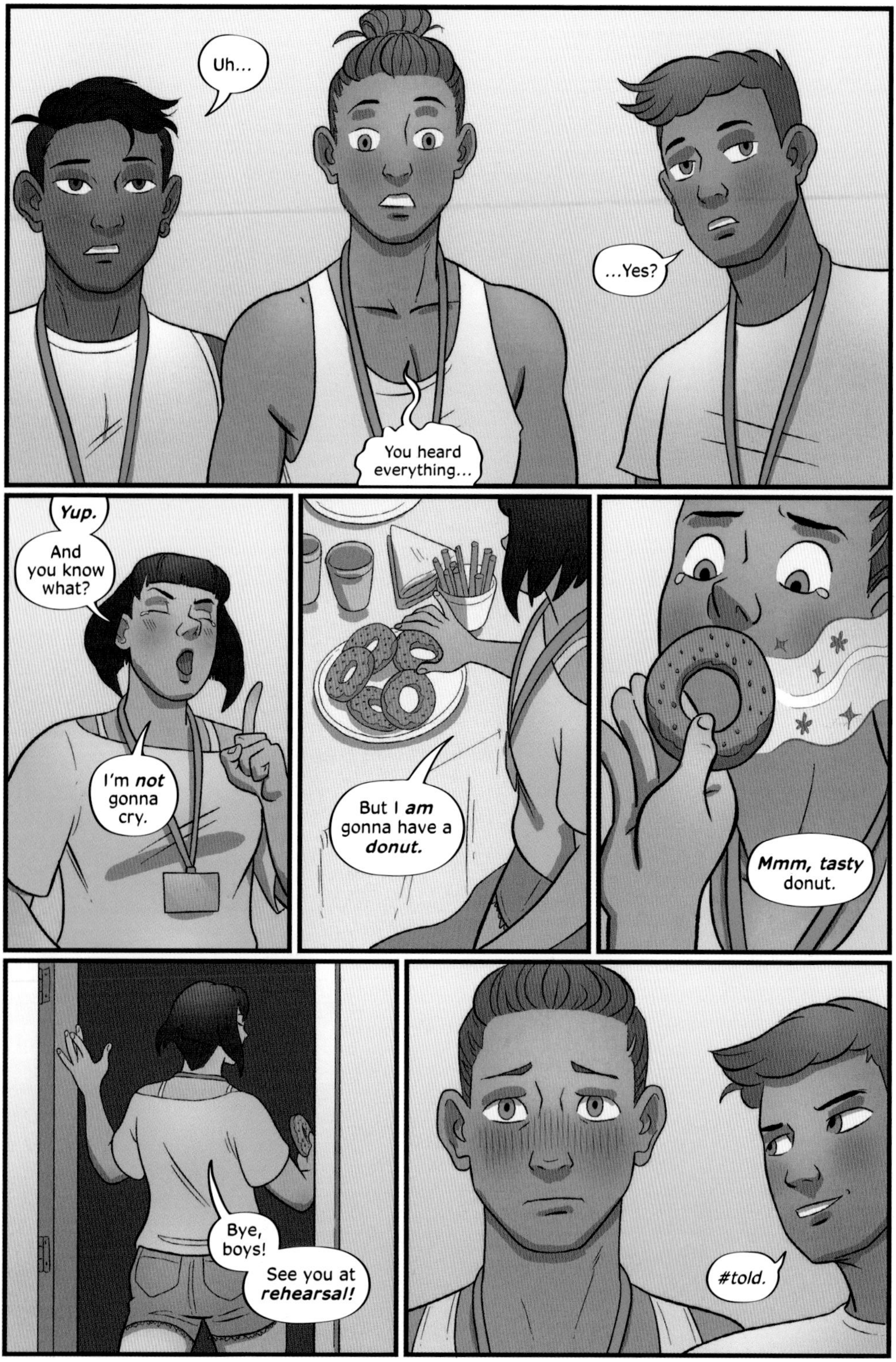
Uh...
...Yes?
You heard everything...
Yup.
And you know what?
I'm ***not*** gonna cry.
But I ***am*** gonna have a ***donut.***
Mmm, tasty donut.
Bye, boys!
See you at ***rehearsal!***
#told.

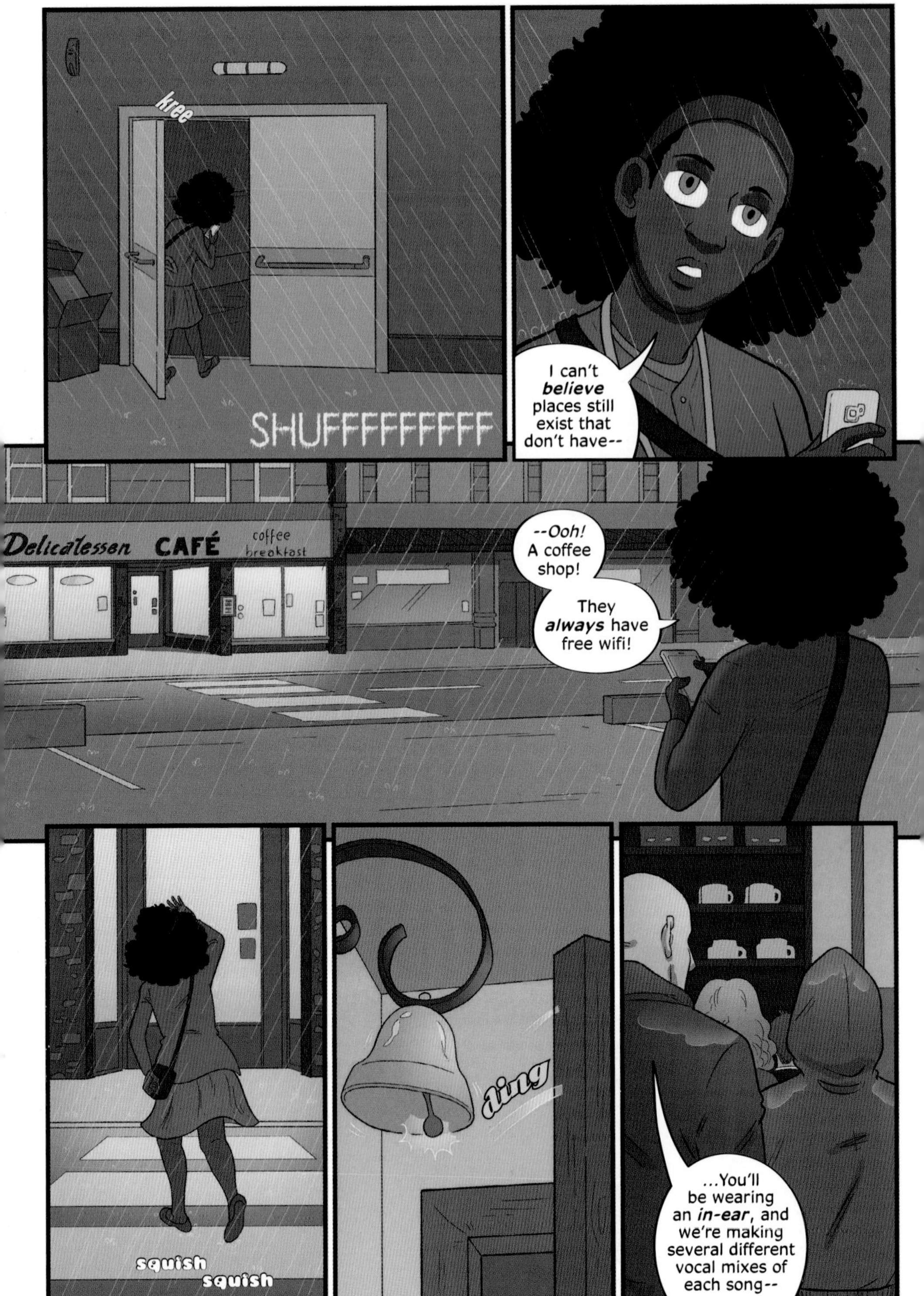
kree
SHUFFFFFFFFF
I can't ***believe*** places still exist that don't have--
Delicatessen CAFÉ coffee breakfast
--Ooh! A coffee shop!
They ***always*** have free wifi!
squish squish
ding
...You'll be wearing an ***in-ear***, and we're making several different vocal mixes of each song--

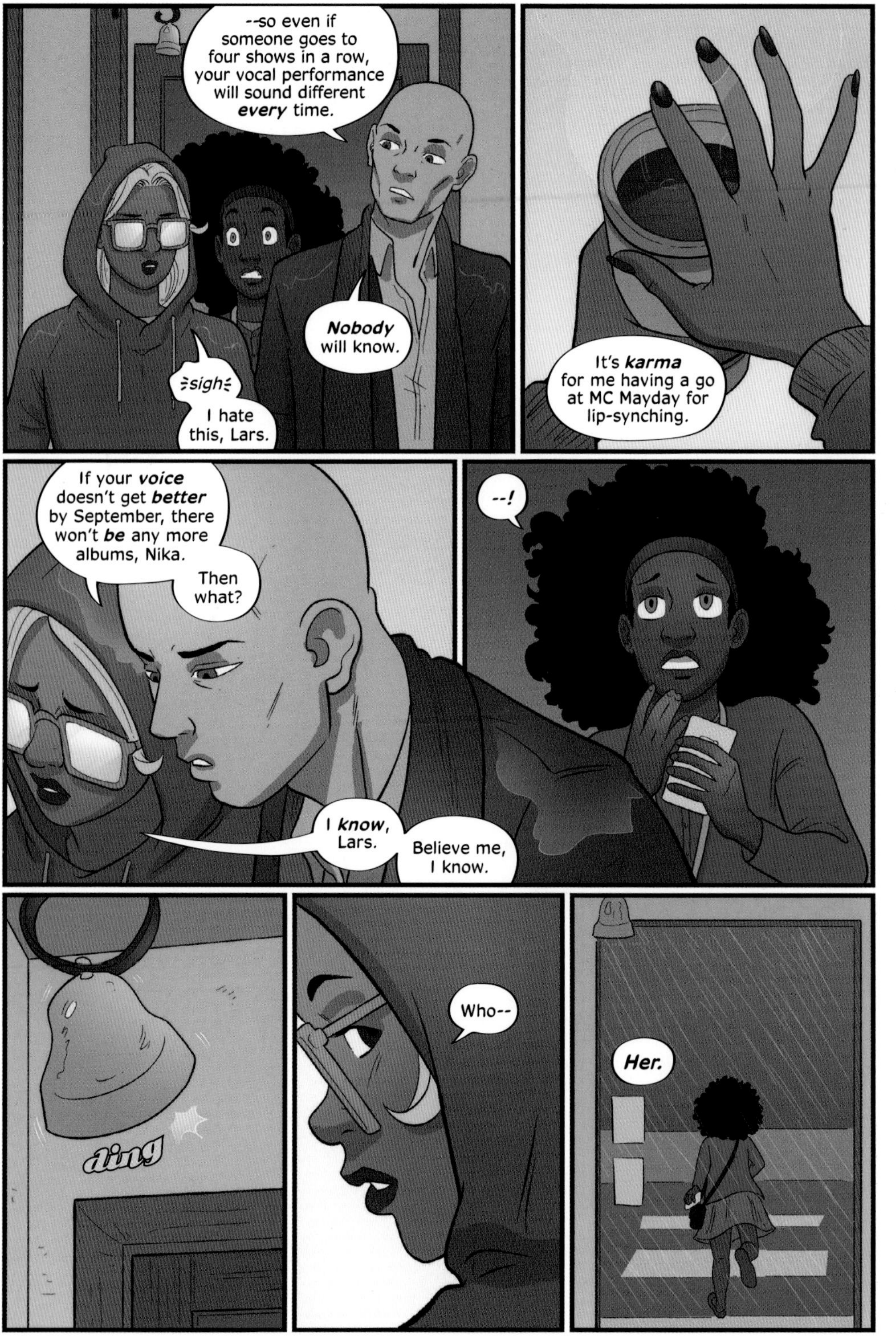
--so even if someone goes to four shows in a row, your vocal performance will sound different *every* time.
Nobody will know.
sigh
I hate this, Lars.
It's ***karma*** for me having a go at MC Mayday for lip-synching.
If your ***voice*** doesn't get ***better*** by September, there won't ***be*** any more albums, Nika.
Then what?
--!
I ***know***, Lars.
Believe me, I know.
ding
Who--
Her.

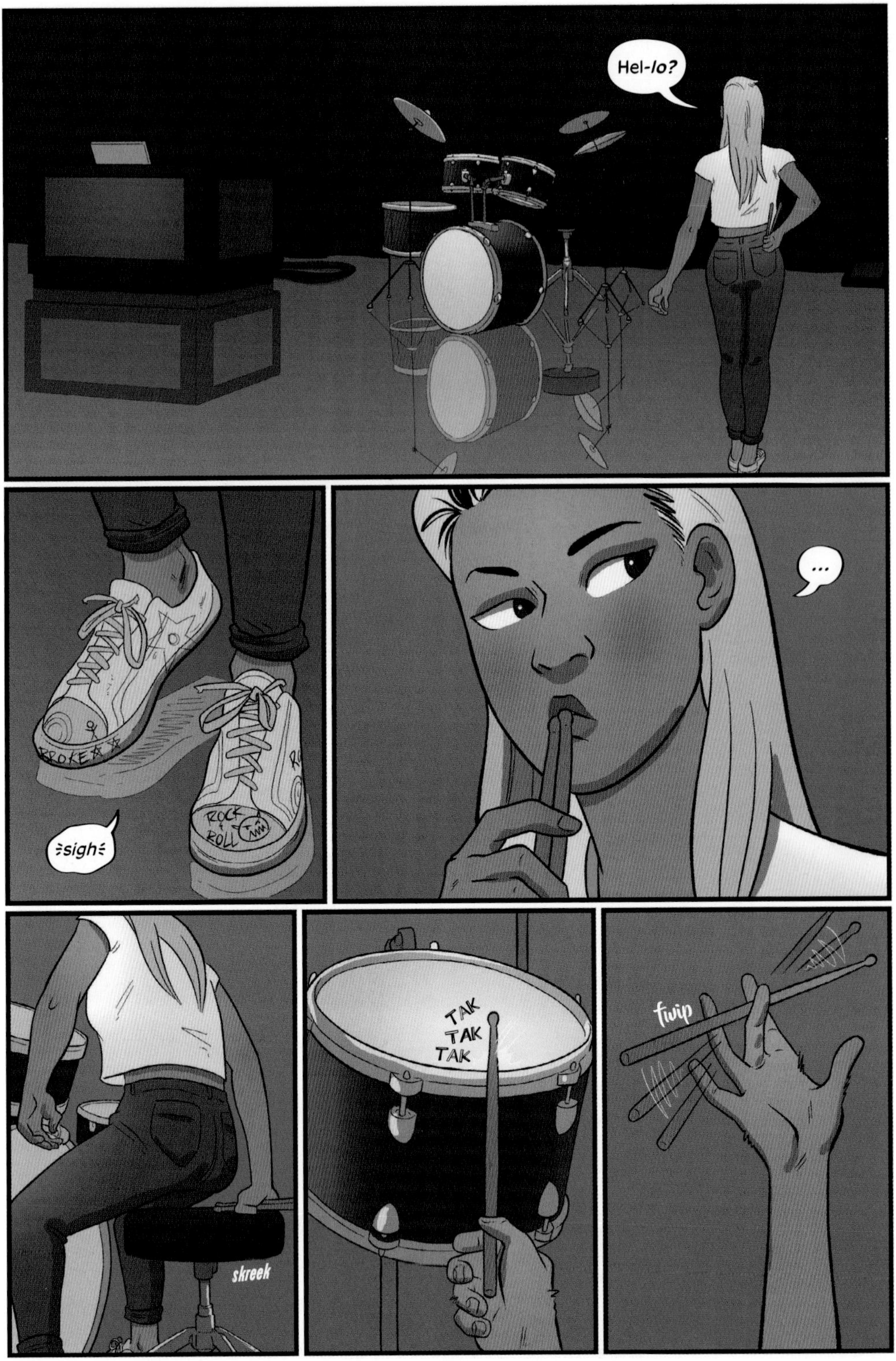
Hel-lo?
BROKE
ROCK & ROLL
sigh
...
skreek
TAK
TAK
TAK
twip

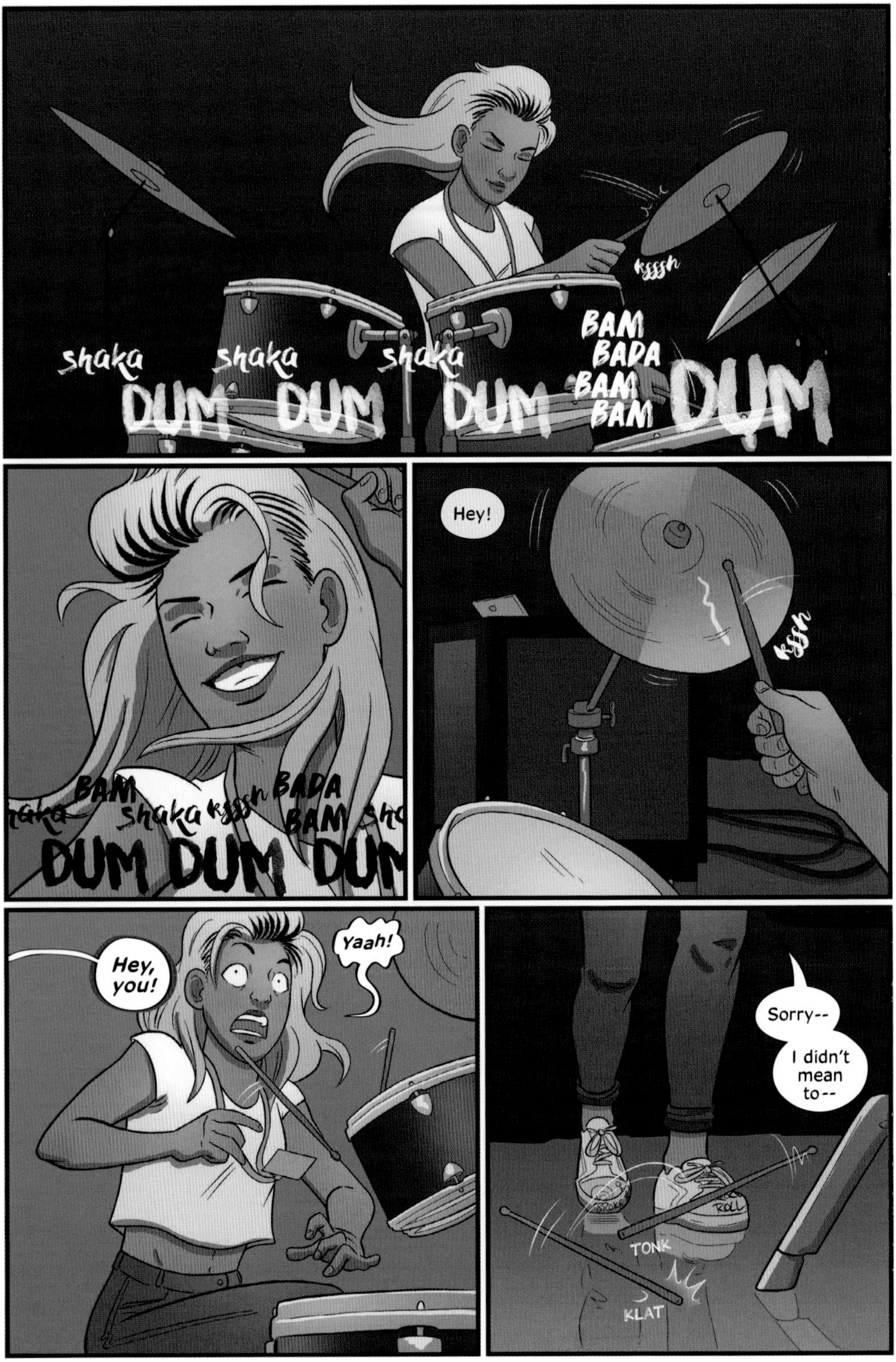
shaka
DUM
shaka
DUM
shaka
DUM
kssh
BAM
BADA
BAM
BAM
DUM
BAM
shaka
kssh
BADA
BAM
DUM DUM DUM
Hey!
kssh
Hey, you!
Yaah!
Sorry--
I didn't mean to--
TONK
KLAT

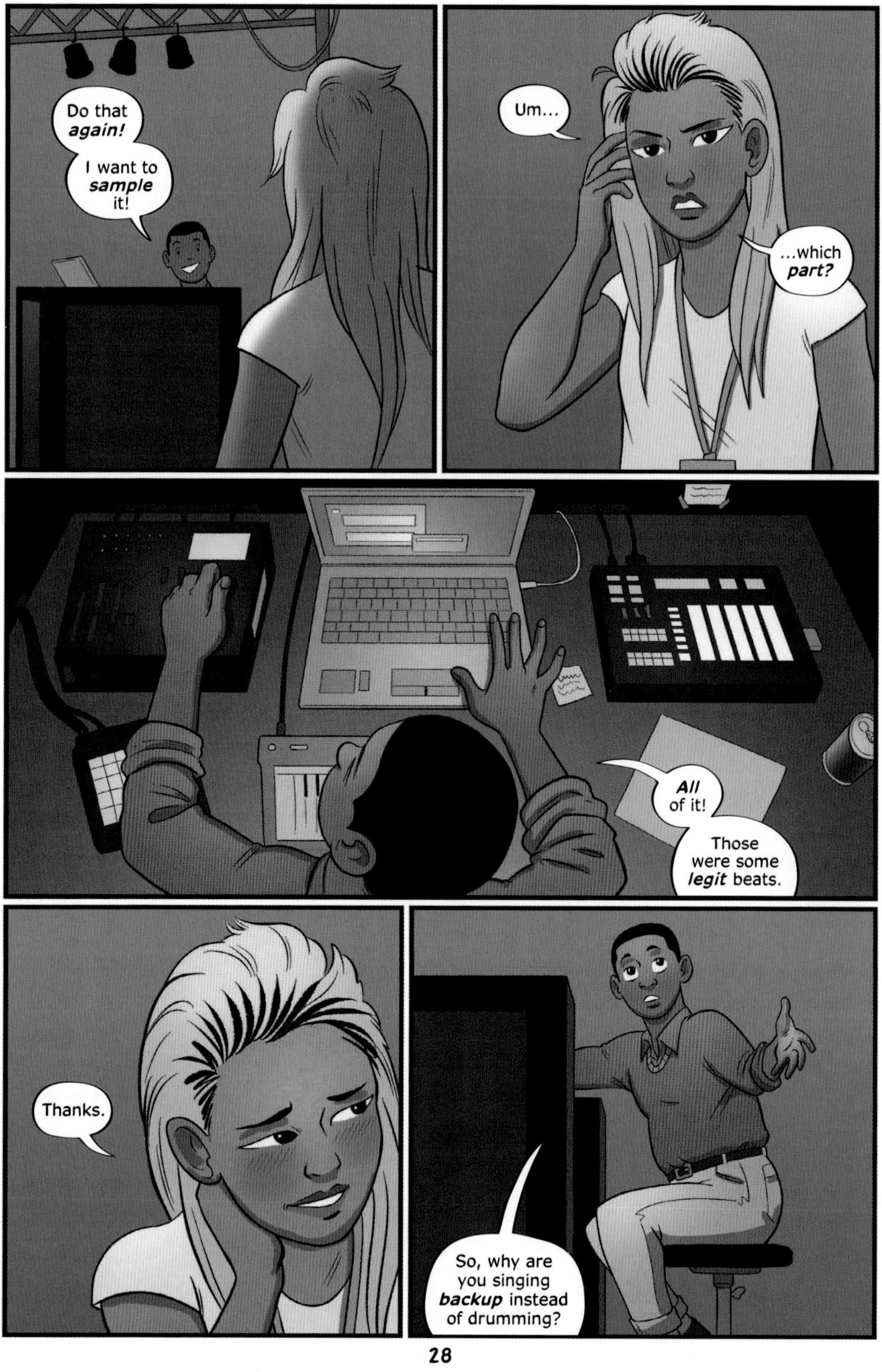

Do that *again!*
I want to *sample* it!
Um...
...which *part?*
All of it!
Those were some *legit* beats.
Thanks.
So, why are you singing *backup* instead of drumming?

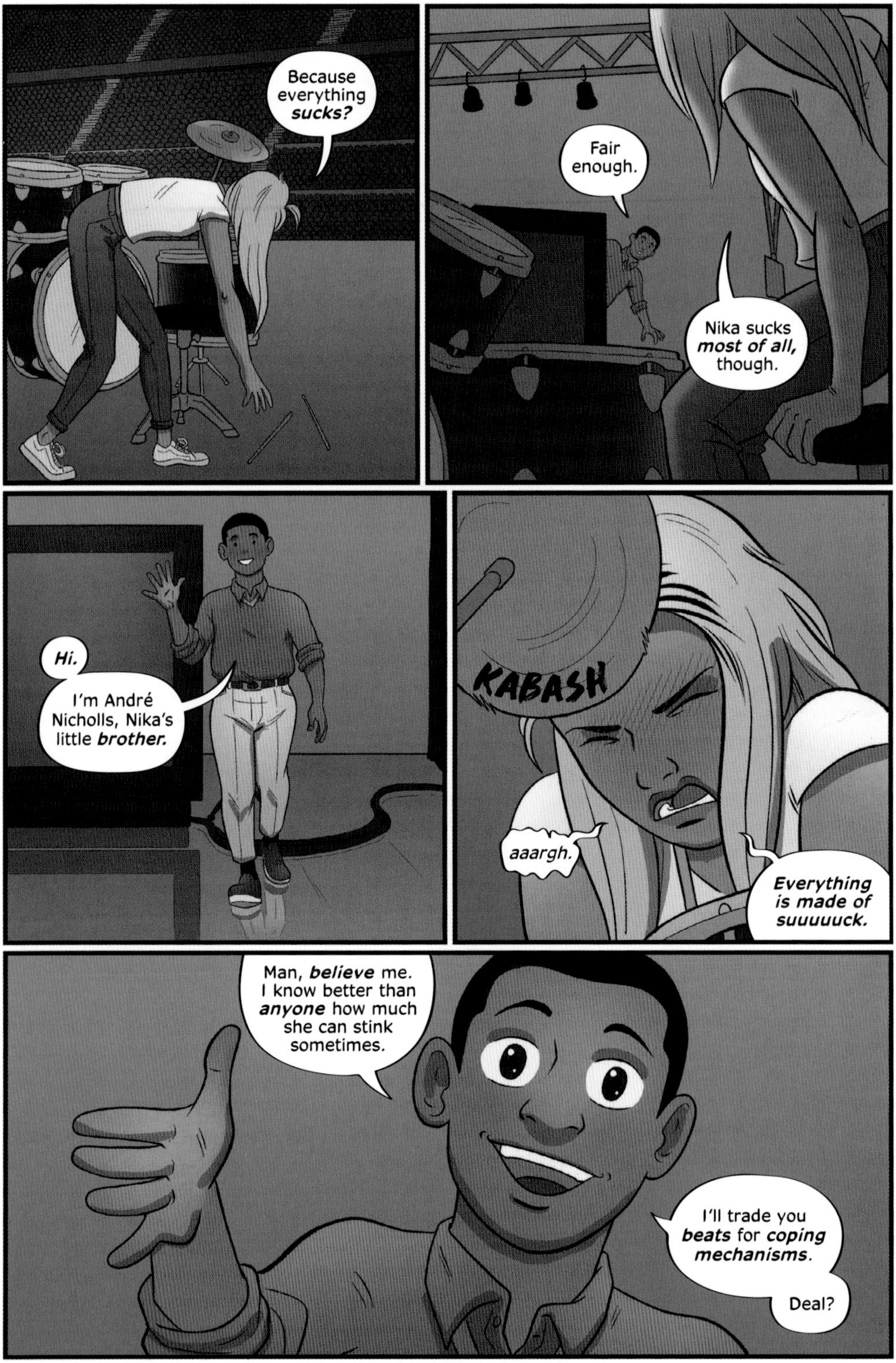
Because everything *sucks?*
Fair enough.
Nika sucks *most of all,* though.
Hi.
I'm André Nicholls, Nika's little *brother.*
KABASH
aaargh.
Everything is made of suuuuuck.
Man, *believe* me. I know better than *anyone* how much she can stink sometimes.
I'll trade you *beats* for *coping mechanisms*.
Deal?

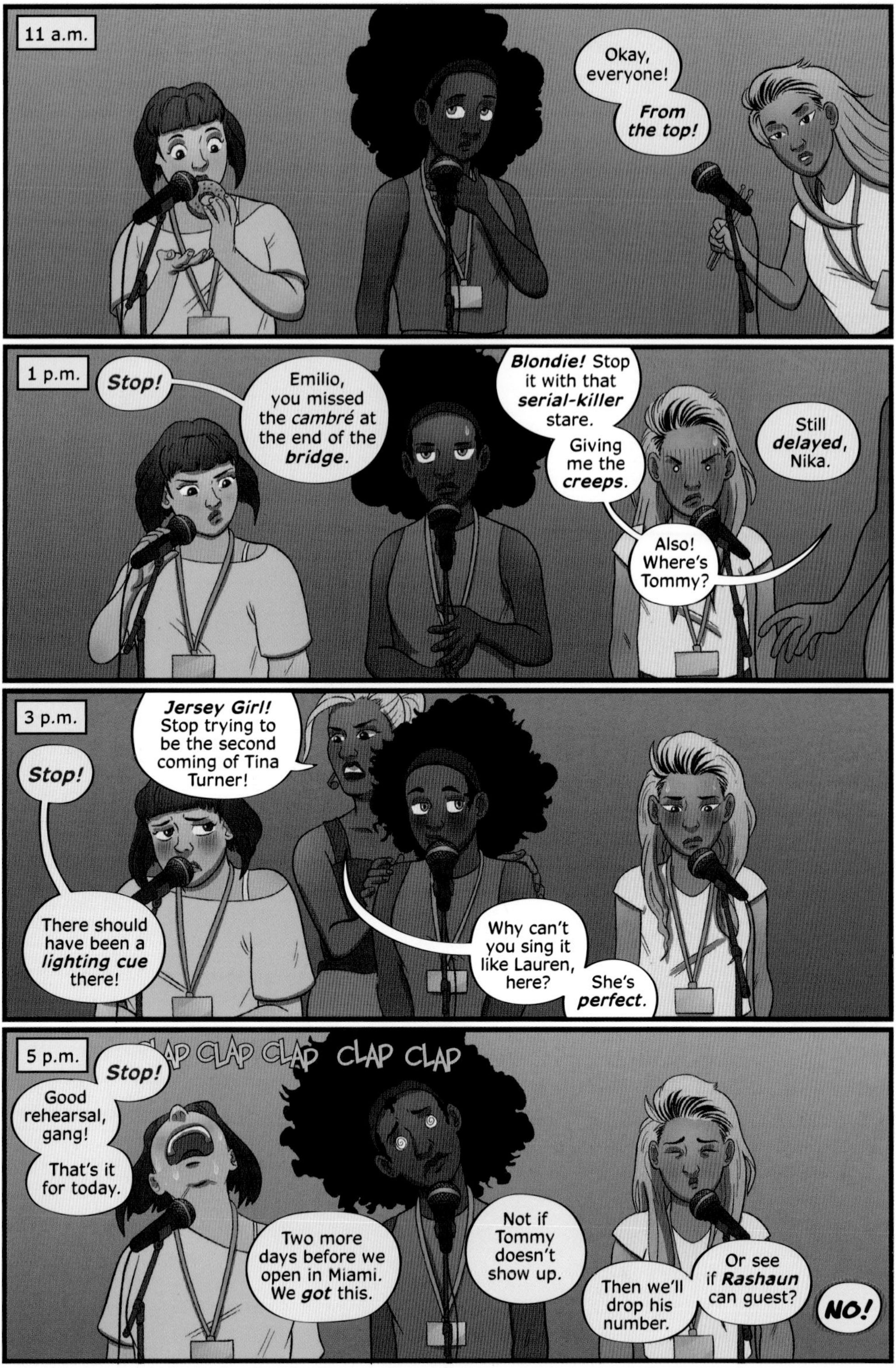
11 a.m.
Okay, everyone!
From the top!
1 p.m.
Stop!
Emilio, you missed the cambré at the end of the bridge.
Blondie! Stop it with that serial-killer stare.
Giving me the creeps.
Still delayed, Nika.
Also! Where's Tommy?
3 p.m.
Jersey Girl! Stop trying to be the second coming of Tina Turner!
Stop!
There should have been a lighting cue there!
Why can't you sing it like Lauren, here?
She's perfect.
5 p.m.
CLAP CLAP CLAP CLAP CLAP
Stop!
Good rehearsal, gang!
That's it for today.
Two more days before we open in Miami. We got this.
Not if Tommy doesn't show up.
Then we'll drop his number.
Or see if Rashaun can guest?
NO!

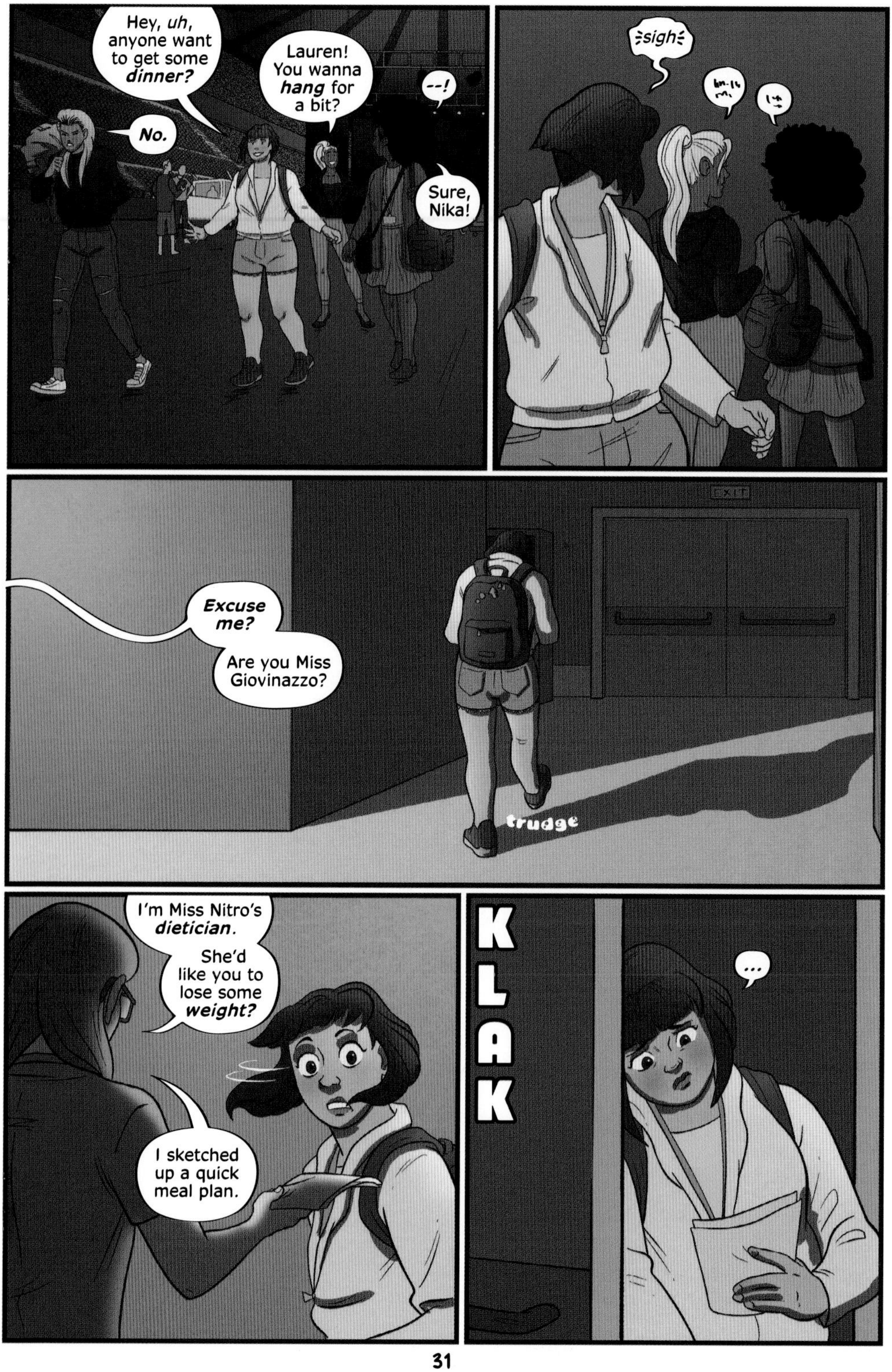
Hey, *uh*, anyone want to get some ***dinner?***
No.
Lauren! You wanna ***hang*** for a bit?
--!
Sure, Nika!
sigh
Excuse me?
Are you Miss Giovinazzo?
trudge
I'm Miss Nitro's ***dietician***.
She'd like you to lose some ***weight?***
I sketched up a quick meal plan.
KLAK
...

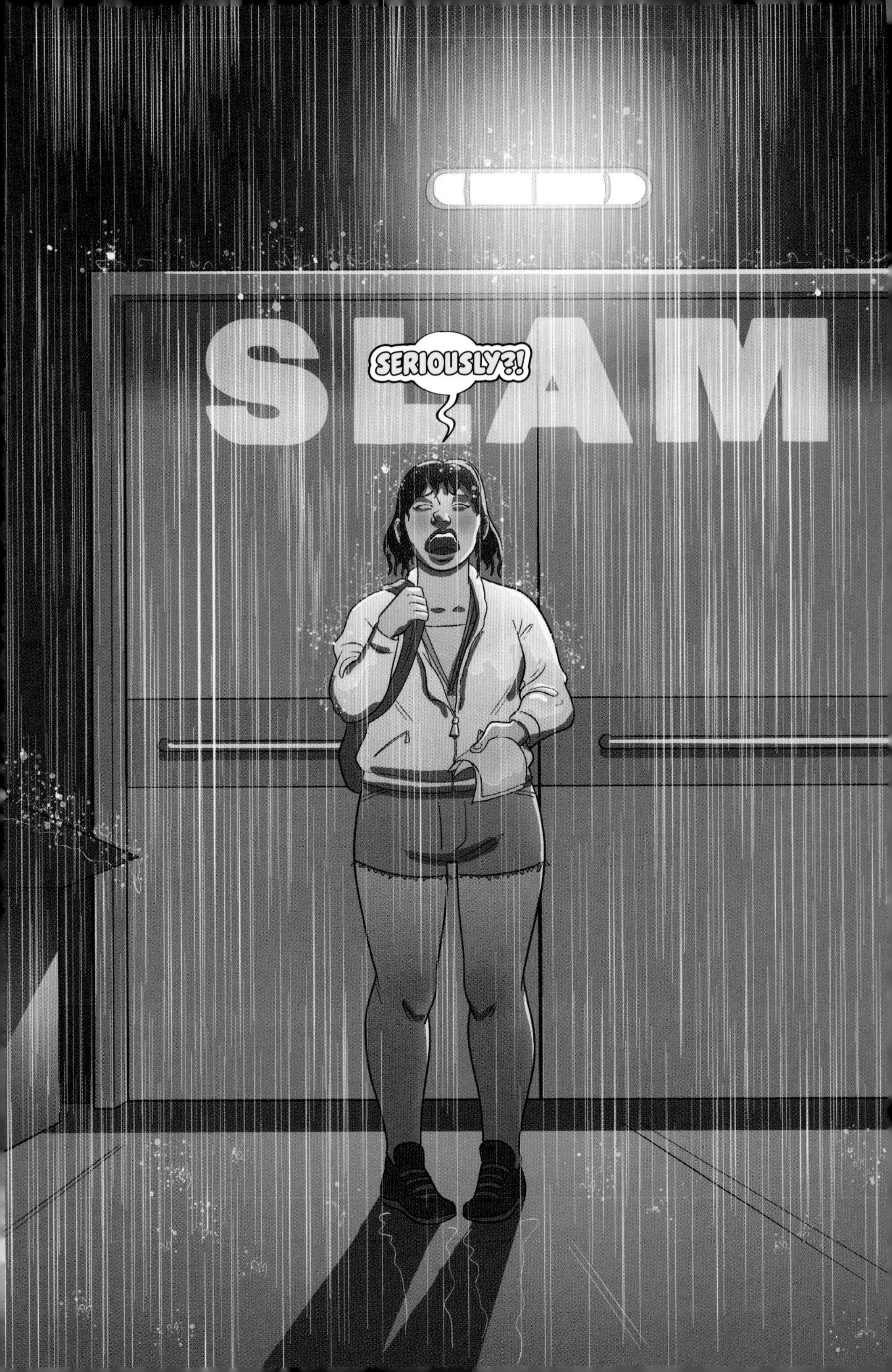
SLAM
SERIOUSLY?!

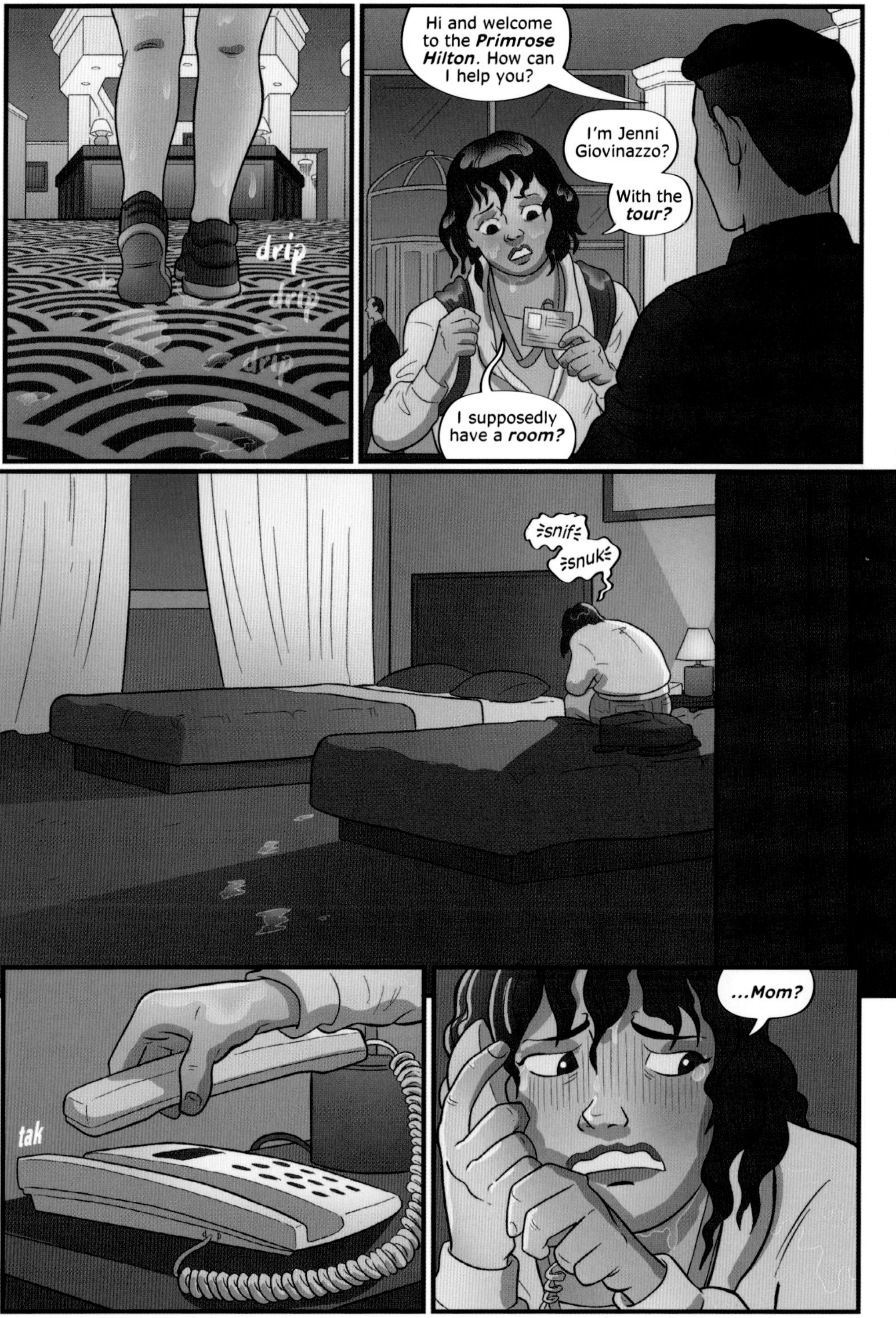
drip
drip
drip
Hi and welcome to the ***Primrose Hilton***. How can I help you?
I'm Jenni Giovinazzo?
With the ***tour?***
I supposedly have a ***room?***
snif
snuk
tak
...Mom?

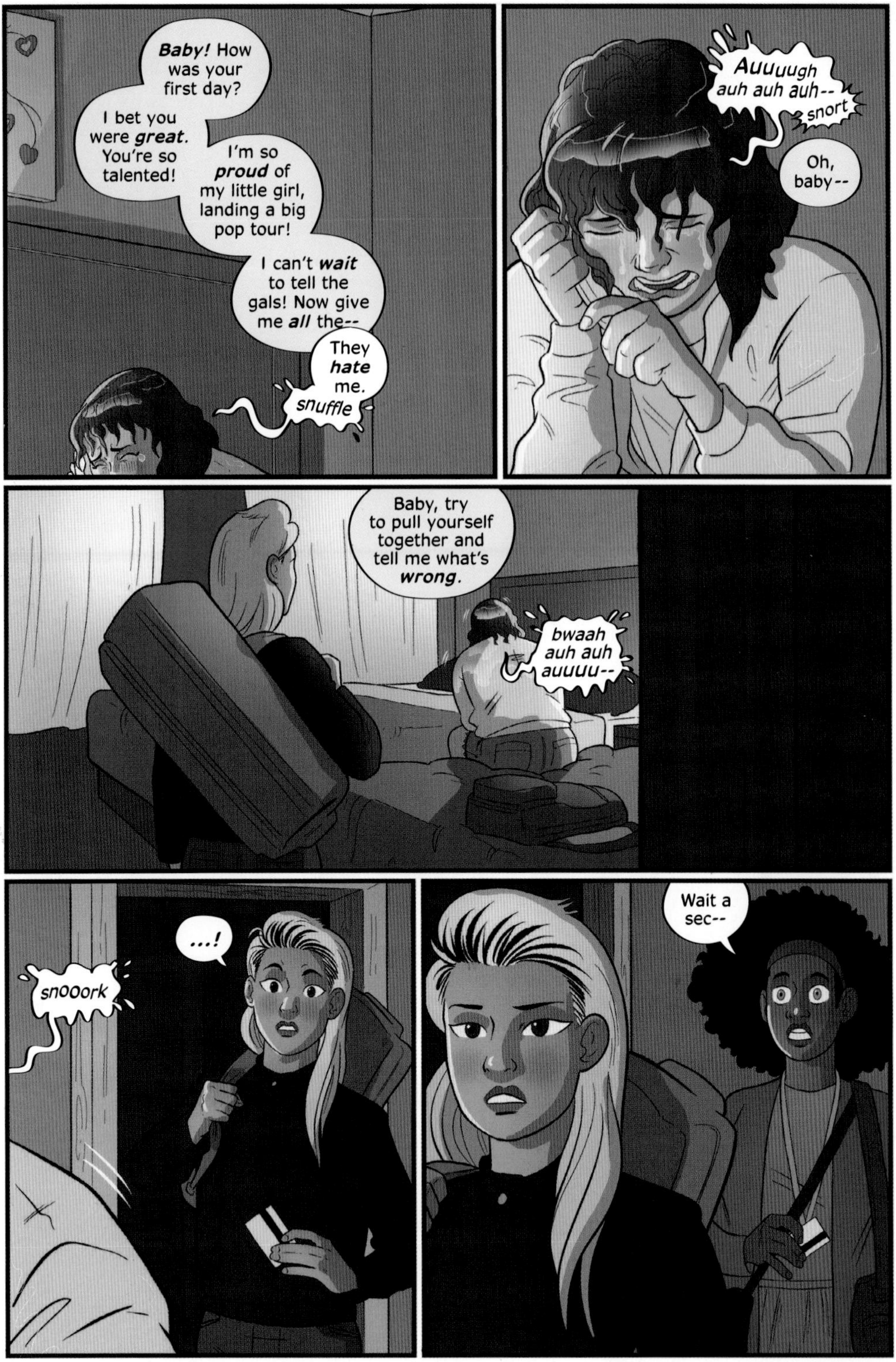

Baby! How was your first day?
I bet you were ***great***. You're so talented!
I'm so ***proud*** of my little girl, landing a big pop tour!
I can't ***wait*** to tell the gals! Now give me ***all*** the--
They ***hate*** me.
snuffle
Auuuugh auh auh auh--
snort
Oh, baby--
Baby, try to pull yourself together and tell me what's ***wrong***.
bwaah auh auh auuuu--
snooork
...!
Wait a sec--

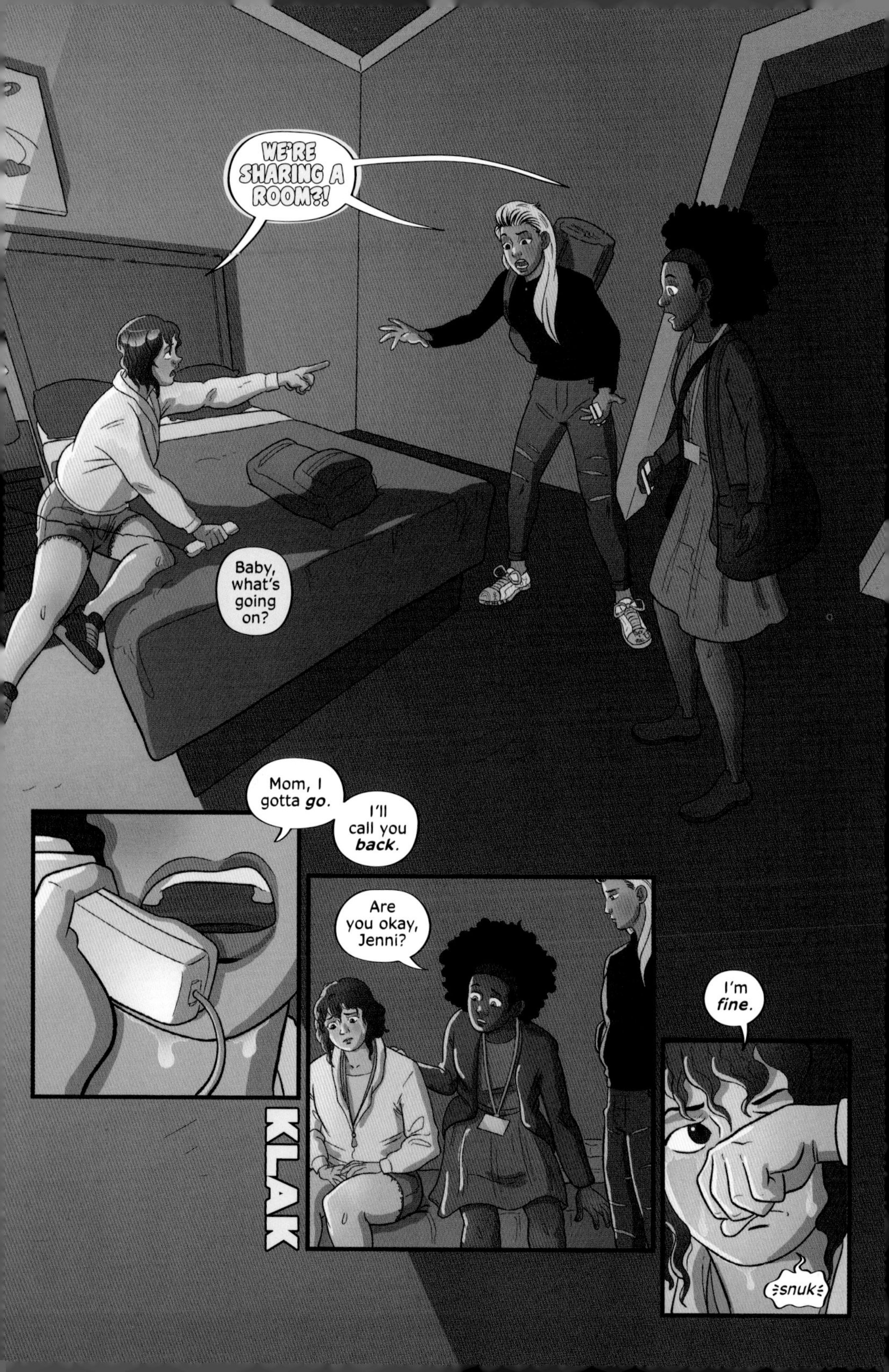
WE'RE SHARING A ROOM?!
Baby, what's going on?
Mom, I gotta *go*.
I'll call you *back*.
KLAK
Are you okay, Jenni?
I'm *fine*.
snuk

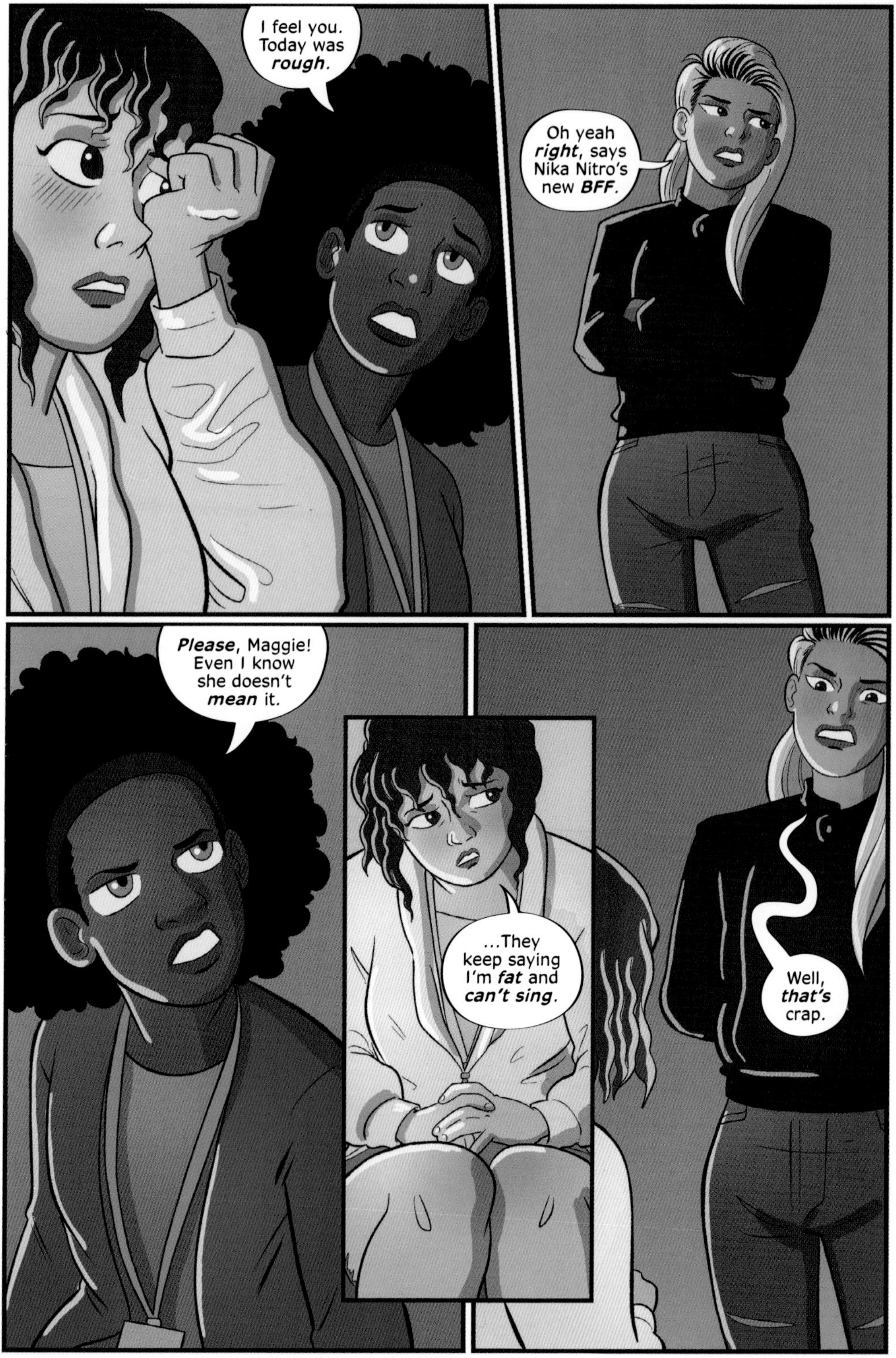
I feel you. Today was *rough*.
Oh yeah *right*, says Nika Nitro's new *BFF*.
Please, Maggie! Even I know she doesn't *mean* it.
...They keep saying I'm *fat* and *can't sing*.
Well, *that's* crap.

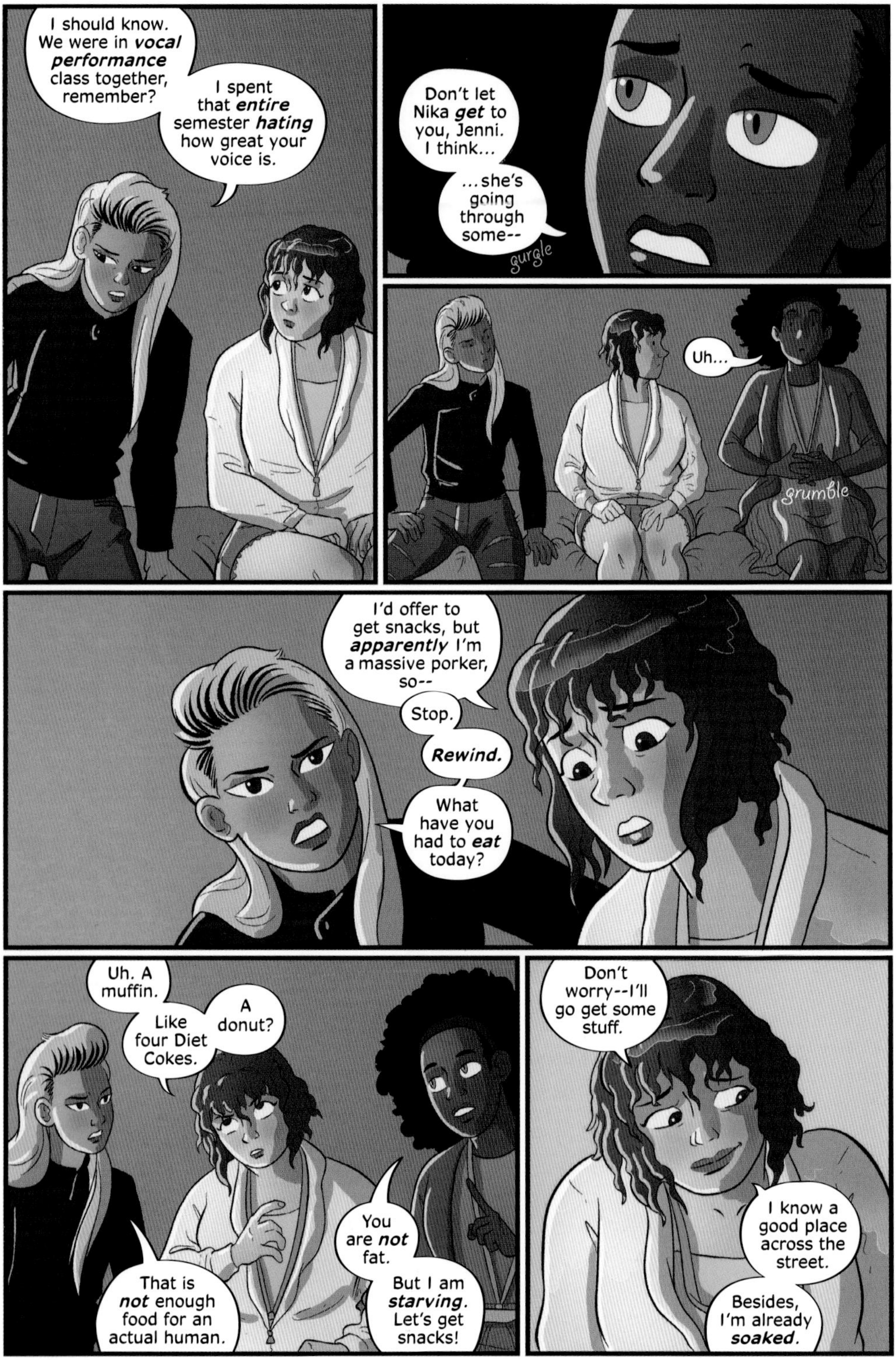
I should know. We were in *vocal performance* class together, remember?
I spent that *entire* semester *hating* how great your voice is.
Don't let Nika *get* to you, Jenni. I think...
...she's going through some--
gurgle
Uh...
grumble
I'd offer to get snacks, but *apparently* I'm a massive porker, so--
Stop.
Rewind.
What have you had to *eat* today?
Uh. A muffin.
Like four Diet Cokes.
A donut?
That is *not* enough food for an actual human.
You are *not* fat.
But I am *starving*. Let's get snacks!
Don't worry--I'll go get some stuff.
I know a good place across the street.
Besides, I'm already *soaked*.

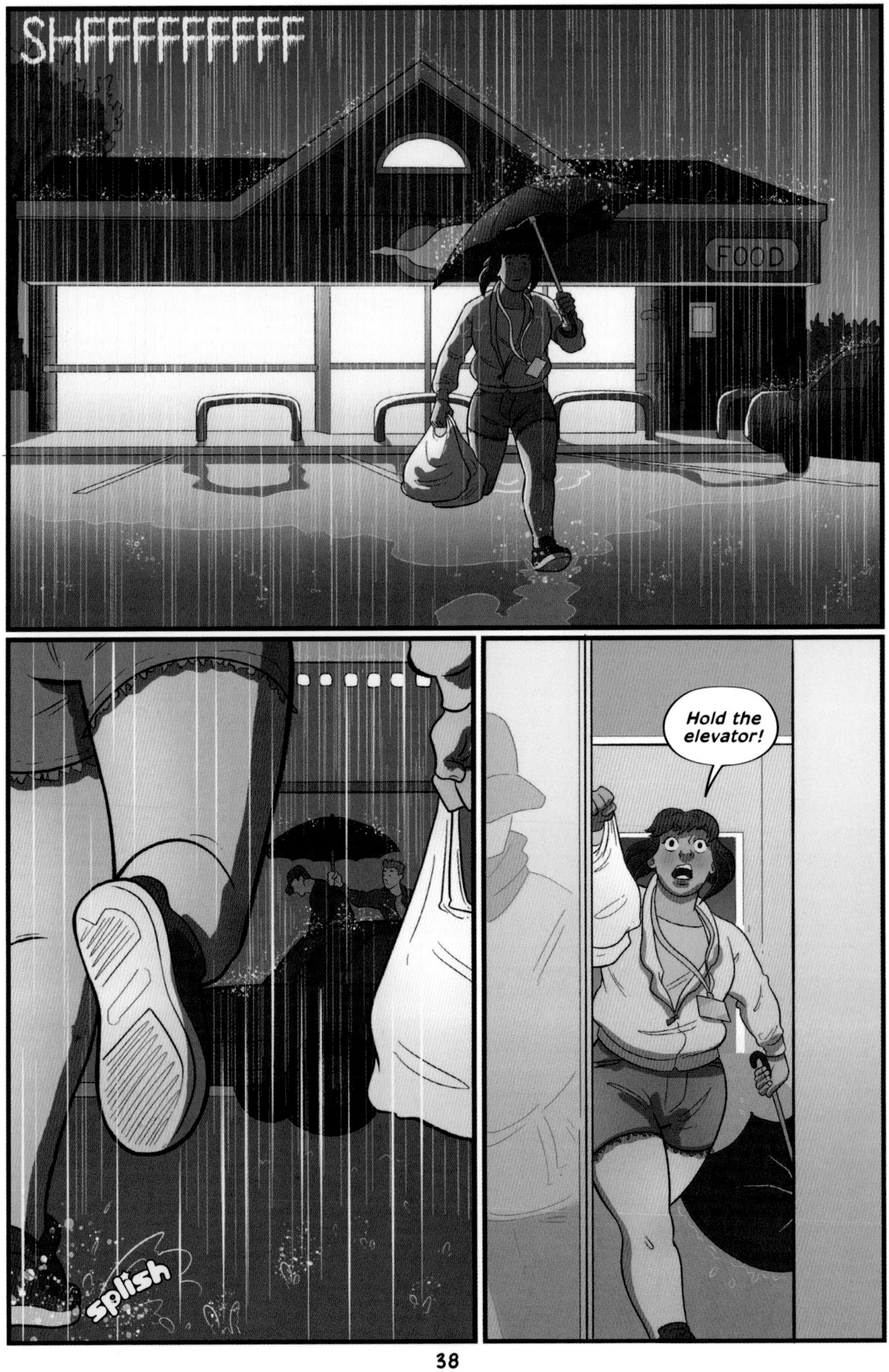
SHFFFFFFFFF
FOOD
splish
Hold the elevator!

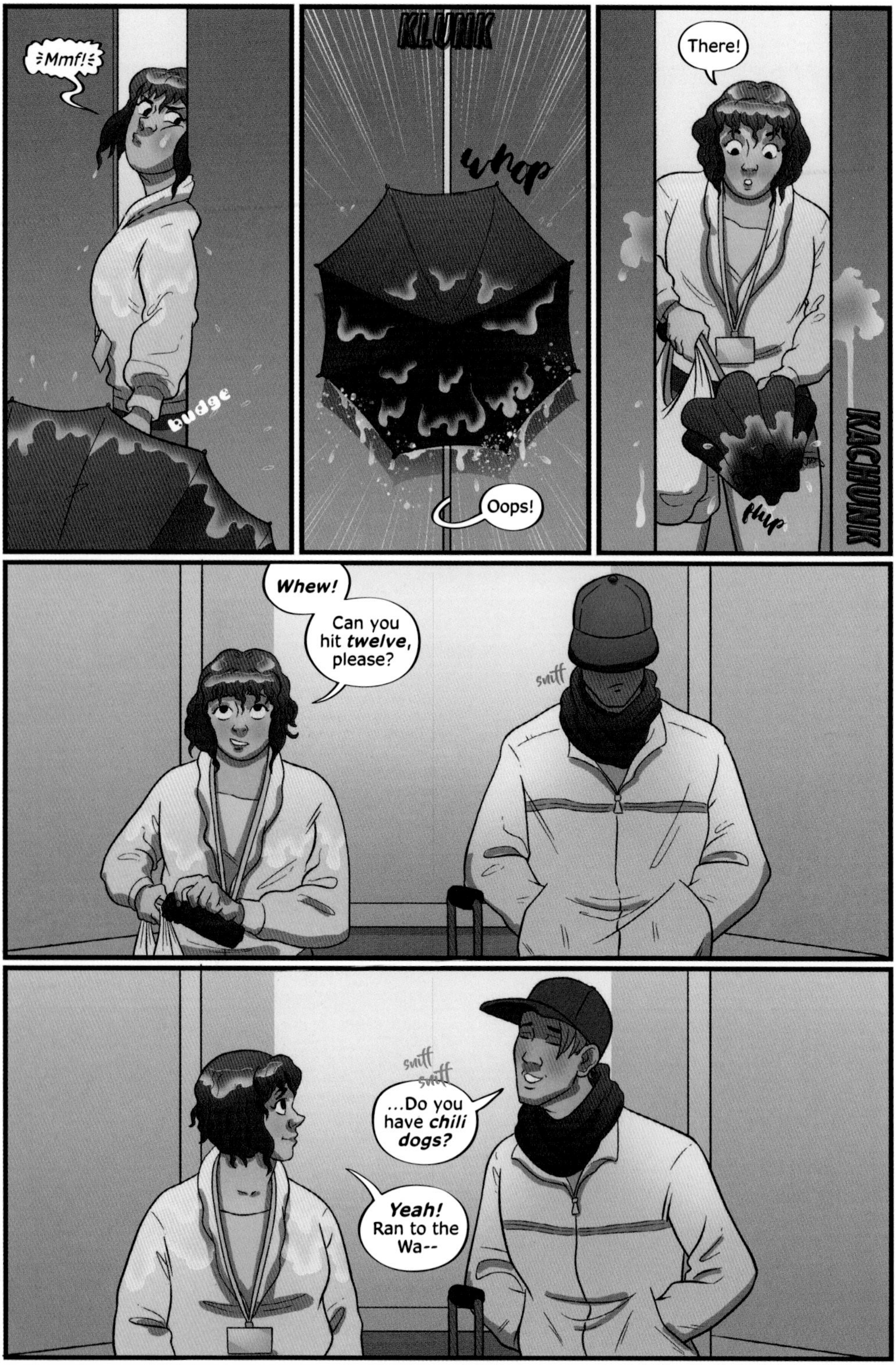
Mmf!
budge
KLUNK
whap
Oops!
There!
KACHUNK
flup
Whew!
Can you hit *twelve*, please?
sniff
sniff
sniff
...Do you have *chili dogs?*
Yeah! Ran to the Wa--

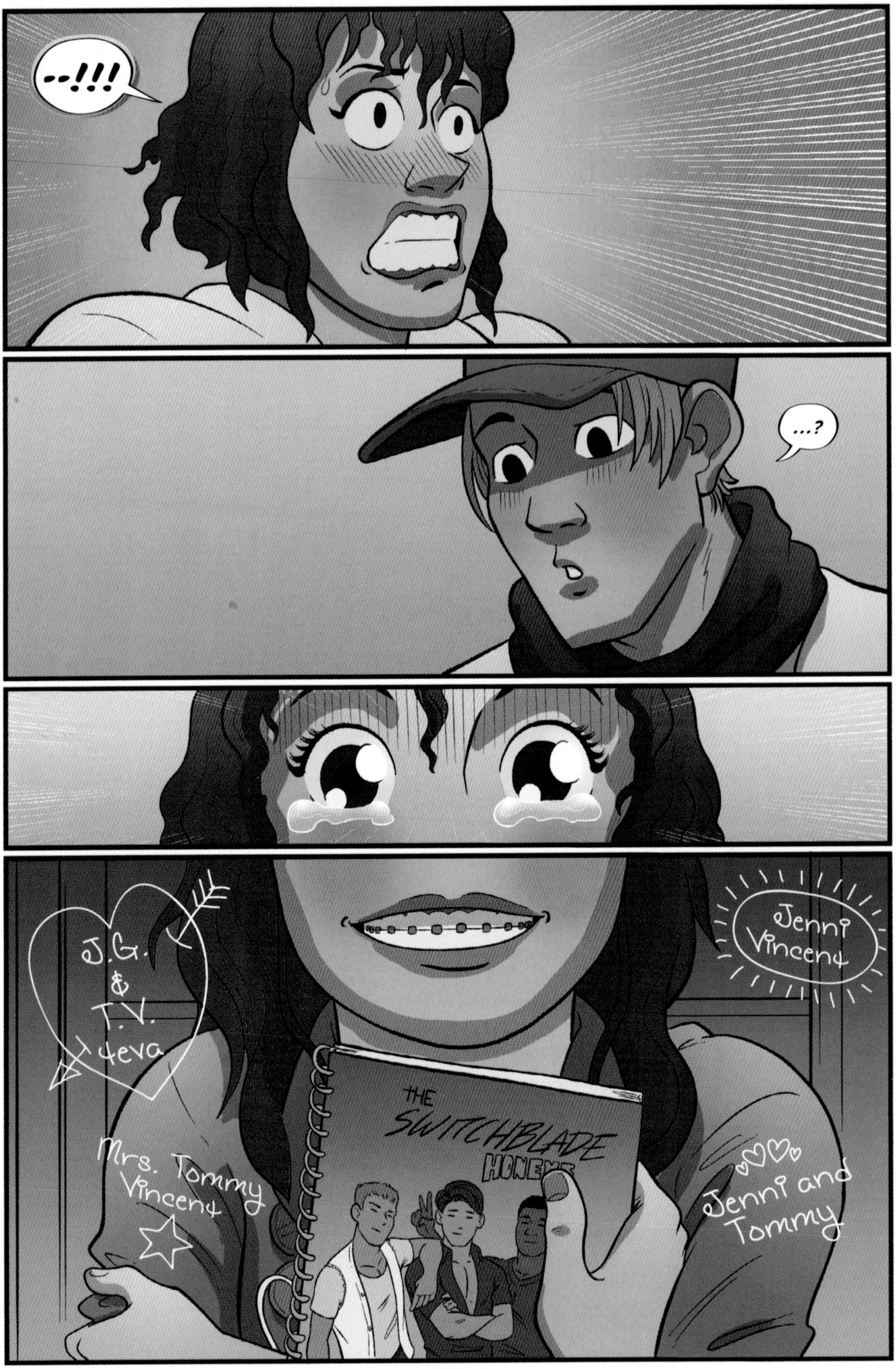
--!!!
...?
J.G. & T.V. 4eva
Jenni Vincent
THE SWITCHBLADE HONEYS
Mrs. Tommy Vincent
Jenni and Tommy

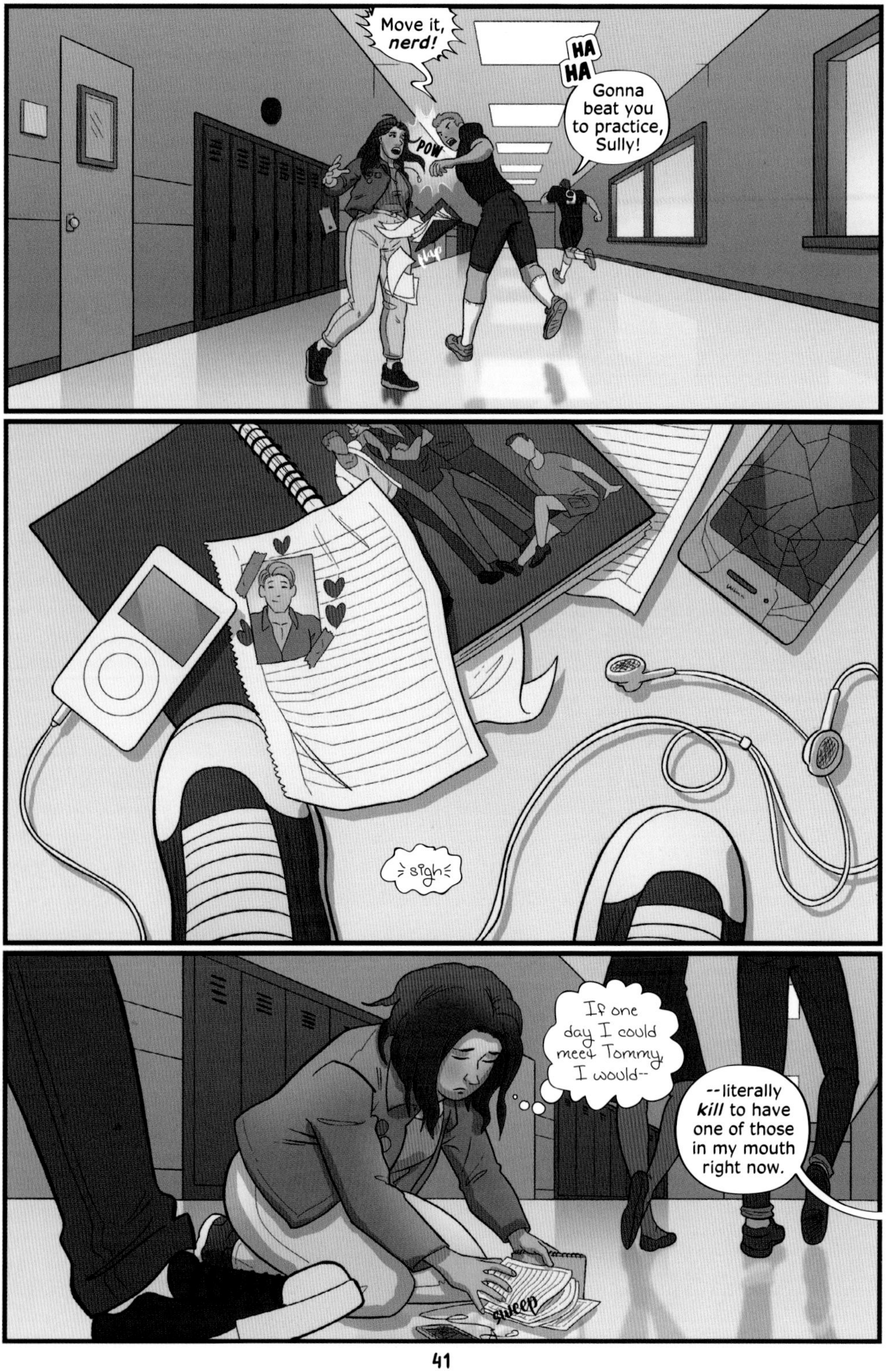
Move it, *nerd!*
HA HA
Gonna beat you to practice, Sully!
POW
flap
sigh
If one day I could meet Tommy, I would--
--literally ***kill*** to have one of those in my mouth right now.
sweep

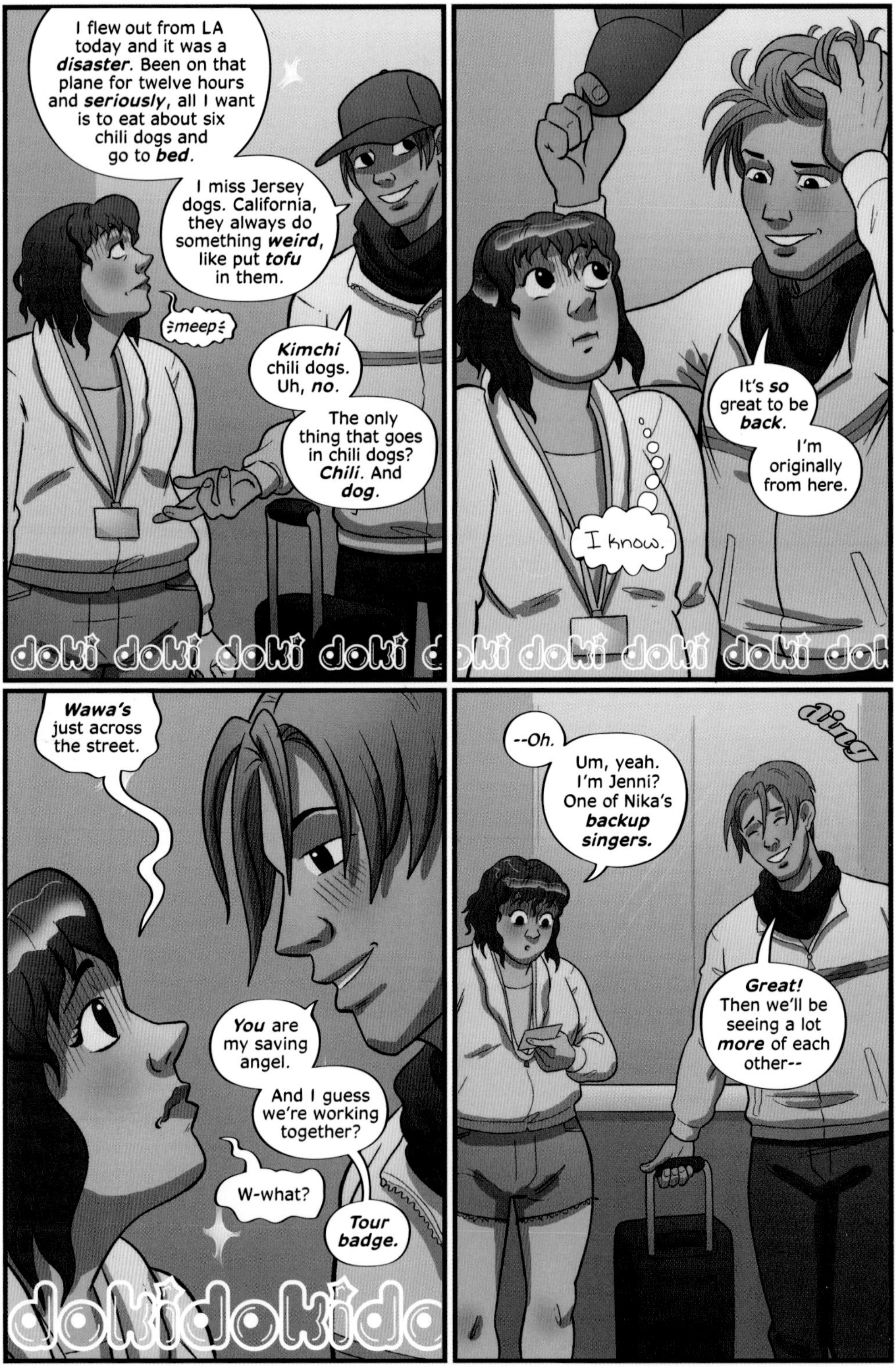

I flew out from LA today and it was a *disaster*. Been on that plane for twelve hours and *seriously*, all I want is to eat about six chili dogs and go to *bed*.
I miss Jersey dogs. California, they always do something *weird*, like put *tofu* in them.
meep
Kimchi chili dogs. Uh, *no*.
The only thing that goes in chili dogs? *Chili*. And *dog*.
doki doki doki doki
It's *so* great to be *back*.
I'm originally from here.
I know.
Wawa's just across the street.
You are my saving angel.
And I guess we're working together?
W-what?
Tour badge.
dokidokido
--Oh.
Um, yeah. I'm Jenni? One of Nika's *backup singers.*
ding
Great! Then we'll be seeing a lot *more* of each other--

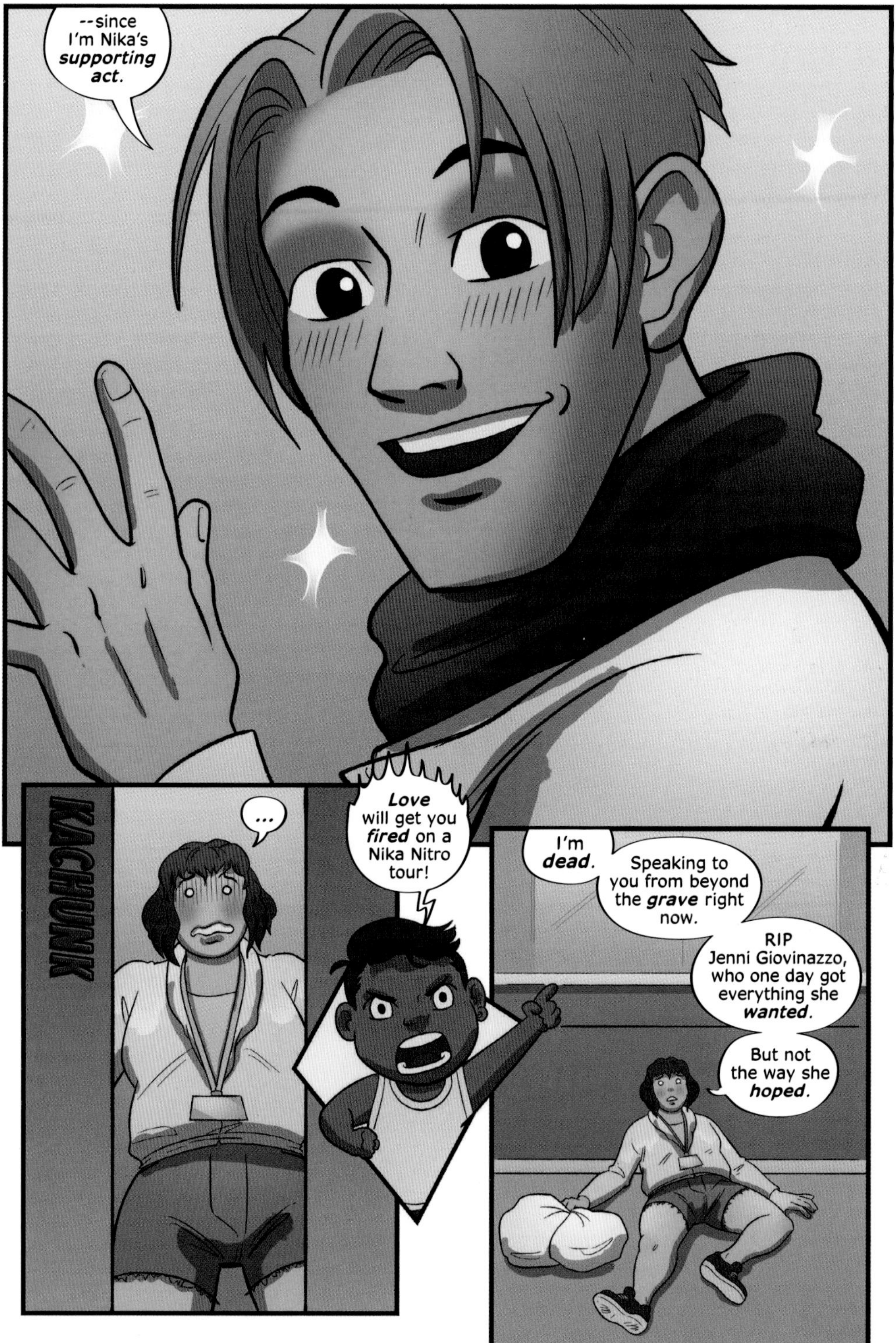
--since I'm Nika's *supporting act*.
KACHUNK
...
Love will get you *fired* on a Nika Nitro tour!
I'm *dead*.
Speaking to you from beyond the *grave* right now.
RIP Jenni Giovinazzo, who one day got everything she *wanted*.
But not the way she *hoped*.

CHAPTER 2

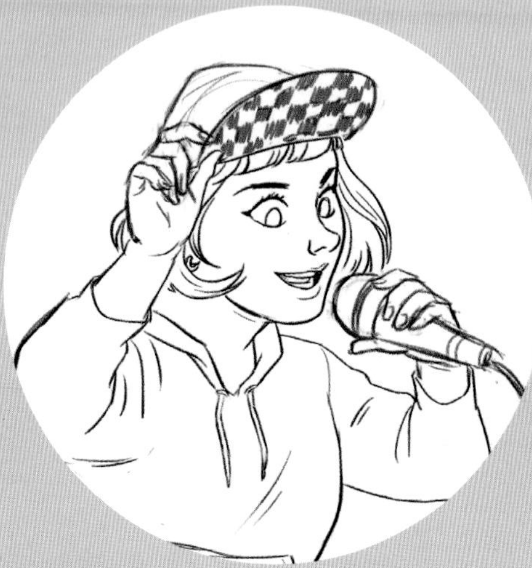

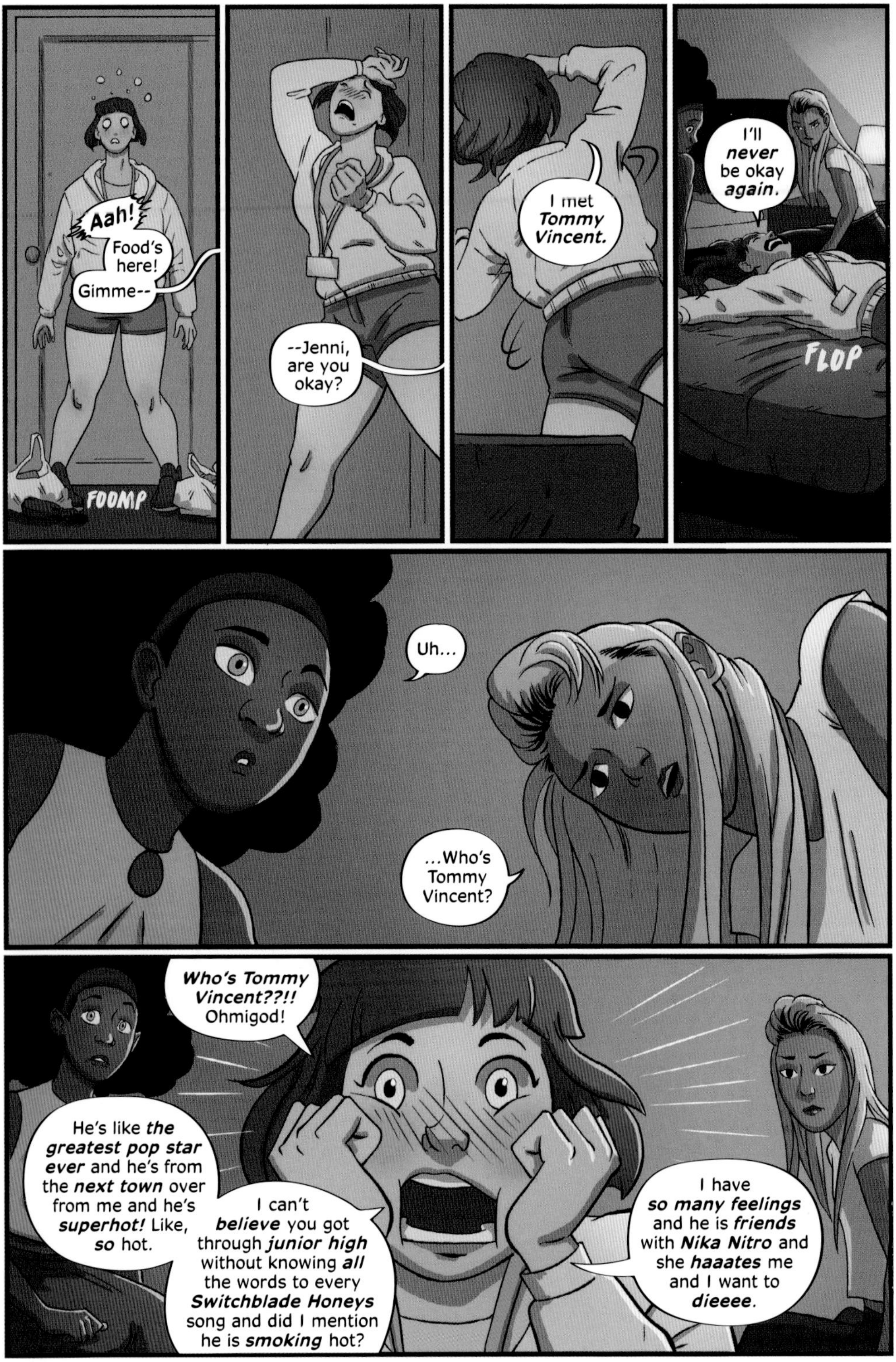
Aah!
Food's here!
Gimme--
--Jenni, are you okay?
FOOMP
I met *Tommy Vincent.*
I'll *never* be okay *again*.
FLOP
Uh...
...Who's Tommy Vincent?
Who's Tommy Vincent??!! Ohmigod!
He's like ***the greatest pop star ever*** and he's from the ***next town*** over from me and he's ***superhot!*** Like, ***so*** hot.
I can't ***believe*** you got through ***junior high*** without knowing ***all*** the words to every ***Switchblade Honeys*** song and did I mention he is ***smoking*** hot?
I have ***so many feelings*** and he is ***friends*** with ***Nika Nitro*** and she ***haaates*** me and I want to ***dieeee.***

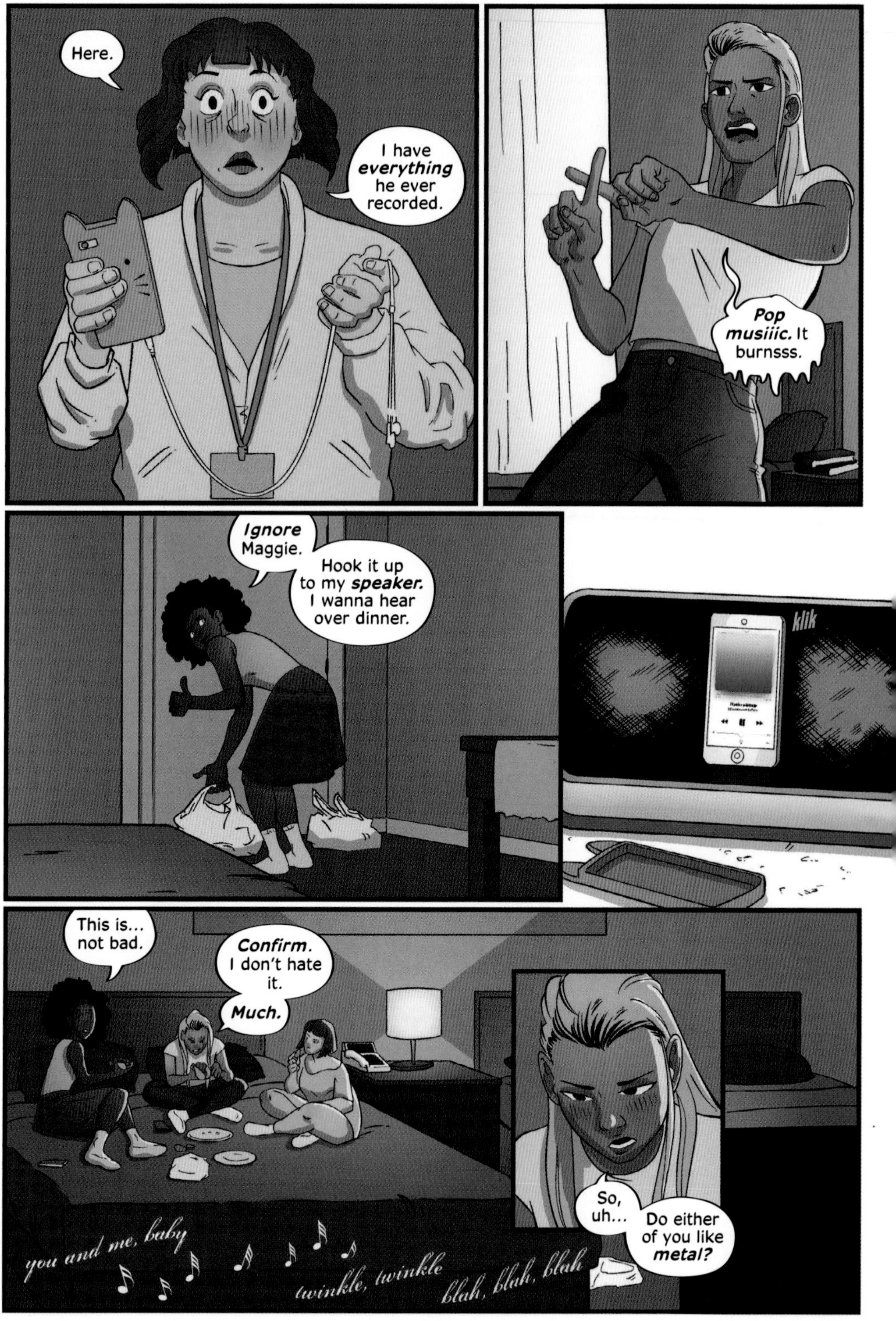
Here.
I have *everything* he ever recorded.
Pop musiiic. It burnsss.
Ignore Maggie.
Hook it up to my ***speaker.*** I wanna hear over dinner.
klik
This is... not bad.
Confirm. I don't hate it.
Much.
So, uh...
Do either of you like ***metal?***
you and me, baby
twinkle, twinkle
blah, blah, blah

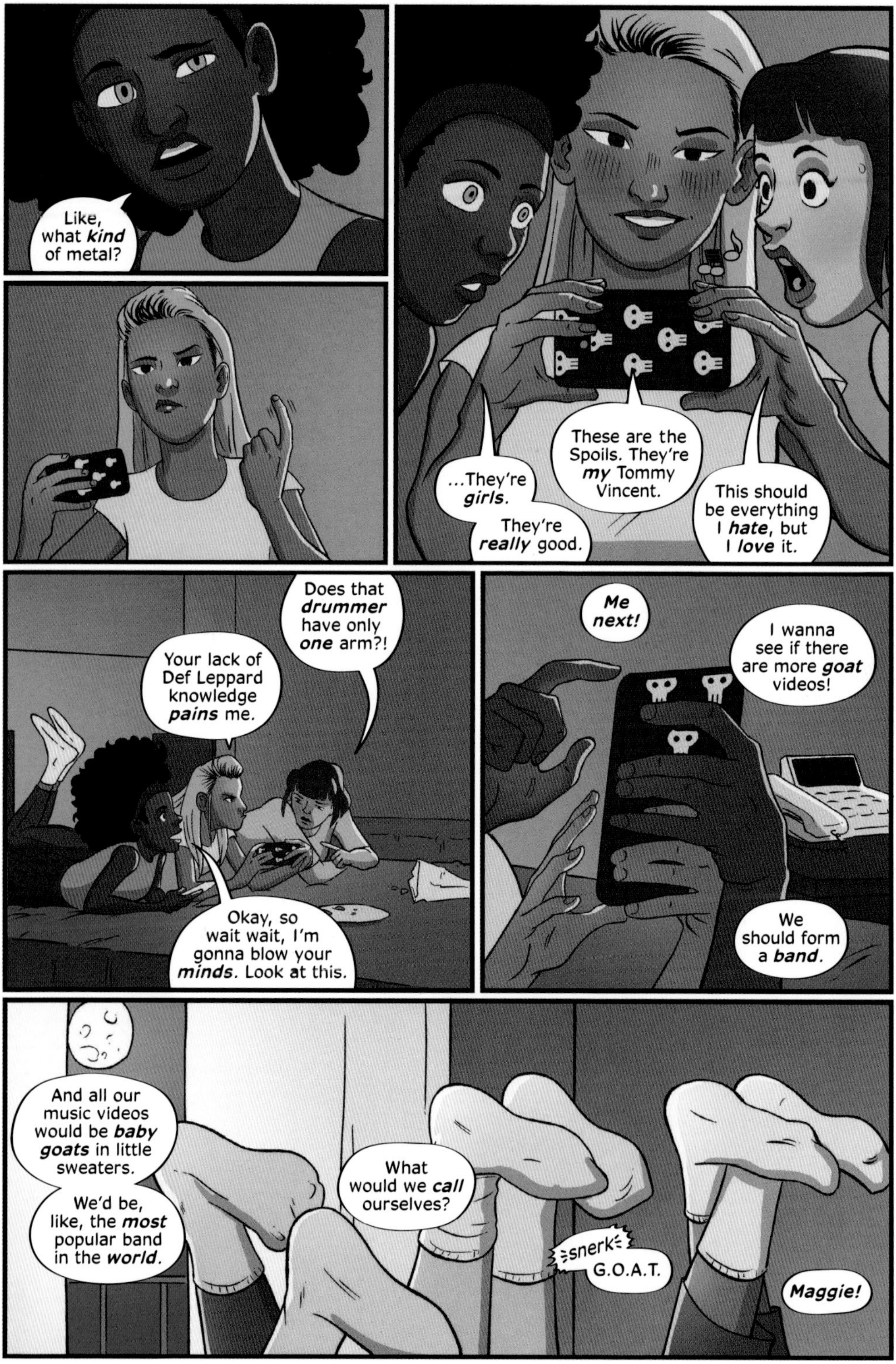
Like, what *kind* of metal?
These are the Spoils. They're *my* Tommy Vincent.
...They're *girls*.
They're *really* good.
This should be everything I *hate*, but I *love* it.
Does that *drummer* have only *one* arm?!
Your lack of Def Leppard knowledge *pains* me.
Okay, so wait wait, I'm gonna blow your *minds*. Look at this.
Me next!
I wanna see if there are more *goat* videos!
We should form a *band*.
And all our music videos would be *baby goats* in little sweaters.
We'd be, like, the *most* popular band in the *world*.
What would we *call* ourselves?
snerk
G.O.A.T.
Maggie!

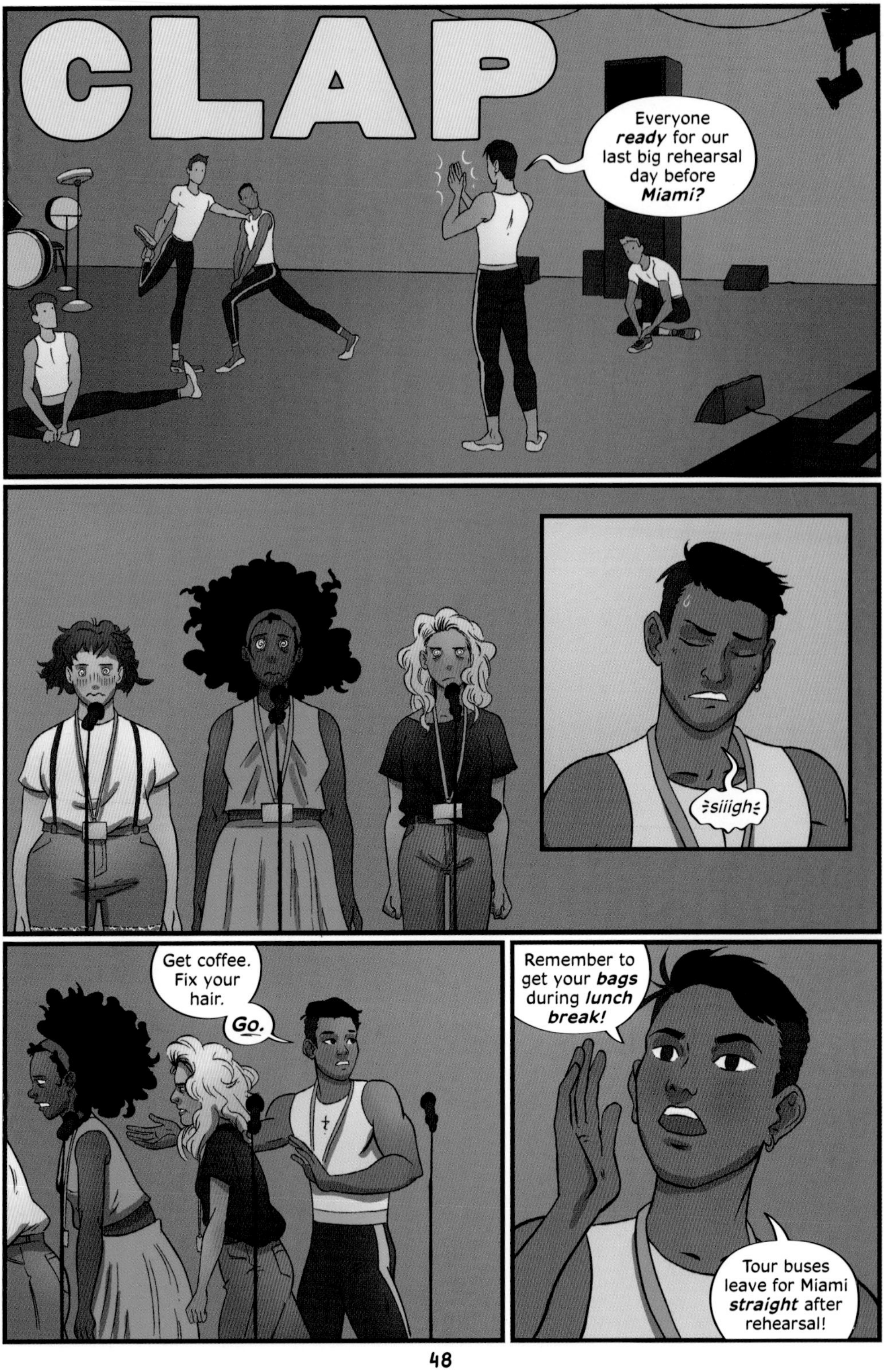
CLAP
Everyone *ready* for our last big rehearsal day before *Miami?*
≷siiigh≶
Get coffee. Fix your hair.
Go.
Remember to get your *bags* during *lunch break!*
Tour buses leave for Miami *straight* after rehearsal!

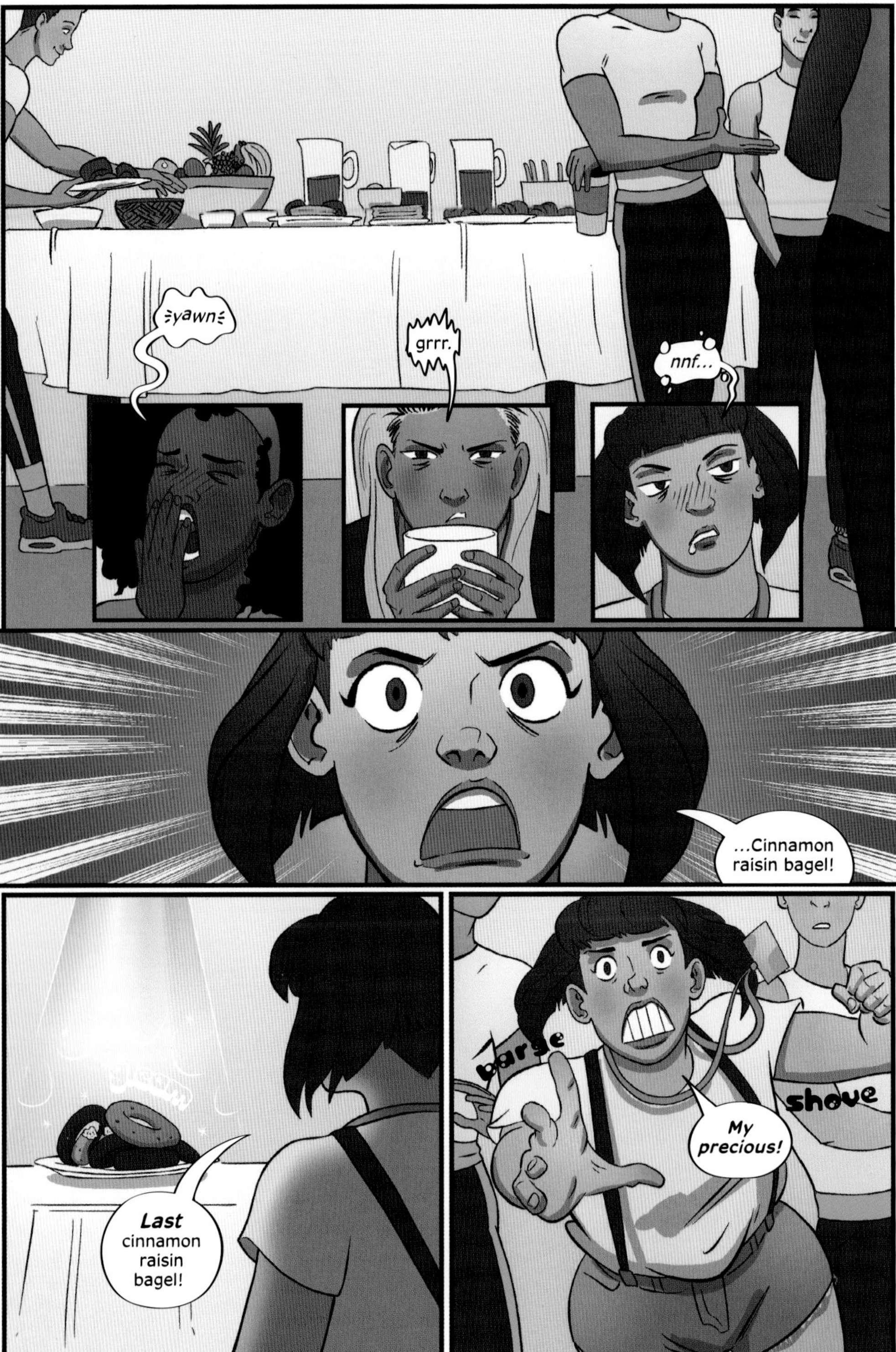
yawn
grrr.
nnf...
...Cinnamon raisin bagel!
Last cinnamon raisin bagel!
barge
shove
My precious!

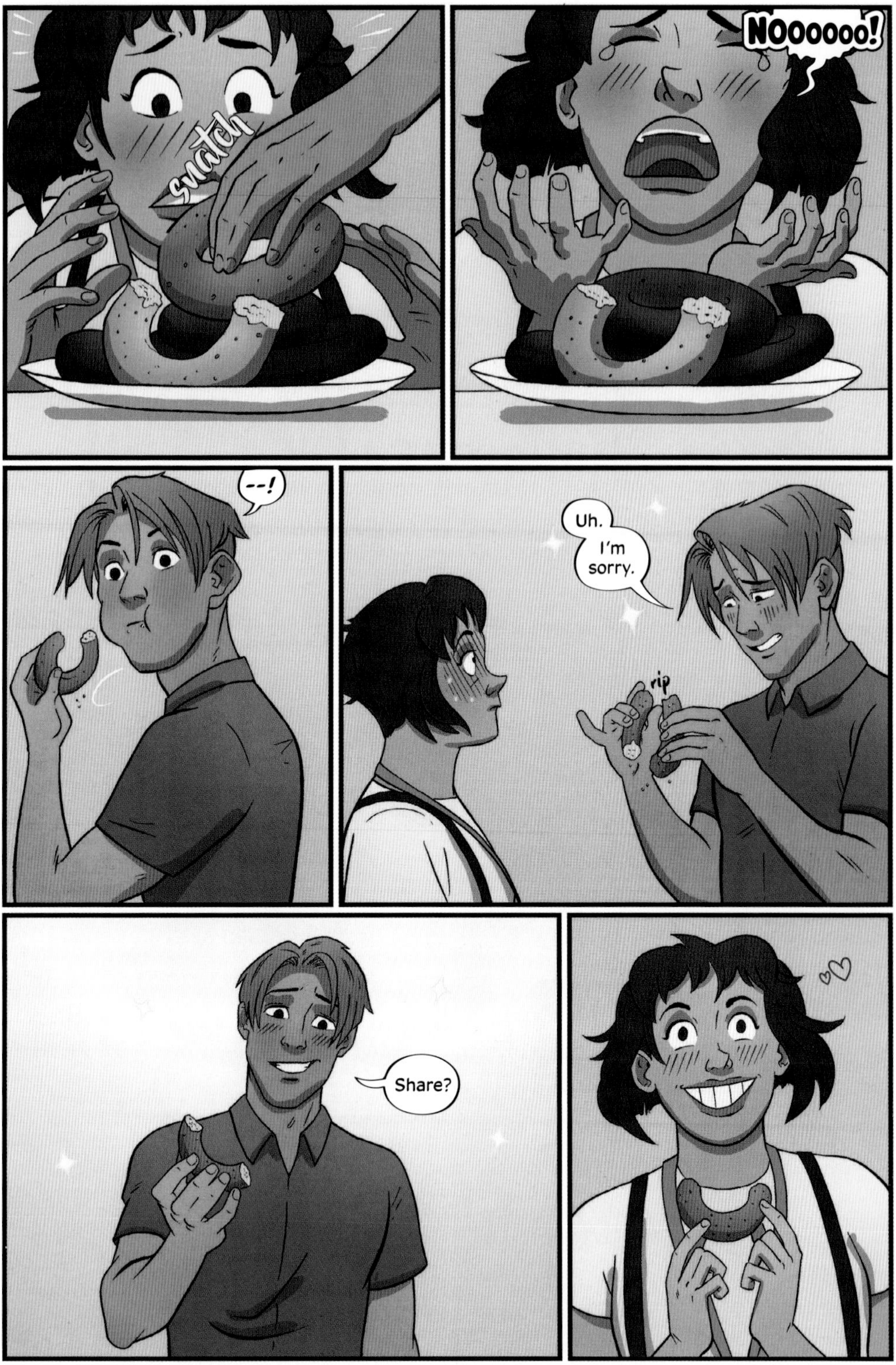
snatch
NOooooo!
--!
Uh.
I'm sorry.
rip
Share?

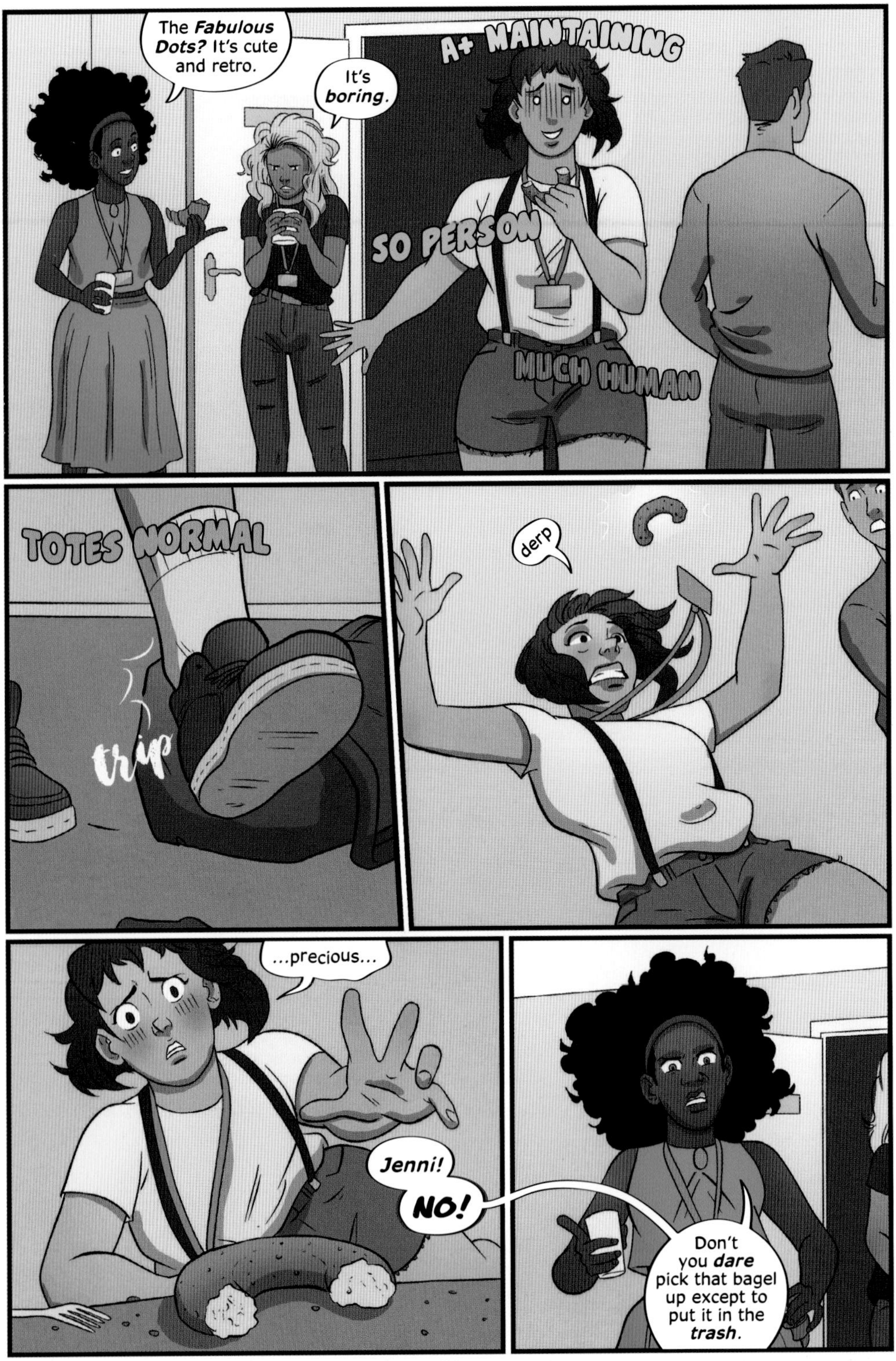
The *Fabulous Dots?* It's cute and retro.
It's *boring*.
A+ MAINTAINING
SO PERSON
MUCH HUMAN
TOTES NORMAL
trip
derp
...precious...
Jenni!
NO!
Don't you *dare* pick that bagel up except to put it in the *trash*.

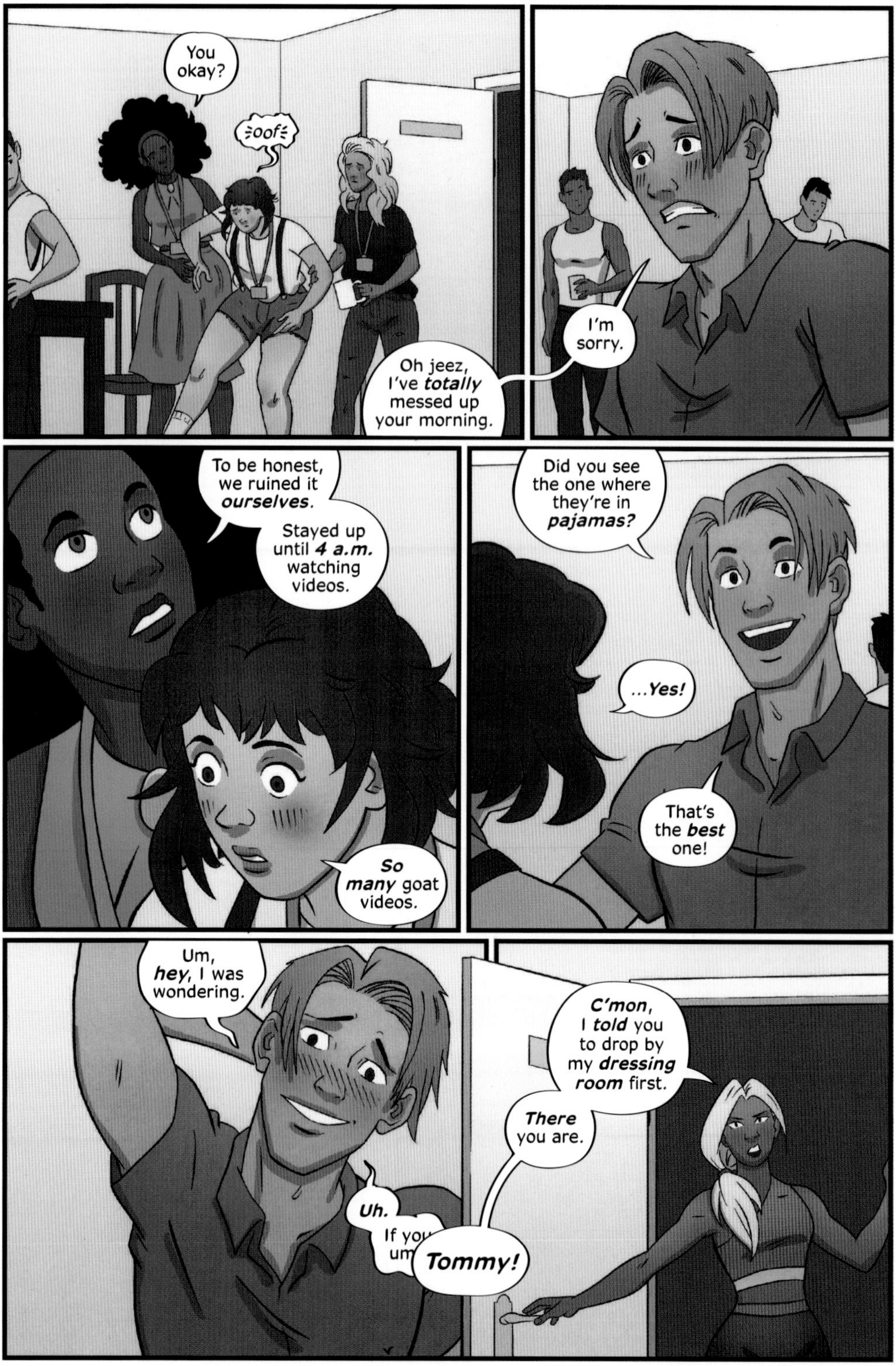
You okay?
oof
Oh jeez, I've *totally* messed up your morning.
I'm sorry.
To be honest, we ruined it *ourselves*.
Stayed up until *4 a.m.* watching videos.
So many goat videos.
Did you see the one where they're in *pajamas?*
...*Yes!*
That's the *best* one!
Um, *hey*, I was wondering.
Uh.
If you um
Tommy!
There you are.
C'mon, I *told* you to drop by my *dressing room* first.

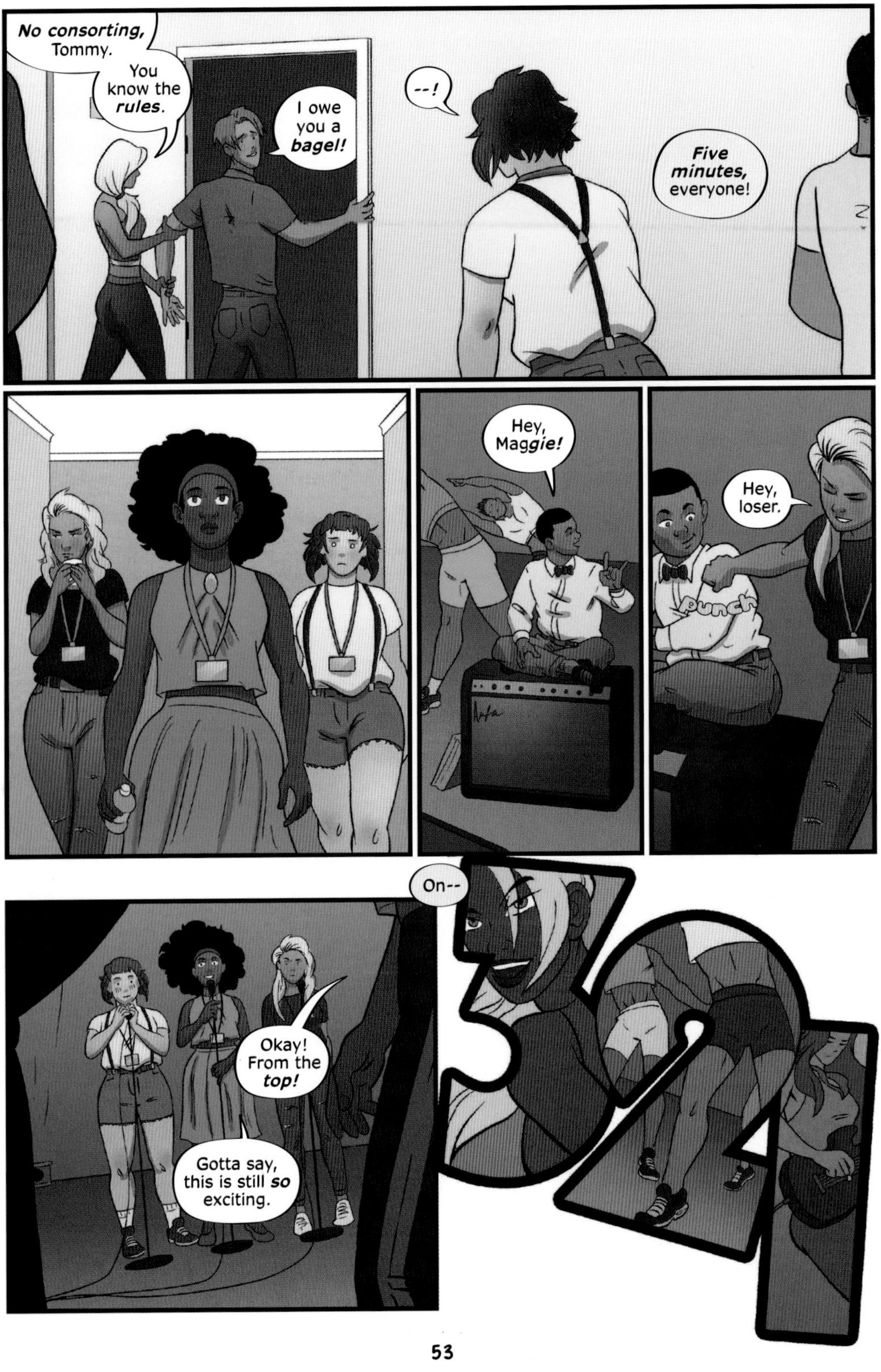

No consorting, Tommy.
You know the *rules*.
I owe you a *bagel!*
--!
Five minutes, everyone!
Hey, Mag*gie!*
Hey, loser.
Punch
On--
Okay! From the *top!*
Gotta say, this is still *so* exciting.

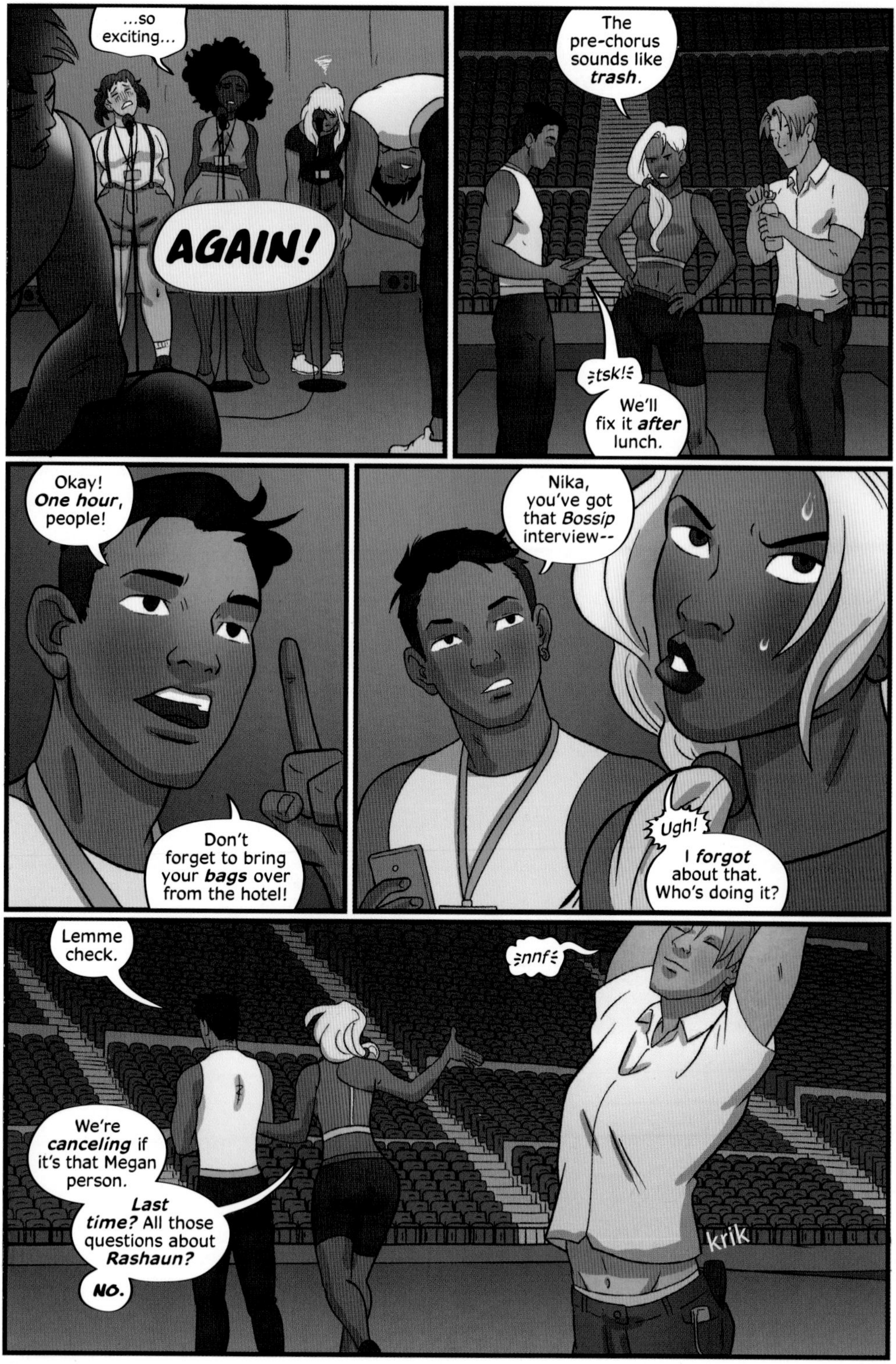
...so exciting...
AGAIN!
The pre-chorus sounds like *trash*.
tsk!
We'll fix it *after* lunch.
Okay! *One hour*, people!
Don't forget to bring your *bags* over from the hotel!
Nika, you've got that *Bossip* interview--
Ugh!
I *forgot* about that. Who's doing it?
Lemme check.
nnf
We're *canceling* if it's that Megan person.
Last time? All those questions about *Rashaun?*
NO.
krik

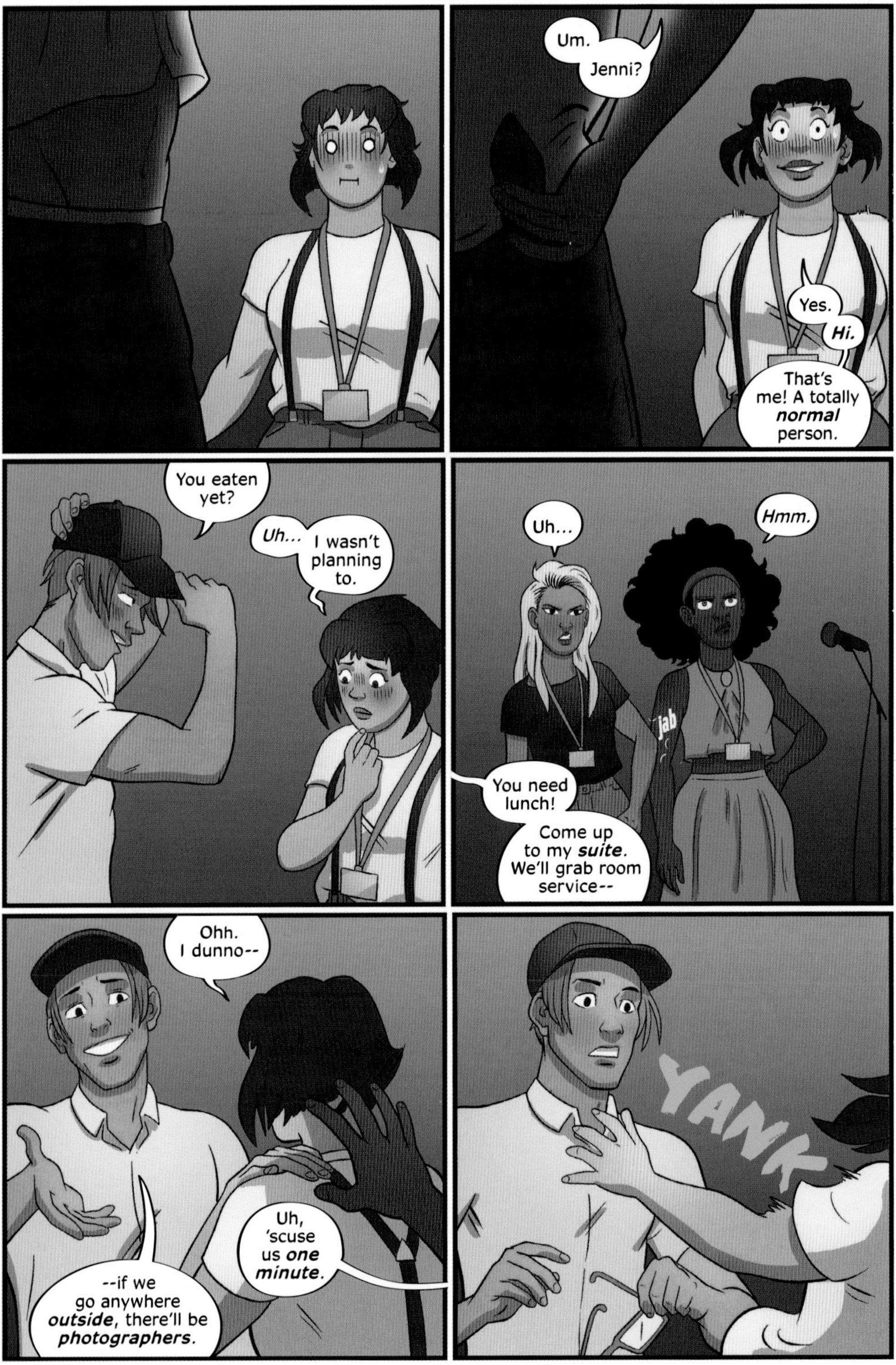
Um.
Jenni?
Yes.
Hi.
That's me! A totally ***normal*** person.
You eaten yet?
Uh... I wasn't planning to.
Uh...
Hmm.
You need lunch!
Come up to my ***suite***. We'll grab room service--
Ohh. I dunno--
--if we go anywhere ***outside***, there'll be ***photographers***.
Uh, 'scuse us ***one minute***.
YANK

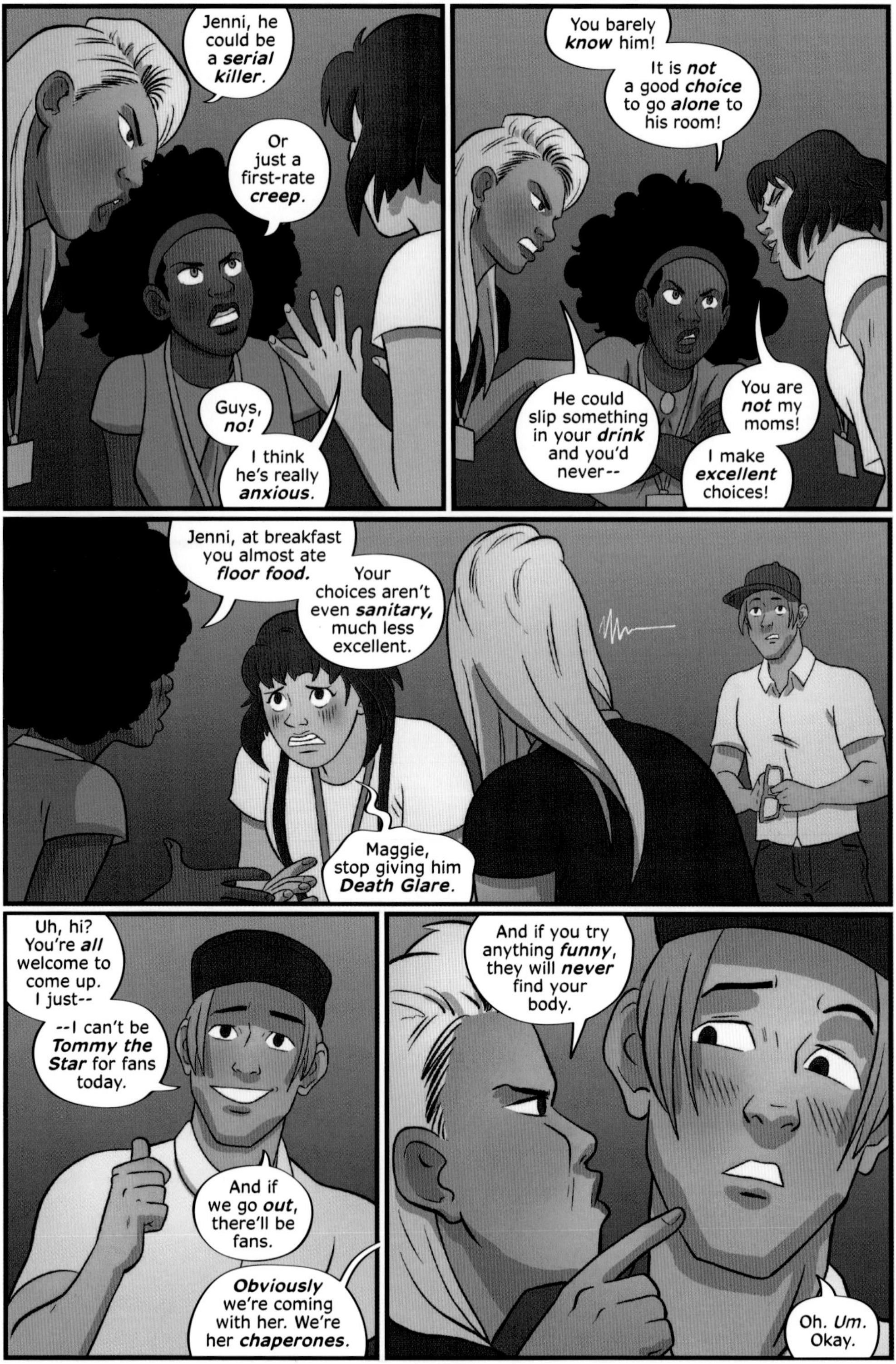
Jenni, he could be a ***serial killer***.
Or just a first-rate ***creep***.
Guys, ***no!***
I think he's really ***anxious***.
You barely ***know*** him!
It is ***not*** a good ***choice*** to go ***alone*** to his room!
He could slip something in your ***drink*** and you'd never--
You are ***not*** my moms!
I make ***excellent*** choices!
Jenni, at breakfast you almost ate ***floor food.***
Your choices aren't even ***sanitary,*** much less excellent.
Maggie, stop giving him ***Death Glare***.
Uh, hi? You're ***all*** welcome to come up. I just--
--I can't be ***Tommy the Star*** for fans today.
And if we go ***out***, there'll be fans.
Obviously we're coming with her. We're her ***chaperones***.
And if you try anything ***funny***, they will ***never*** find your body.
Oh. *Um*. Okay.

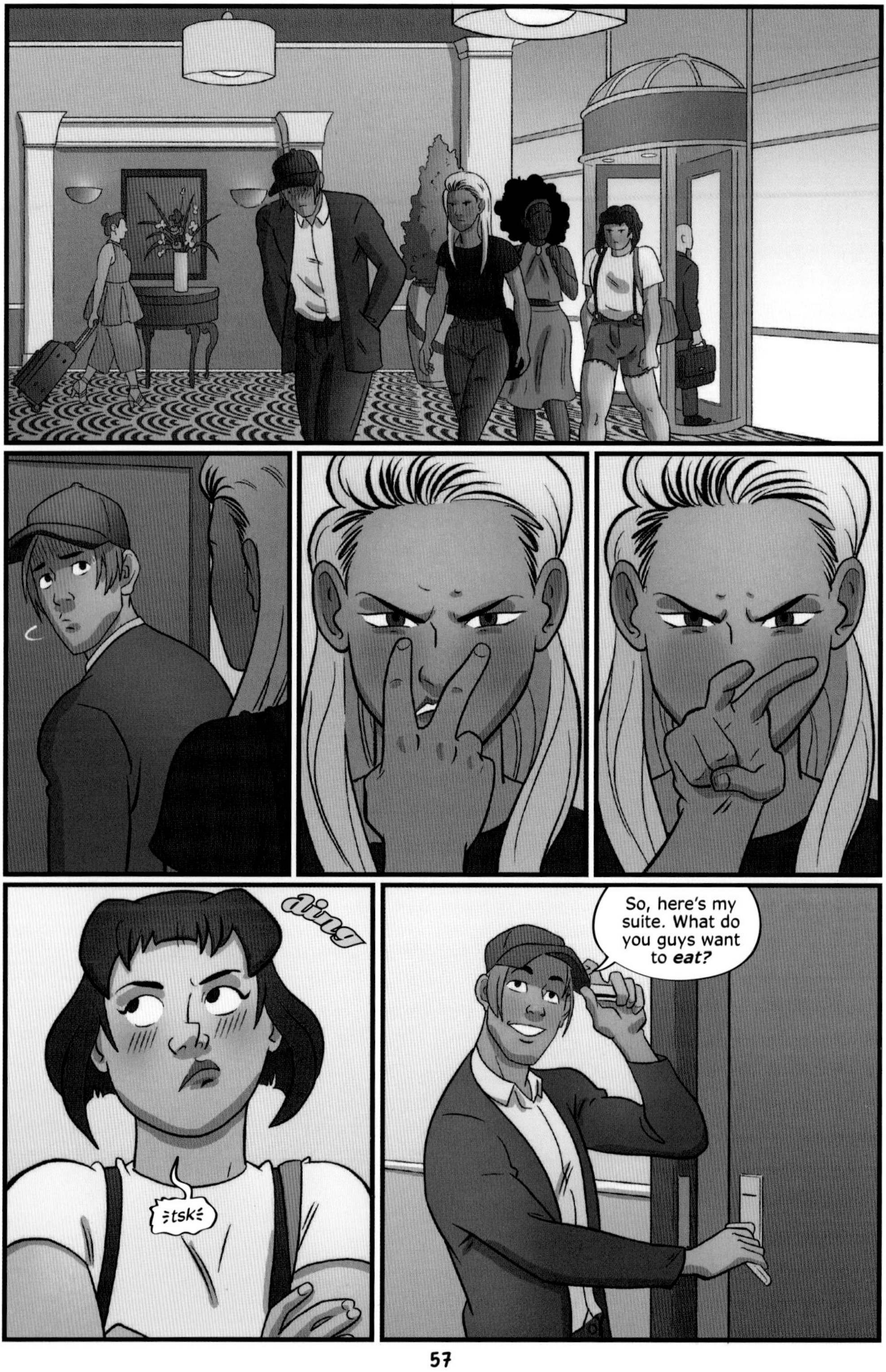
ding
tsk
So, here's my suite. What do you guys want to *eat?*

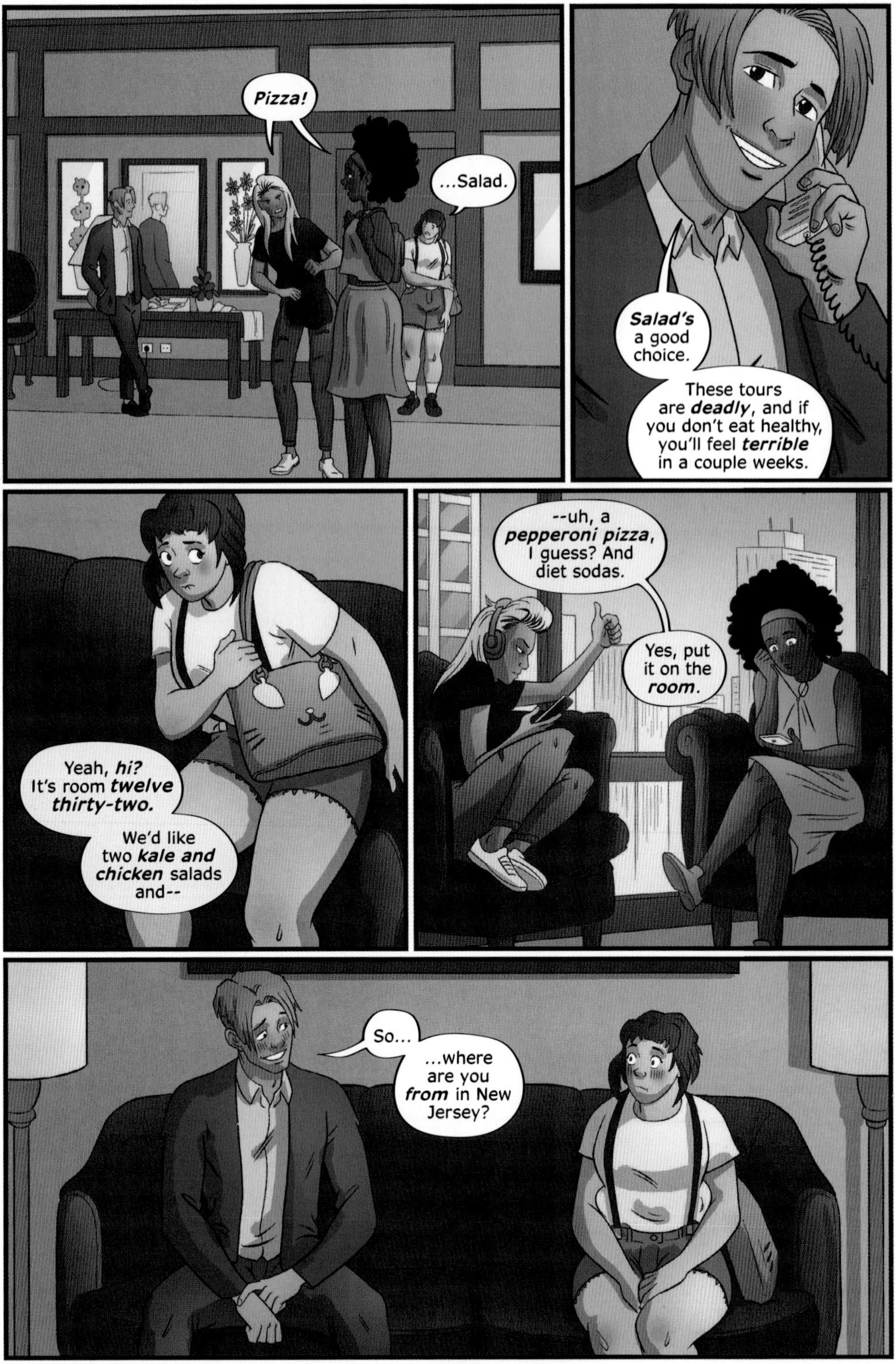
Pizza!
...Salad.
Salad's a good choice.
These tours are deadly, and if you don't eat healthy, you'll feel terrible in a couple weeks.
Yeah, hi? It's room twelve thirty-two.
We'd like two kale and chicken salads and--
--uh, a pepperoni pizza, I guess? And diet sodas.
Yes, put it on the room.
So...
...where are you from in New Jersey?

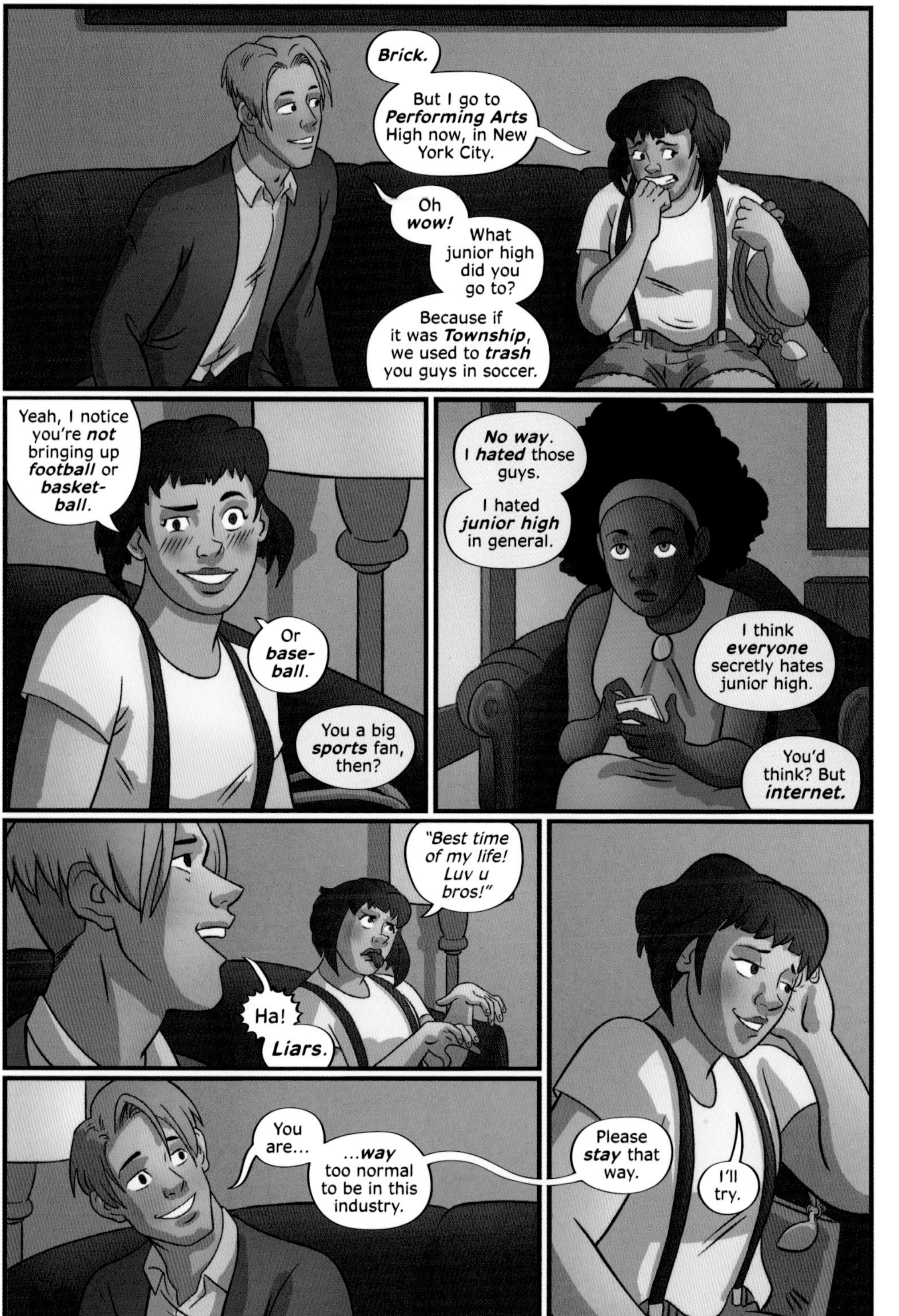
Brick.
But I go to *Performing Arts* High now, in New York City.
Oh *wow!*
What junior high did you go to?
Because if it was *Township*, we used to *trash* you guys in soccer.
Yeah, I notice you're *not* bringing up *football* or *basket-ball*.
Or *base-ball*.
You a big *sports* fan, then?
No way. I *hated* those guys.
I hated *junior high* in general.
I think *everyone* secretly hates junior high.
You'd think? But *internet.*
"Best time of my life! Luv u bros!"
Ha!
Liars.
You are...
...*way* too normal to be in this industry.
Please *stay* that way.
I'll try.

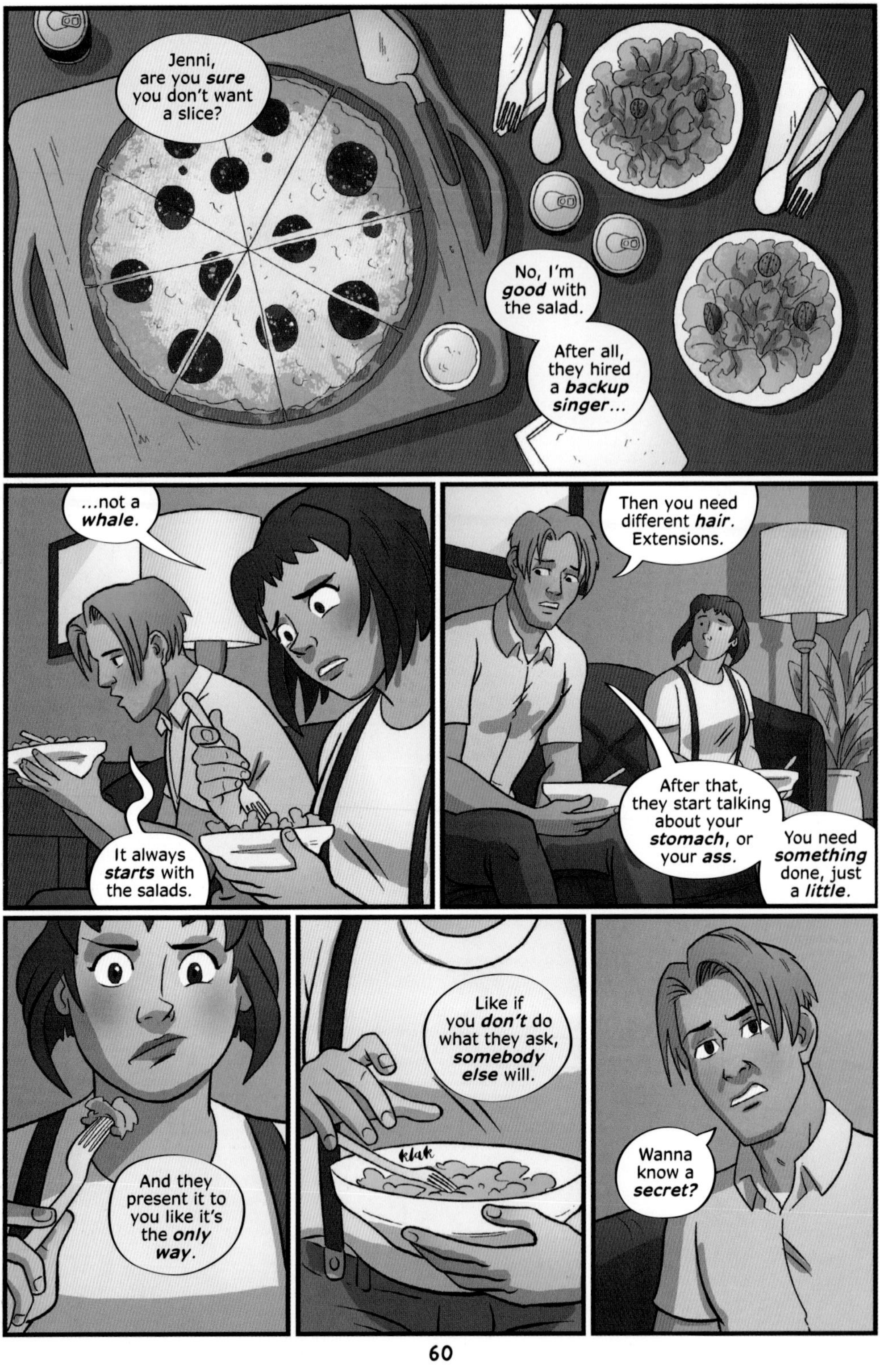
Jenni, are you *sure* you don't want a slice?
No, I'm *good* with the salad.
After all, they hired a *backup singer*...
...not a *whale*.
It always *starts* with the salads.
Then you need different *hair*. Extensions.
After that, they start talking about your *stomach*, or your *ass*.
You need *something* done, just a *little*.
And they present it to you like it's the *only way*.
Like if you *don't* do what they ask, *somebody else* will.
klak
Wanna know a *secret?*

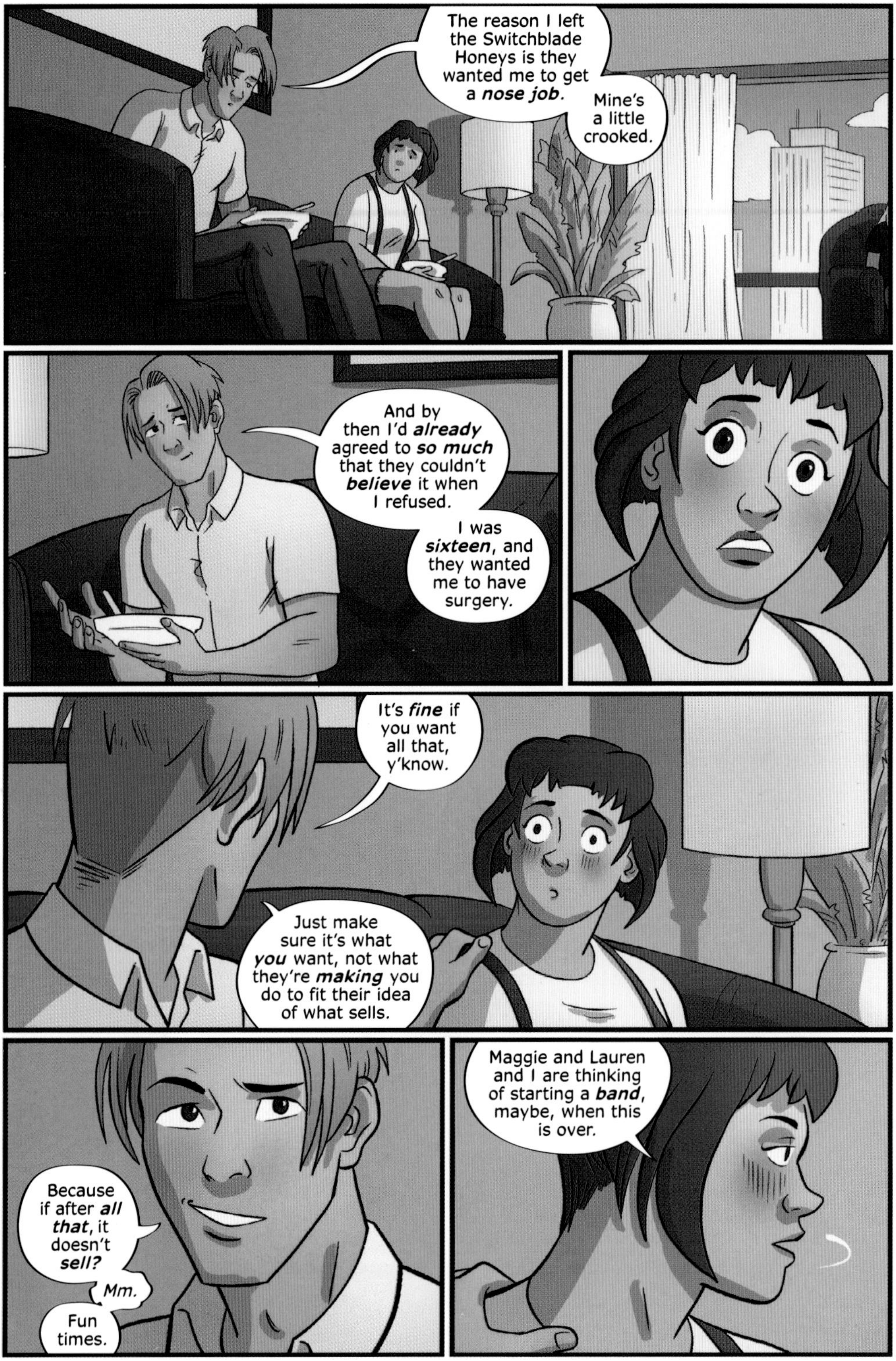
The reason I left the Switchblade Honeys is they wanted me to get a ***nose job***.
Mine's a little crooked.
And by then I'd ***already*** agreed to ***so much*** that they couldn't ***believe*** it when I refused.
I was ***sixteen***, and they wanted me to have surgery.
It's ***fine*** if you want all that, y'know.
Just make sure it's what ***you*** want, not what they're ***making*** you do to fit their idea of what sells.
Because if after ***all that***, it doesn't ***sell?***
Mm.
Fun times.
Maggie and Lauren and I are thinking of starting a ***band***, maybe, when this is over.

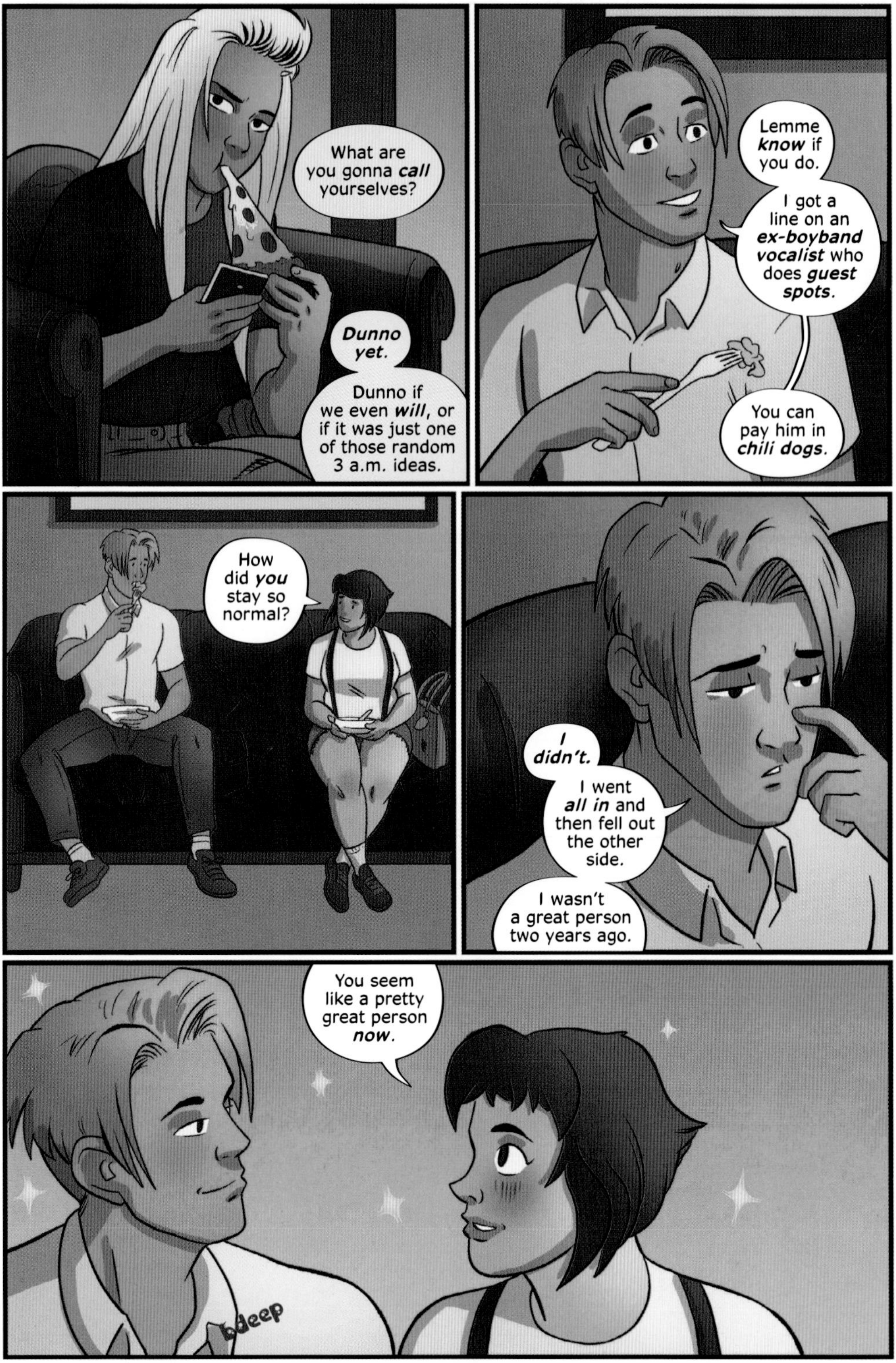
What are you gonna *call* yourselves?
Dunno yet.
Dunno if we even ***will***, or if it was just one of those random 3 a.m. ideas.
Lemme ***know*** if you do.
I got a line on an ***ex-boyband vocalist*** who does ***guest spots***.
You can pay him in ***chili dogs***.
How did ***you*** stay so normal?
I didn't.
I went ***all in*** and then fell out the other side.
I wasn't a great person two years ago.
You seem like a pretty great person ***now***.
bdeep

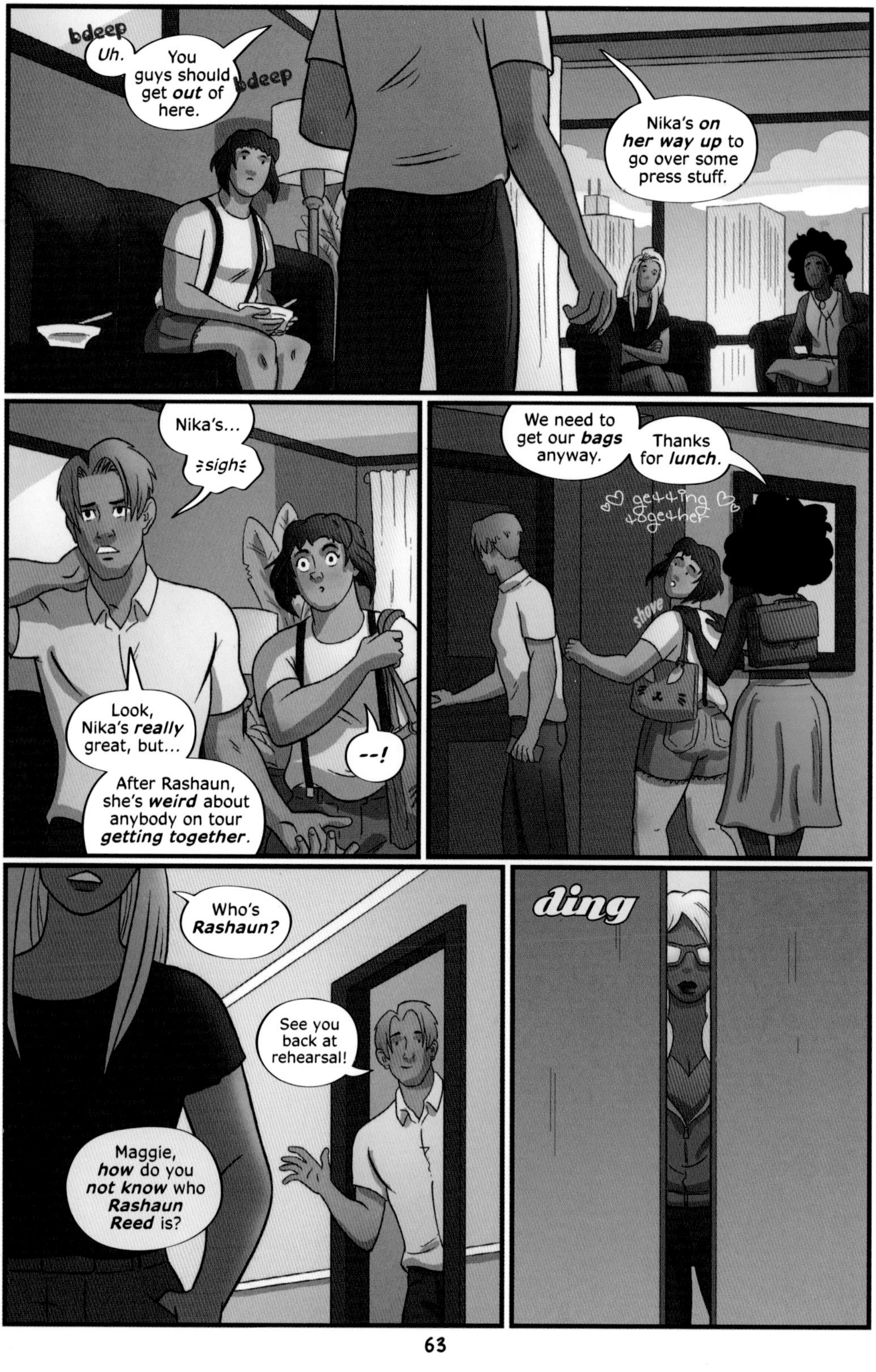
bdeep
Uh.
You guys should get *out* of here.
bdeep
Nika's ***on her way up*** to go over some press stuff.
Nika's...
⁼sigh⁼
Look, Nika's ***really*** great, but...
After Rashaun, she's ***weird*** about anybody on tour ***getting together***.
--!
We need to get our ***bags*** anyway.
Thanks for ***lunch***.
getting together
shove
Who's ***Rashaun?***
See you back at rehearsal!
Maggie, ***how*** do you ***not know*** who ***Rashaun Reed*** is?
ding

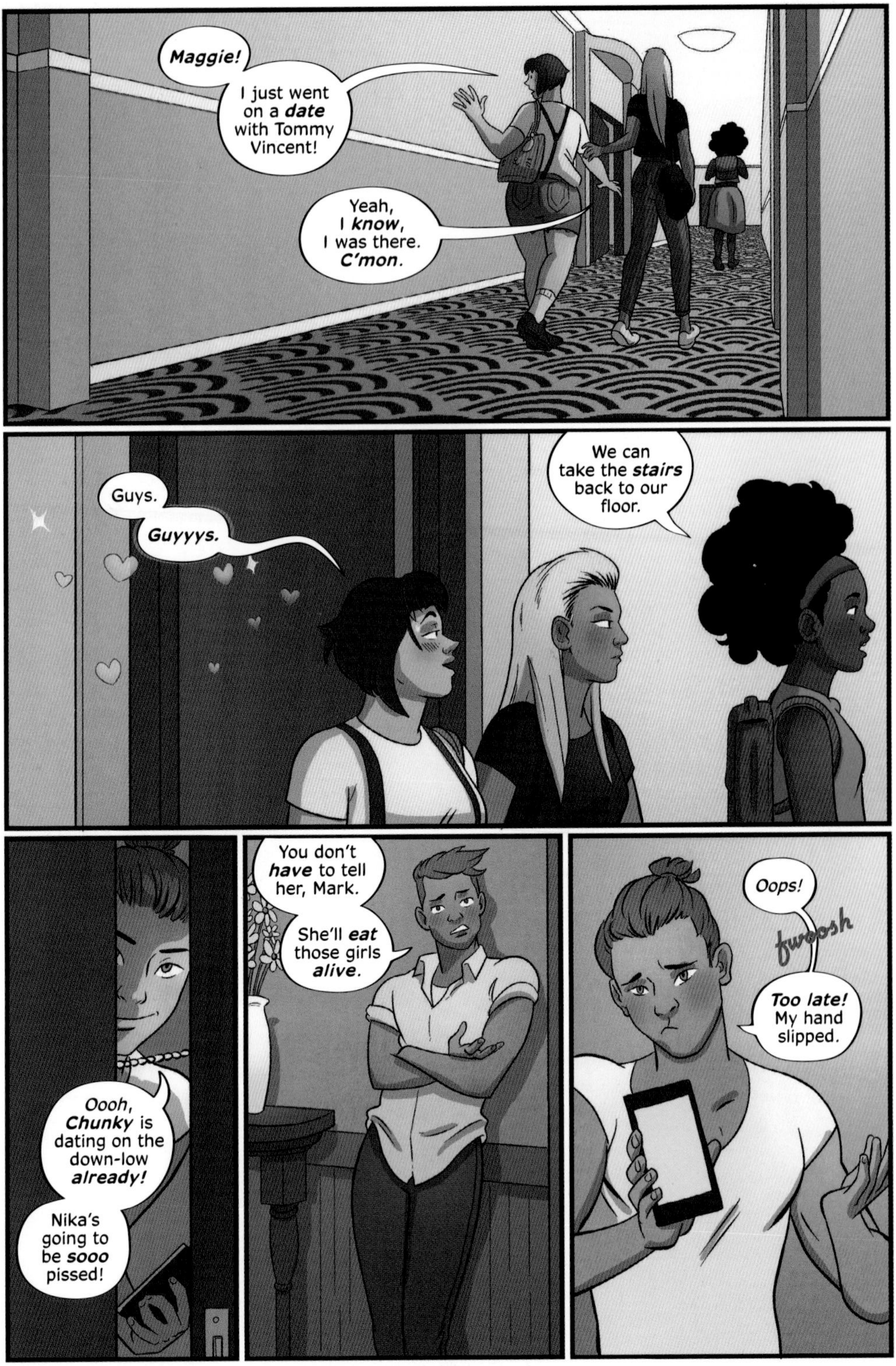
Maggie!
I just went on a ***date*** with Tommy Vincent!
Yeah, I ***know***, I was there. ***C'mon***.
Guys.
Guyyys.
We can take the ***stairs*** back to our floor.
Oooh, ***Chunky*** is dating on the down-low ***already!***
Nika's going to be ***sooo*** pissed!
You don't ***have*** to tell her, Mark.
She'll ***eat*** those girls ***alive***.
Oops!
fwoosh
Too late! My hand slipped.

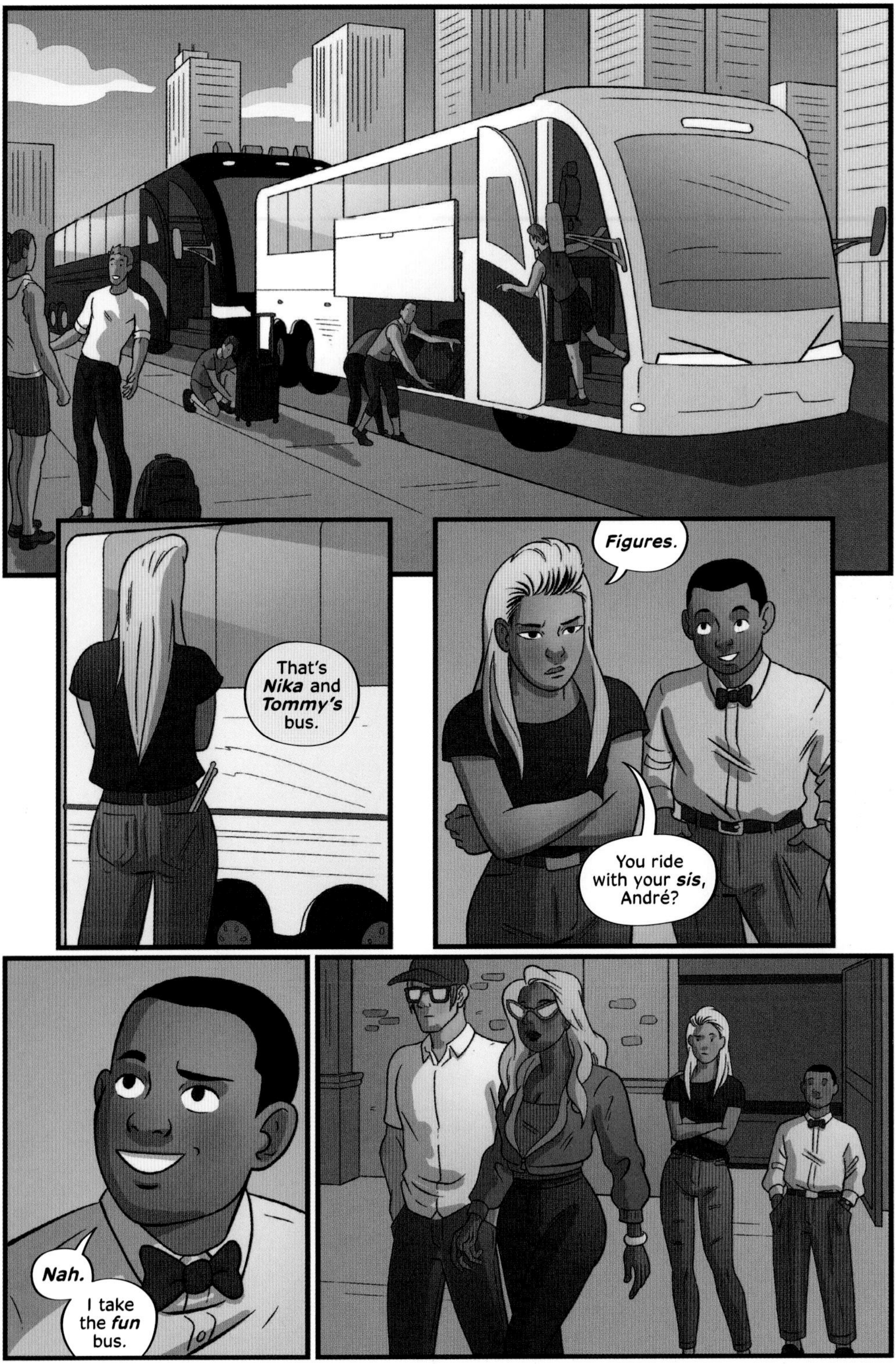
That's *Nika* and *Tommy's* bus.
Figures.
You ride with your *sis*, André?
Nah.
I take the *fun* bus.

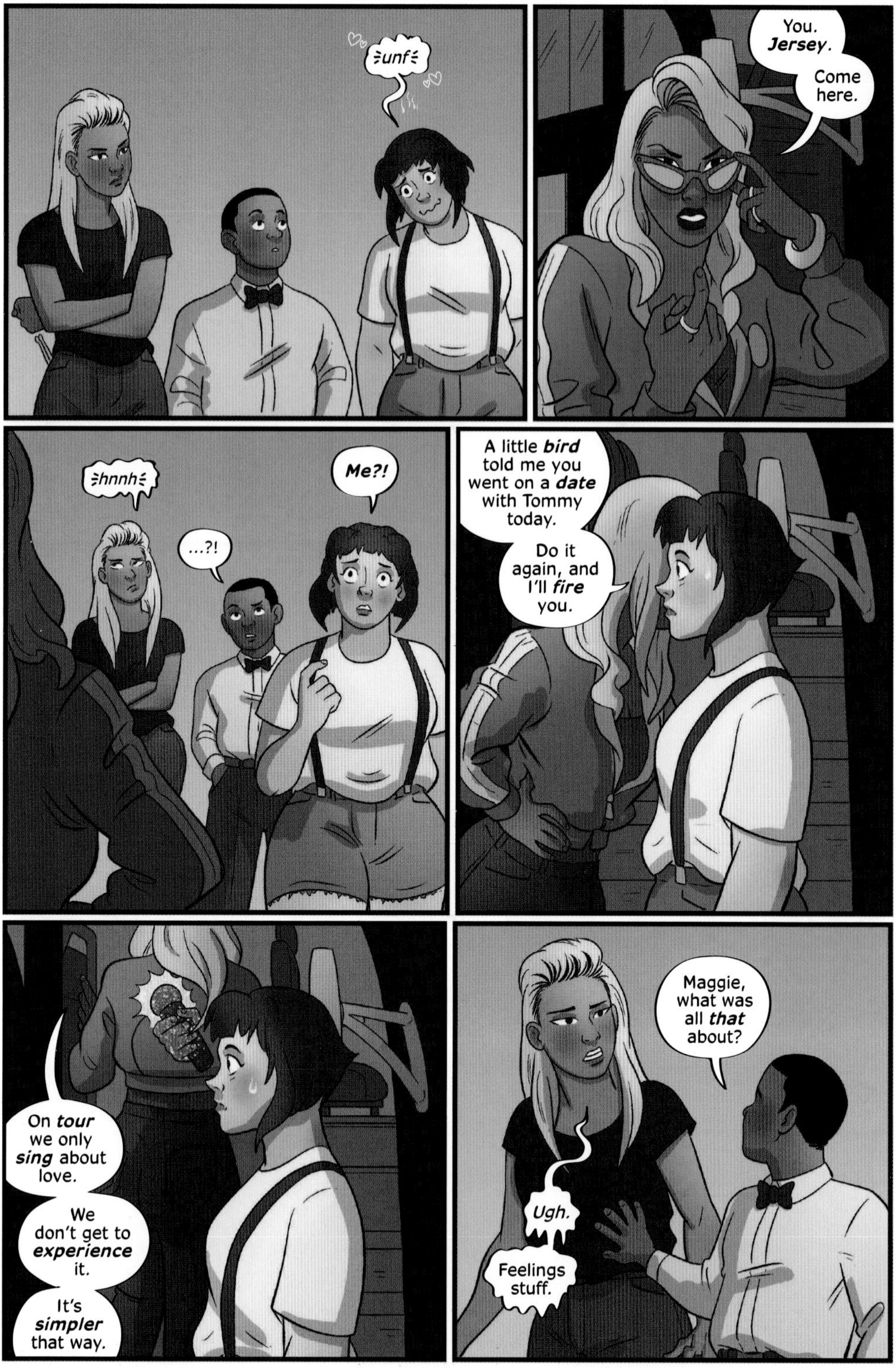
unf
You. Jersey.
Come here.
hnnh
...?!
Me?!
A little bird told me you went on a date with Tommy today.
Do it again, and I'll fire you.
On tour we only sing about love.
We don't get to experience it.
It's simpler that way.
Maggie, what was all that about?
Ugh.
Feelings stuff.

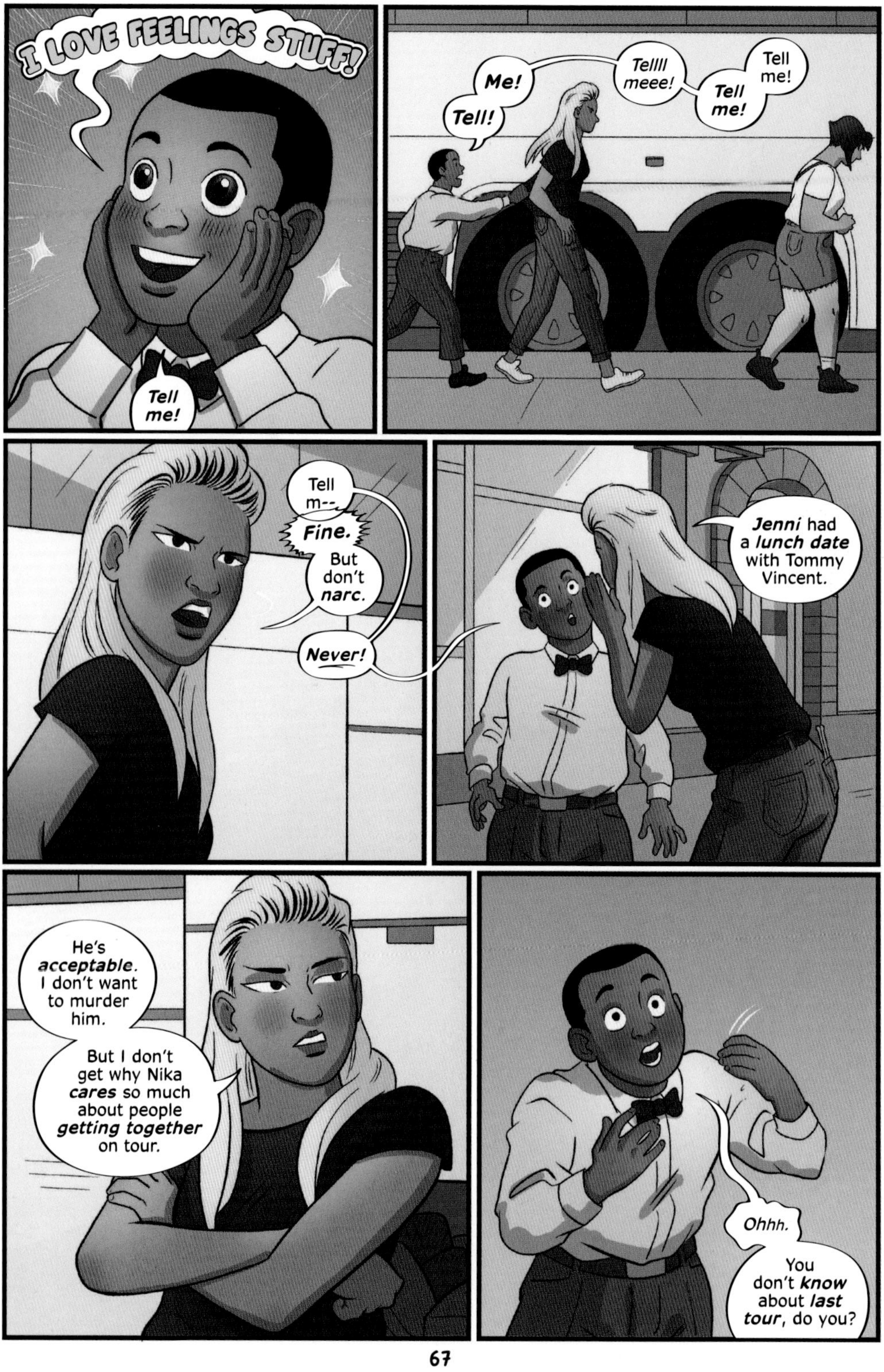
I LOVE FEELINGS STUFF!
Tell me!
Me!
Tell!
Tellll meee!
Tell me!
Tell me!
Tell m--
Fine.
But don't narc.
Never!
Jenni had a lunch date with Tommy Vincent.
He's acceptable. I don't want to murder him.
But I don't get why Nika cares so much about people getting together on tour.
Ohhh.
You don't know about last tour, do you?

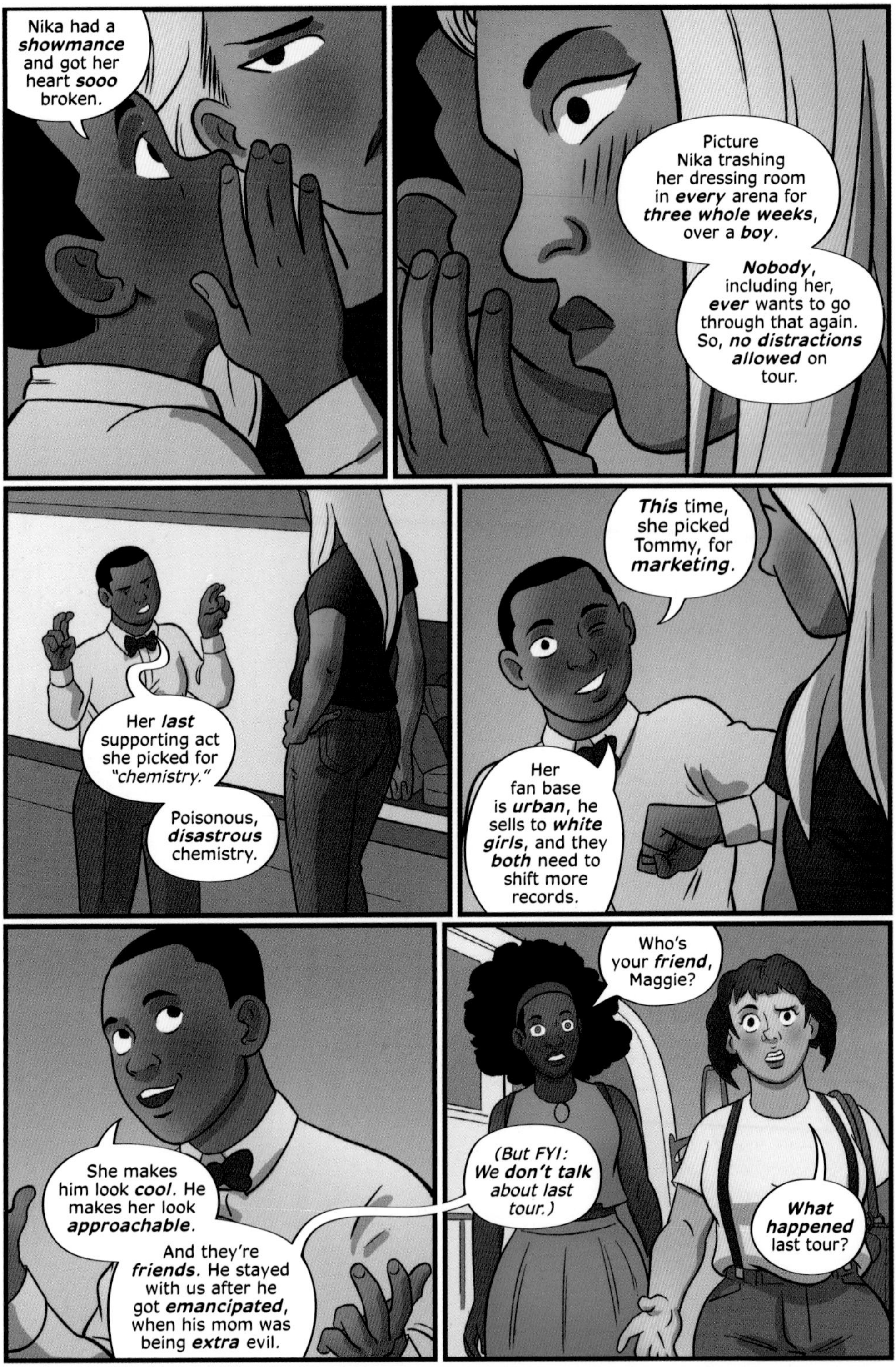
Nika had a *showmance* and got her heart *sooo* broken.
Picture Nika trashing her dressing room in *every* arena for *three whole weeks*, over a *boy*.
Nobody, including her, *ever* wants to go through that again. So, *no distractions allowed* on tour.
Her *last* supporting act she picked for *"chemistry."*
Poisonous, *disastrous* chemistry.
This time, she picked Tommy, for *marketing*.
Her fan base is *urban*, he sells to *white girls*, and they *both* need to shift more records.
She makes him look *cool*. He makes her look *approachable*.
And they're *friends*. He stayed with us after he got *emancipated*, when his mom was being *extra* evil.
Who's your *friend*, Maggie?
(But FYI: We don't talk about last tour.)
What happened last tour?

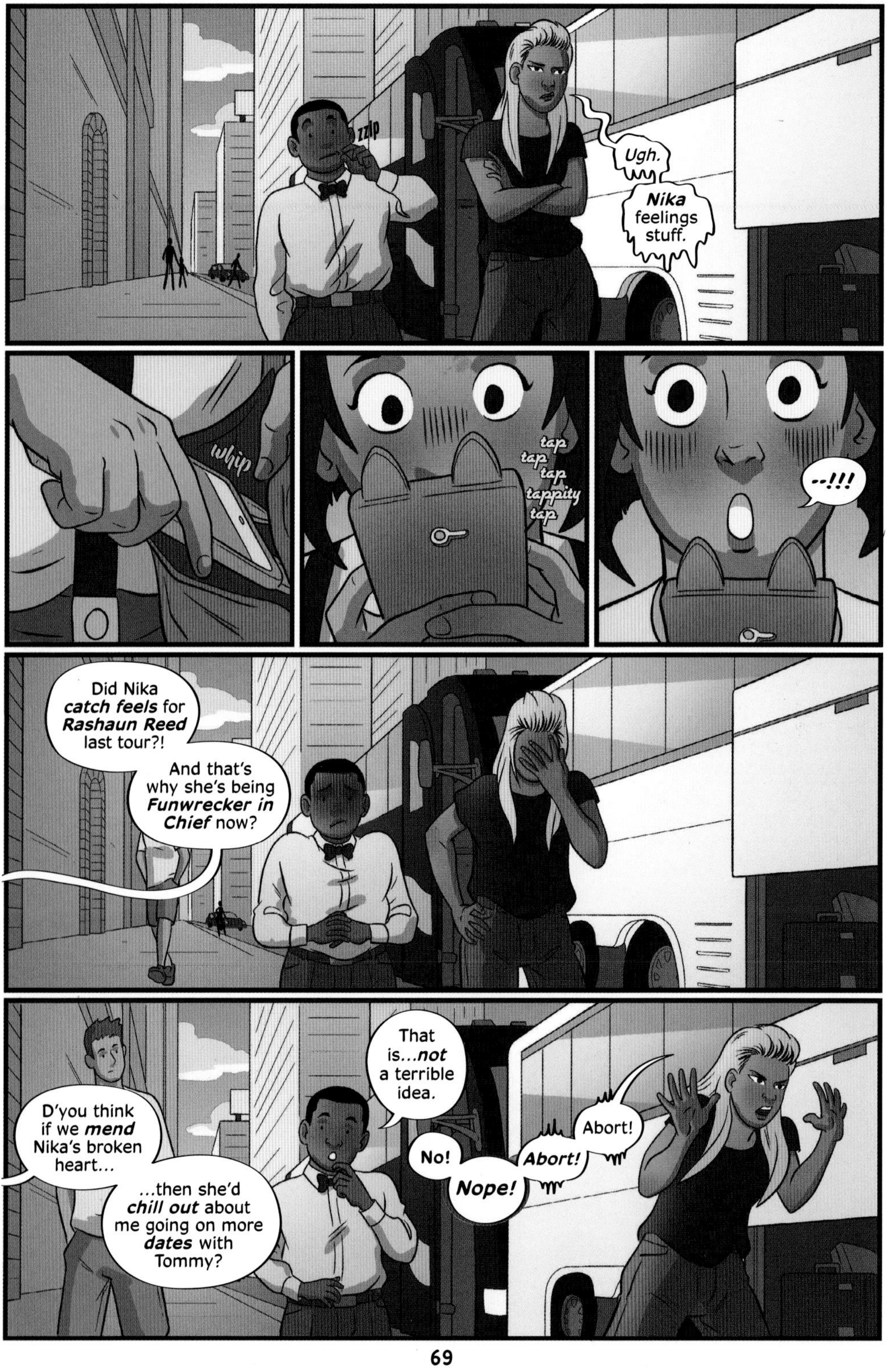
zzip
Ugh.
Nika feelings stuff.
whip
tap tap tap tappity tap
--!!!
Did Nika ***catch feels*** for ***Rashaun Reed*** last tour?!
And that's why she's being ***Funwrecker in Chief*** now?
D'you think if we ***mend*** Nika's broken heart...
...then she'd ***chill out*** about me going on more ***dates*** with Tommy?
That is...***not*** a terrible idea.
No!
Nope!
Abort!
Abort!

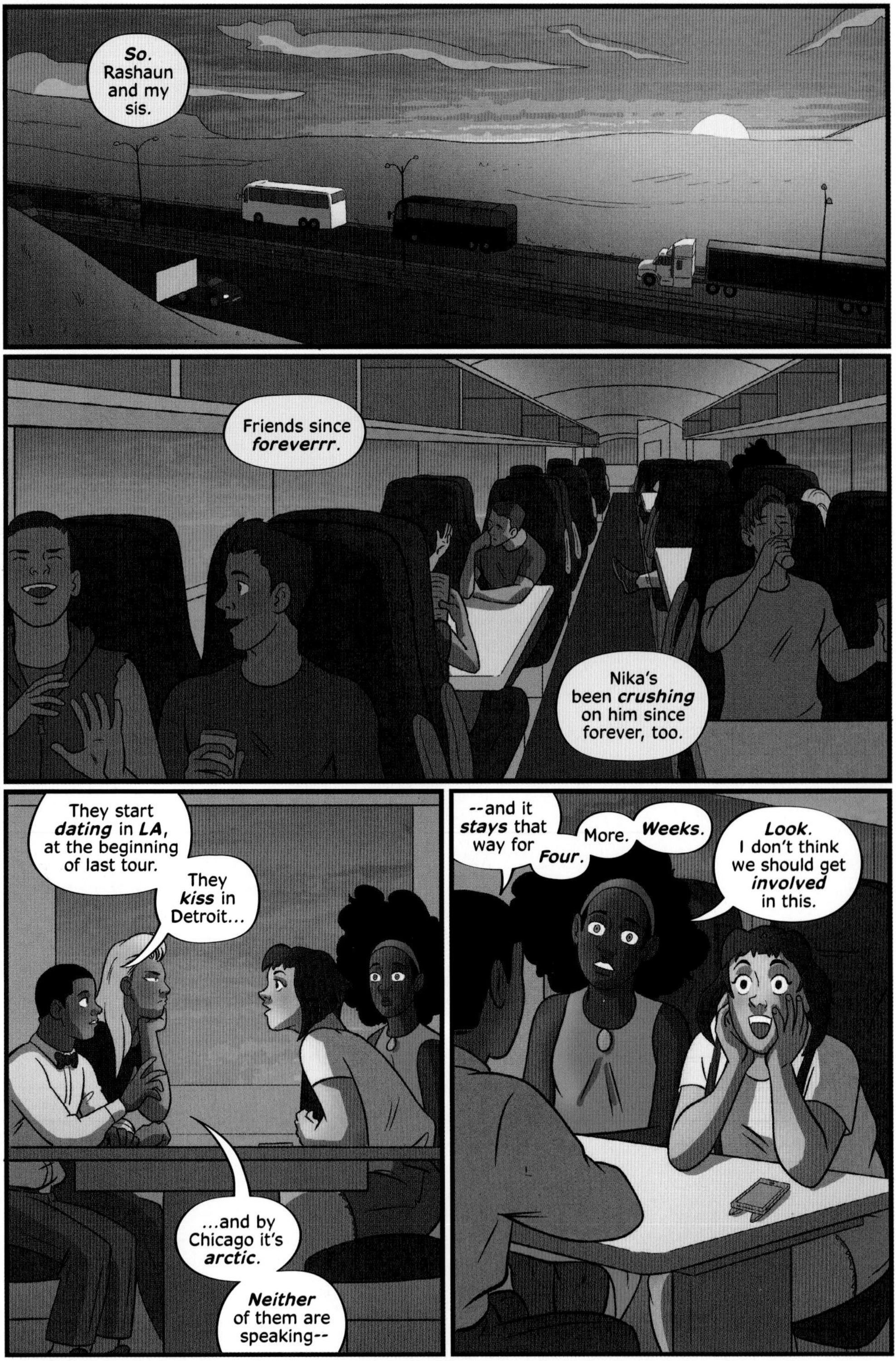
So.
Rashaun and my sis.
Friends since *foreverrr*.
Nika's been ***crushing*** on him since forever, too.
They start ***dating*** in ***LA***, at the beginning of last tour.
They ***kiss*** in Detroit...
...and by Chicago it's ***arctic***.
Neither of them are speaking--
--and it ***stays*** that way for
Four.
More.
Weeks.
Look. I don't think we should get ***involved*** in this.

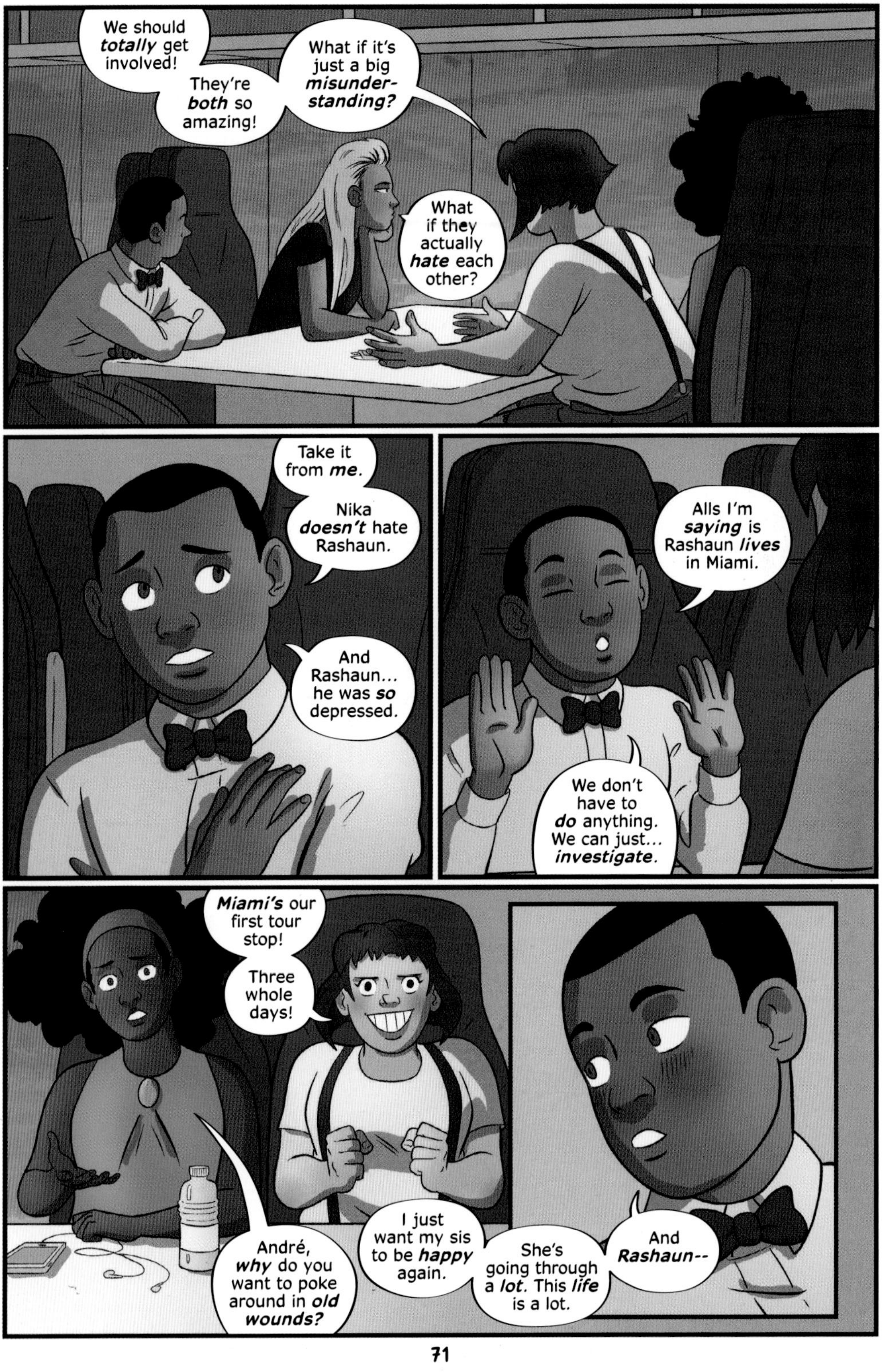
We should *totally* get involved!
They're *both* so amazing!
What if it's just a big ***misunder-standing?***
What if they actually ***hate*** each other?
Take it from ***me.***
Nika ***doesn't*** hate Rashaun.
And Rashaun... he was ***so*** depressed.
Alls I'm ***saying*** is Rashaun ***lives*** in Miami.
We don't have to ***do*** anything. We can just... ***investigate.***
Miami's our first tour stop!
Three whole days!
André, ***why*** do you want to poke around in ***old wounds?***
I just want my sis to be ***happy*** again.
She's going through a ***lot.*** This ***life*** is a lot.
And ***Rashaun--***

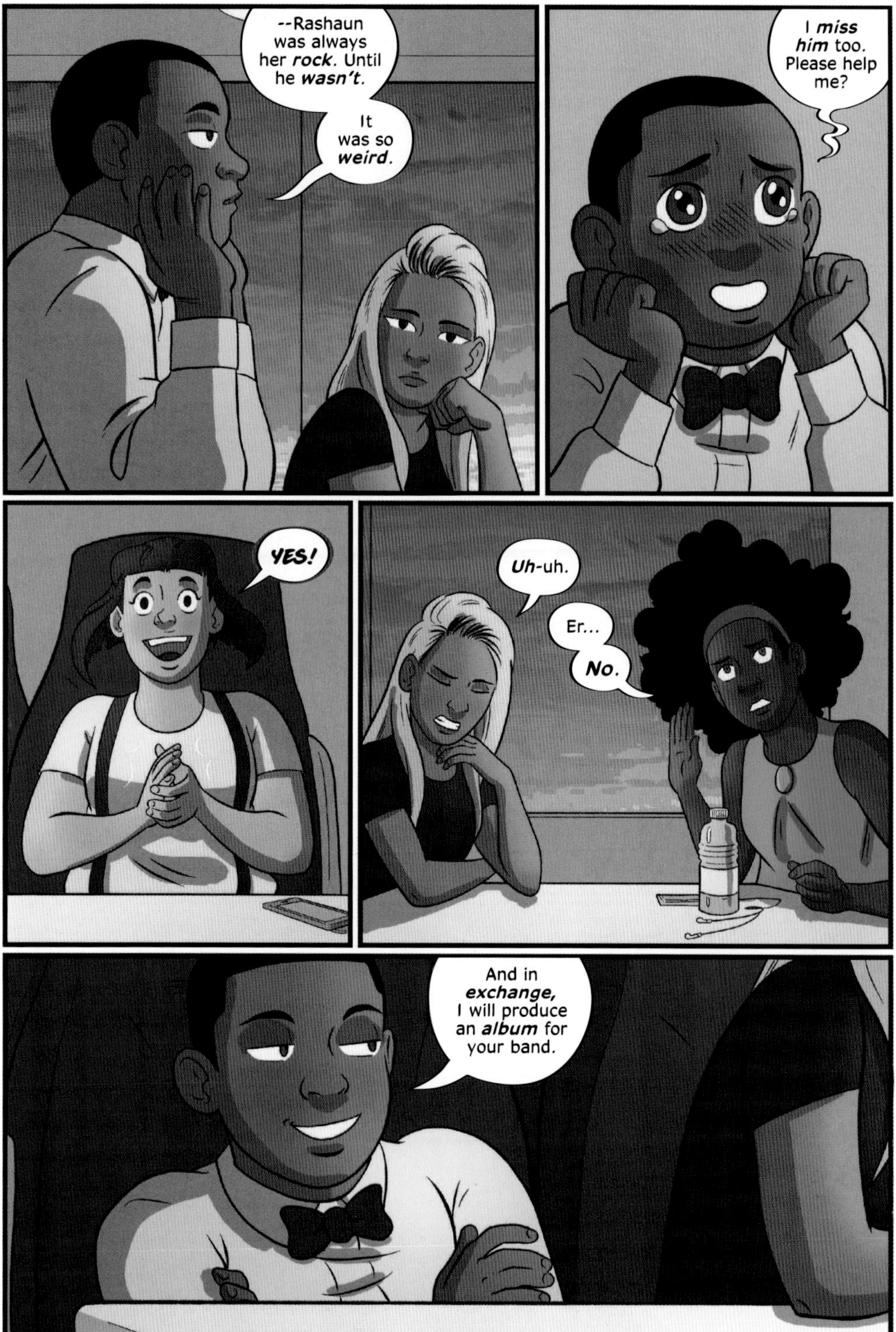
--Rashaun was always her ***rock***. Until he ***wasn't***.
It was so ***weird***.
I ***miss him*** too. Please help me?
YES!
Uh-uh.
Er...
No.
And in ***exchange,*** I will produce an ***album*** for your band.

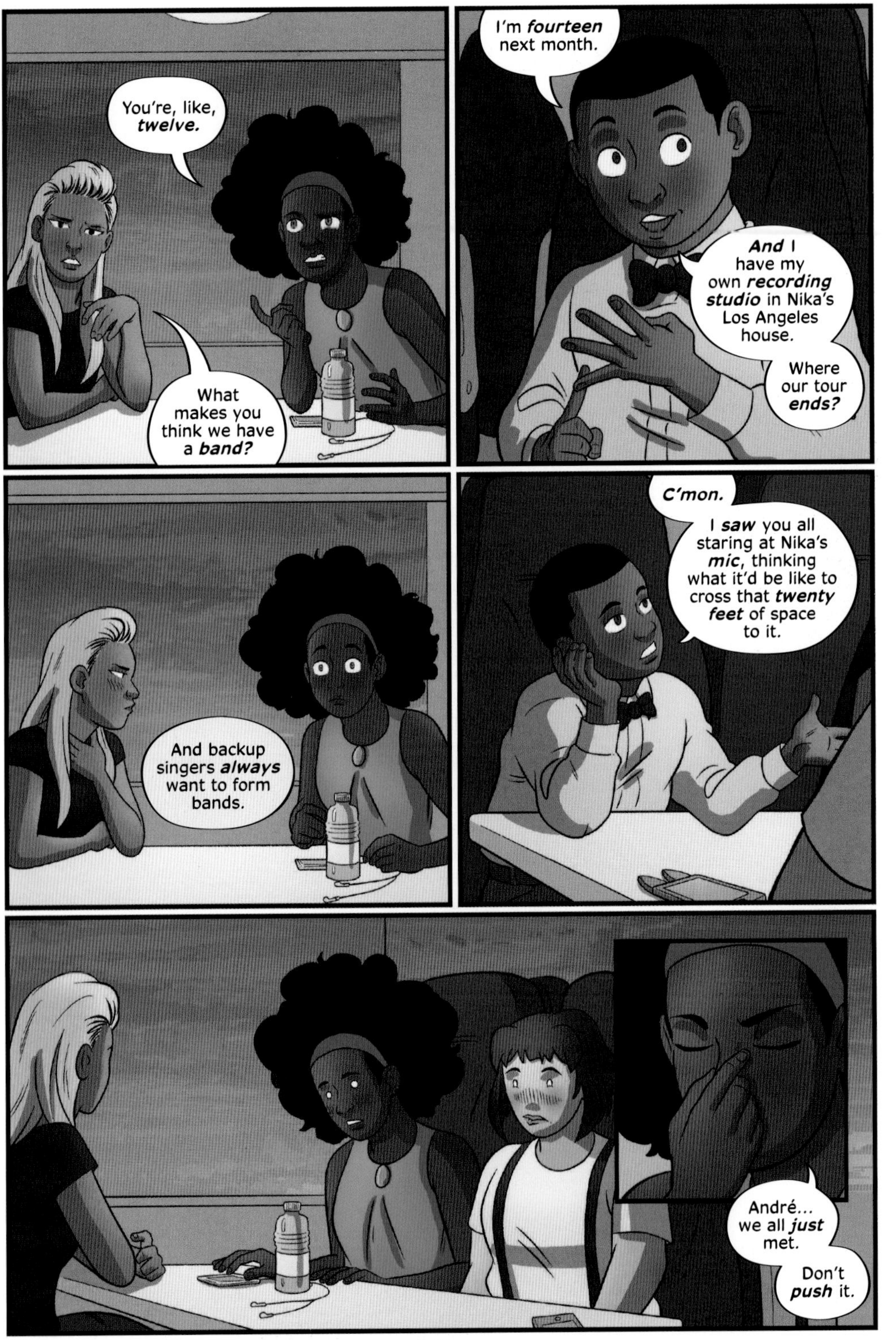
You're, like, *twelve.*
What makes you think we have a *band?*
I'm *fourteen* next month.
And I have my own *recording studio* in Nika's Los Angeles house.
Where our tour *ends?*
And backup singers *always* want to form bands.
C'mon.
I *saw* you all staring at Nika's *mic*, thinking what it'd be like to cross that *twenty feet* of space to it.
André... we all *just* met.
Don't *push* it.

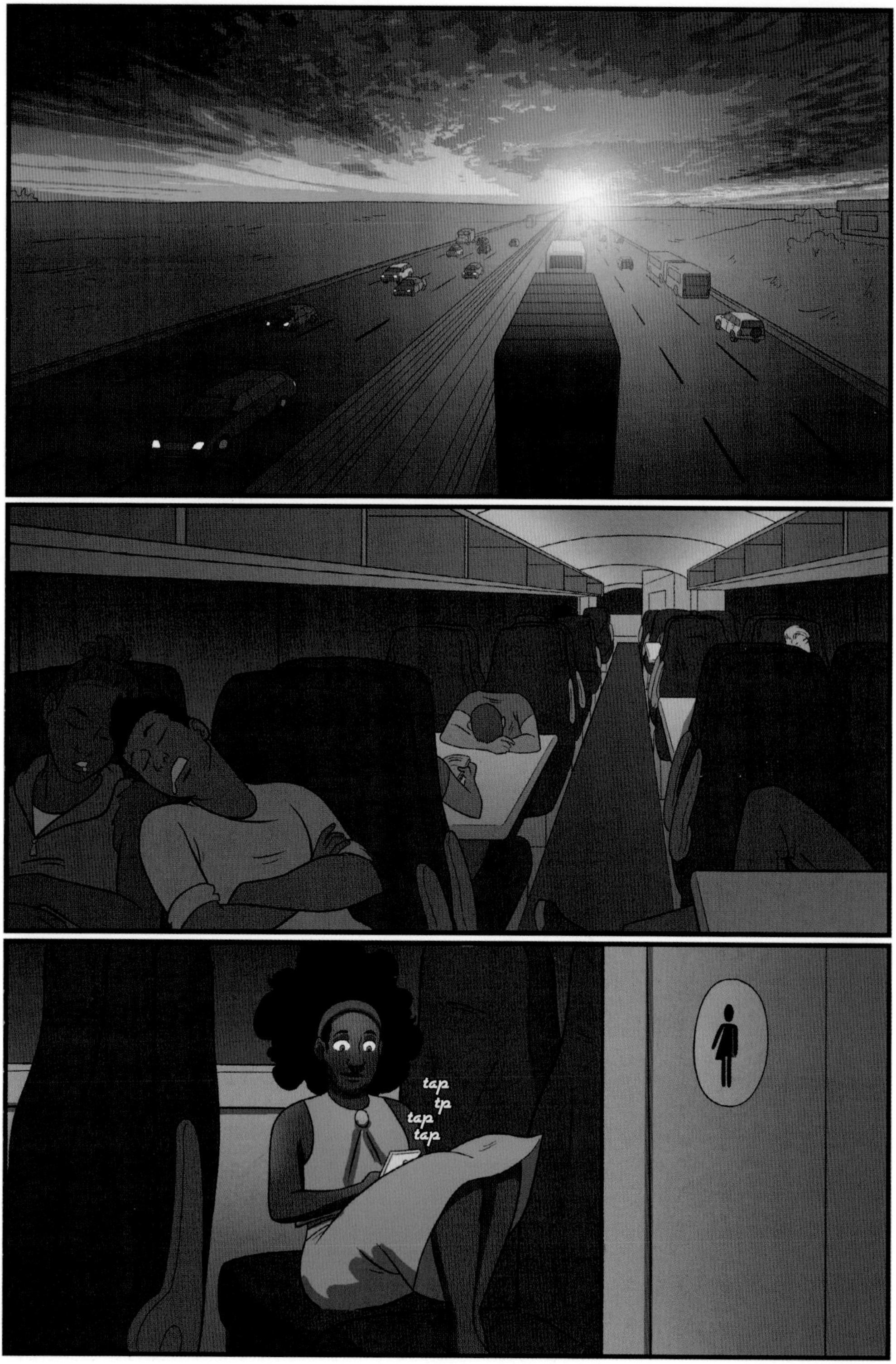
tap
tp
tap
tap

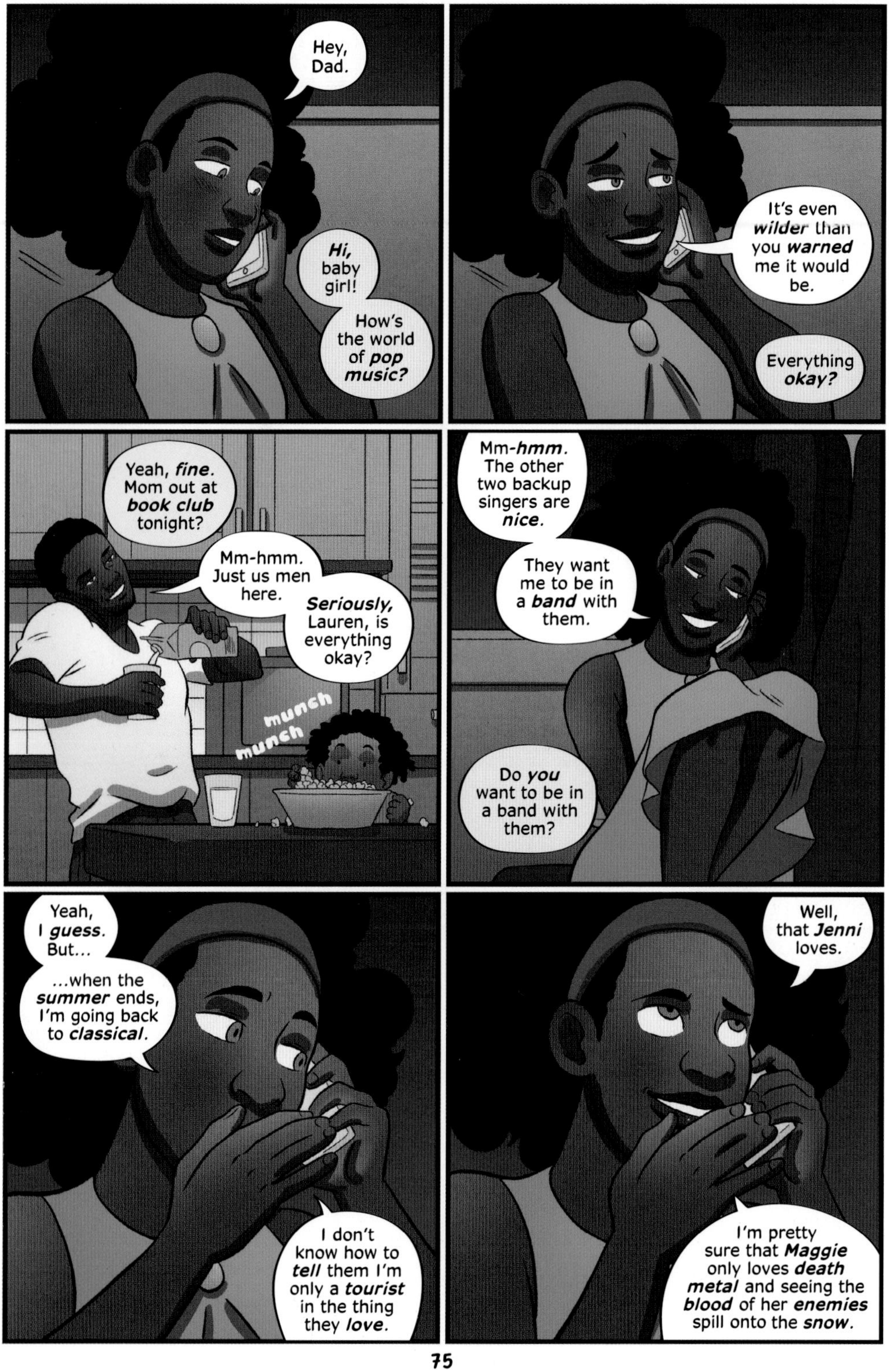
Hey, Dad.
Hi, baby girl!
How's the world of *pop music?*
It's even *wilder* than you *warned* me it would be.
Everything *okay?*
Yeah, *fine.* Mom out at *book club* tonight?
Mm-hmm. Just us men here.
Seriously, Lauren, is everything okay?
munch munch
Mm-*hmm*. The other two backup singers are *nice*.
They want me to be in a *band* with them.
Do *you* want to be in a band with them?
Yeah, I *guess*. But...
...when the *summer* ends, I'm going back to *classical*.
I don't know how to *tell* them I'm only a *tourist* in the thing they *love*.
Well, that *Jenni* loves.
I'm pretty sure that *Maggie* only loves *death metal* and seeing the *blood* of her *enemies* spill onto the *snow*.

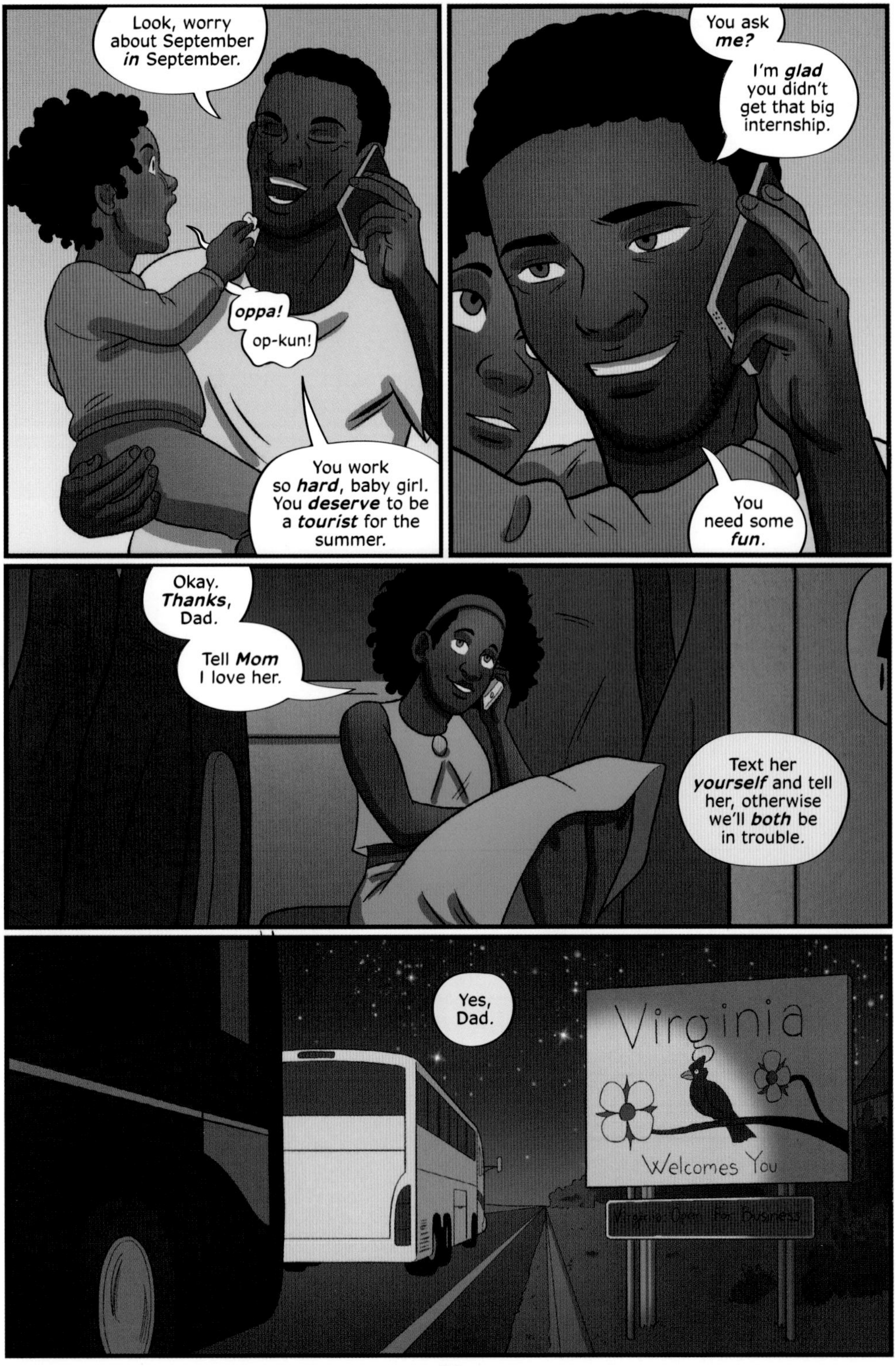
Look, worry about September *in* September.
oppa!
op-kun!
You work so ***hard***, baby girl. You ***deserve*** to be a ***tourist*** for the summer.
You ask ***me?***
I'm ***glad*** you didn't get that big internship.
You need some ***fun***.
Okay. ***Thanks***, Dad.
Tell ***Mom*** I love her.
Text her ***yourself*** and tell her, otherwise we'll ***both*** be in trouble.
Yes, Dad.
Virginia
Welcomes You
Virginia: Open for Business

CHAPTER
3

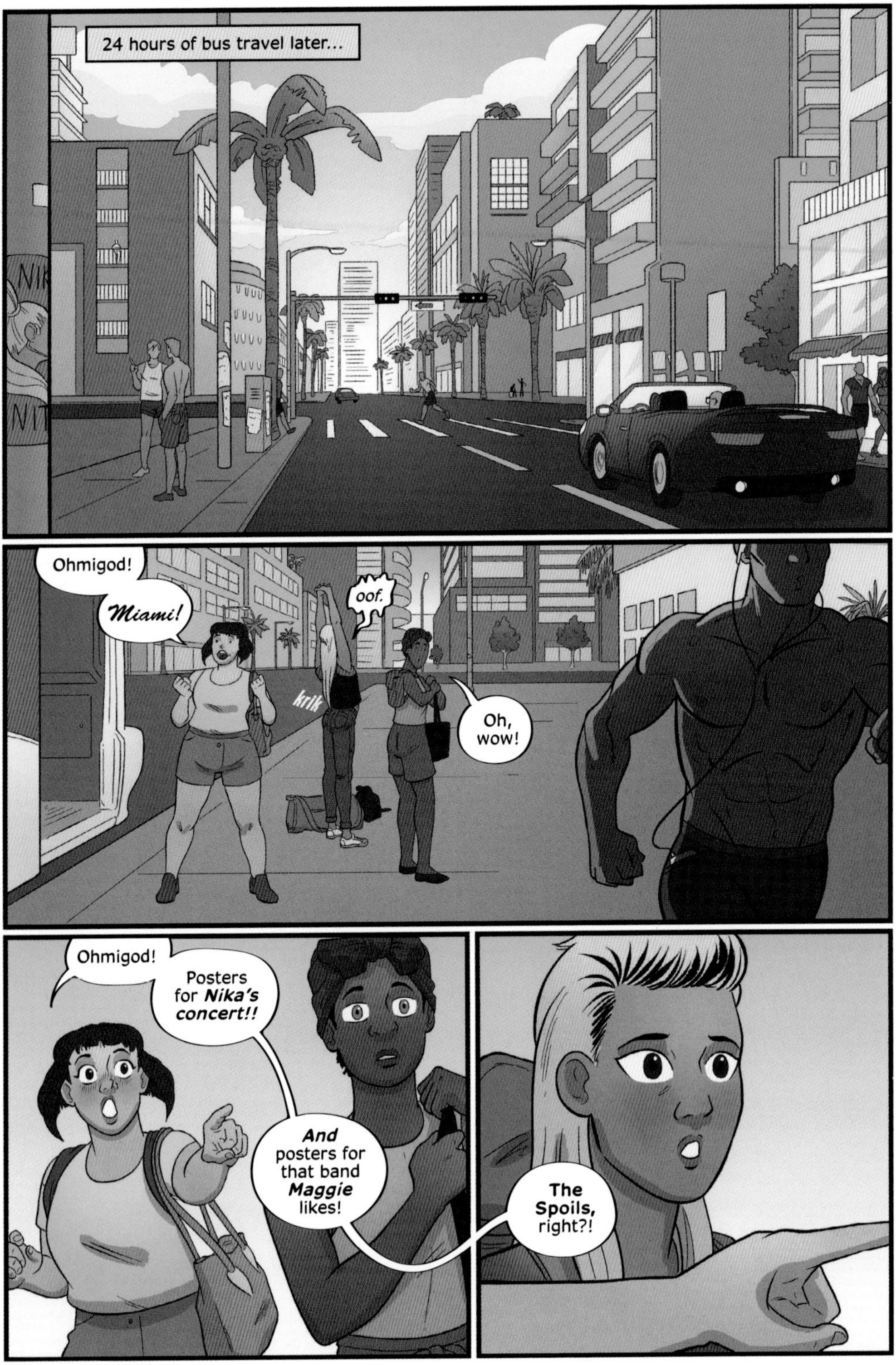
24 hours of bus travel later...
Ohmigod!
Miami!
oof.
krik
Oh, wow!
Ohmigod!
Posters for ***Nika's concert!!***
And posters for that band ***Maggie*** likes!
The Spoils, right?!

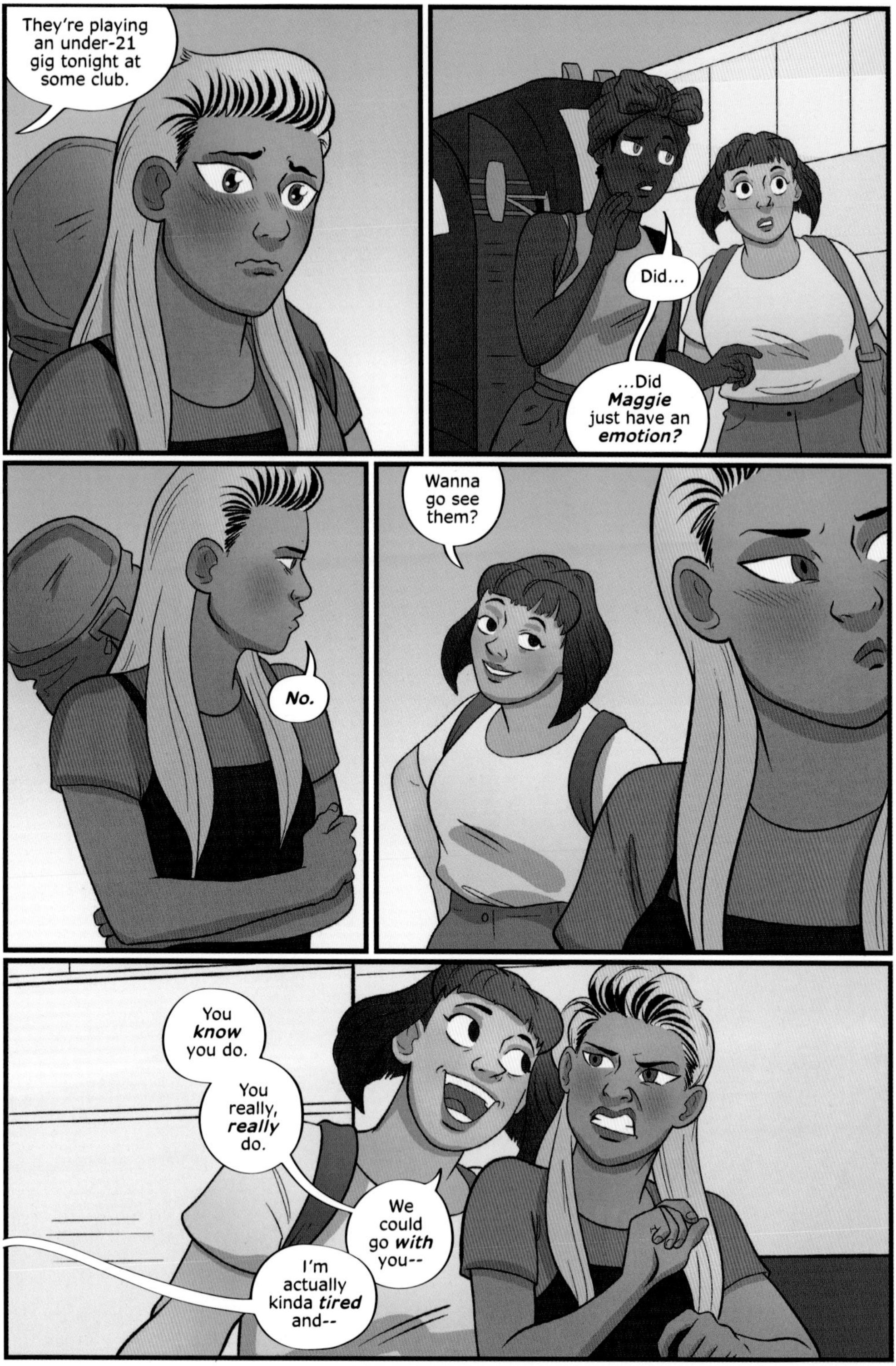
They're playing an under-21 gig tonight at some club.
Did...
...Did *Maggie* just have an *emotion?*
No.
Wanna go see them?
You *know* you do.
You really, *really* do.
We could go *with* you--
I'm actually kinda *tired* and--

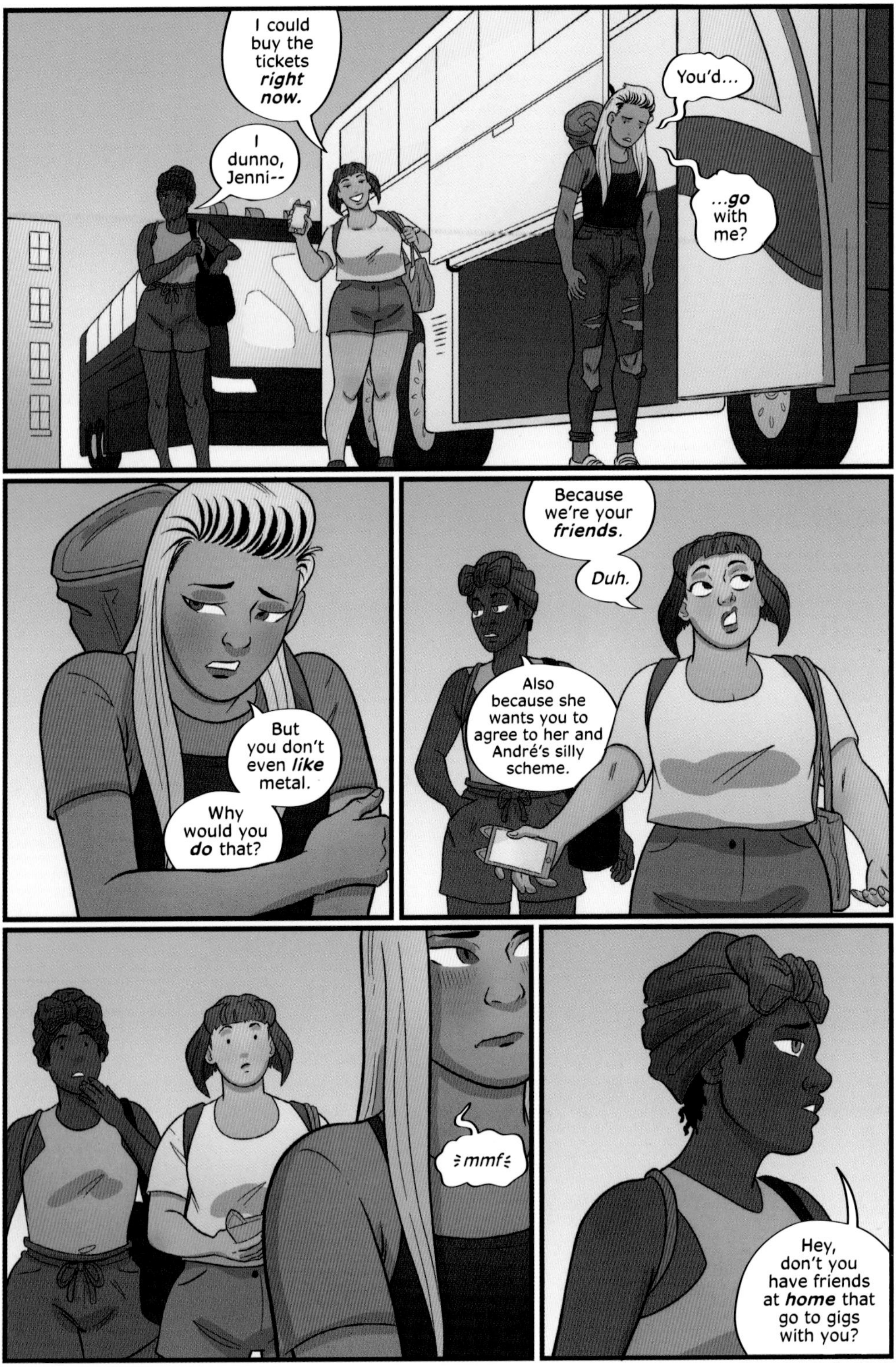
I could buy the tickets *right now.*
I dunno, Jenni--
You'd...
...*go* with me?
But you don't even *like* metal.
Why would you *do* that?
Because we're your *friends*.
Duh.
Also because she wants you to agree to her and André's silly scheme.
mmf
Hey, don't you have friends at *home* that go to gigs with you?

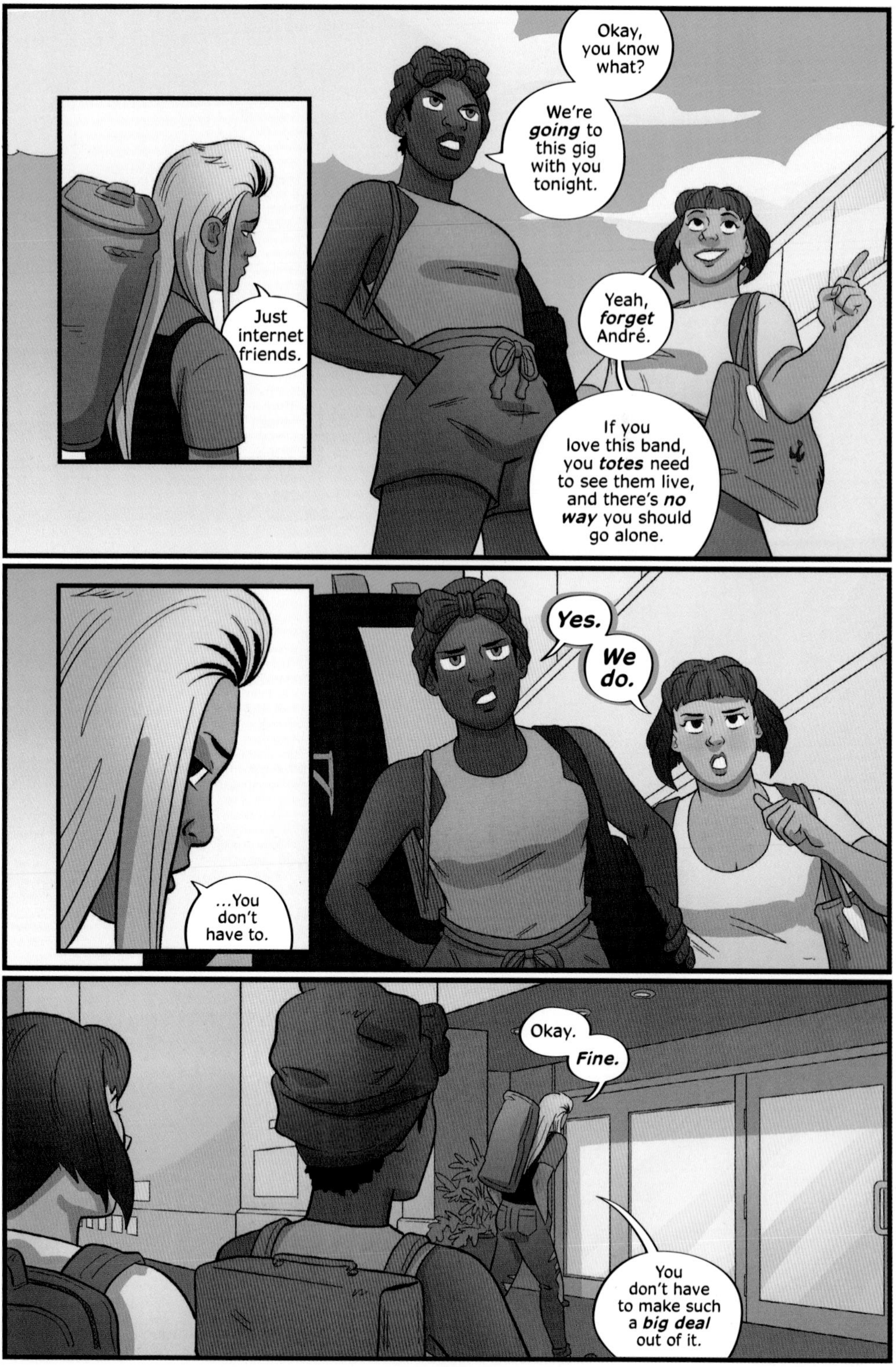
Just internet friends.
Okay, you know what?
We're *going* to this gig with you tonight.
Yeah, *forget* André.
If you love this band, you *totes* need to see them live, and there's *no way* you should go alone.
...You don't have to.
Yes.
We do.
Okay.
Fine.
You don't have to make such a *big deal* out of it.

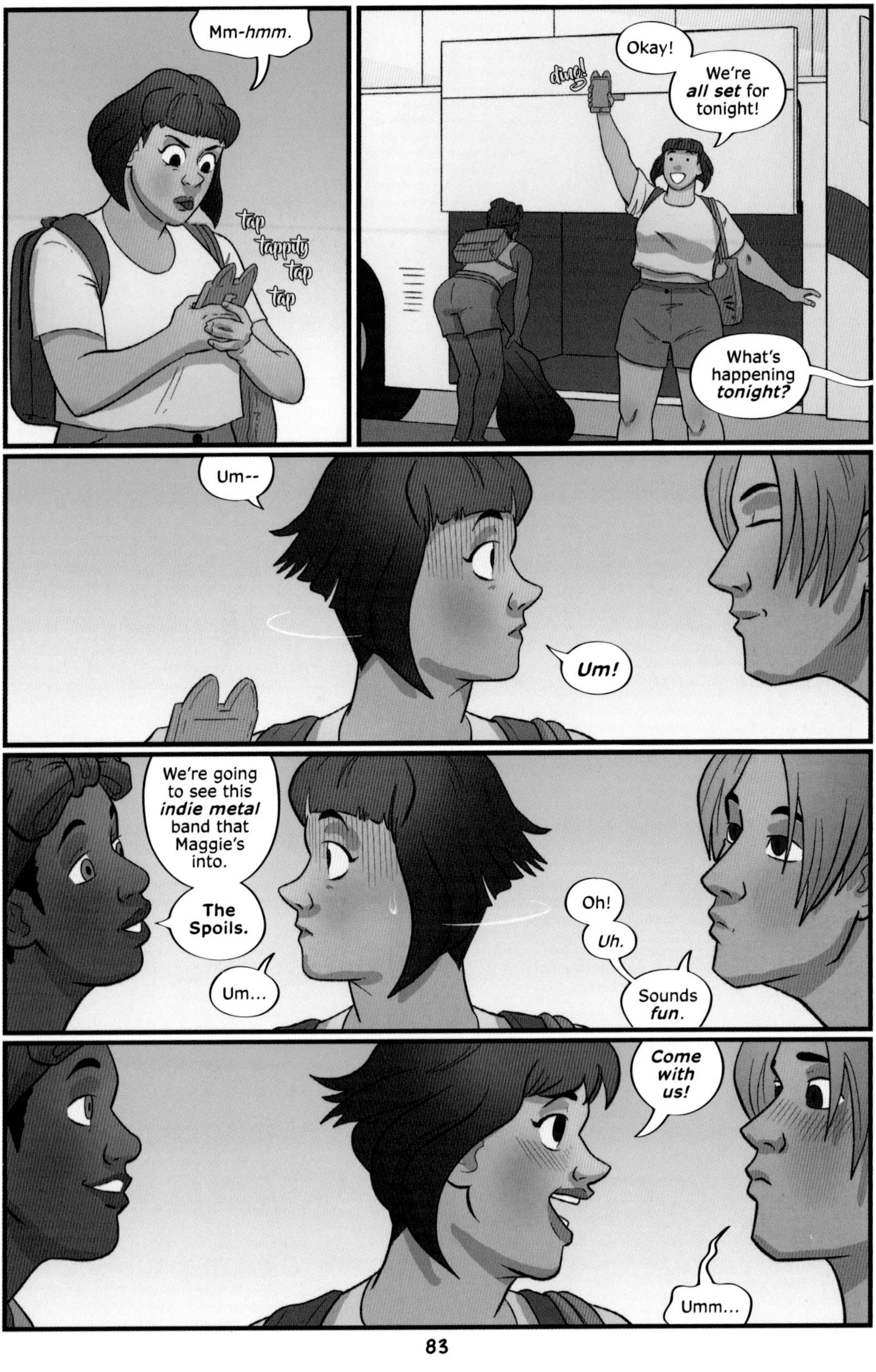
Mm-*hmm.*
tap
tappity
tap
tap
ding!
Okay!
We're *all set* for tonight!
What's happening *tonight?*
Um--
Um!
We're going to see this *indie metal* band that Maggie's into.
The Spoils.
Um...
Oh!
Uh.
Sounds *fun.*
Come with us!
Umm...

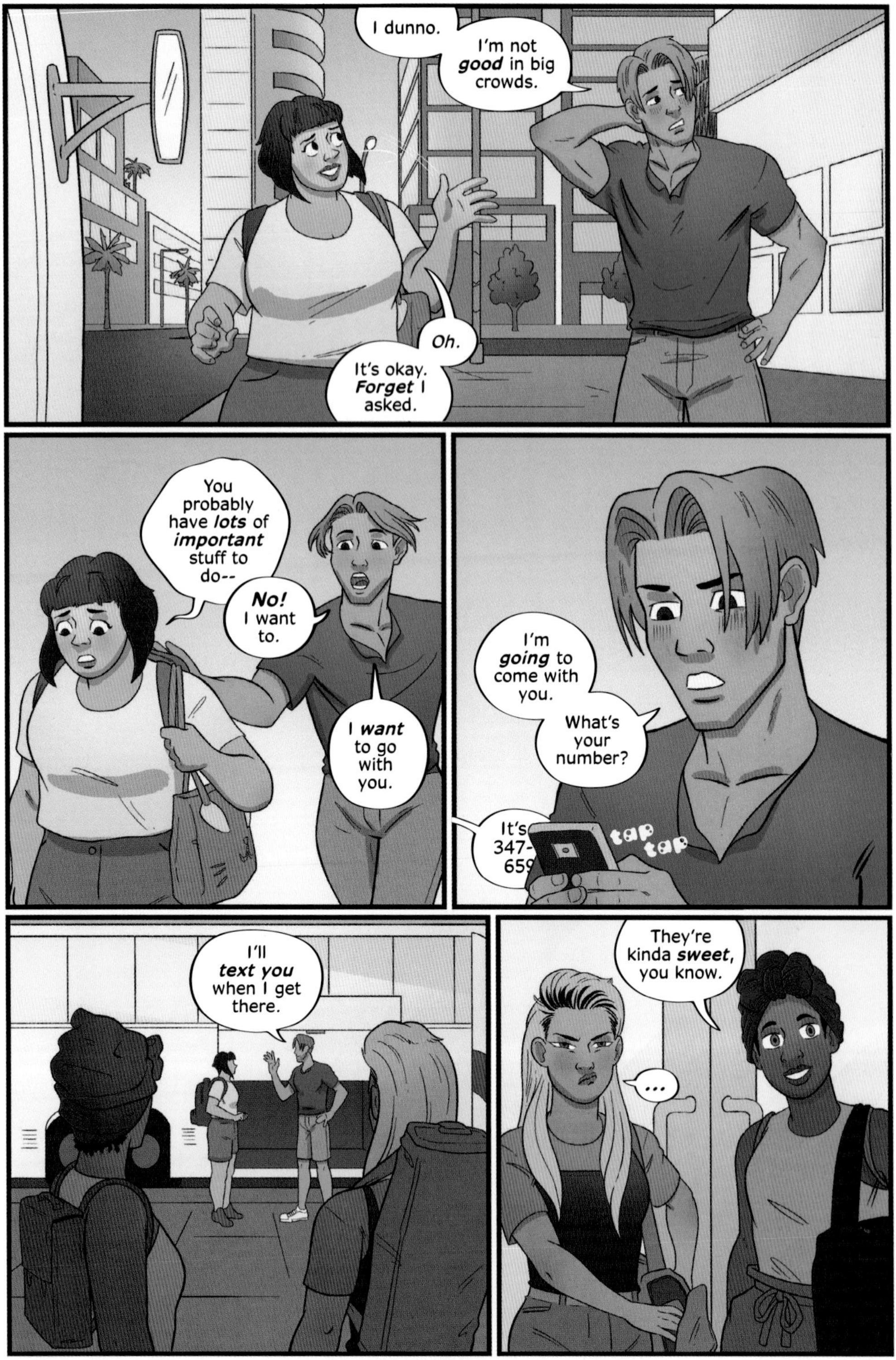
I dunno.
I'm not *good* in big crowds.
Oh.
It's okay. *Forget* I asked.
You probably have *lots* of *important* stuff to do--
No! I want to.
I *want* to go with you.
I'm *going* to come with you.
What's your number?
It's 347-65
tap tap
I'll *text you* when I get there.
They're kinda *sweet*, you know.
...

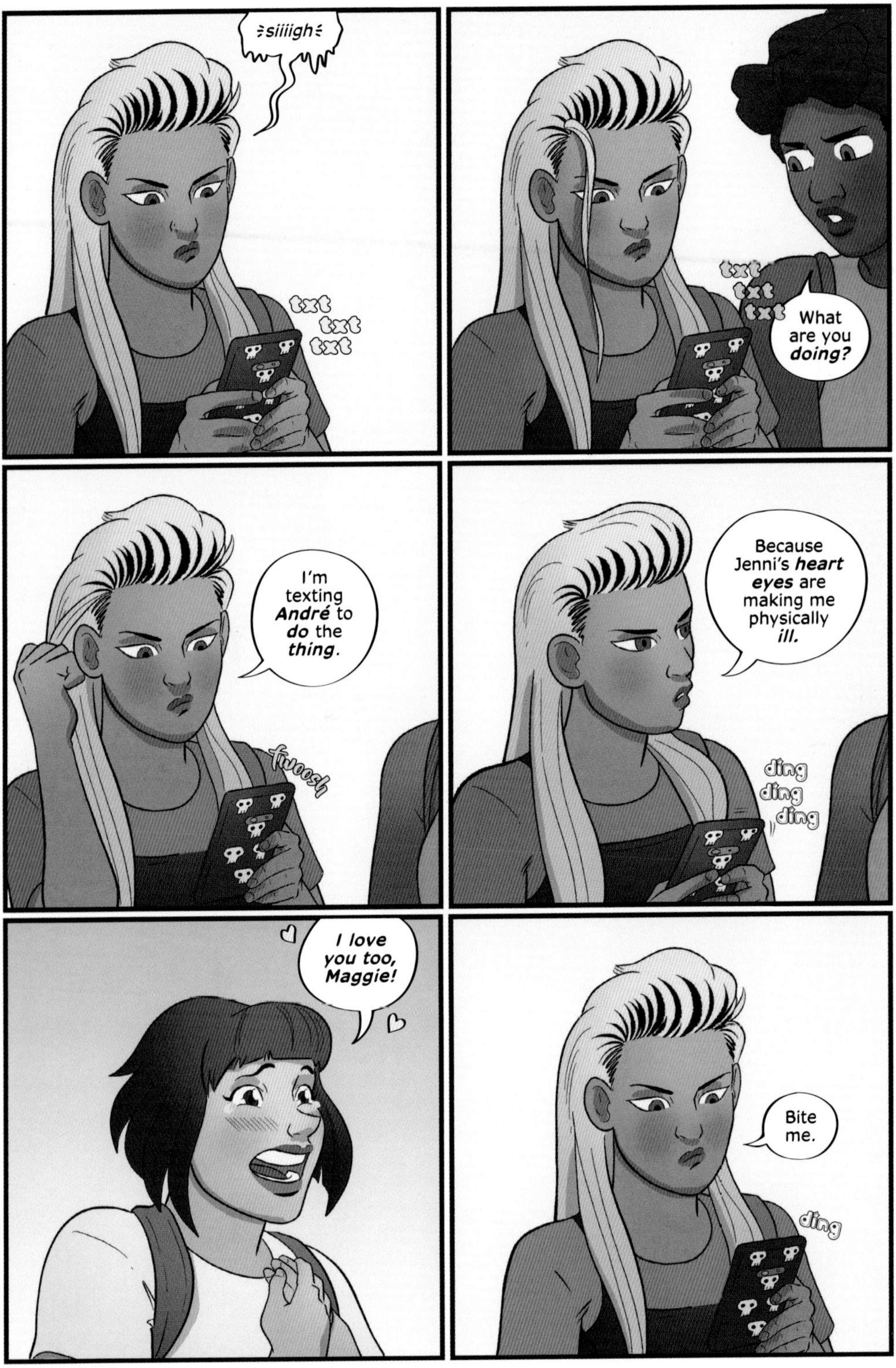
siiiigh
txt txt txt
txt txt txt
What are you *doing?*
I'm texting ***André*** to ***do*** the ***thing***.
fwoosh
Because Jenni's ***heart eyes*** are making me physically ***ill.***
ding ding ding
I love you too, Maggie!
Bite me.
ding

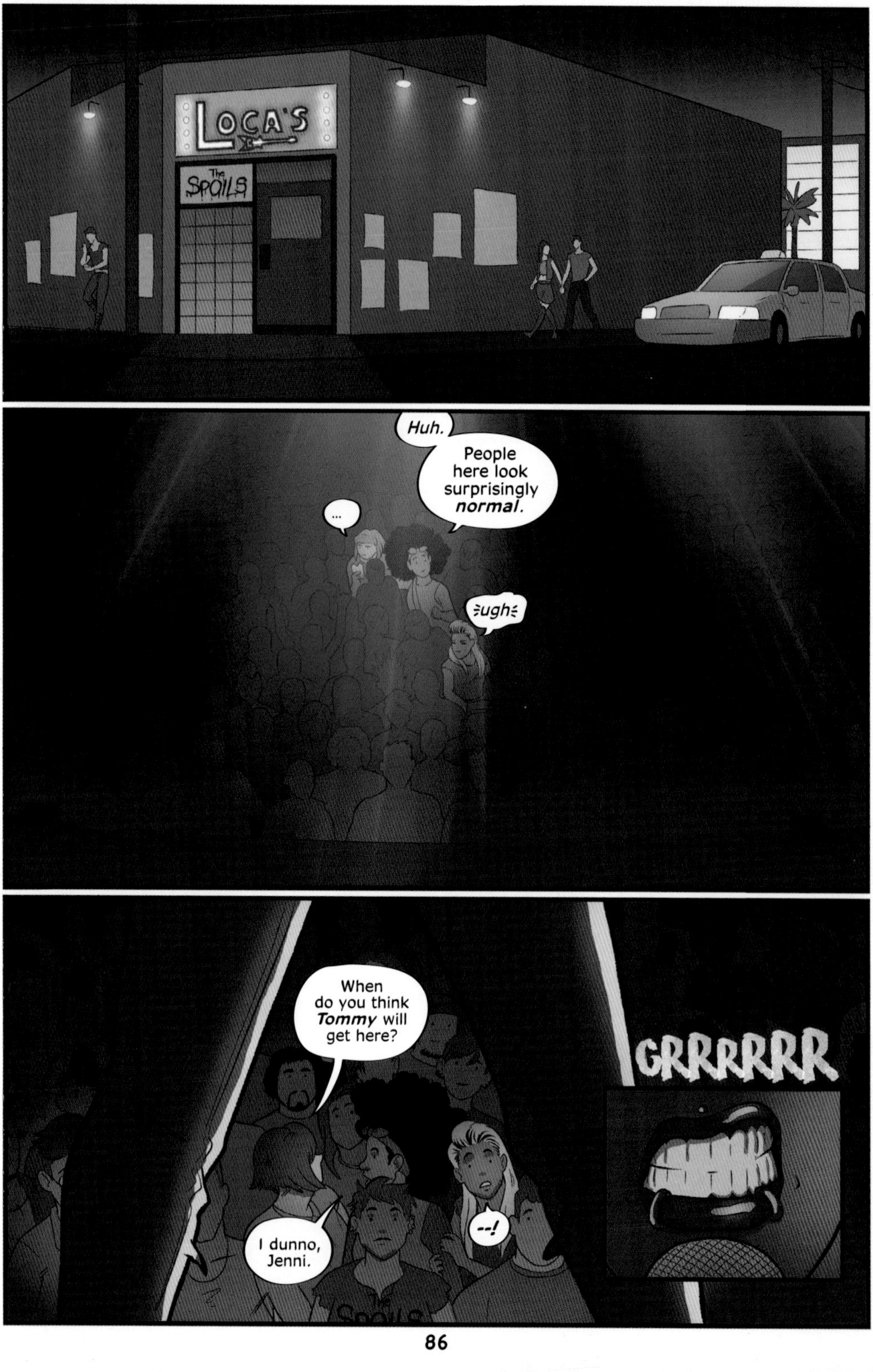
LOCA'S
The SPOILS
Huh.
People here look surprisingly *normal*.
...
ugh
When do you think *Tommy* will get here?
I dunno, Jenni.
--!
GRRRRRR
The SPOILS

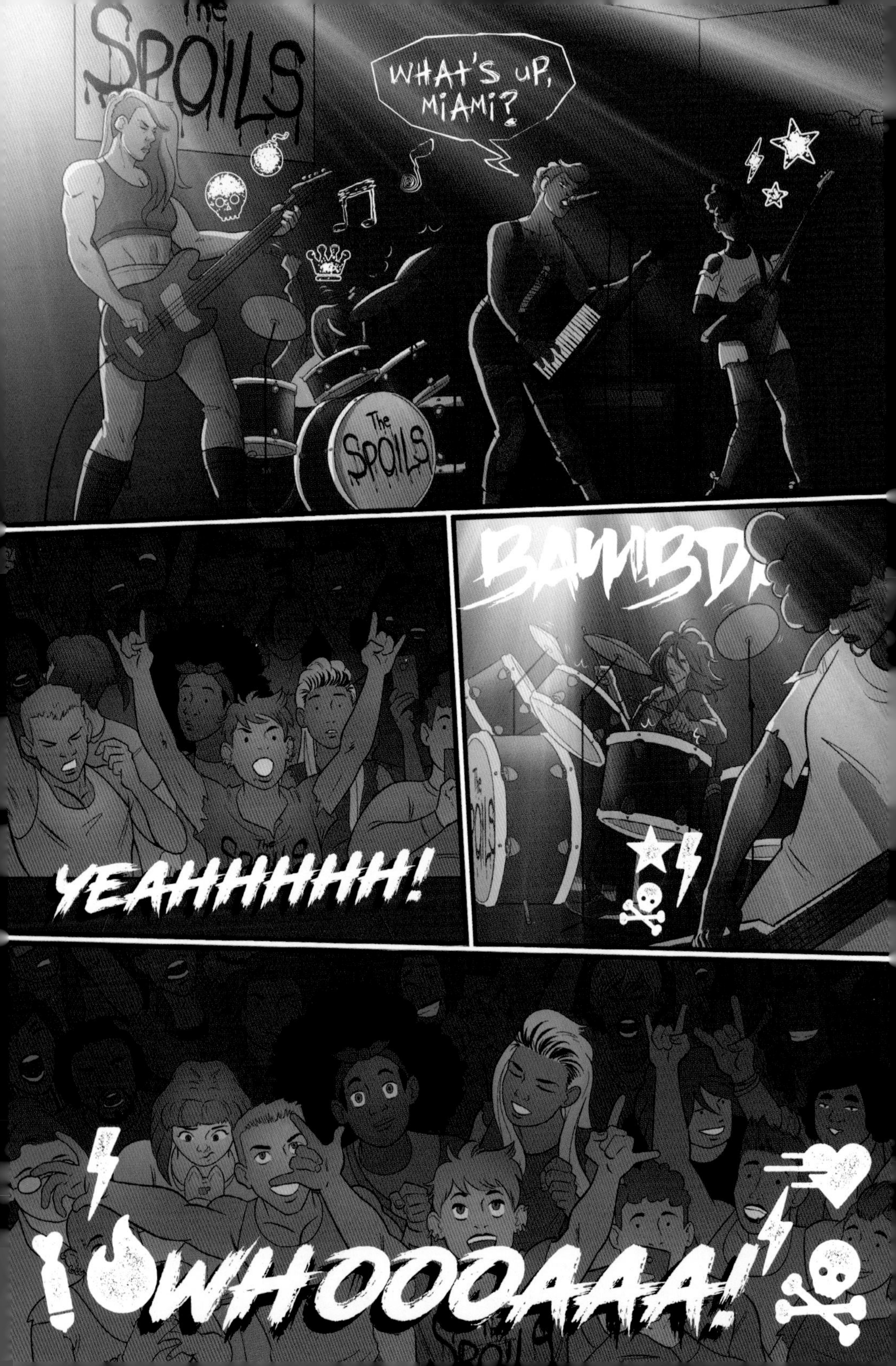
The SPOILS
WHAT'S UP, MIAMI?
The SPOILS
YEAHHHHHH!
BAMBD!
The SPOILS
WHOOOAAA!

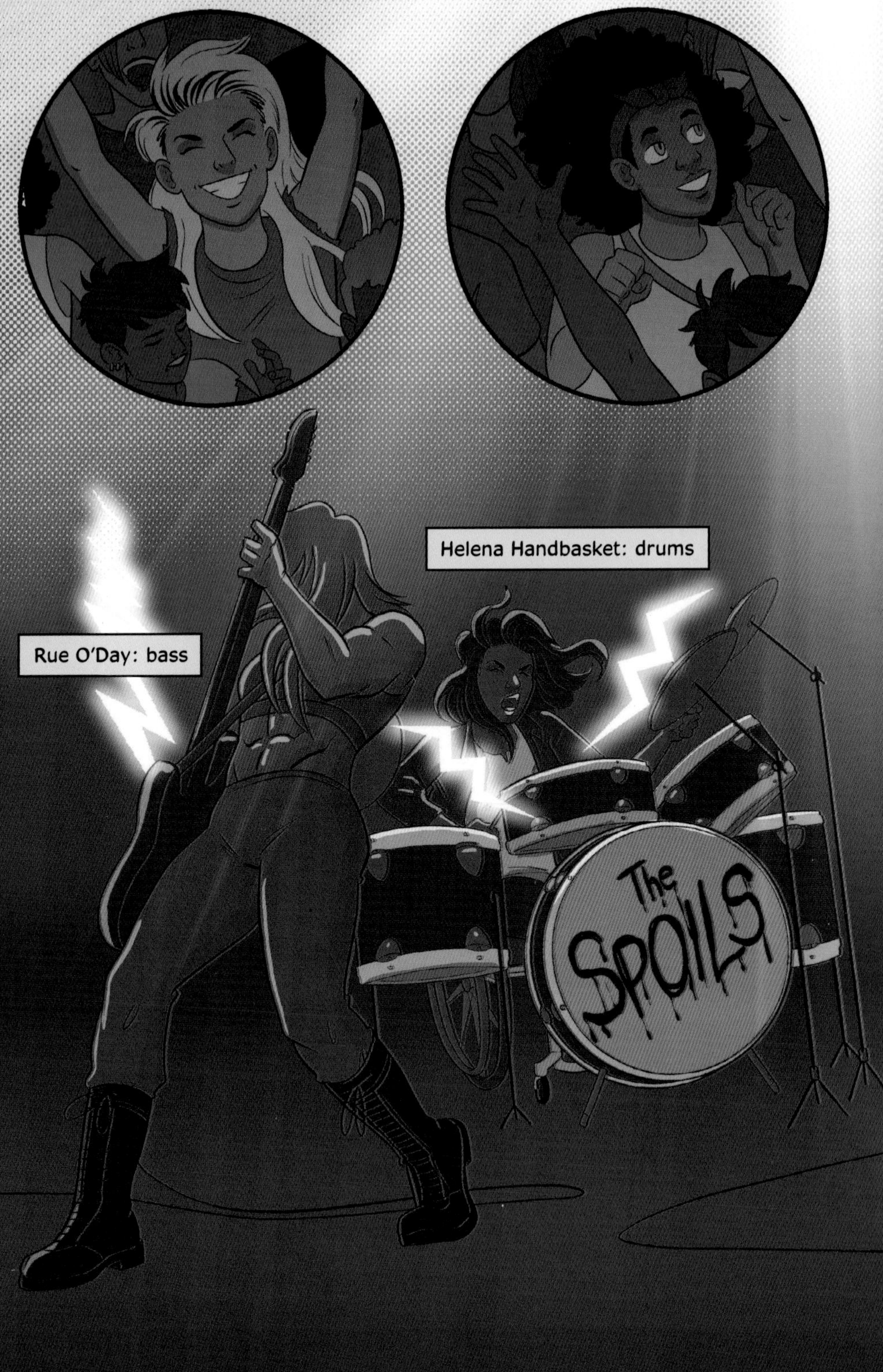
Helena Handbasket: drums
Rue O'Day: bass
The SPOILS

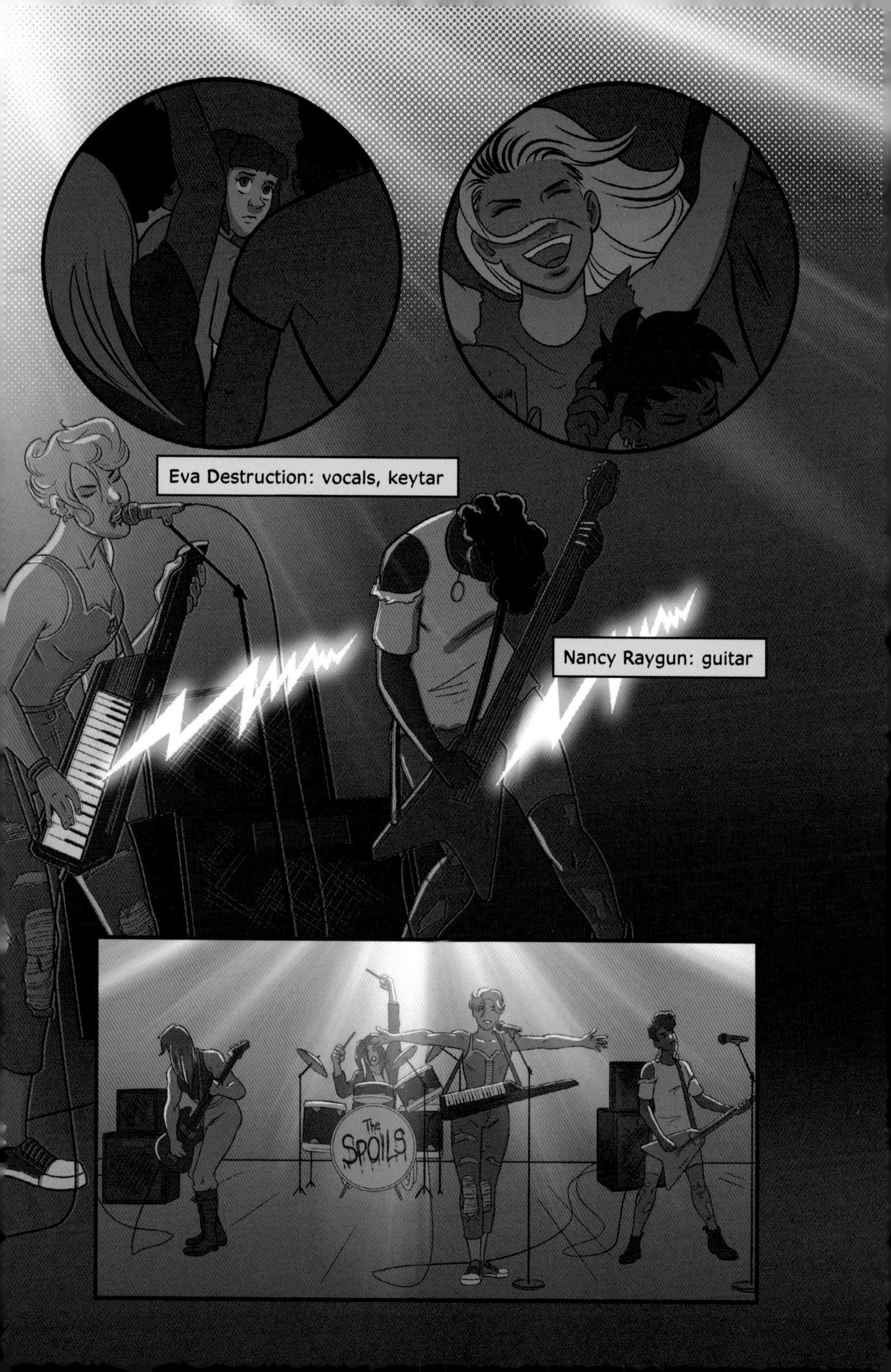
Eva Destruction: vocals, keytar
Nancy Raygun: guitar
The SPOILS

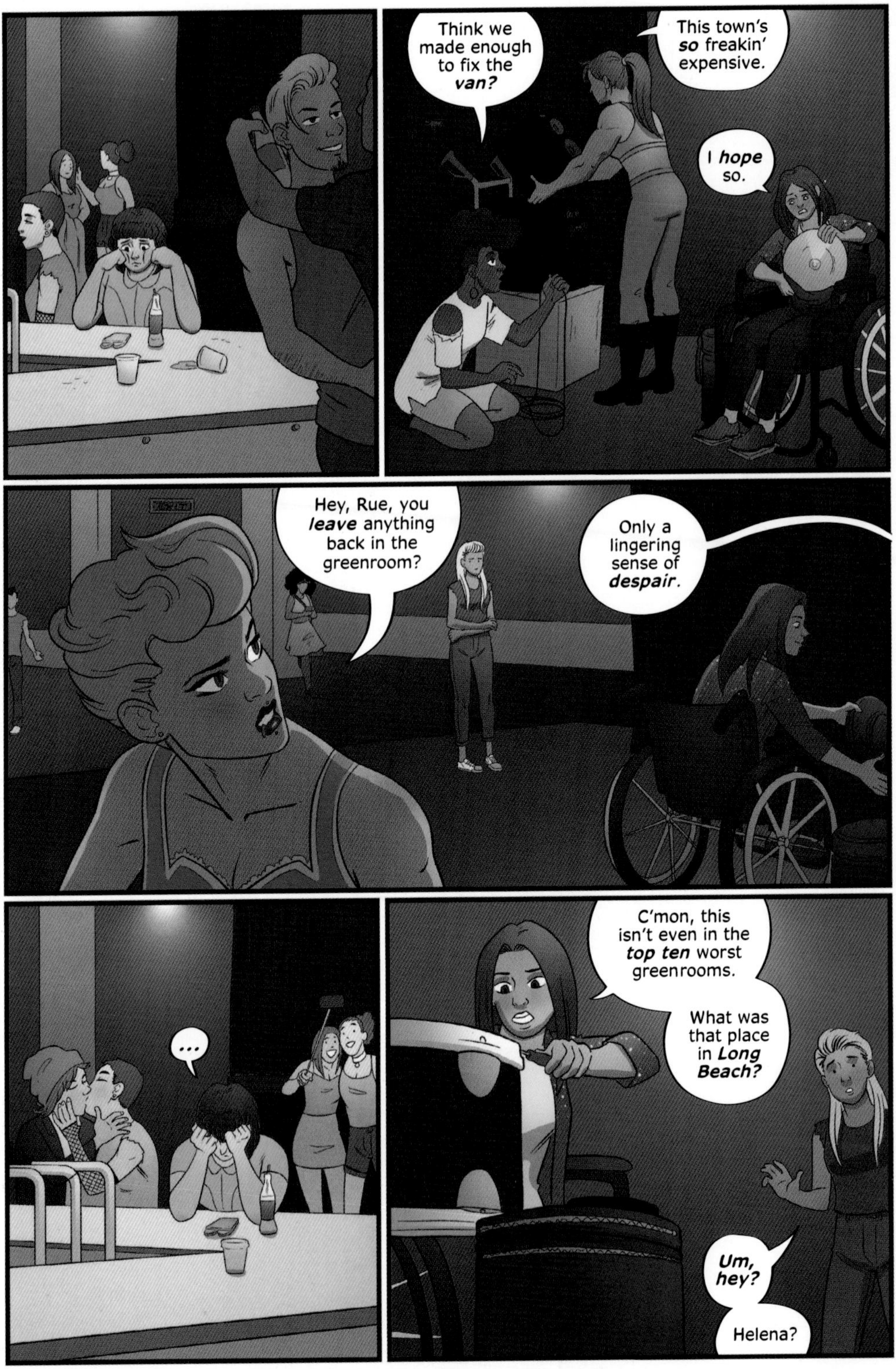

Think we made enough to fix the ***van?***
This town's ***so*** freakin' expensive.
I ***hope*** so.
Hey, Rue, you ***leave*** anything back in the greenroom?
Only a lingering sense of ***despair.***
...
C'mon, this isn't even in the ***top ten*** worst greenrooms.
What was that place in ***Long Beach?***
Um, hey?
Helena?

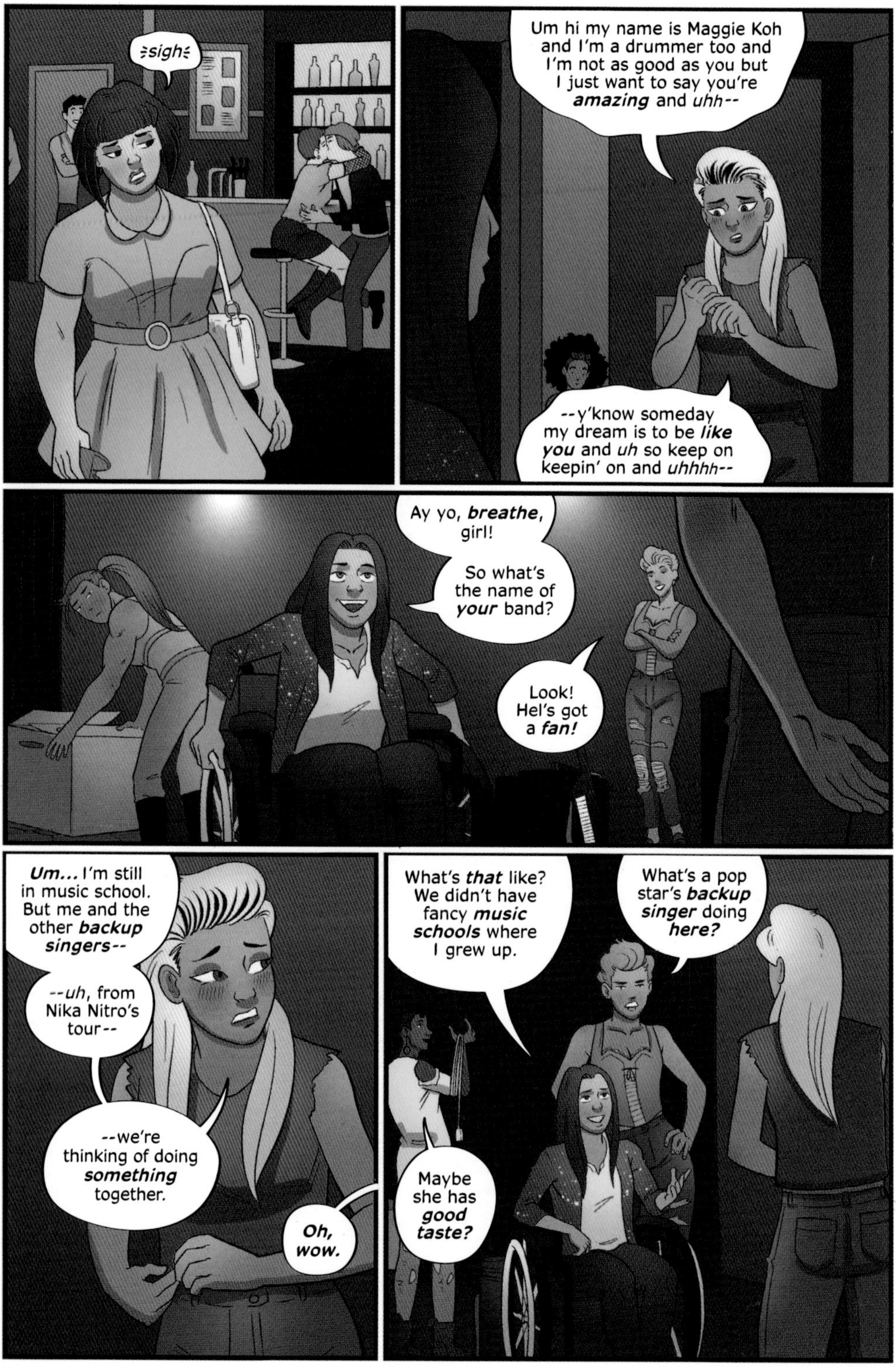
⩫sigh⩪
Um hi my name is Maggie Koh and I'm a drummer too and I'm not as good as you but I just want to say you're ***amazing*** and *uhh*--
--y'know someday my dream is to be ***like you*** and *uh* so keep on keepin' on and *uhhhh*--
Ay yo, ***breathe***, girl!
So what's the name of ***your*** band?
Look! Hel's got a ***fan!***
Um... I'm still in music school. But me and the other ***backup singers***--
--*uh*, from Nika Nitro's tour--
--we're thinking of doing ***something*** together.
Oh, wow.
What's ***that*** like? We didn't have fancy ***music schools*** where I grew up.
What's a pop star's ***backup singer*** doing ***here?***
Maybe she has ***good taste?***

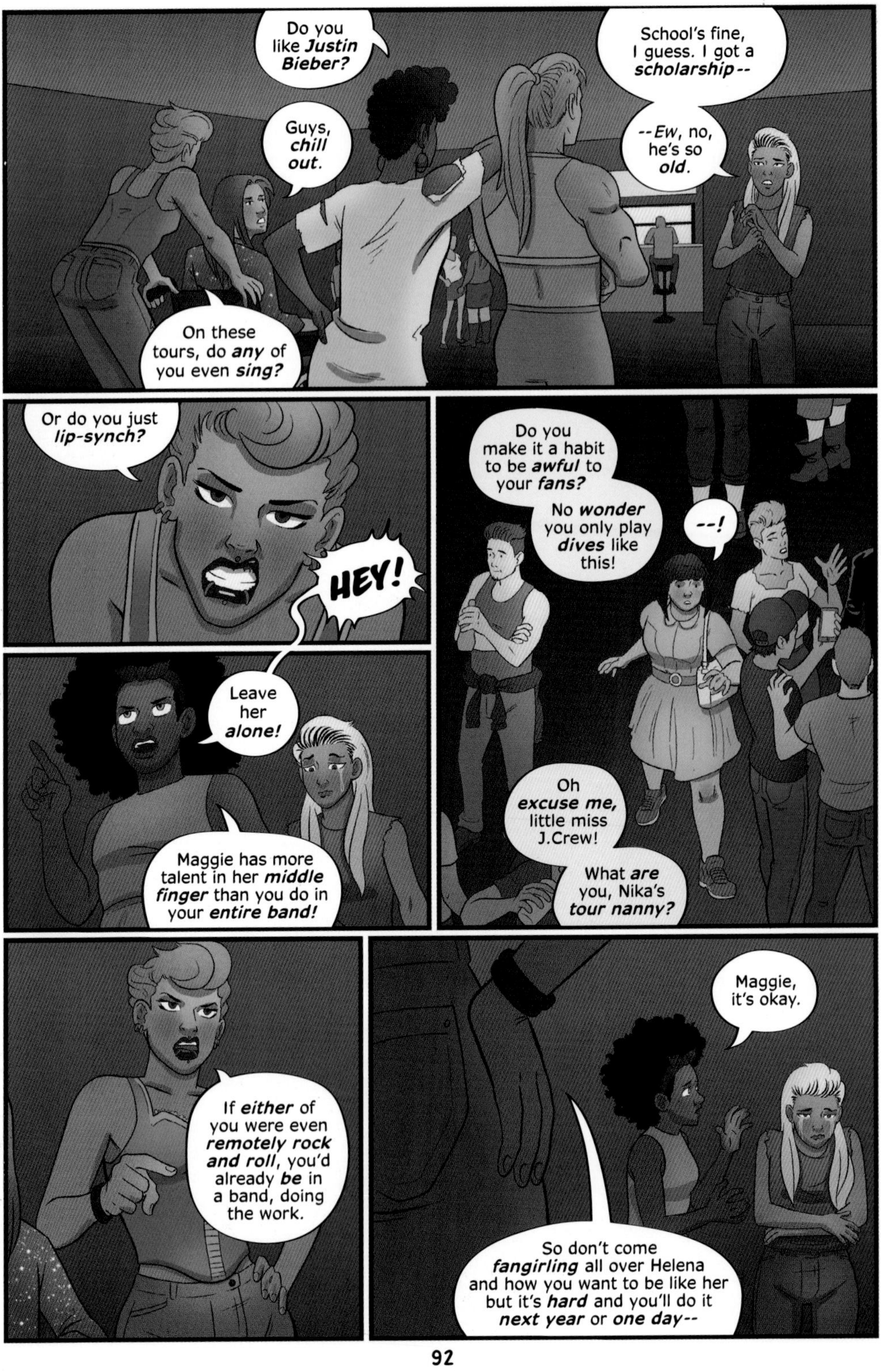
Do you like ***Justin Bieber?***
School's fine, I guess. I got a ***scholarship--***
Guys, ***chill out***.
--*Ew*, no, he's so ***old***.
On these tours, do ***any*** of you even ***sing?***
Or do you just ***lip-synch?***
HEY!
Leave her ***alone!***
Maggie has more talent in her ***middle finger*** than you do in your ***entire band!***
Do you make it a habit to be ***awful*** to your ***fans?***
No ***wonder*** you only play ***dives*** like this!
--!
Oh ***excuse me,*** little miss J.Crew!
What ***are*** you, Nika's ***tour nanny?***
If ***either*** of you were even ***remotely rock and roll***, you'd already ***be*** in a band, doing the work.
Maggie, it's okay.
So don't come ***fangirling*** all over Helena and how you want to be like her but it's ***hard*** and you'll do it ***next year*** or ***one day--***

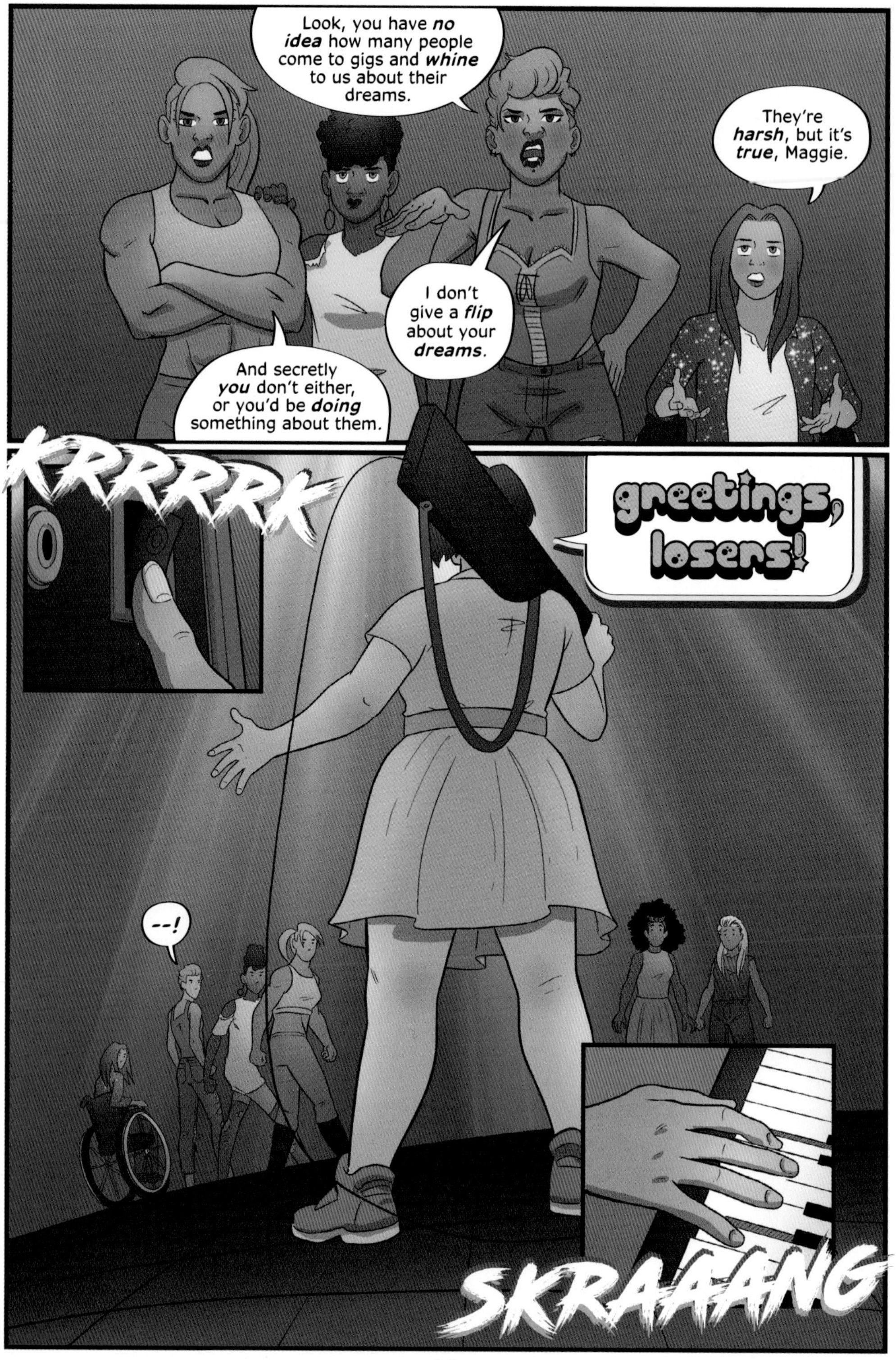

Look, you have *no* *idea* how many people come to gigs and *whine* to us about their dreams.
They're *harsh*, but it's *true*, Maggie.
I don't give a *flip* about your *dreams*.
And secretly *you* don't either, or you'd be *doing* something about them.
KRRRRK
greetings, losers!
--!
SKRAAAANG

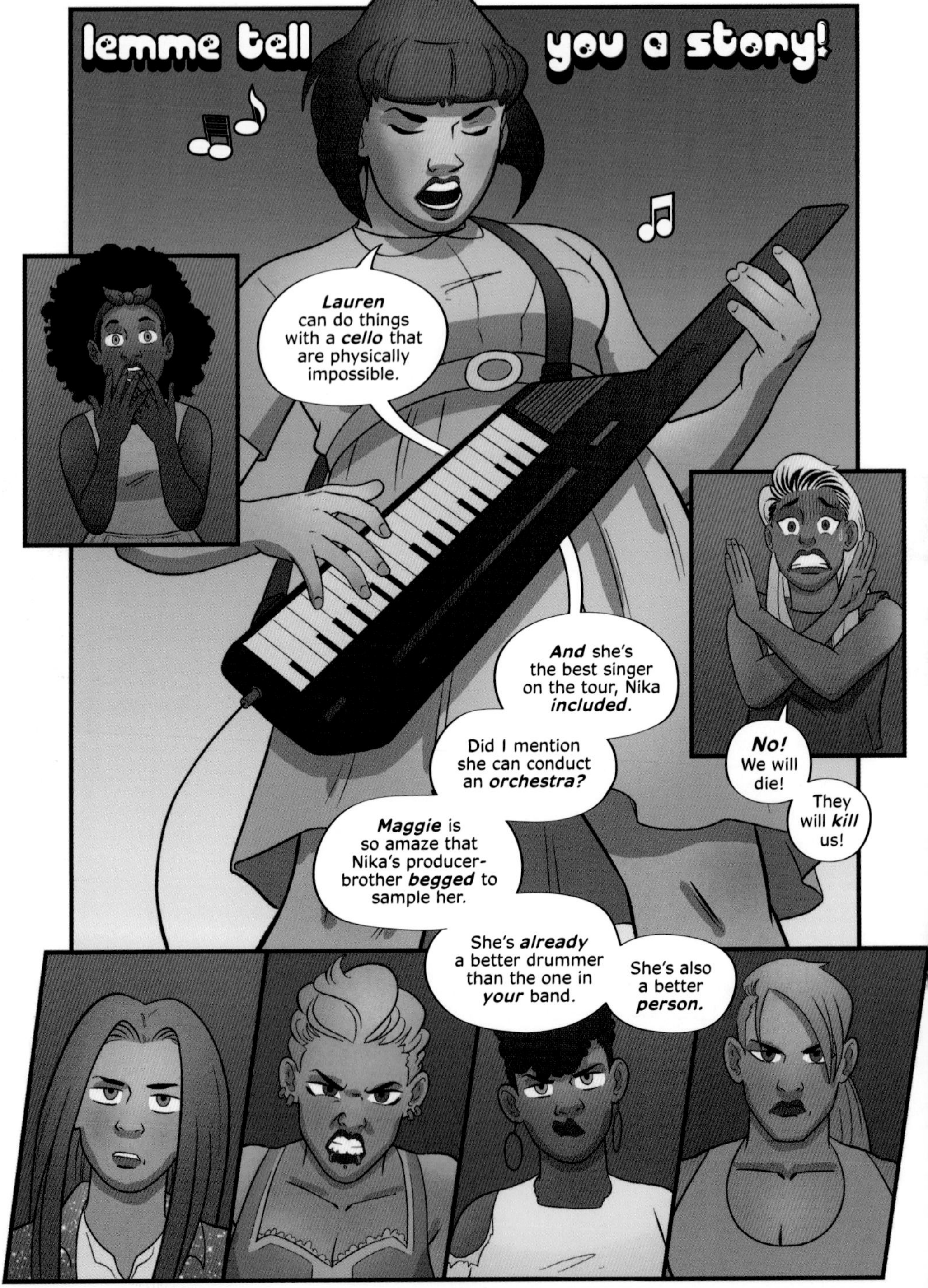
lemme tell you a story!
Lauren can do things with a *cello* that are physically impossible.
And she's the best singer on the tour, Nika ***included.***
Did I mention she can conduct an ***orchestra?***
No! We will die!
They will ***kill*** us!
Maggie is so amaze that Nika's producer-brother ***begged*** to sample her.
She's ***already*** a better drummer than the one in ***your*** band.
She's also a better ***person.***

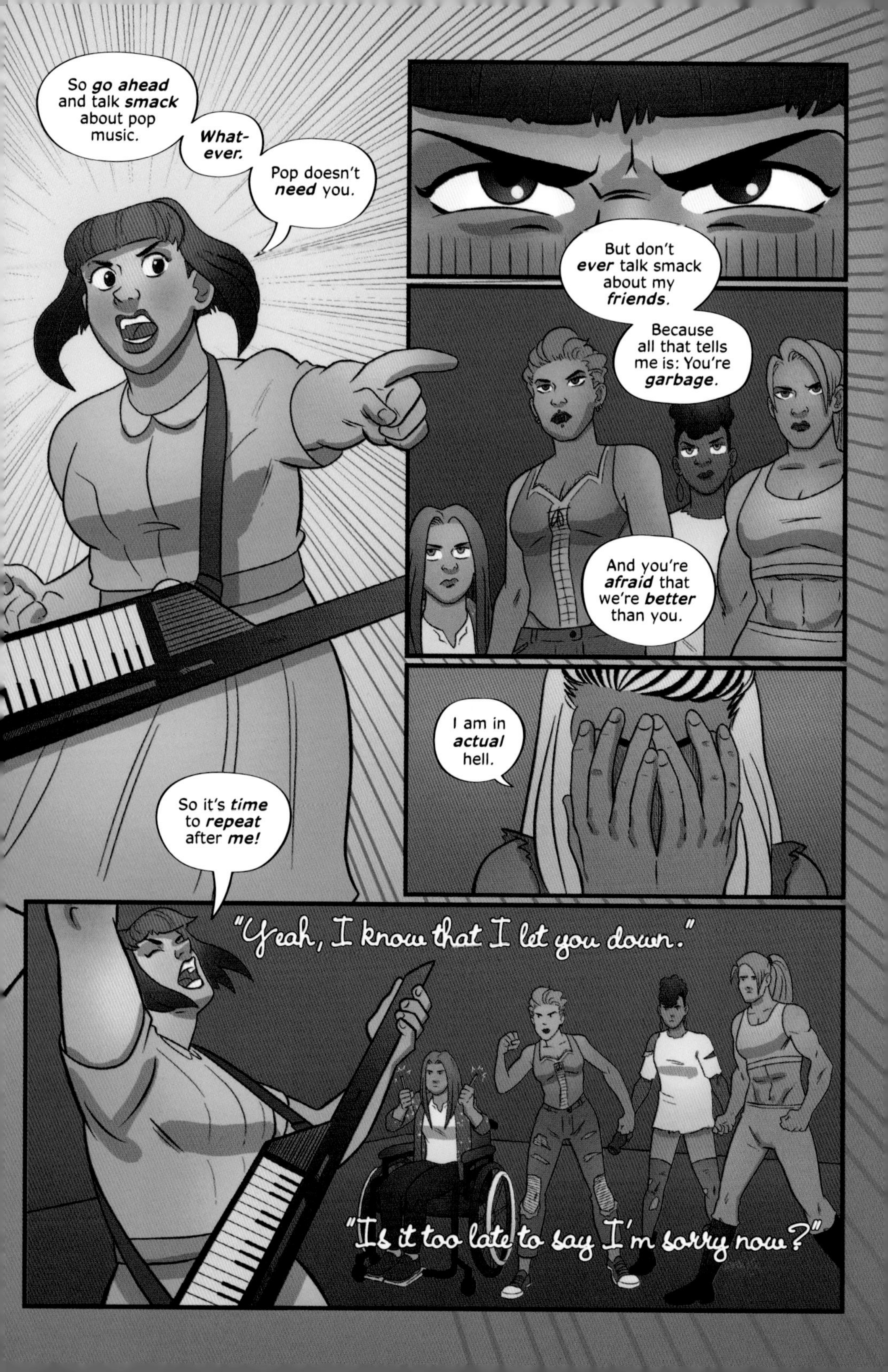
So *go ahead* and talk *smack* about pop music.
What-ever.
Pop doesn't *need* you.
But don't *ever* talk smack about my *friends*.
Because all that tells me is: You're *garbage*.
And you're *afraid* that we're *better* than you.
I am in *actual* hell.
So it's *time* to *repeat* after *me!*
"Yeah, I know that I let you down."
"Is it too late to say I'm sorry now?"

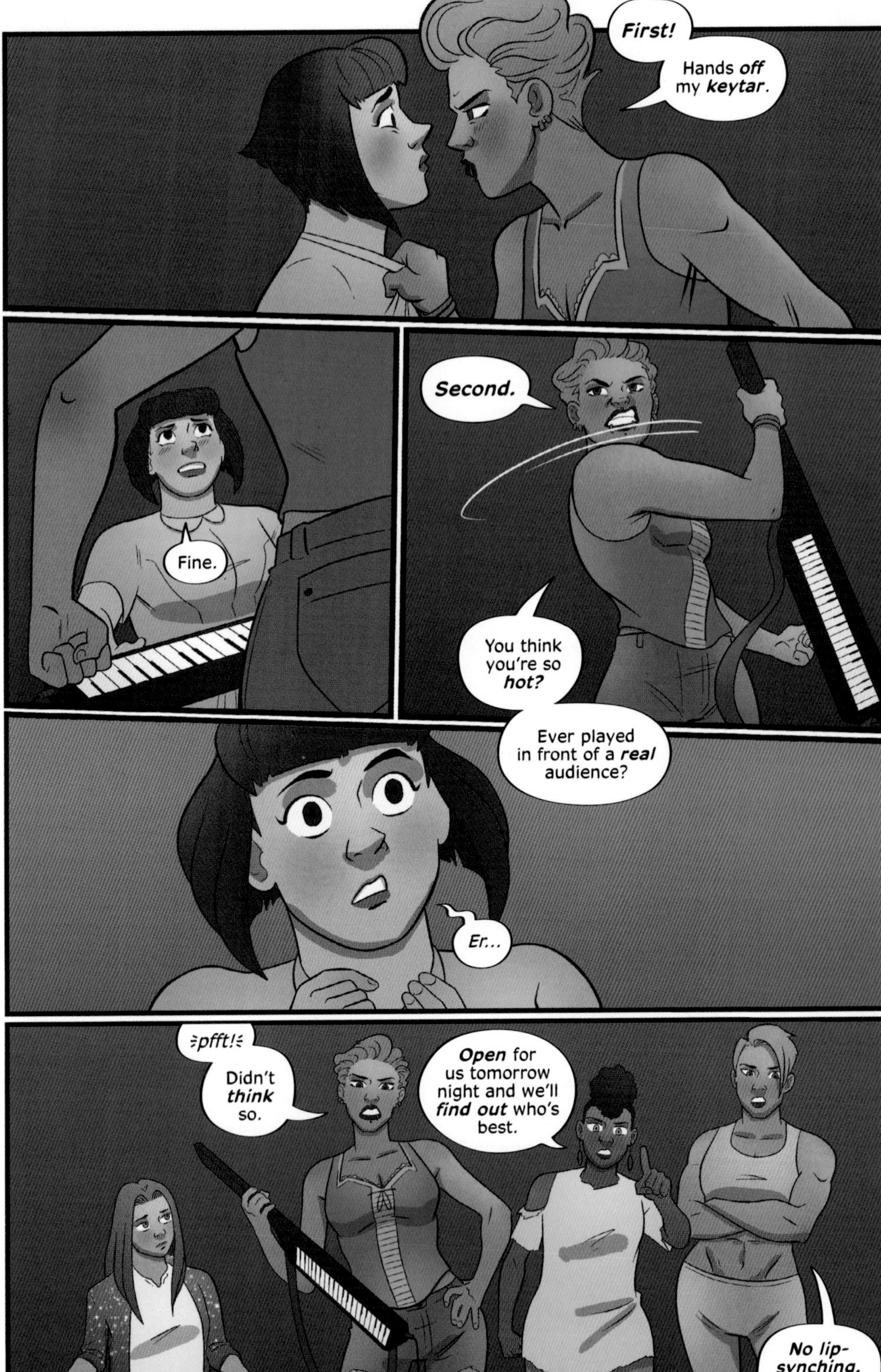

First!
Hands *off* my *keytar*.
Second.
Fine.
You think you're so *hot?*
Ever played in front of a *real* audience?
Er...
pfft!
Didn't *think* so.
Open for us tomorrow night and we'll *find out* who's best.
No lip-synching.

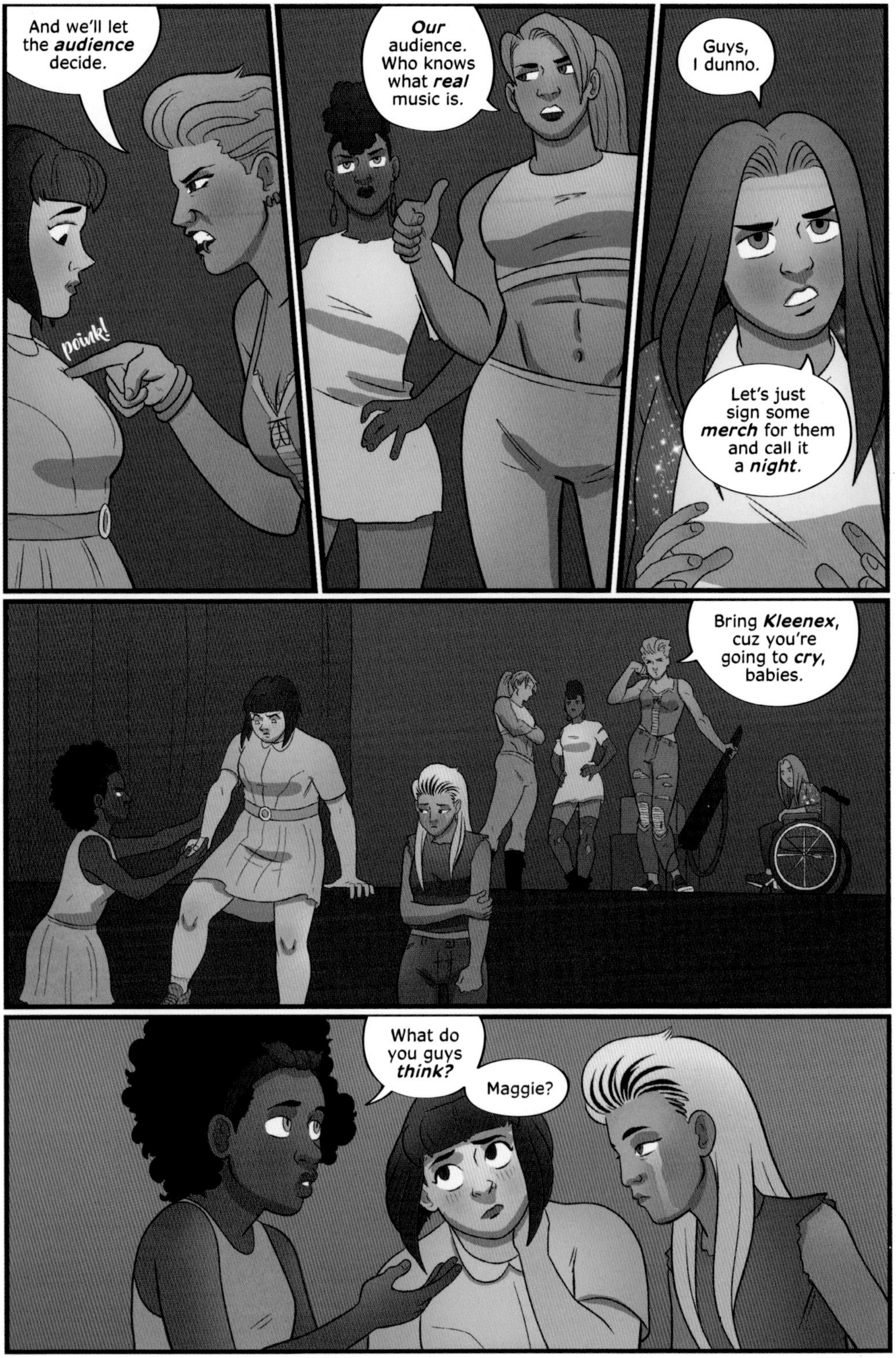
And we'll let the *audience* decide.
poink!
Our audience. Who knows what *real* music is.
Guys, I dunno.
Let's just sign some *merch* for them and call it a *night*.
Bring *Kleenex*, cuz you're going to *cry*, babies.
What do you guys *think?*
Maggie?

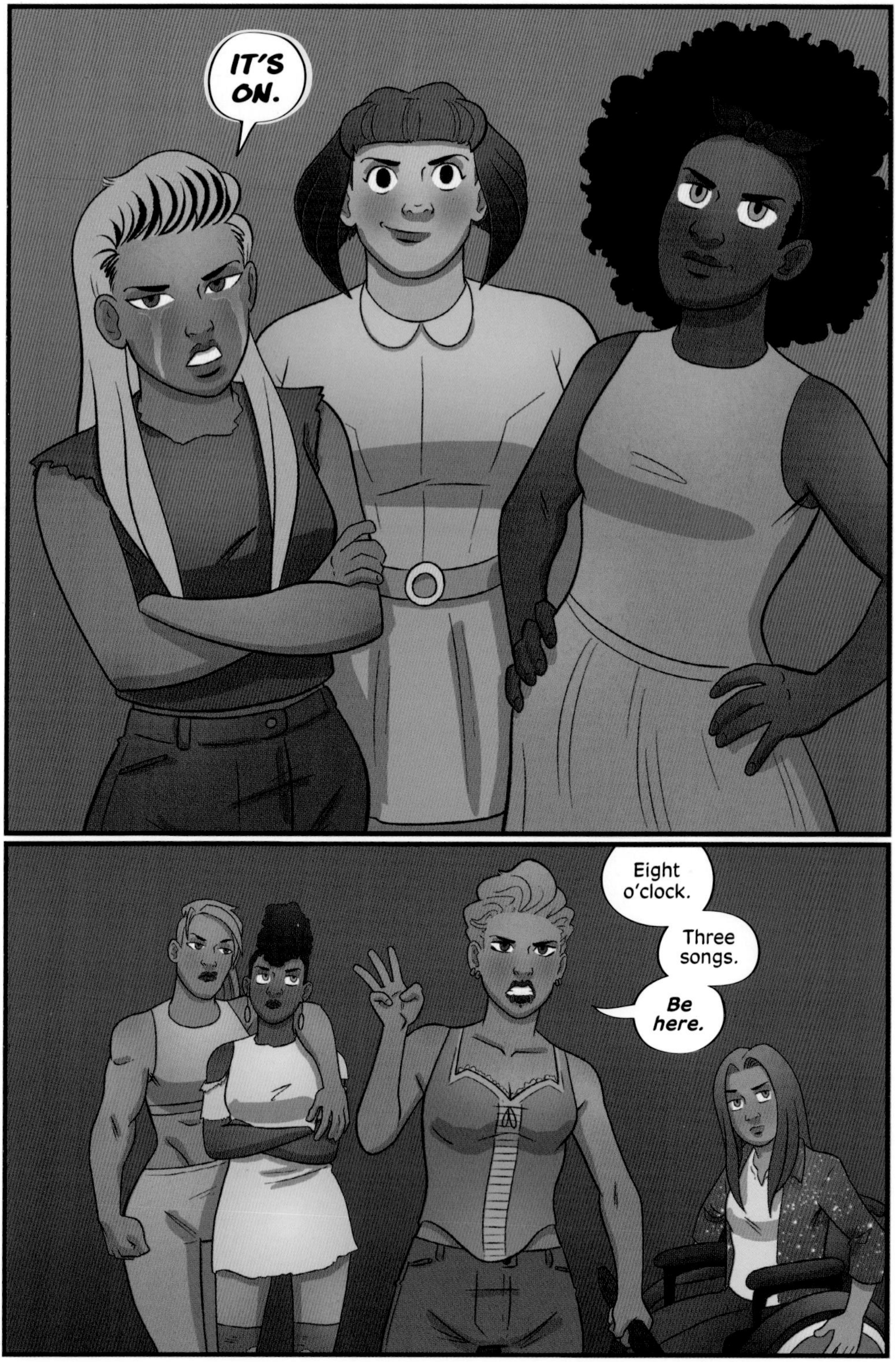
IT'S ON.
Eight o'clock.
Three songs.
Be here.

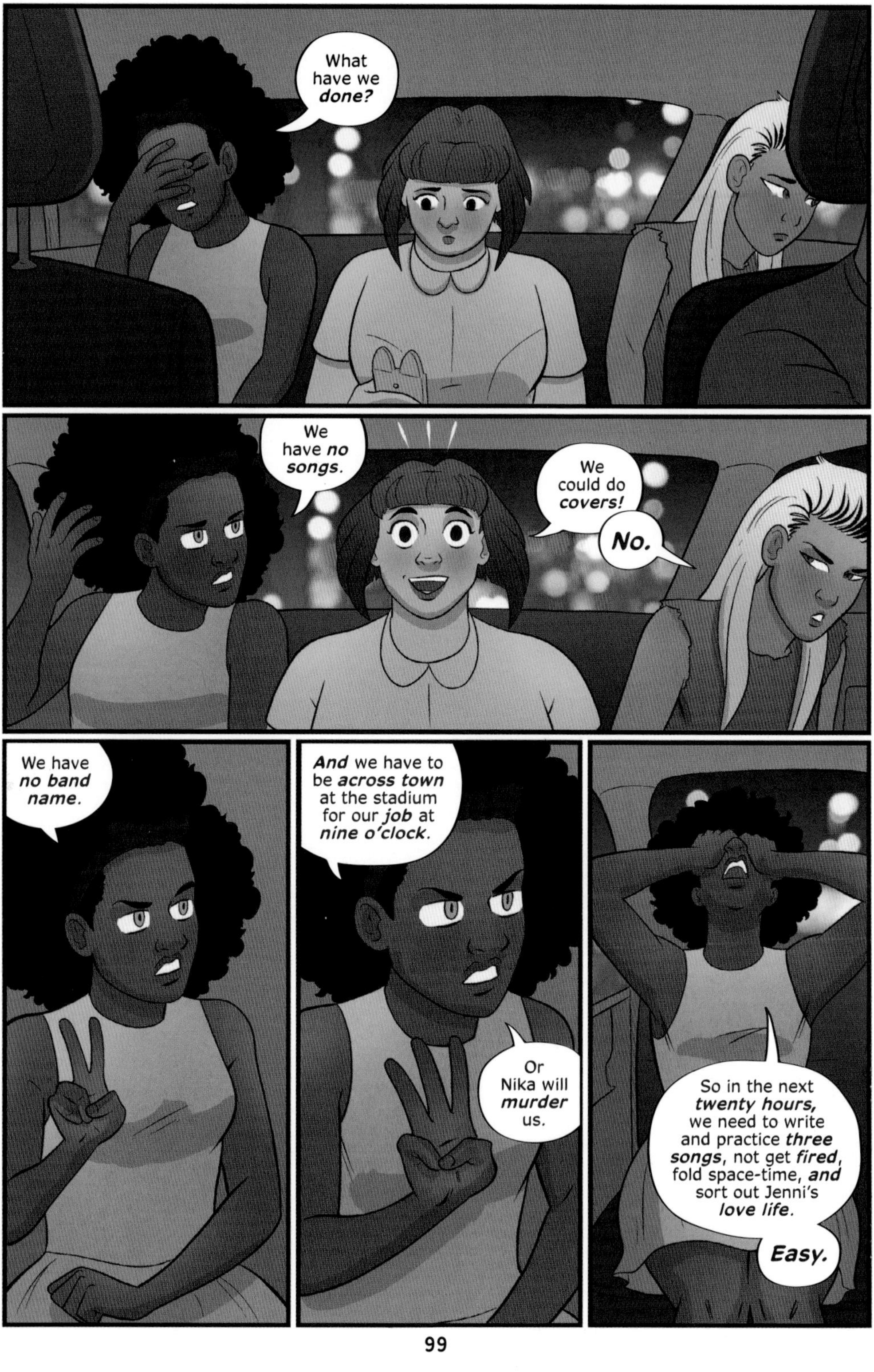
What have we *done?*
We have *no songs*.
We could do *covers!*
No.
We have *no band name*.
And we have to be ***across town*** at the stadium for our ***job*** at ***nine o'clock***.
Or Nika will ***murder*** us.
So in the next ***twenty hours,*** we need to write and practice ***three songs***, not get ***fired***, fold space-time, ***and*** sort out Jenni's ***love life***.
Easy.

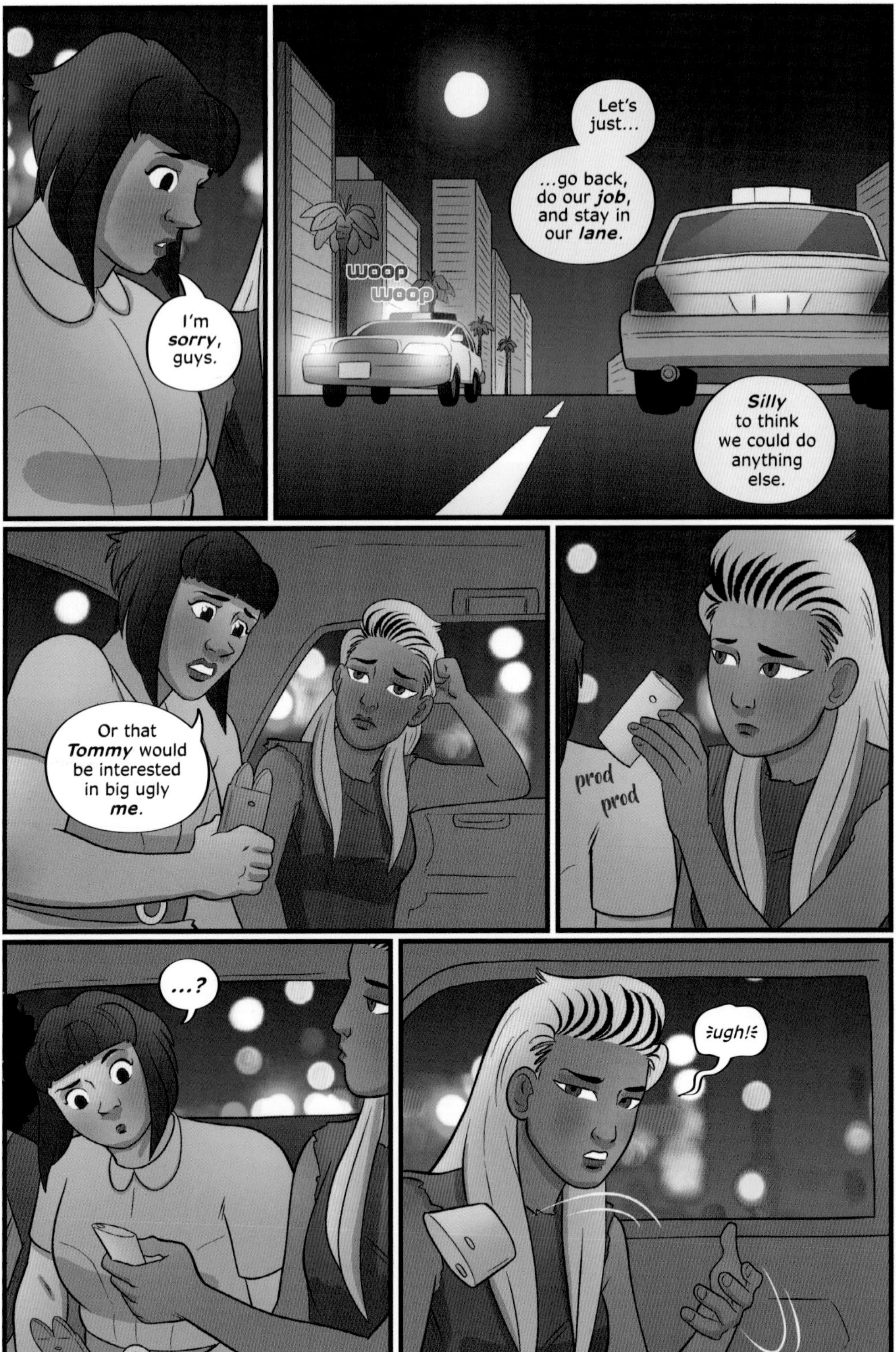
I'm *sorry*, guys.
Let's just...
...go back, do our ***job***, and stay in our ***lane***.
woop
woop
Silly to think we could do anything else.
Or that ***Tommy*** would be interested in big ugly ***me***.
prod
prod
...?
ugh!

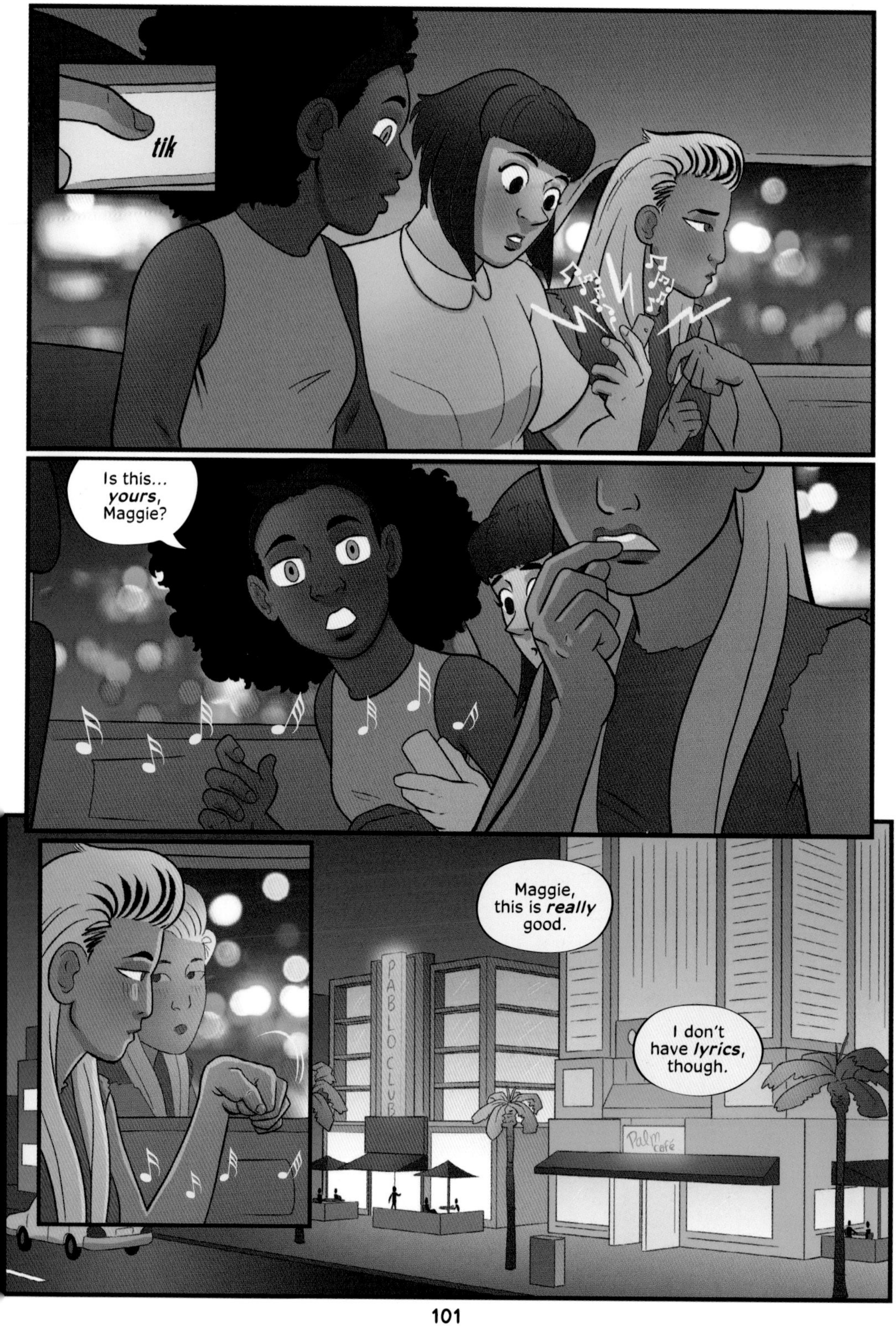
tik
Is this... *yours*, Maggie?
Maggie, this is *really* good.
PABLO CLUB
Palm café
I don't have *lyrics*, though.

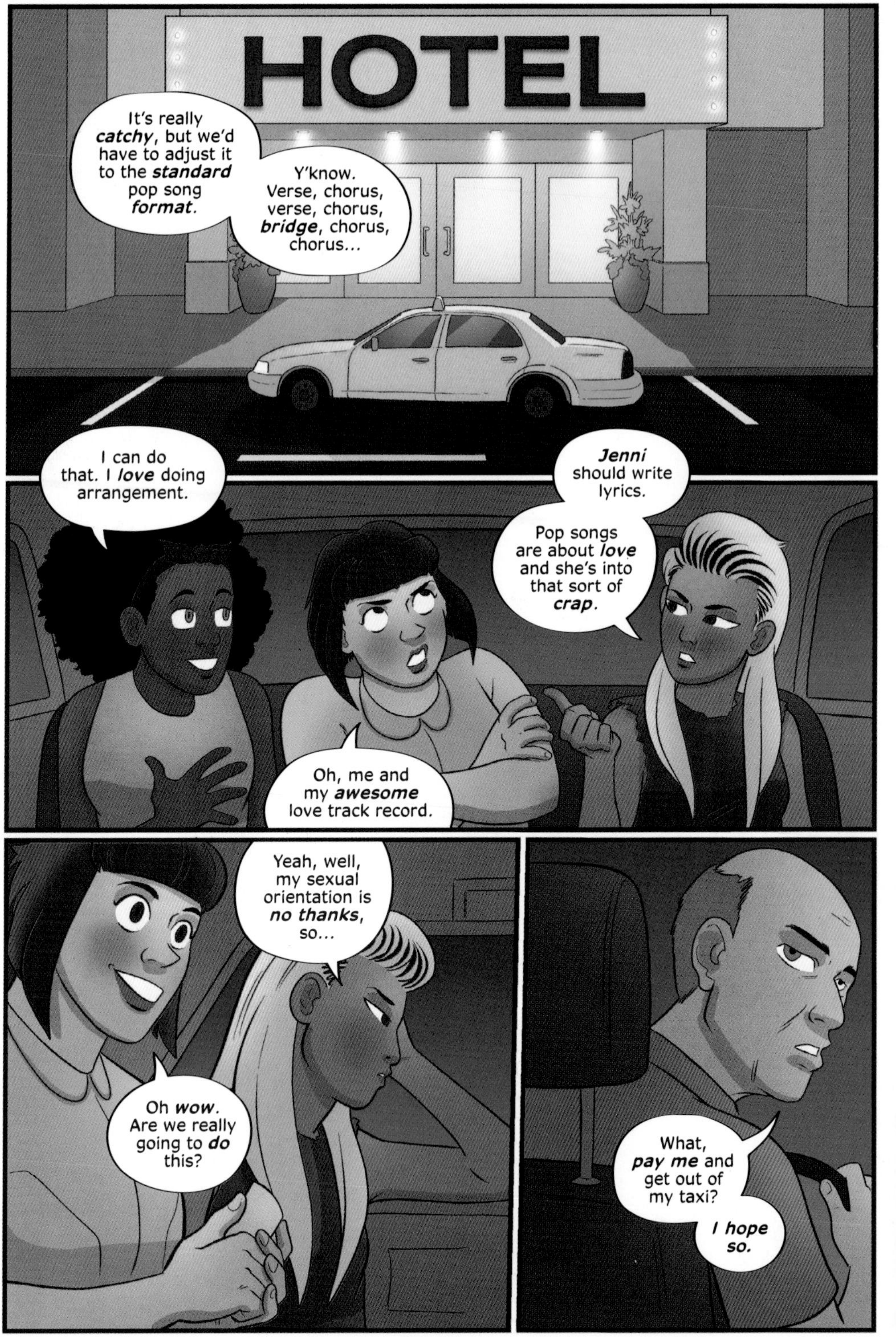
HOTEL
It's really *catchy*, but we'd have to adjust it to the *standard* pop song *format*.
Y'know. Verse, chorus, verse, chorus, *bridge*, chorus, chorus...
I can do that. I *love* doing arrangement.
Jenni should write lyrics.
Pop songs are about *love* and she's into that sort of *crap*.
Oh, me and my *awesome* love track record.
Yeah, well, my sexual orientation is *no thanks*, so...
Oh *wow*. Are we really going to *do* this?
What, *pay me* and get out of my taxi?
I hope so.

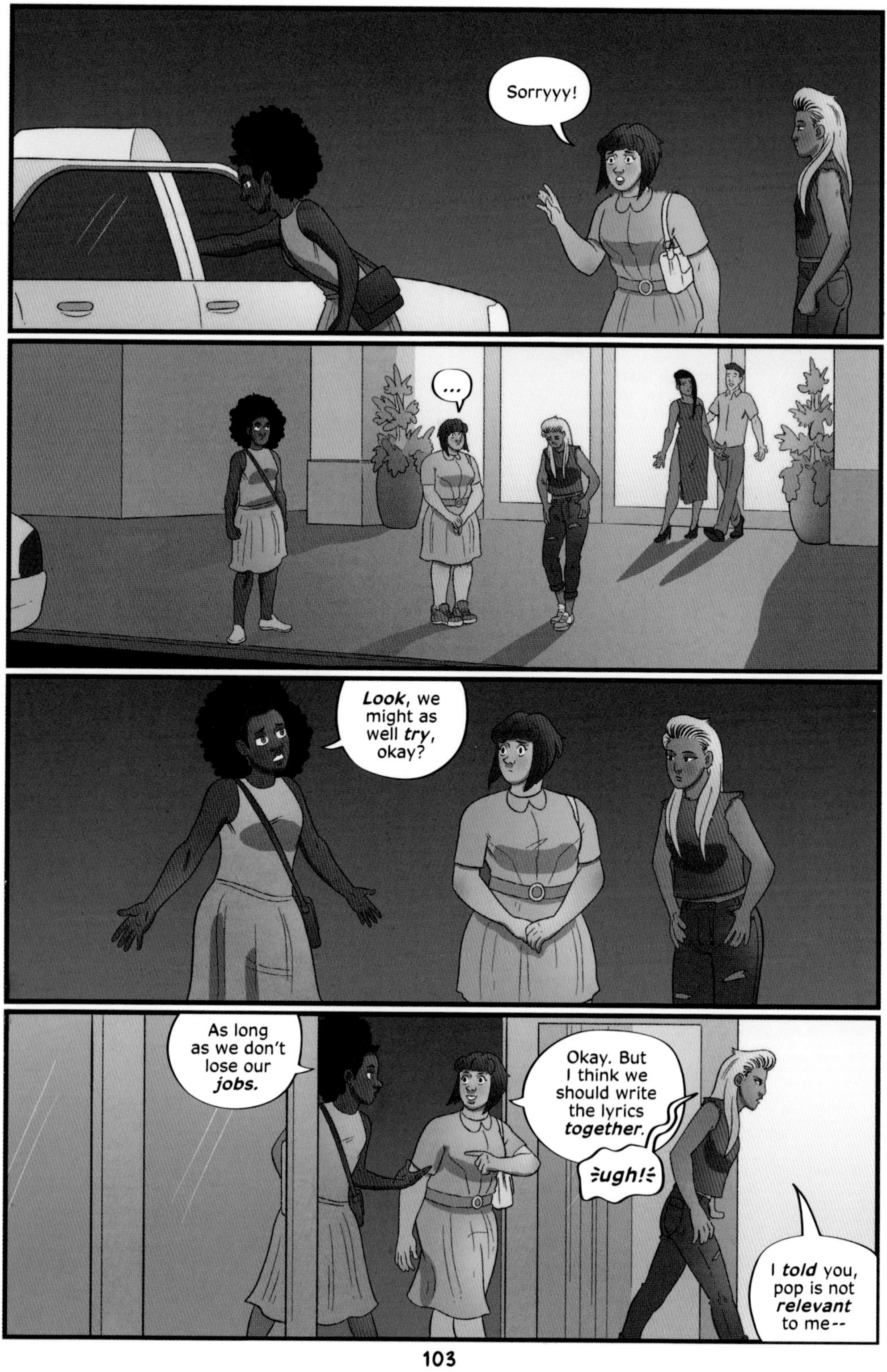
Sorryyy!
...
Look, we might as well *try*, okay?
As long as we don't lose our *jobs.*
Okay. But I think we should write the lyrics *together*.
ugh!
I *told* you, pop is not *relevant* to me--

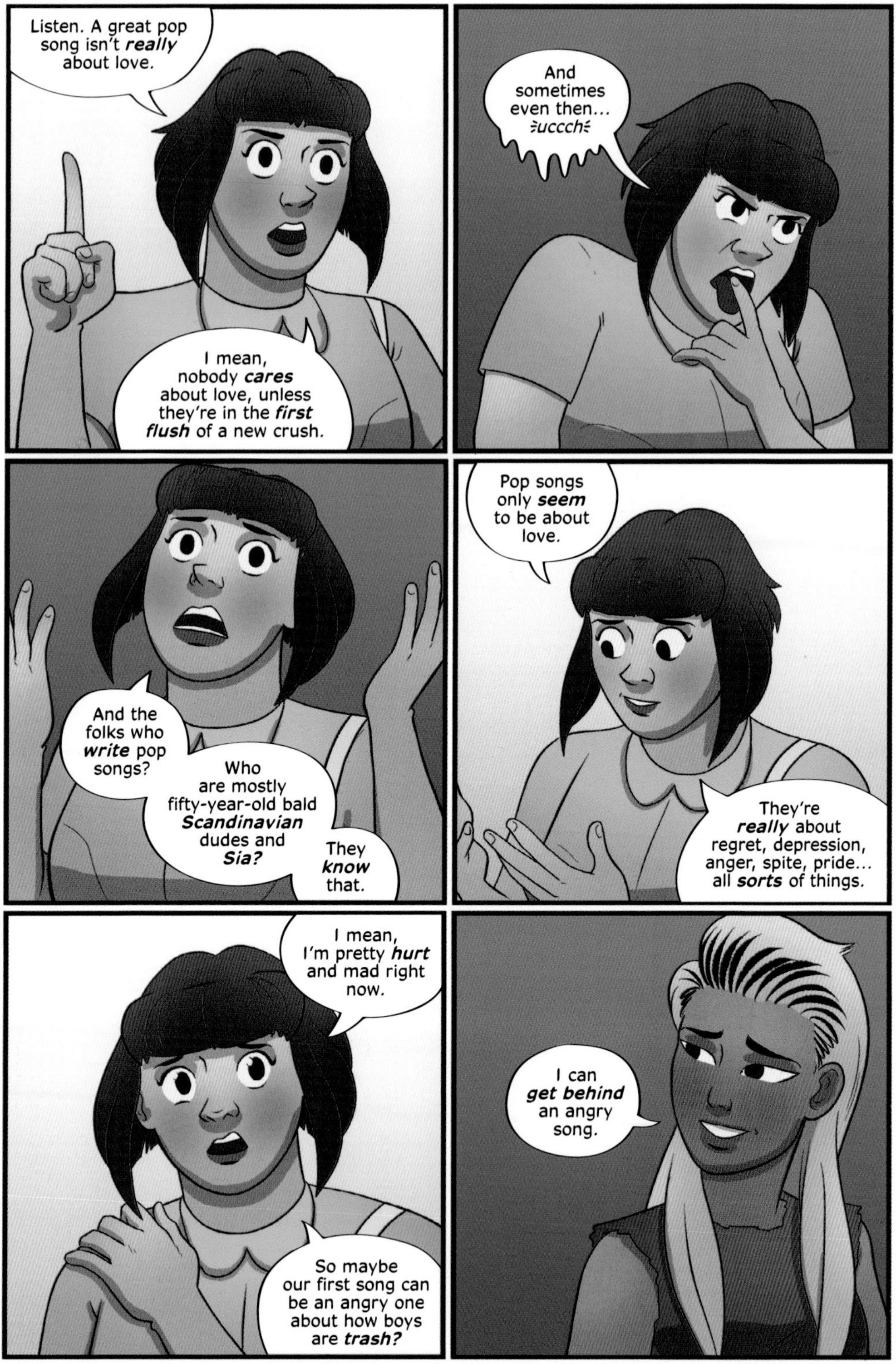
Listen. A great pop song isn't ***really*** about love.
I mean, nobody ***cares*** about love, unless they're in the ***first flush*** of a new crush.
And sometimes even then... *uccch*
And the folks who ***write*** pop songs?
Who are mostly fifty-year-old bald ***Scandinavian*** dudes and ***Sia?***
They ***know*** that.
Pop songs only ***seem*** to be about love.
They're ***really*** about regret, depression, anger, spite, pride... all ***sorts*** of things.
I mean, I'm pretty ***hurt*** and mad right now.
So maybe our first song can be an angry one about how boys are ***trash?***
I can ***get behind*** an angry song.

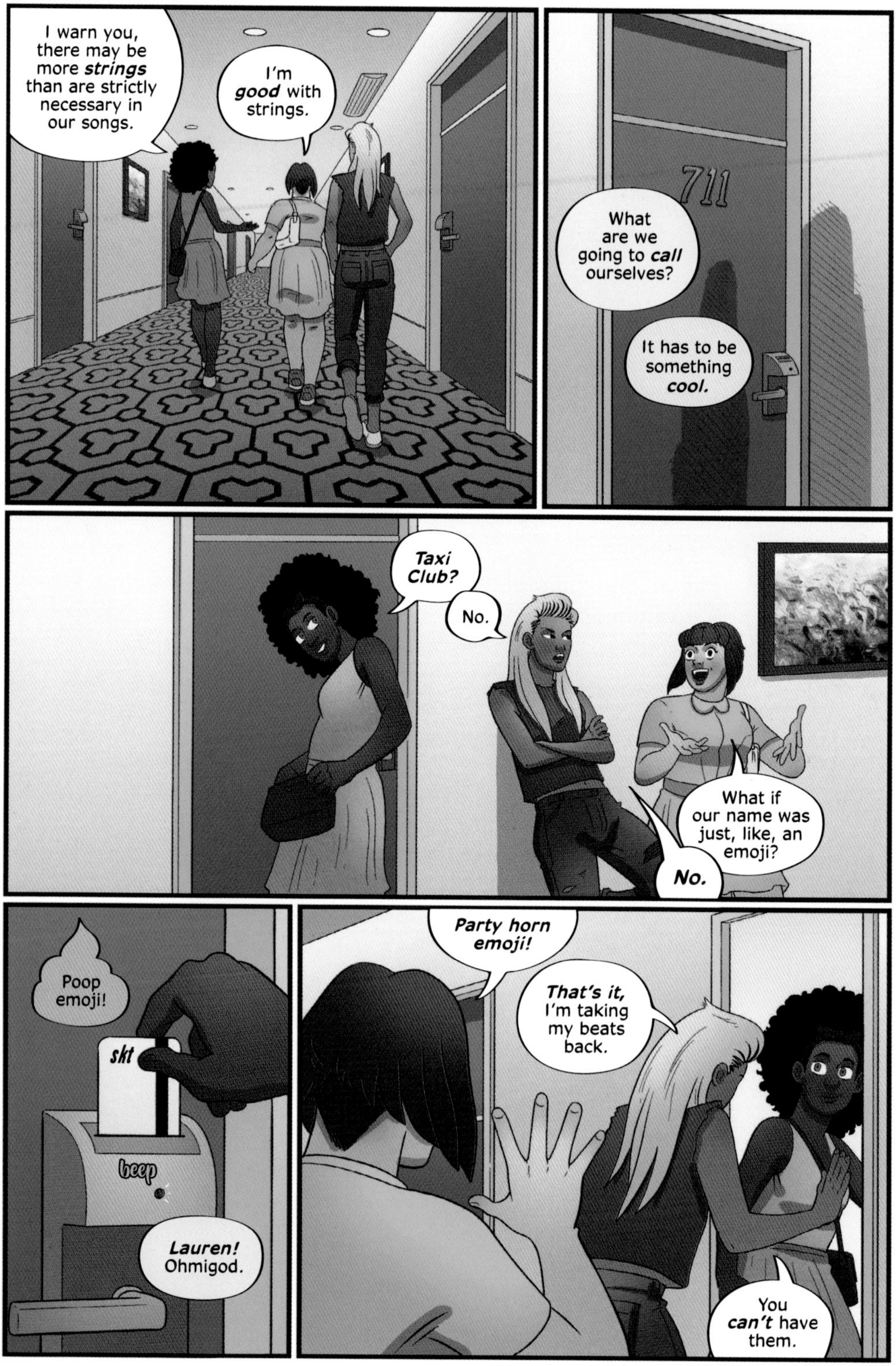
I warn you, there may be more ***strings*** than are strictly necessary in our songs.
I'm ***good*** with strings.
711
What are we going to ***call*** ourselves?
It has to be something ***cool.***
Taxi Club?
No.
What if our name was just, like, an emoji?
No.
Poop emoji!
skt
beep
Lauren! Ohmigod.
Party horn emoji!
That's it, I'm taking my beats back.
You ***can't*** have them.

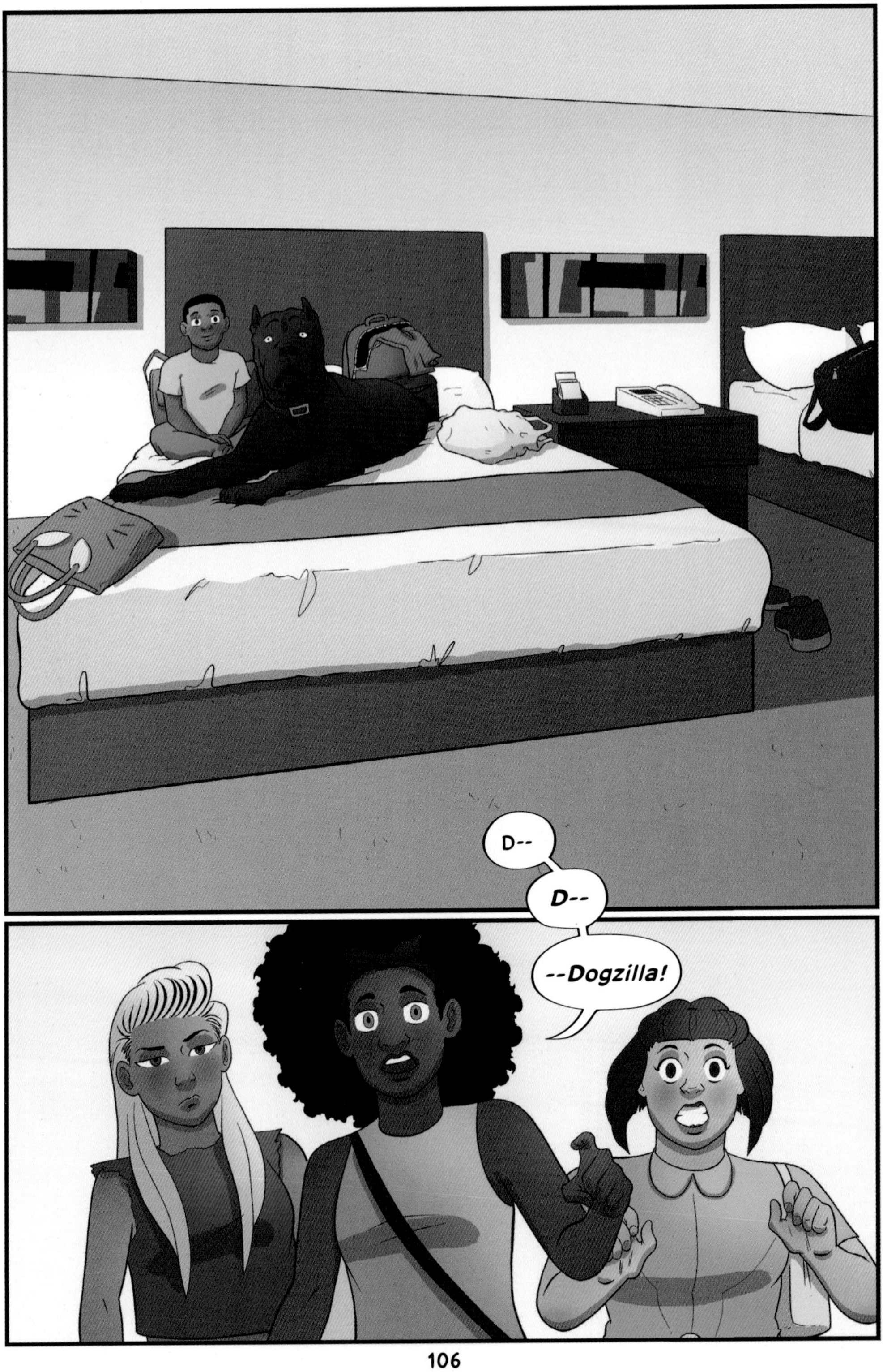
D--
D--
--Dogzilla!

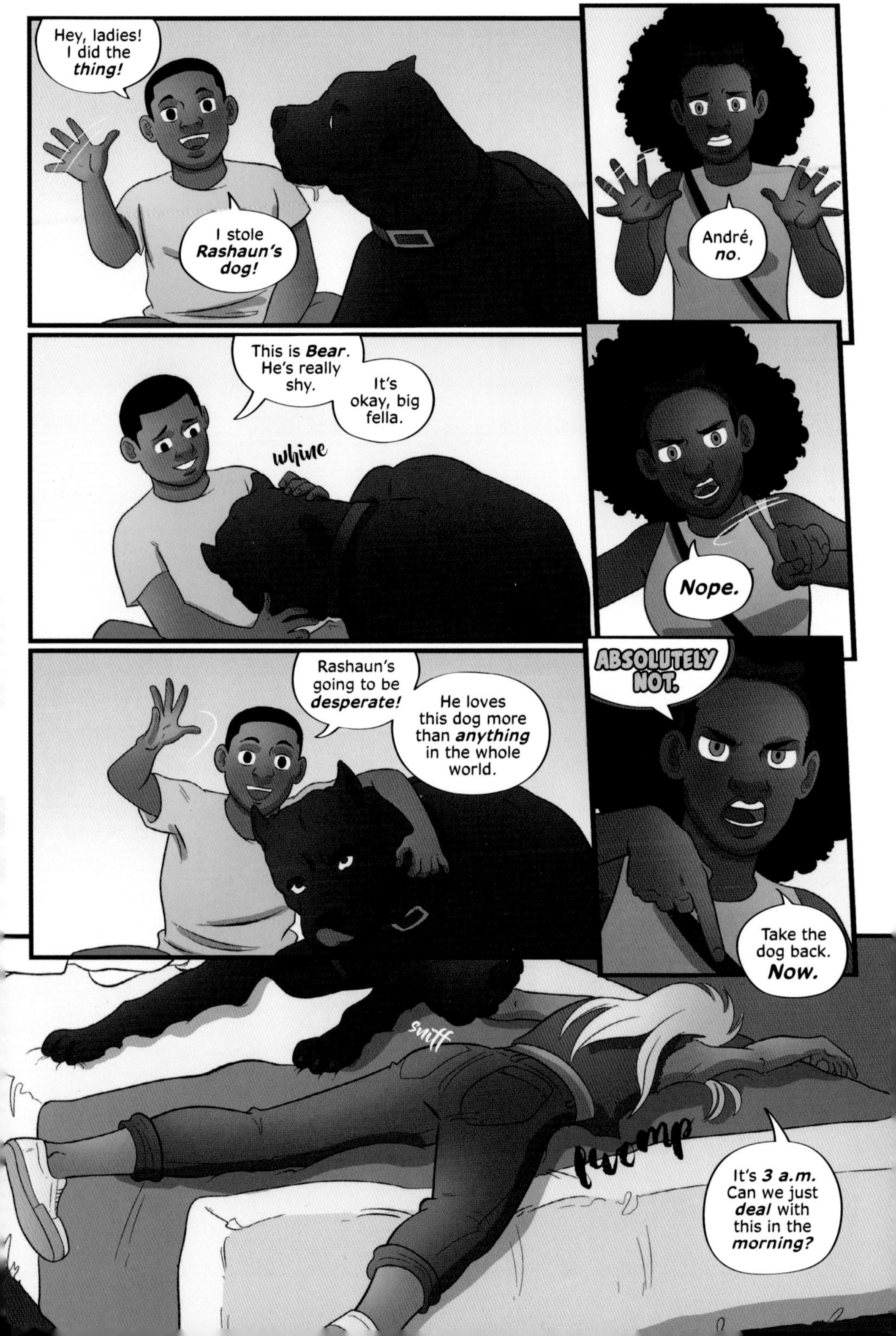
Hey, ladies! I did the *thing!*
I stole *Rashaun's dog!*
André, *no*.
This is *Bear*. He's really shy.
It's okay, big fella.
whine
Nope.
Rashaun's going to be *desperate!*
He loves this dog more than *anything* in the whole world.
ABSOLUTELY NOT.
Take the dog back. **Now.**
sniff
fwomp
It's *3 a.m.* Can we just *deal* with this in the *morning?*

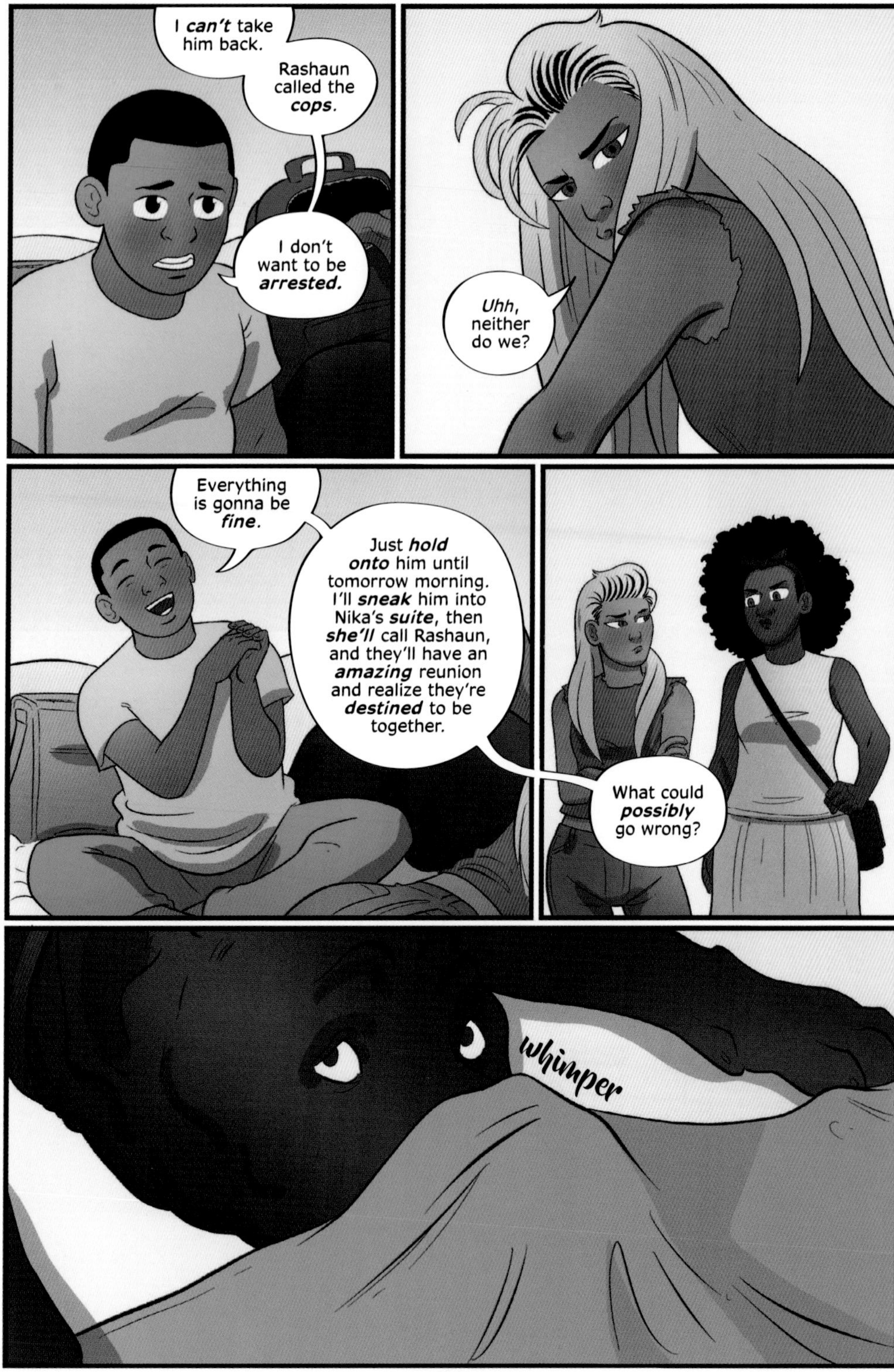
I *can't* take him back.
Rashaun called the *cops*.
I don't want to be ***arrested.***
Uhh, neither do we?
Everything is gonna be ***fine***.
Just ***hold onto*** him until tomorrow morning. I'll ***sneak*** him into Nika's ***suite***, then ***she'll*** call Rashaun, and they'll have an ***amazing*** reunion and realize they're ***destined*** to be together.
What could ***possibly*** go wrong?
whimper

CHAPTER
4

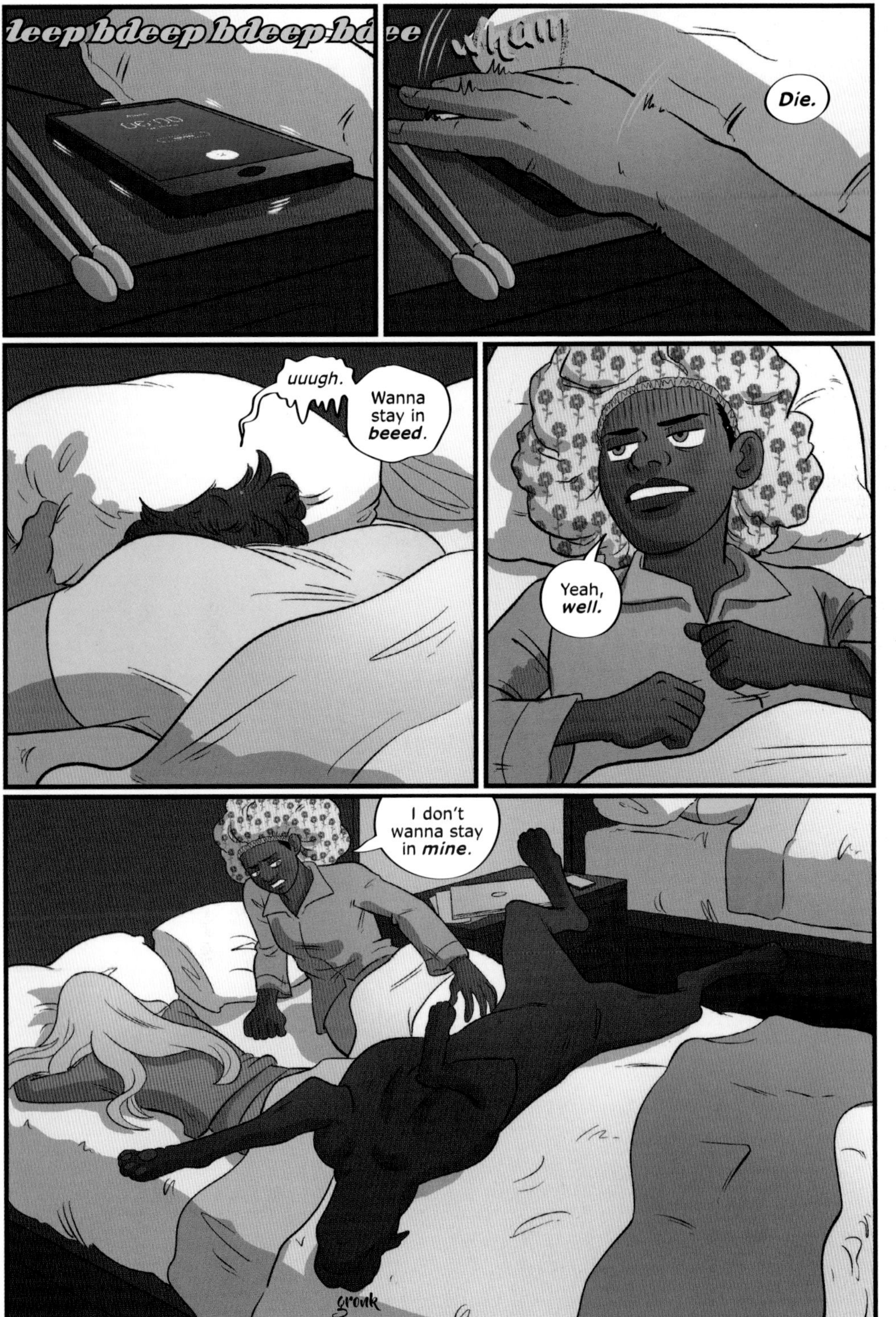
deep bdeep bdeep bdee
wham
Die.
uuugh.
Wanna stay in *beeed*.
Yeah, *well*.
I don't wanna stay in *mine*.
gronk

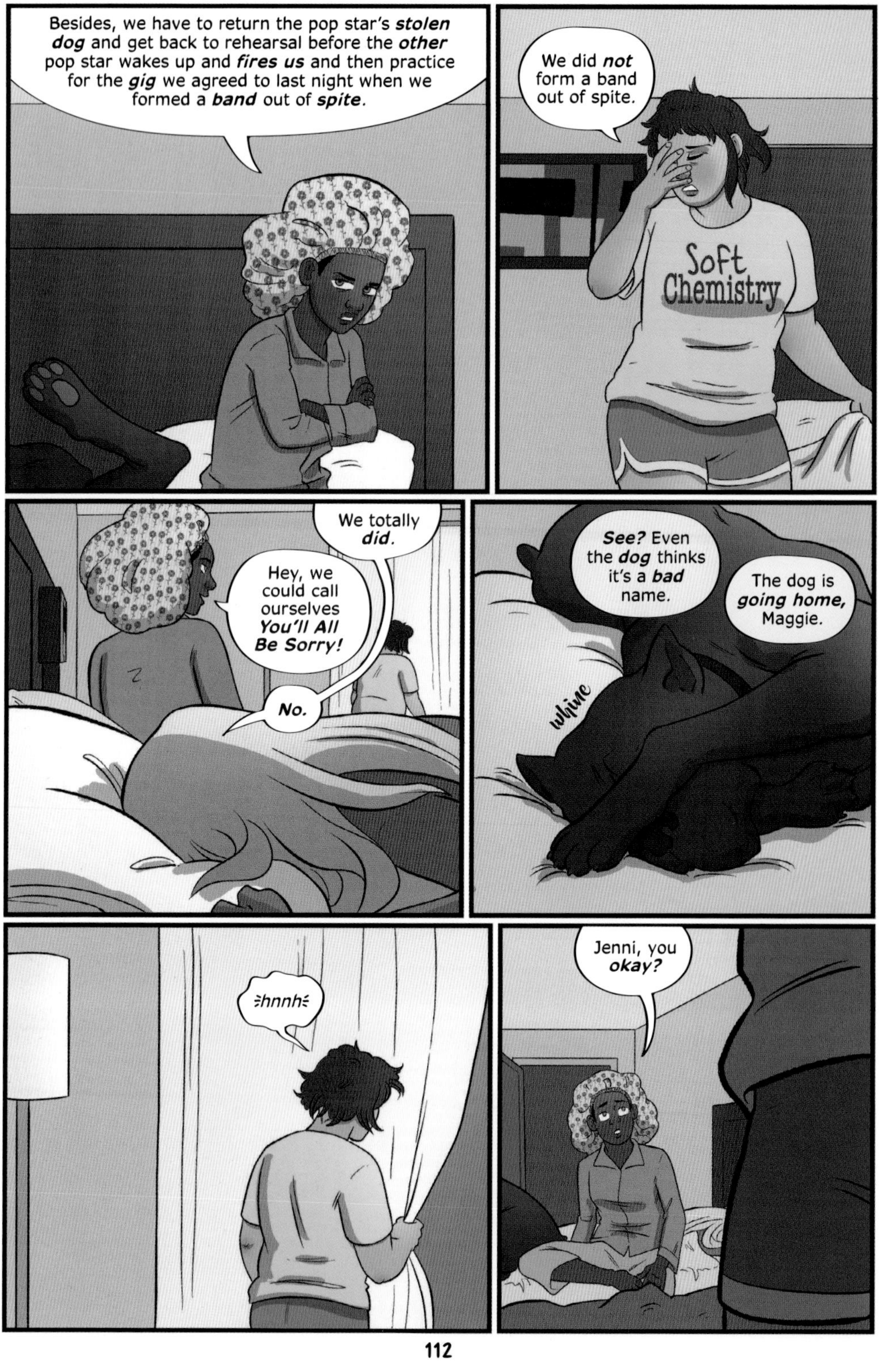

Besides, we have to return the pop star's ***stolen dog*** and get back to rehearsal before the ***other*** pop star wakes up and ***fires us*** and then practice for the ***gig*** we agreed to last night when we formed a ***band*** out of ***spite***.
We did ***not*** form a band out of spite.
Soft Chemistry
Hey, we could call ourselves ***You'll All Be Sorry!***
We totally ***did***.
No.
See? Even the ***dog*** thinks it's a ***bad*** name.
whine
The dog is ***going home,*** Maggie.
hnnh
Jenni, you ***okay?***

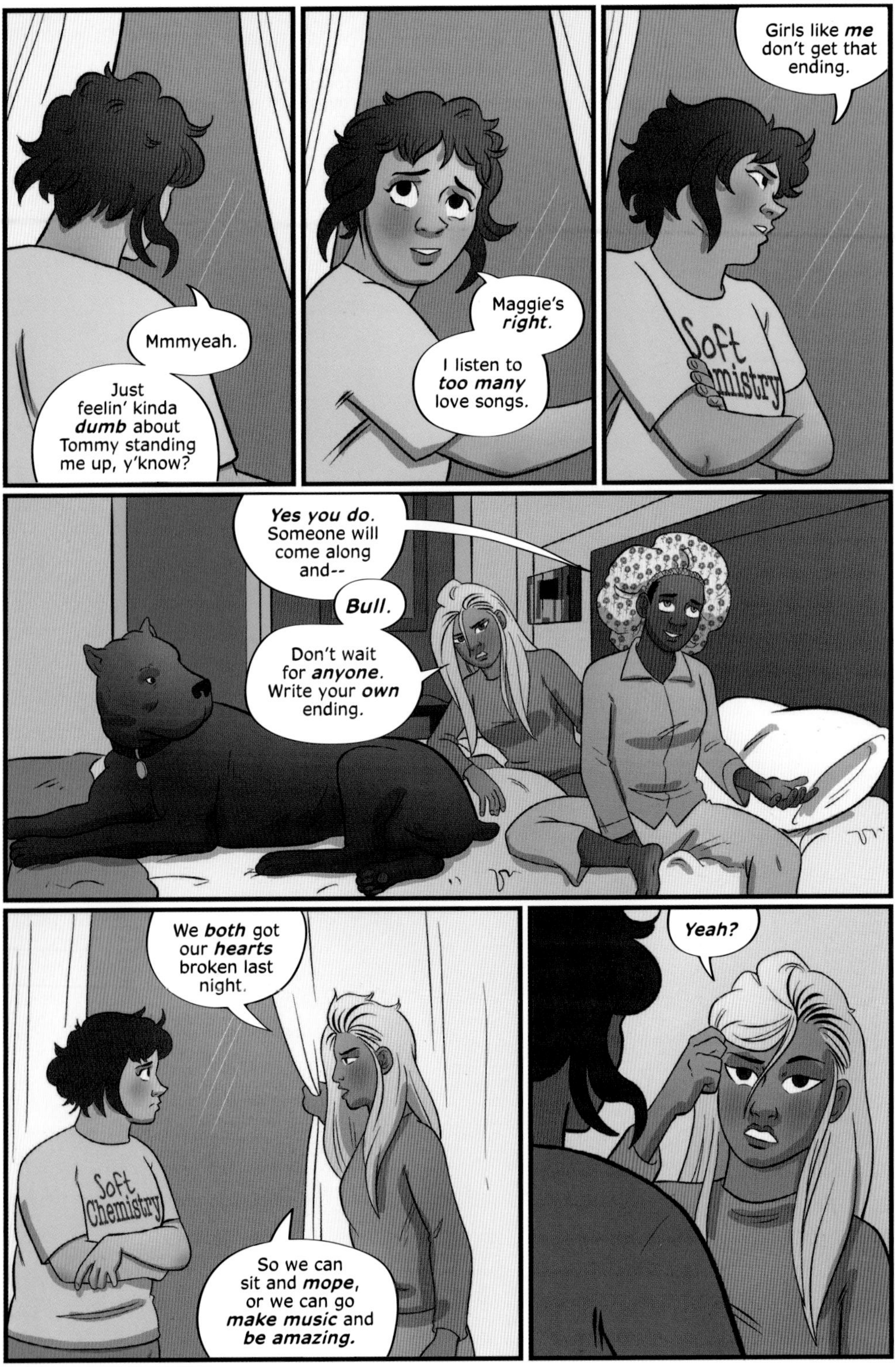
Mmmyeah.
Just feelin' kinda ***dumb*** about Tommy standing me up, y'know?
Maggie's ***right***.
I listen to ***too many*** love songs.
Girls like ***me*** don't get that ending.
Soft Chemistry
Yes you do. Someone will come along and--
Bull.
Don't wait for ***anyone***. Write your ***own*** ending.
We ***both*** got our ***hearts*** broken last night.
So we can sit and ***mope***, or we can go ***make music*** and ***be amazing.***
Yeah?

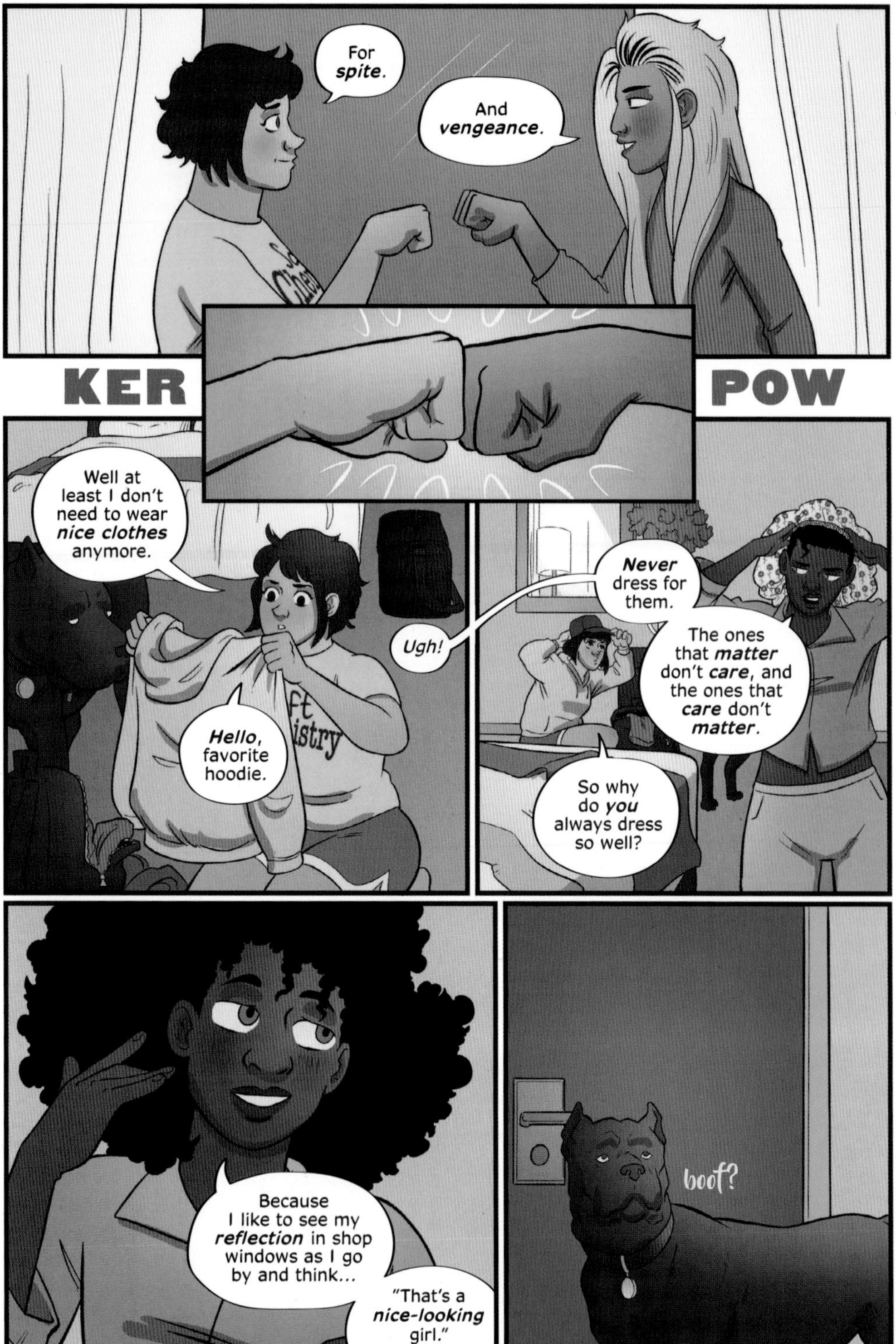
For *spite*.
And *vengeance*.
KER
POW
Well at least I don't need to wear *nice clothes* anymore.
Hello, favorite hoodie.
Ugh!
Never dress for them.
The ones that *matter* don't *care*, and the ones that *care* don't *matter*.
So why do *you* always dress so well?
Because I like to see my *reflection* in shop windows as I go by and think...
"That's a *nice-looking* girl."
boof?

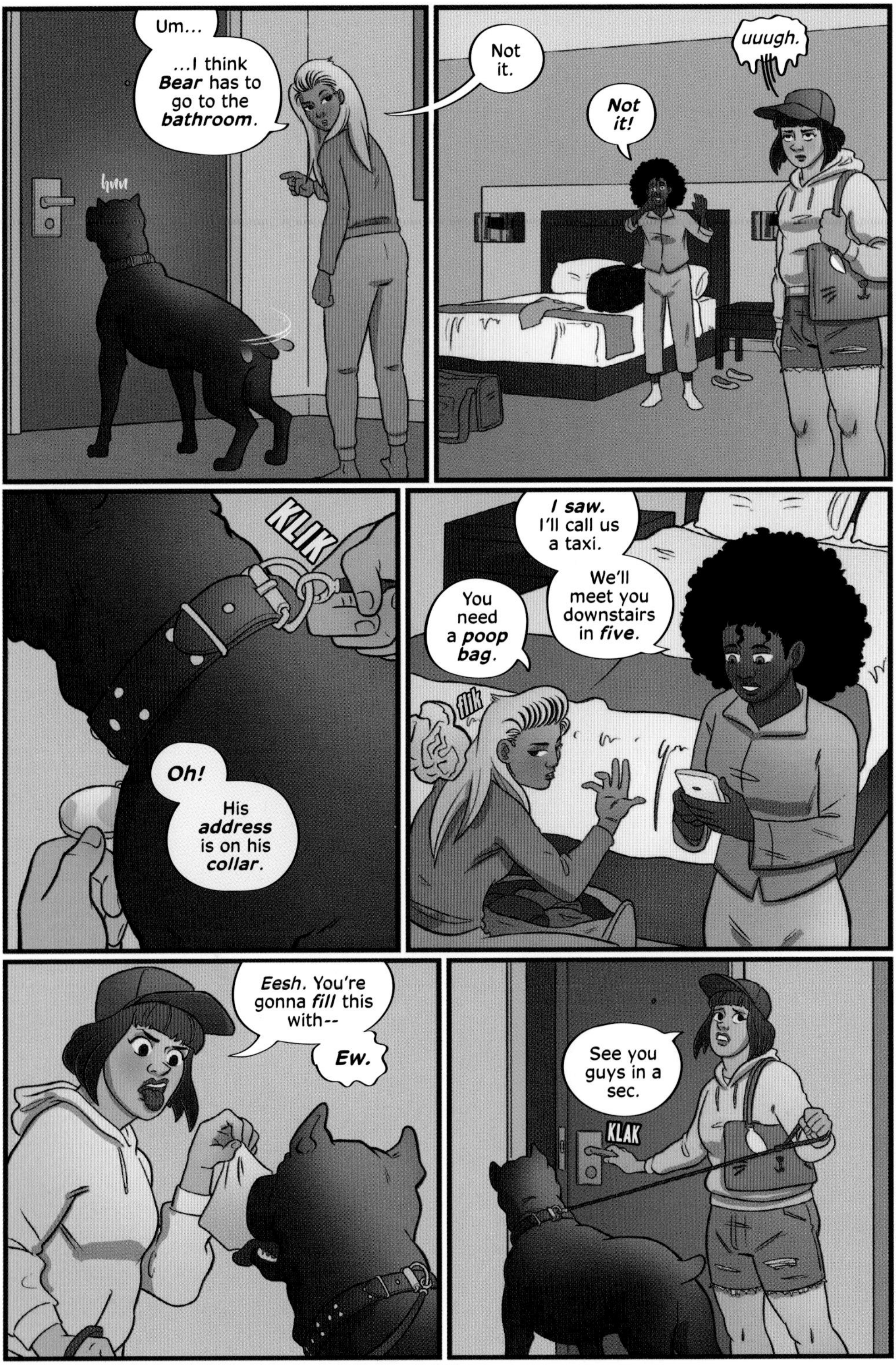
Um...
...I think *Bear* has to go to the *bathroom*.
hnn
Not it.
Not it!
uuugh.
KLIK
Oh!
His *address* is on his *collar*.
I saw. I'll call us a taxi.
We'll meet you downstairs in *five*.
You need a *poop bag*.
flik
Eesh. You're gonna *fill* this with--
Ew.
See you guys in a sec.
KLAK

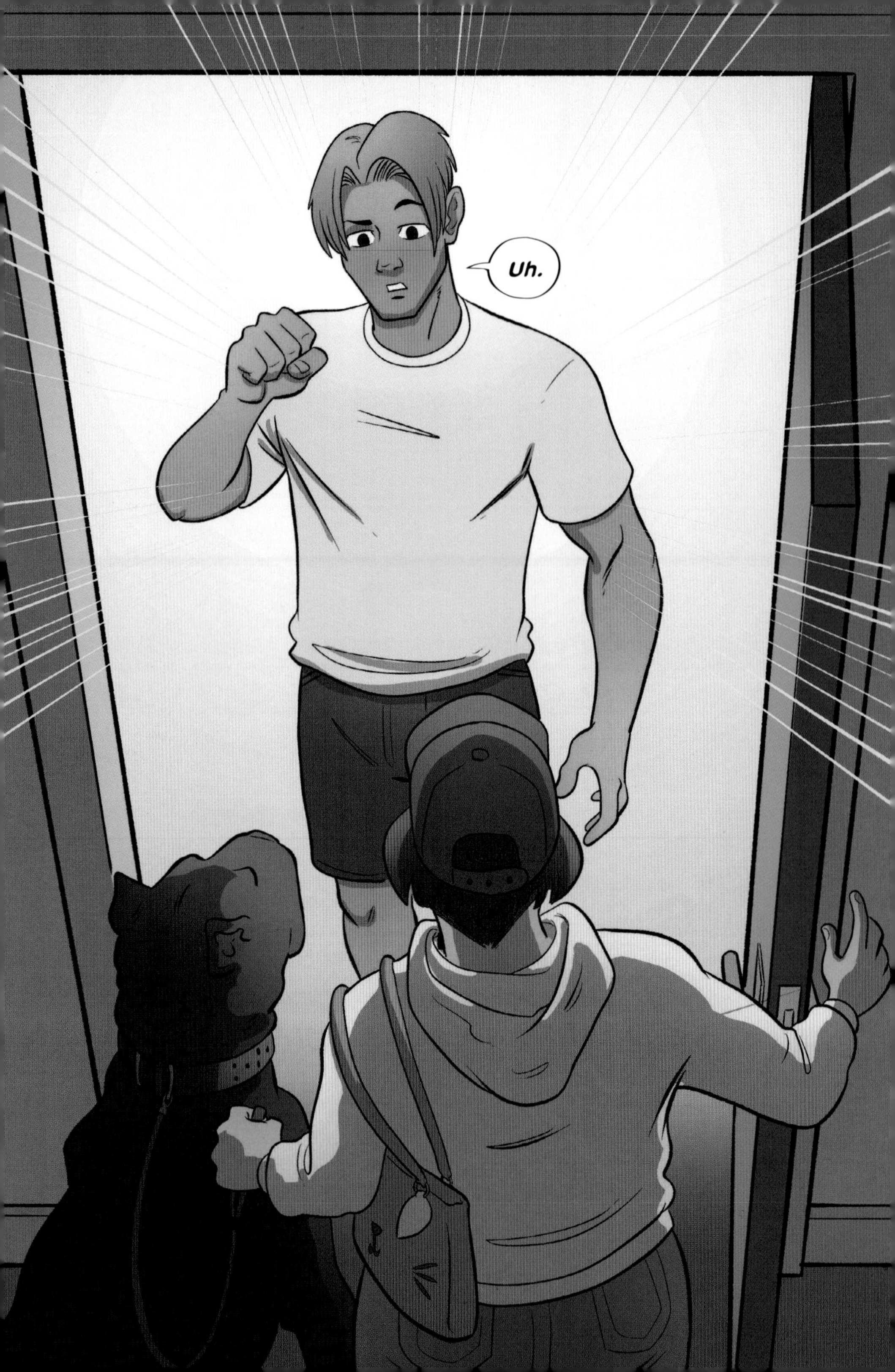
Uh.

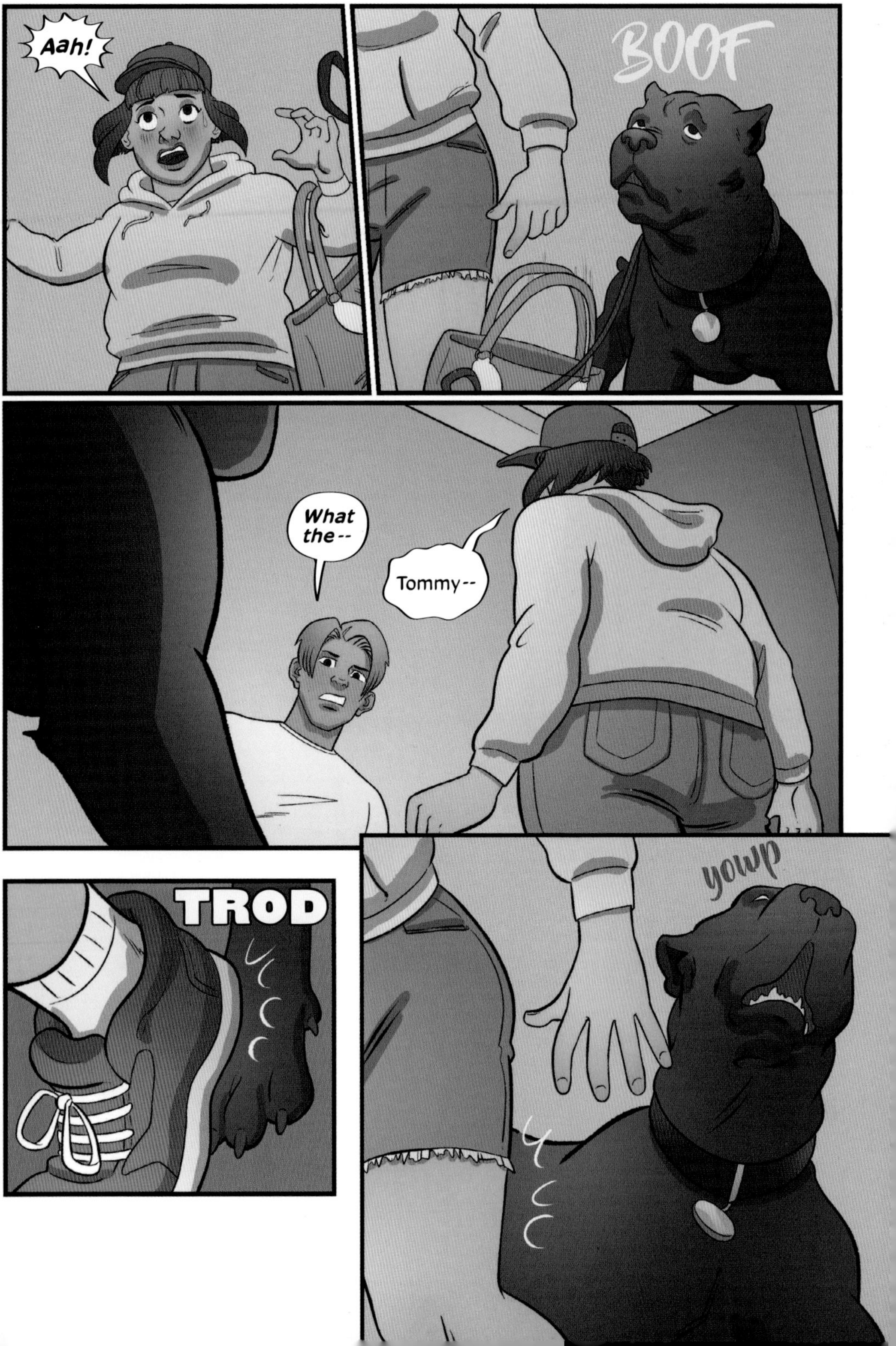
Aah!
BOOF
What the--
Tommy--
TROD
yowp

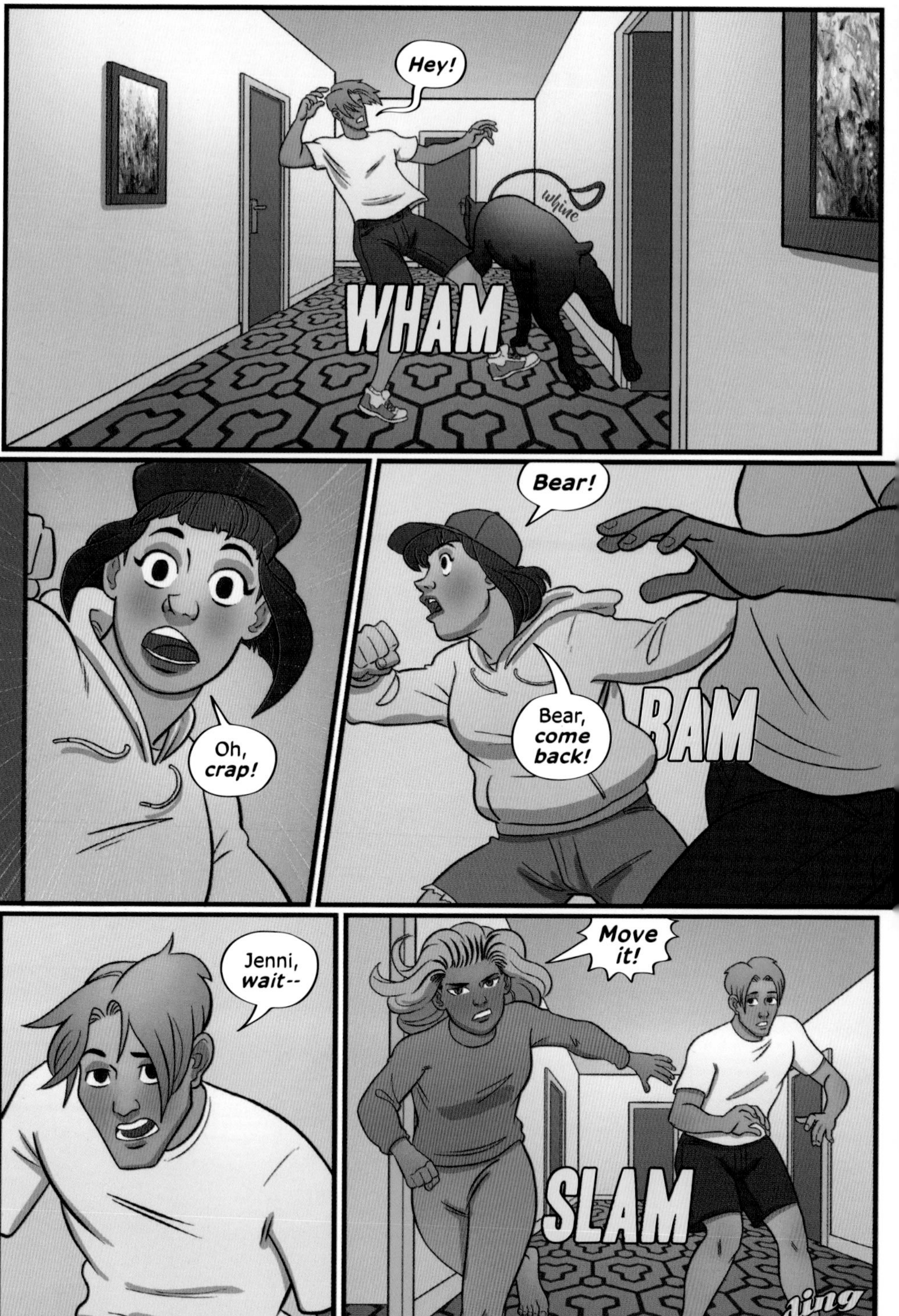
Hey!
whine
WHAM
Oh, crap!
Bear!
Bear, come back!
BAM
Jenni, wait--
Move it!
SLAM
ding

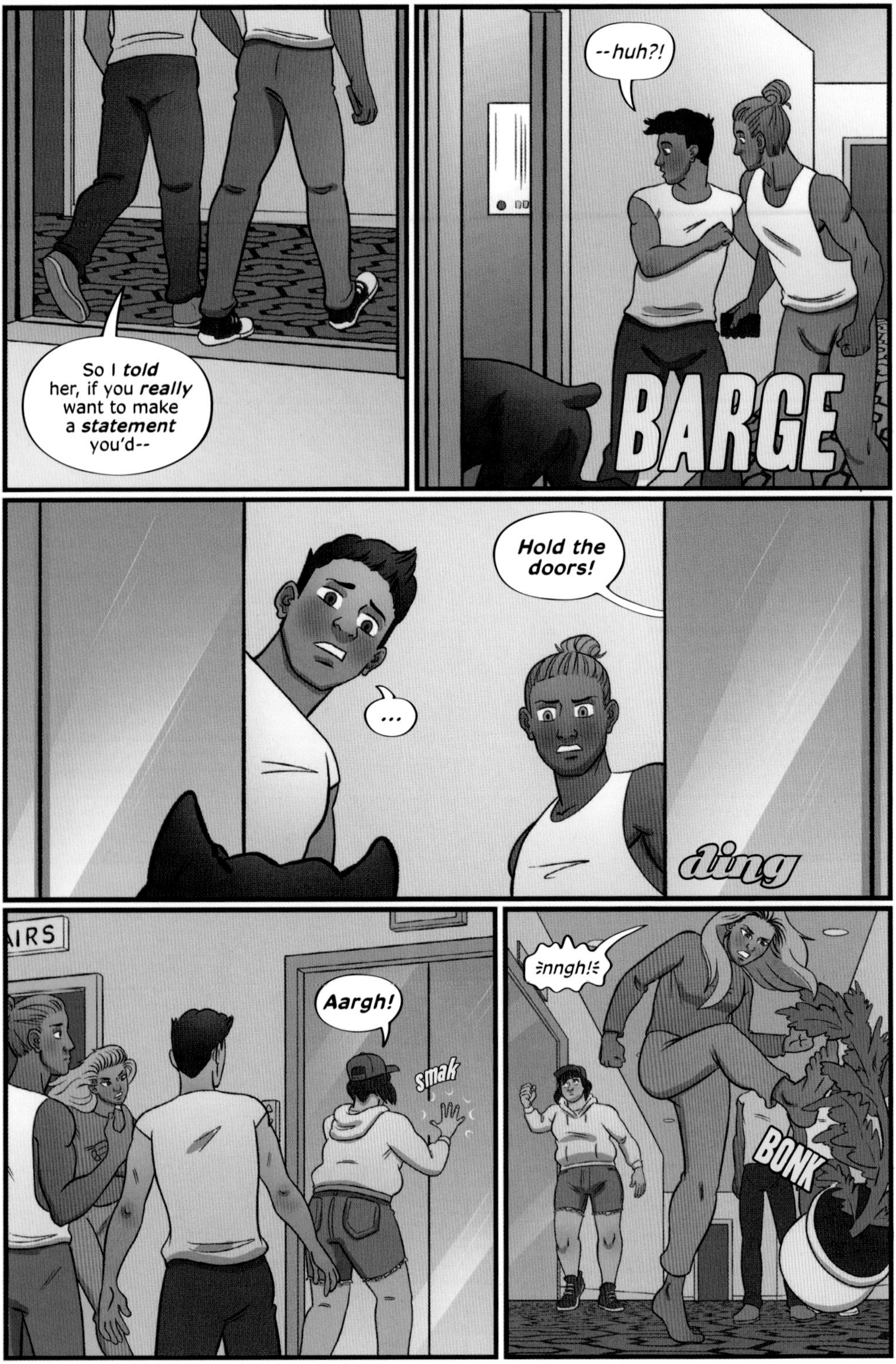
So I *told* her, if you *really* want to make a *statement* you'd--
--huh?!
BARGE
Hold the doors!
...
ding
AIRS
Aargh!
smak
≑nngh!≑
BONK

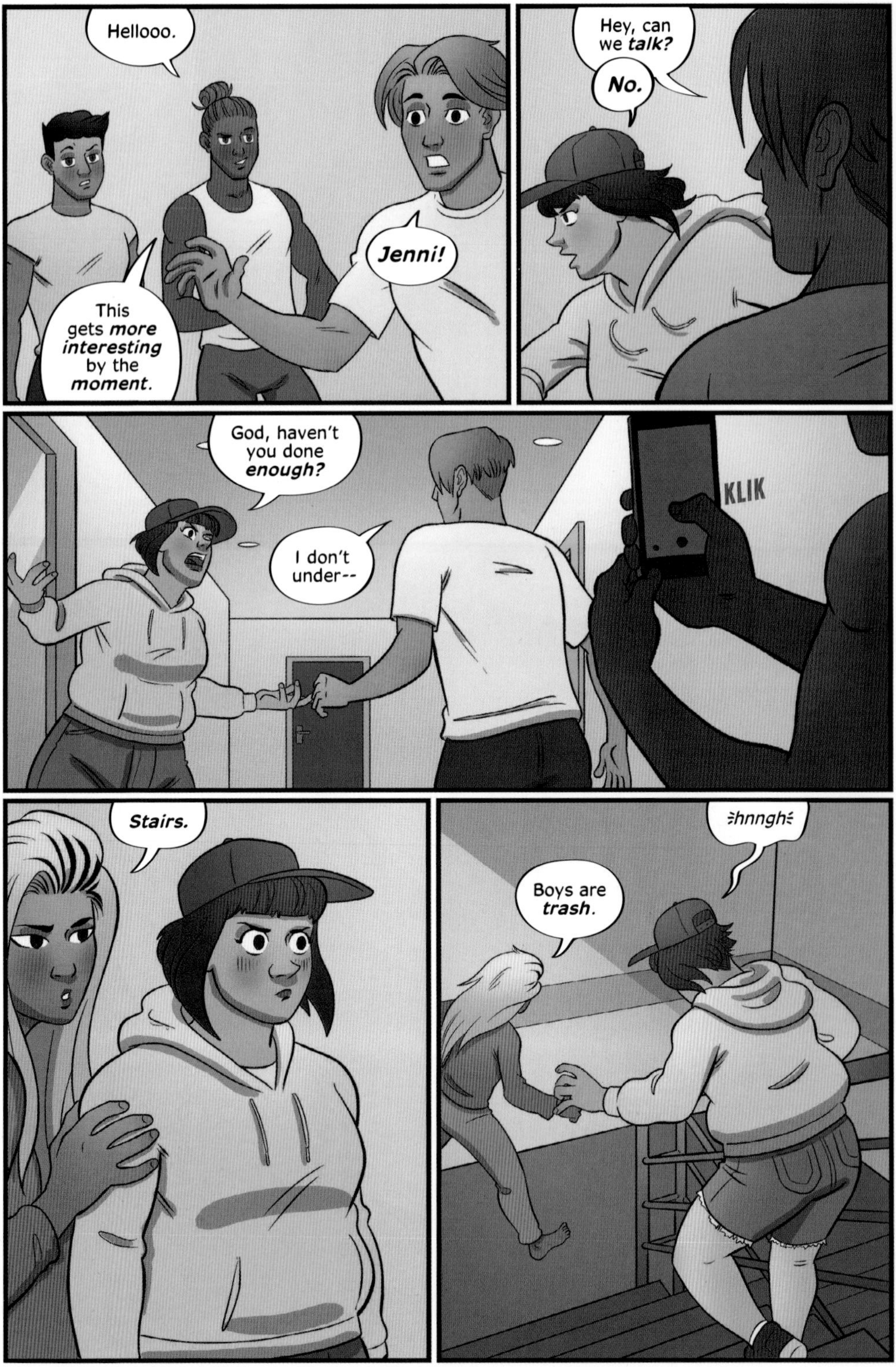
Hellooo.
This gets *more interesting* by the *moment*.
Jenni!
Hey, can we *talk?*
No.
God, haven't you done *enough?*
I don't under--
KLIK
Stairs.
Boys are trash.
hnngh

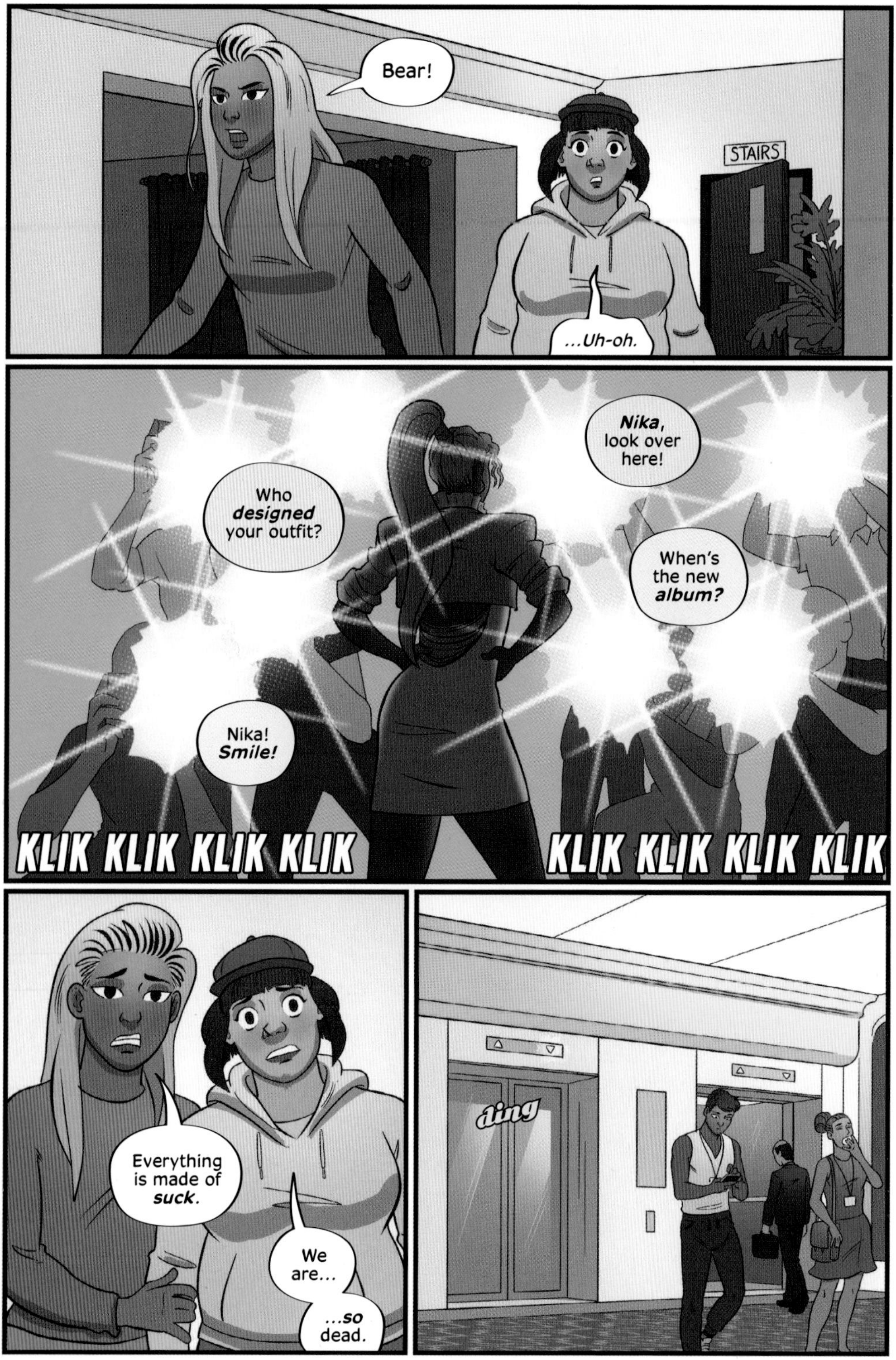
Bear!
STAIRS
...Uh-oh.
Nika, look over here!
Who *designed* your outfit?
When's the new *album?*
Nika! *Smile!*
KLIK KLIK KLIK KLIK
KLIK KLIK KLIK KLIK
Everything is made of *suck*.
We are...
...*so* dead.
ding

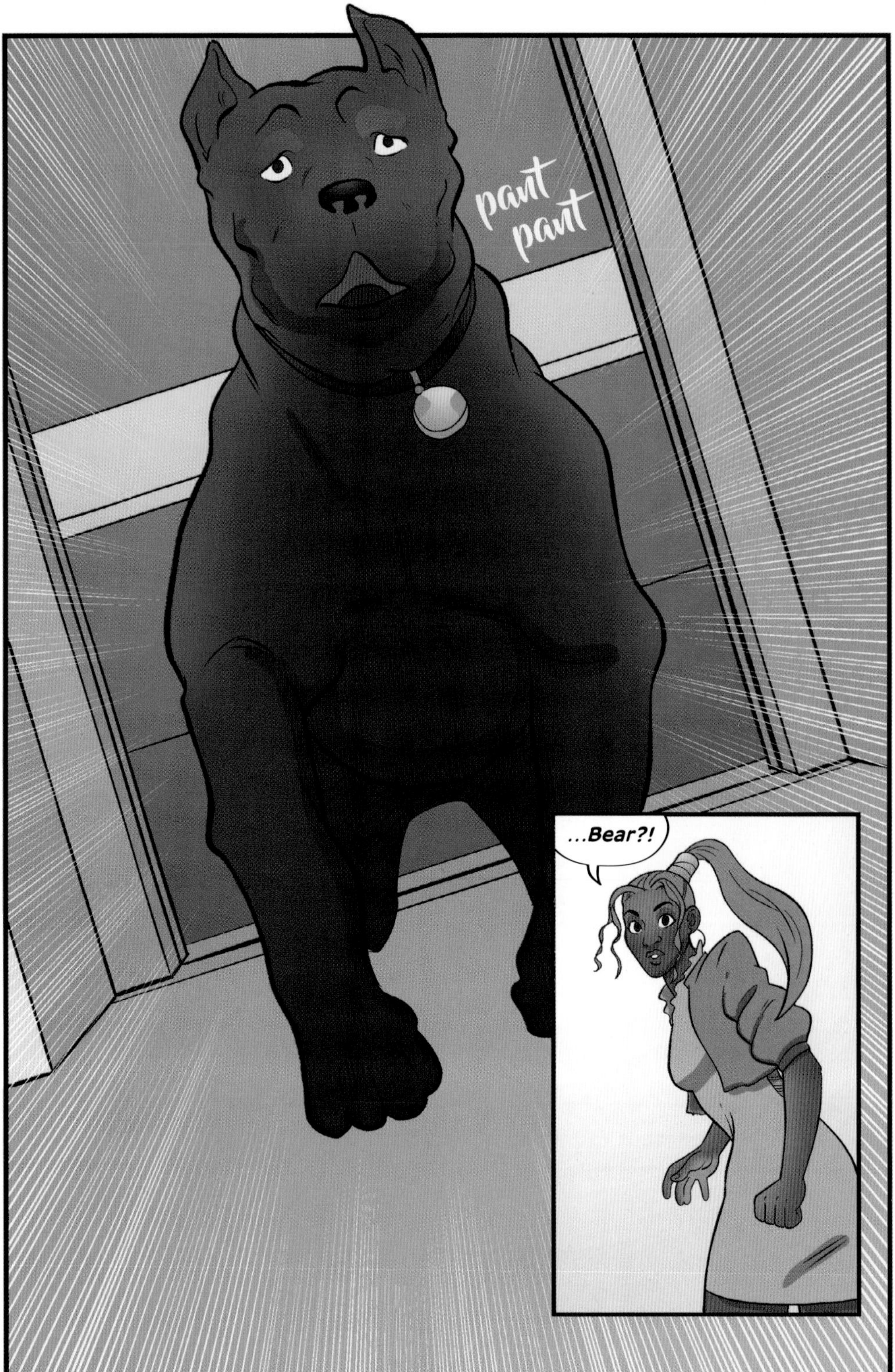
pant
pant
...Bear?!

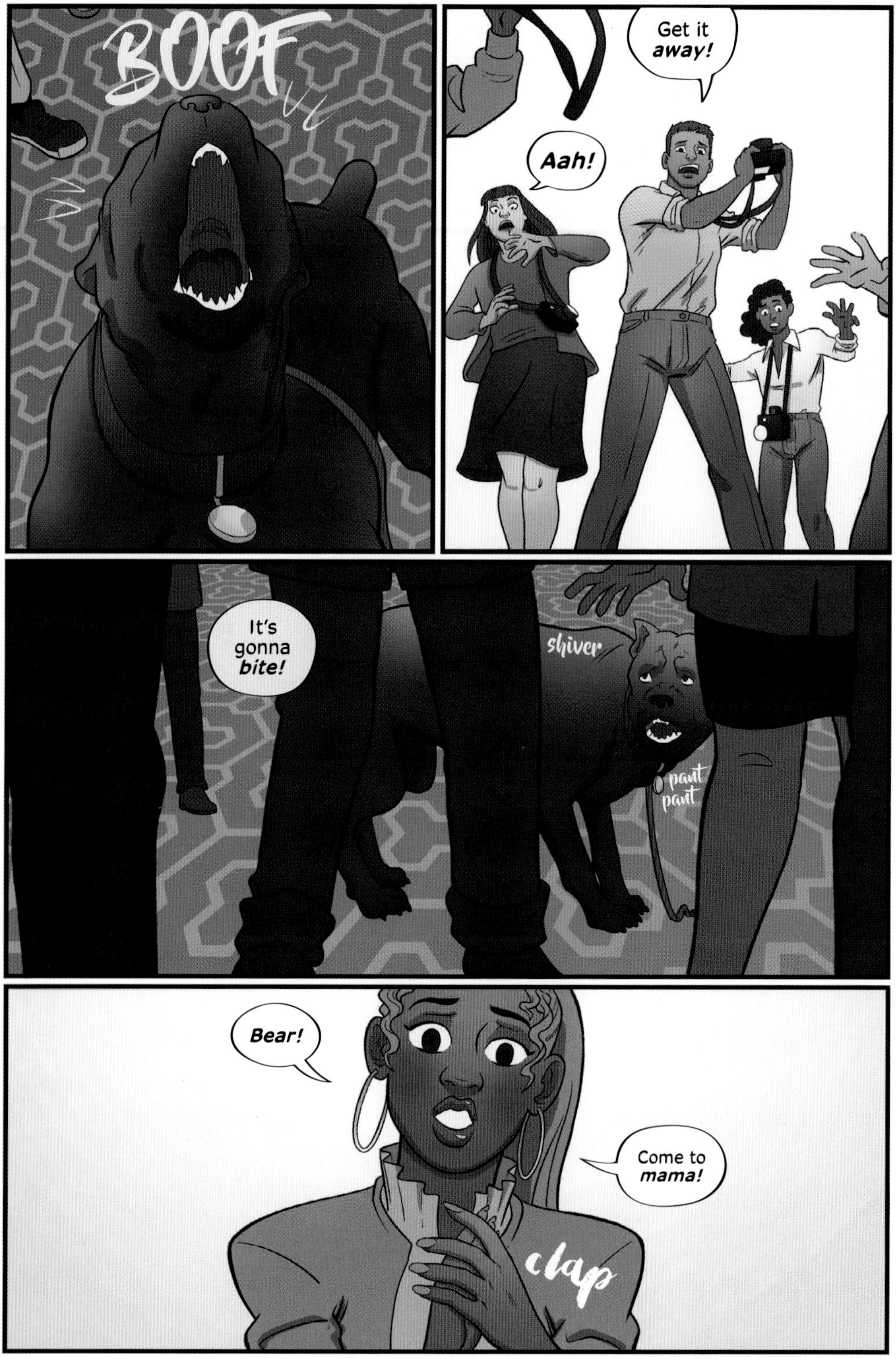
BOOF
Get it away!
Aah!
It's gonna bite!
shiver
pant pant
Bear!
Come to mama!
clap

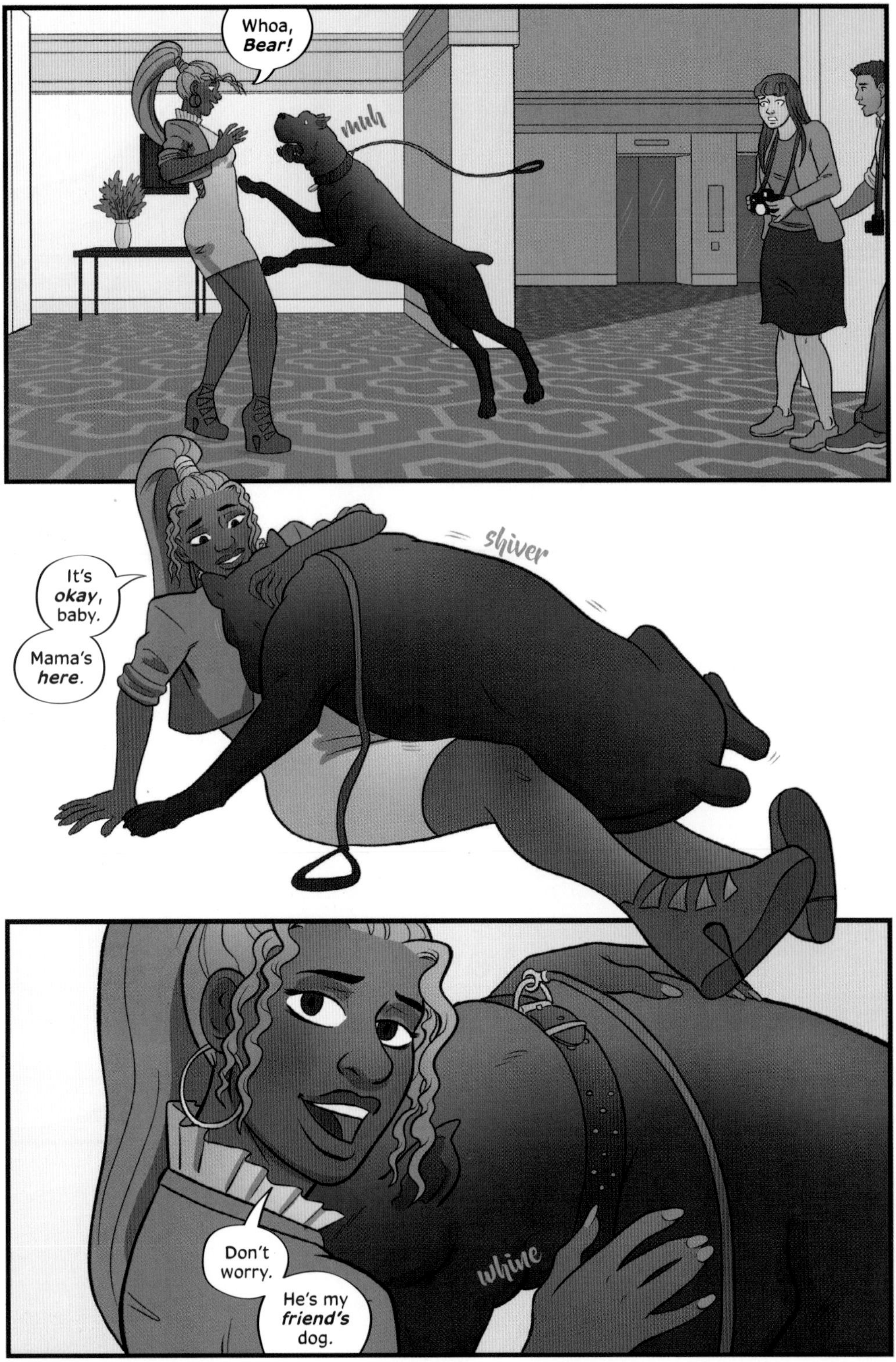
Whoa, *Bear!*
muh
shiver
It's *okay*, baby.
Mama's *here*.
Don't worry.
He's my *friend's* dog.
whine

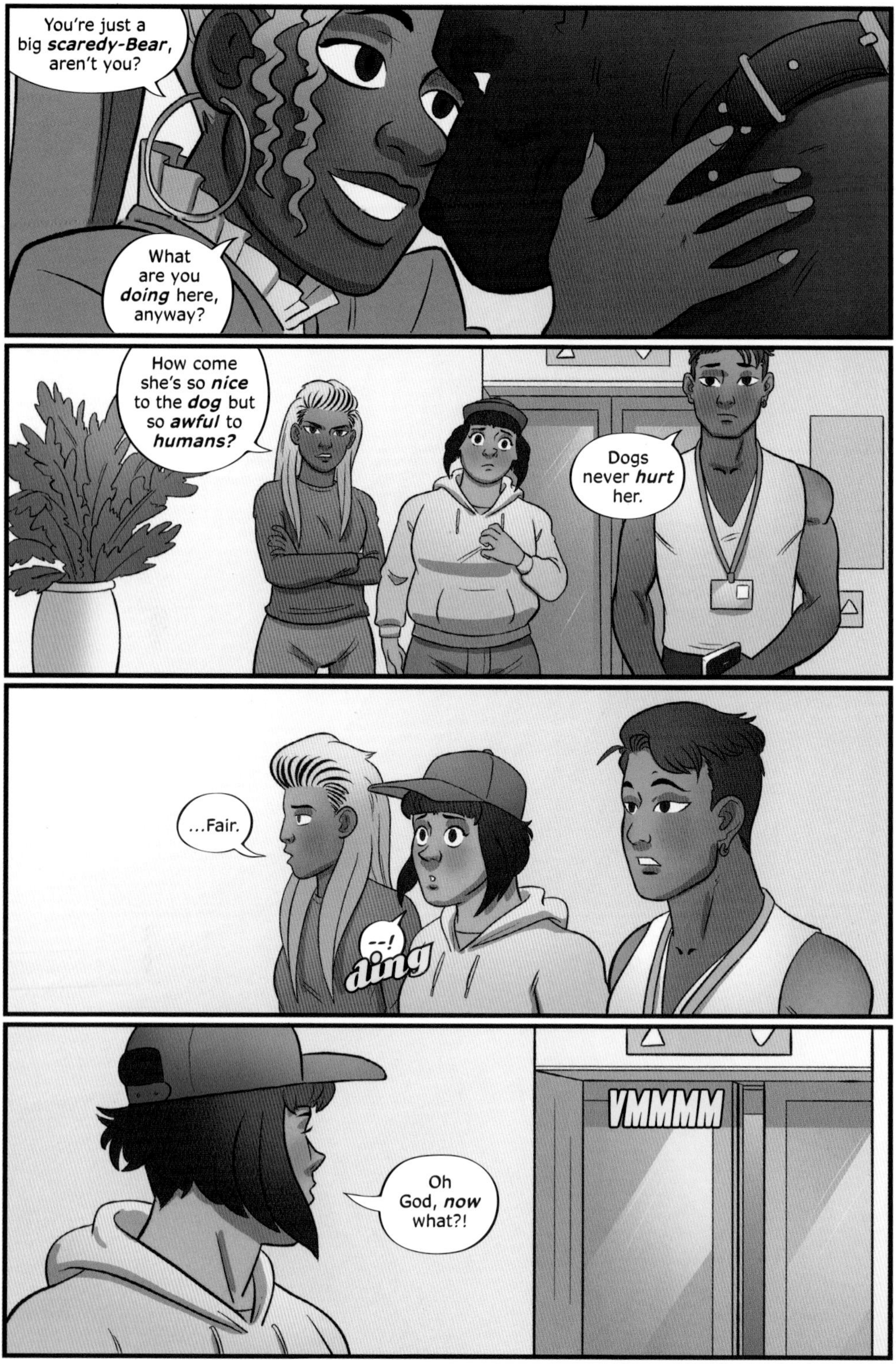
You're just a big scaredy-Bear, aren't you?
What are you doing here, anyway?
How come she's so nice to the dog but so awful to humans?
Dogs never hurt her.
...Fair.
--!
ding
Oh God, now what?!
VMMMM

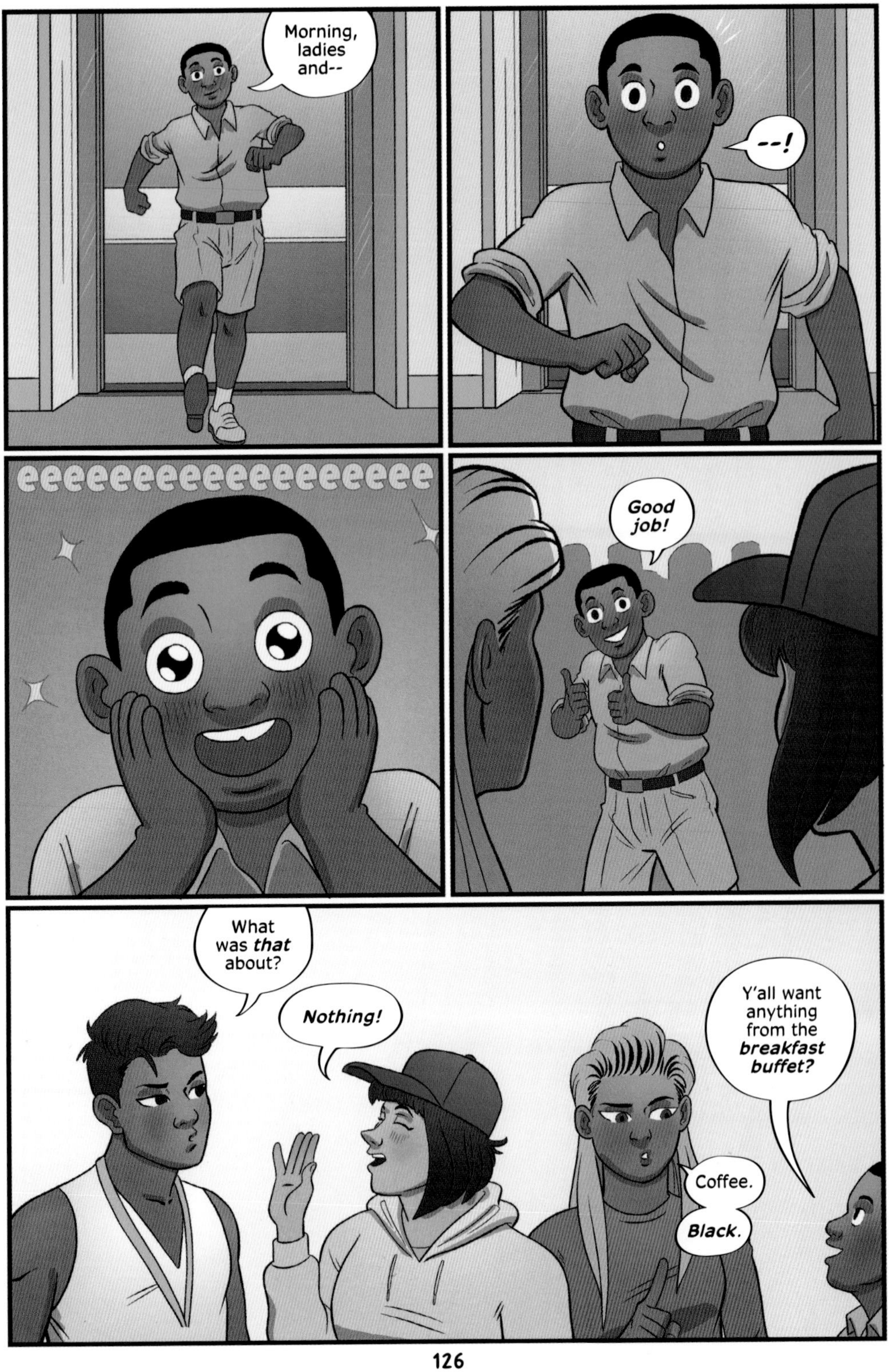
Morning, ladies and--
--!
eeeeeeeeeeeeeeeeeeee
Good job!
What was *that* about?
Nothing!
Y'all want anything from the *breakfast buffet?*
Coffee.
Black.

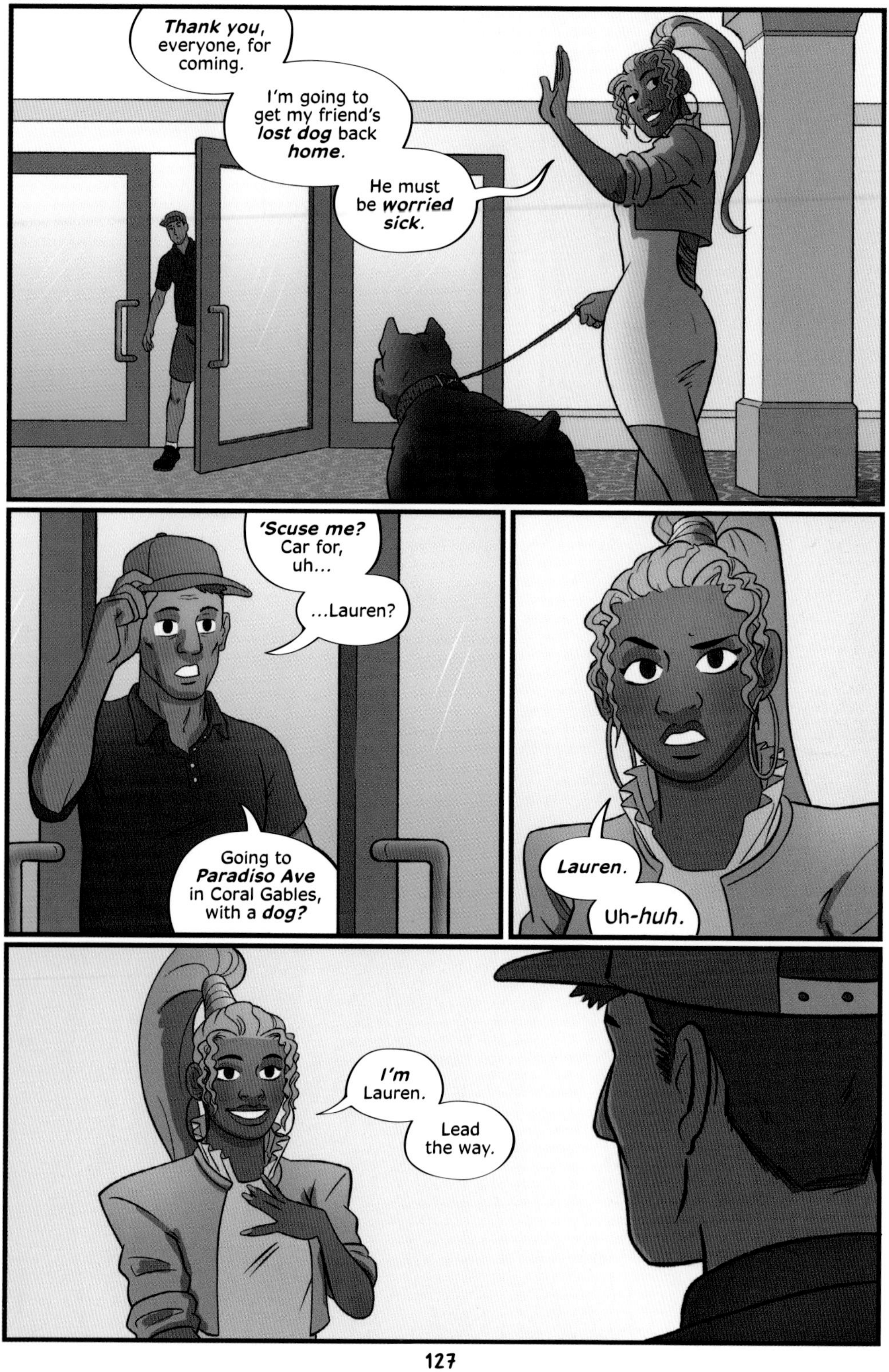
Thank you, everyone, for coming.
I'm going to get my friend's ***lost dog*** back ***home***.
He must be ***worried sick***.
'Scuse me? Car for, uh...
...Lauren?
Going to ***Paradiso Ave*** in Coral Gables, with a ***dog?***
Lauren.
Uh-*huh*.
I'm Lauren.
Lead the way.

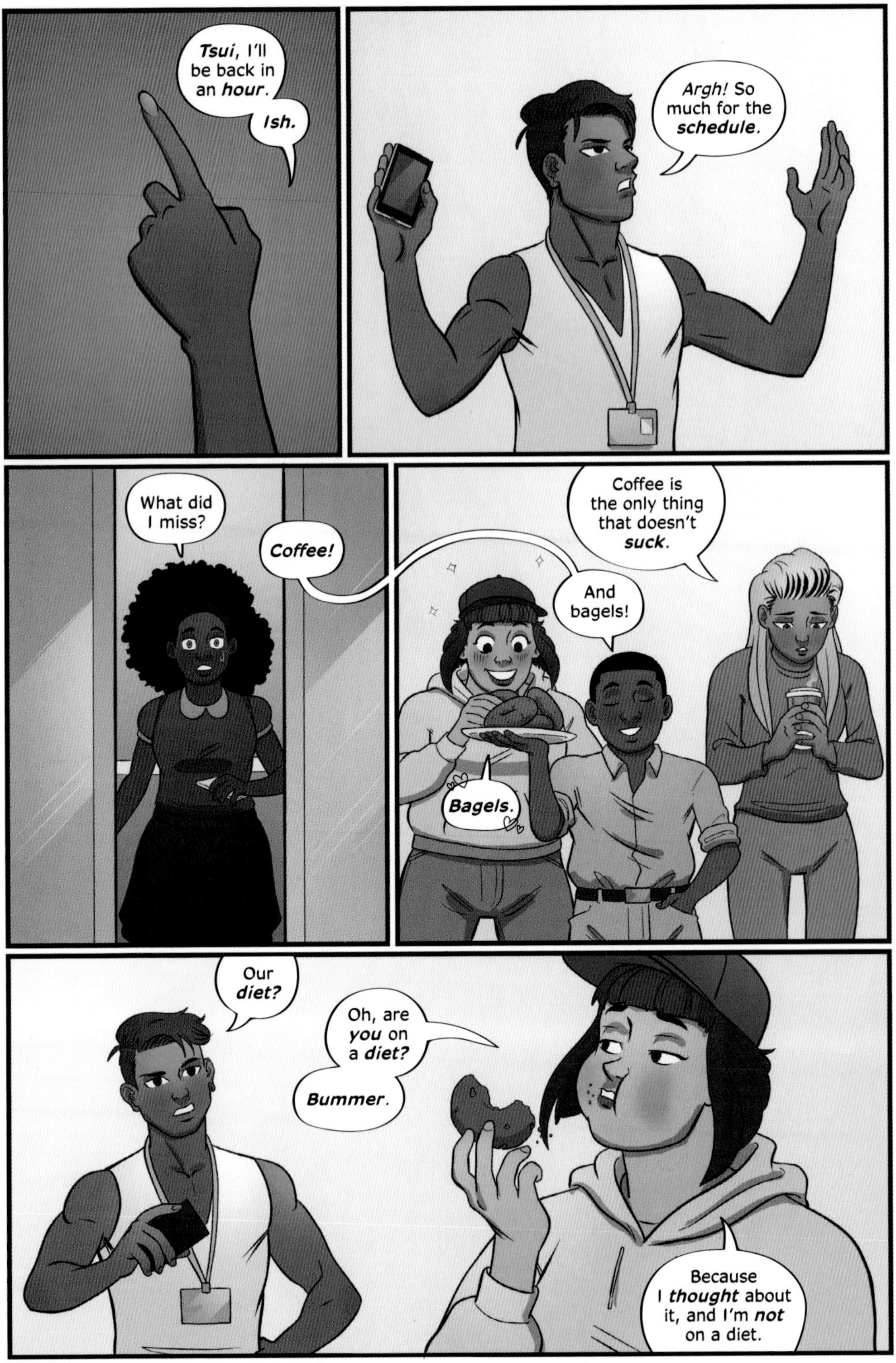
Tsui, I'll be back in an *hour*.
Ish.
Argh! So much for the *schedule*.
What did I miss?
Coffee!
Coffee is the only thing that doesn't *suck*.
And bagels!
Bagels.
Our *diet?*
Oh, are *you* on a *diet?*
Bummer.
Because I *thought* about it, and I'm *not* on a diet.

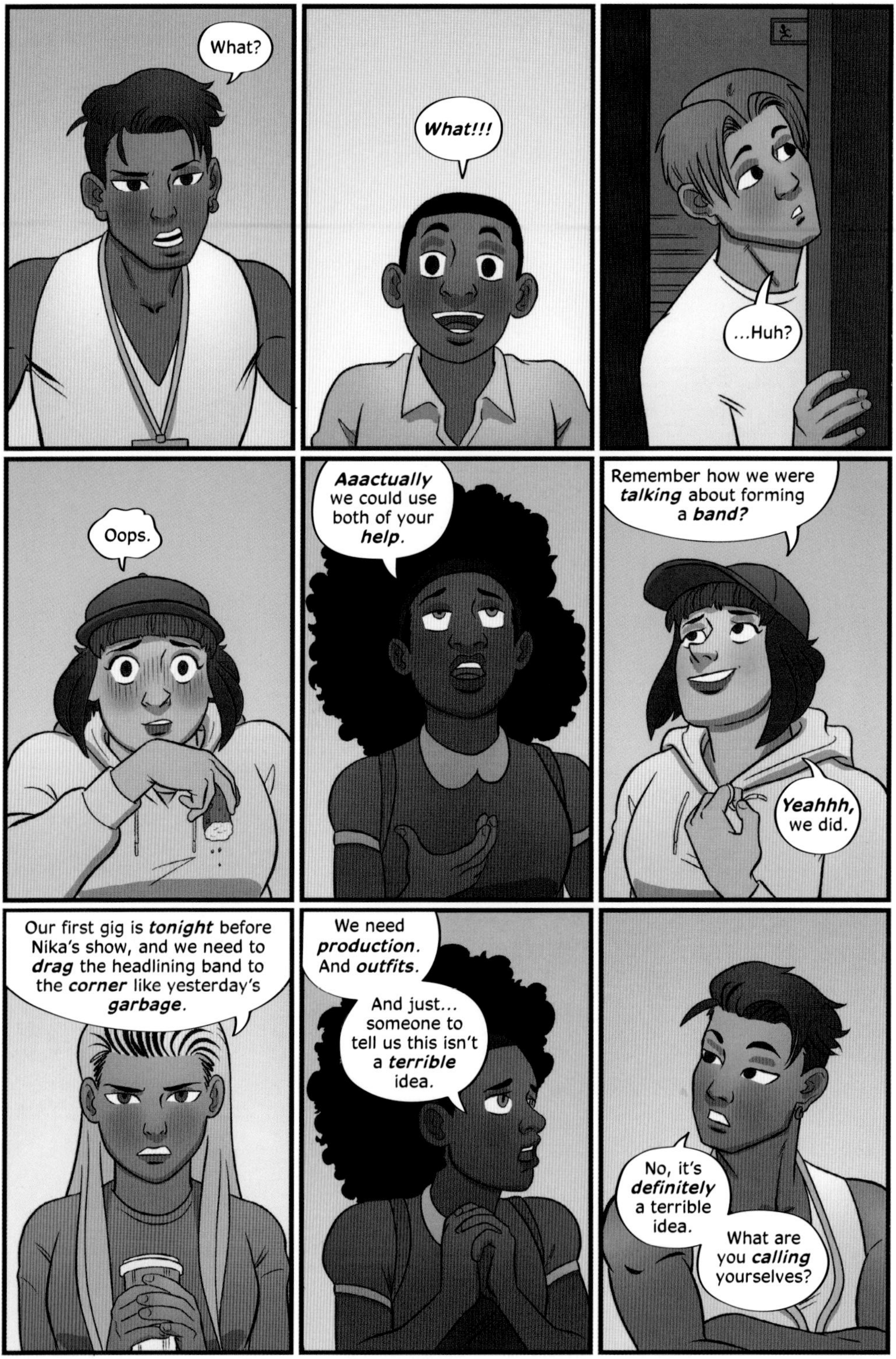
What?
What!!!
...Huh?
Oops.
Aaactually we could use both of your ***help***.
Remember how we were ***talking*** about forming a ***band?***
Yeahhh, we did.
Our first gig is ***tonight*** before Nika's show, and we need to ***drag*** the headlining band to the ***corner*** like yesterday's ***garbage***.
We need ***production***. And ***outfits***.
And just... someone to tell us this isn't a ***terrible*** idea.
No, it's ***definitely*** a terrible idea.
What are you ***calling*** yourselves?

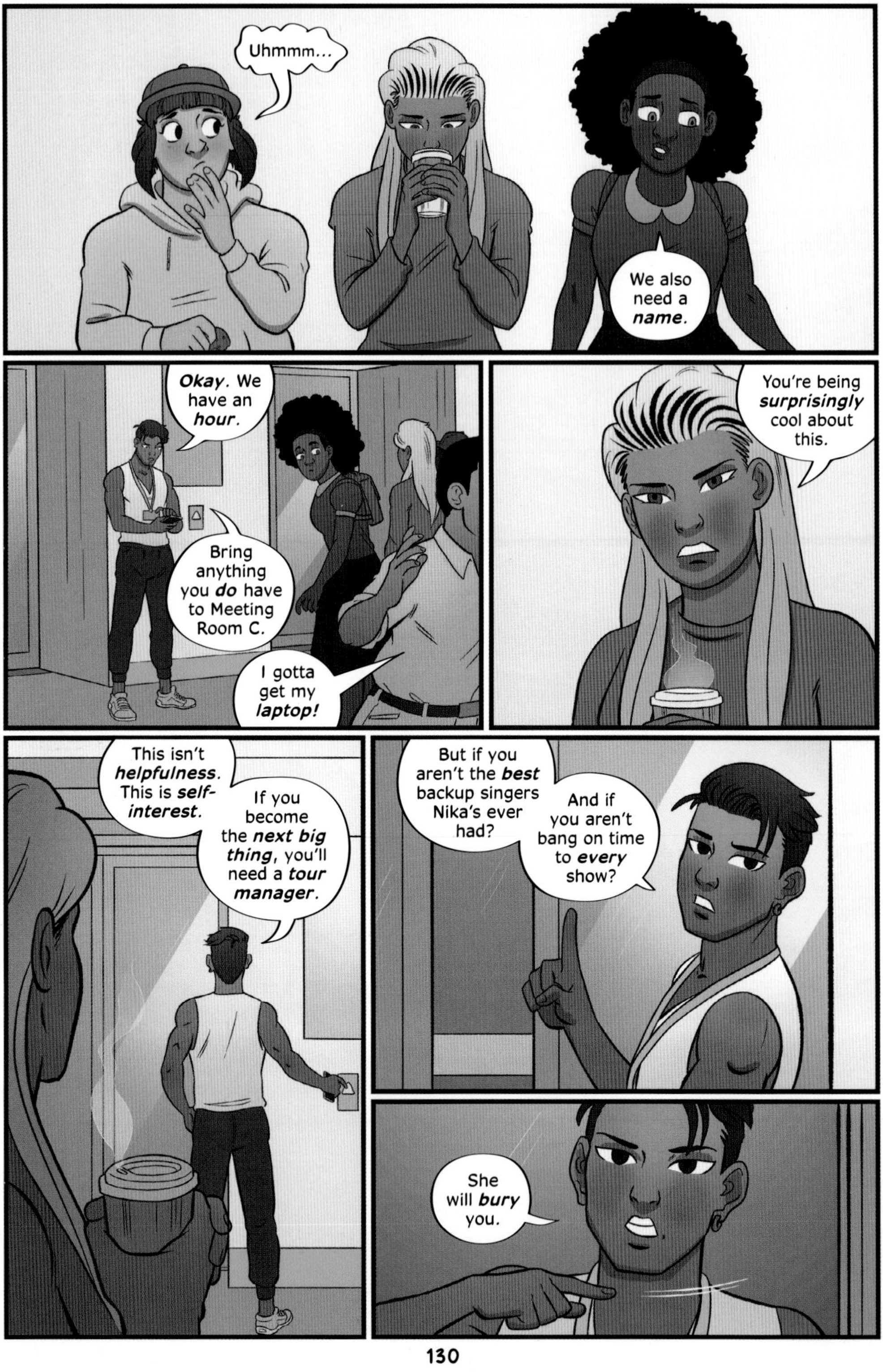
Uhmmm...
We also need a *name*.
Okay. We have an *hour*.
Bring anything you *do* have to Meeting Room C.
I gotta get my *laptop!*
You're being *surprisingly* cool about this.
This isn't *helpfulness*. This is *self-interest*.
If you become the *next big thing*, you'll need a *tour manager*.
But if you aren't the *best* backup singers Nika's ever had?
And if you aren't bang on time to *every* show?
She will *bury* you.

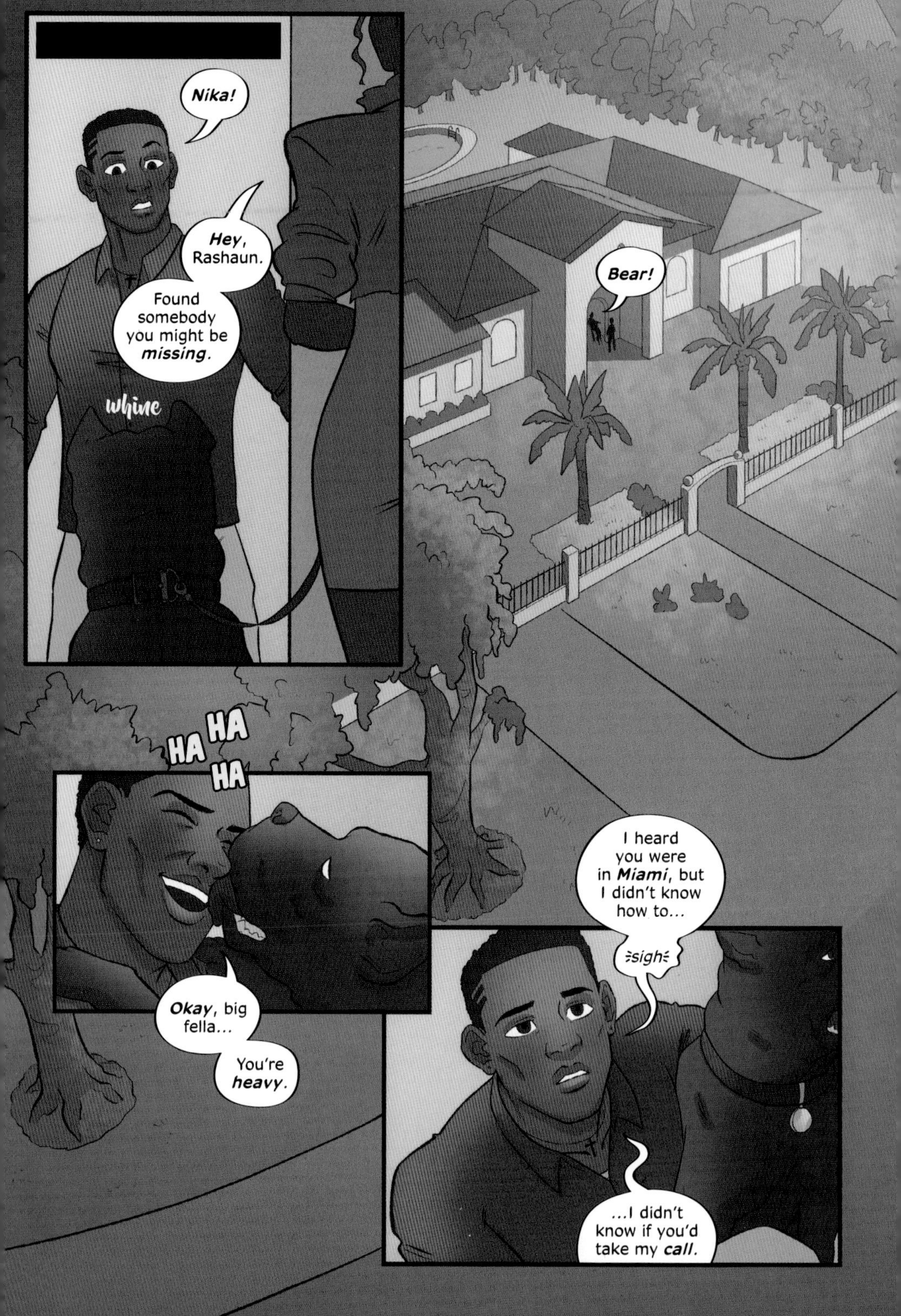
[redacted]
Nika!
Bear!
Hey, Rashaun.
Found somebody you might be missing.
whine
HA HA HA
Okay, big fella...
You're heavy.
I heard you were in Miami, but I didn't know how to...
≑sigh≑
...I didn't know if you'd take my call.

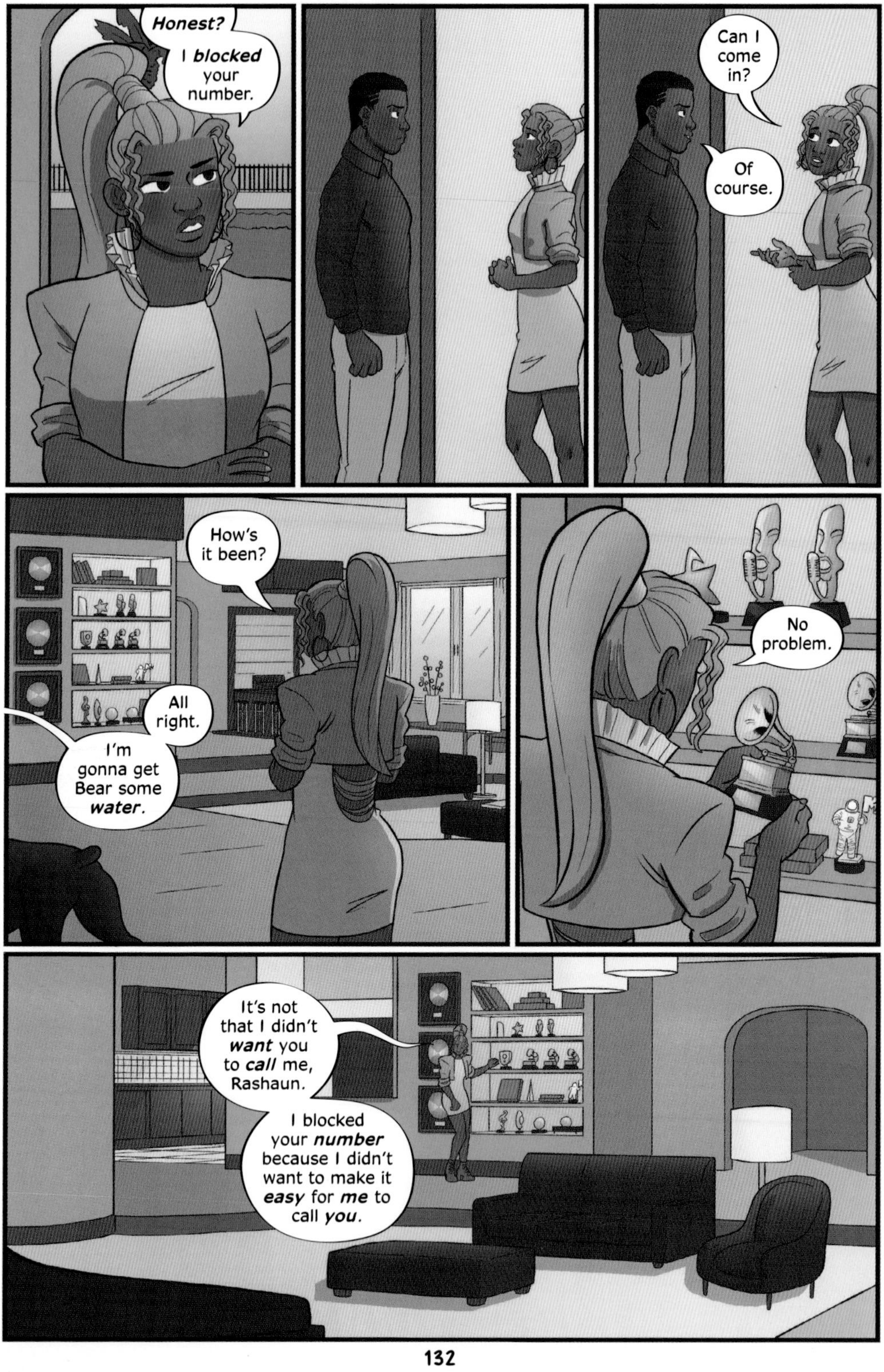

Honest?
I *blocked* your number.
Can I come in?
Of course.
How's it been?
All right.
I'm gonna get Bear some *water*.
No problem.
It's not that I didn't *want* you to *call* me, Rashaun.
I blocked your *number* because I didn't want to make it *easy* for *me* to call *you*.

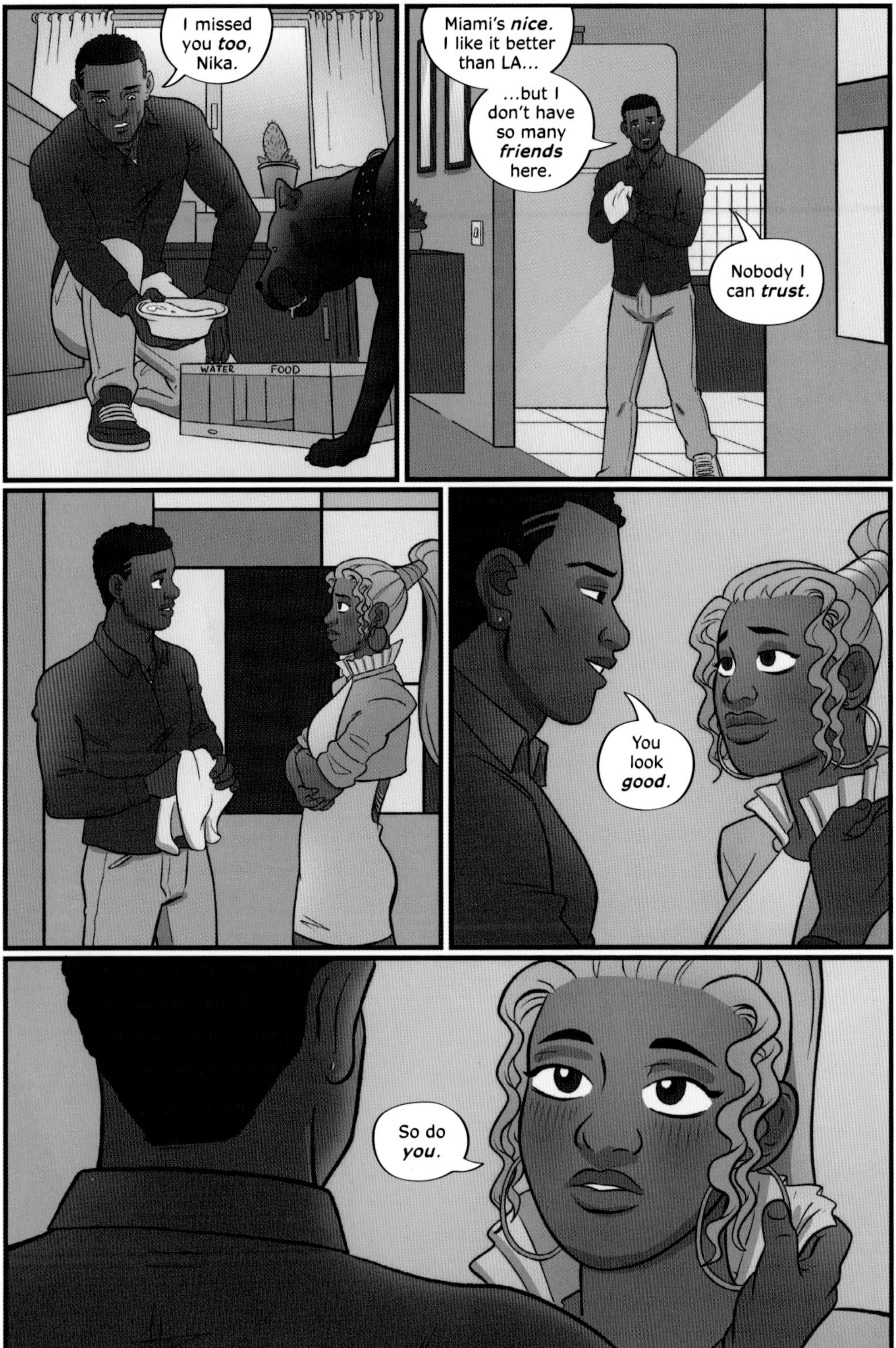
I missed you *too*, Nika.
WATER
FOOD
Miami's *nice*. I like it better than LA...
...but I don't have so many *friends* here.
Nobody I can *trust*.
You look *good*.
So do *you*.

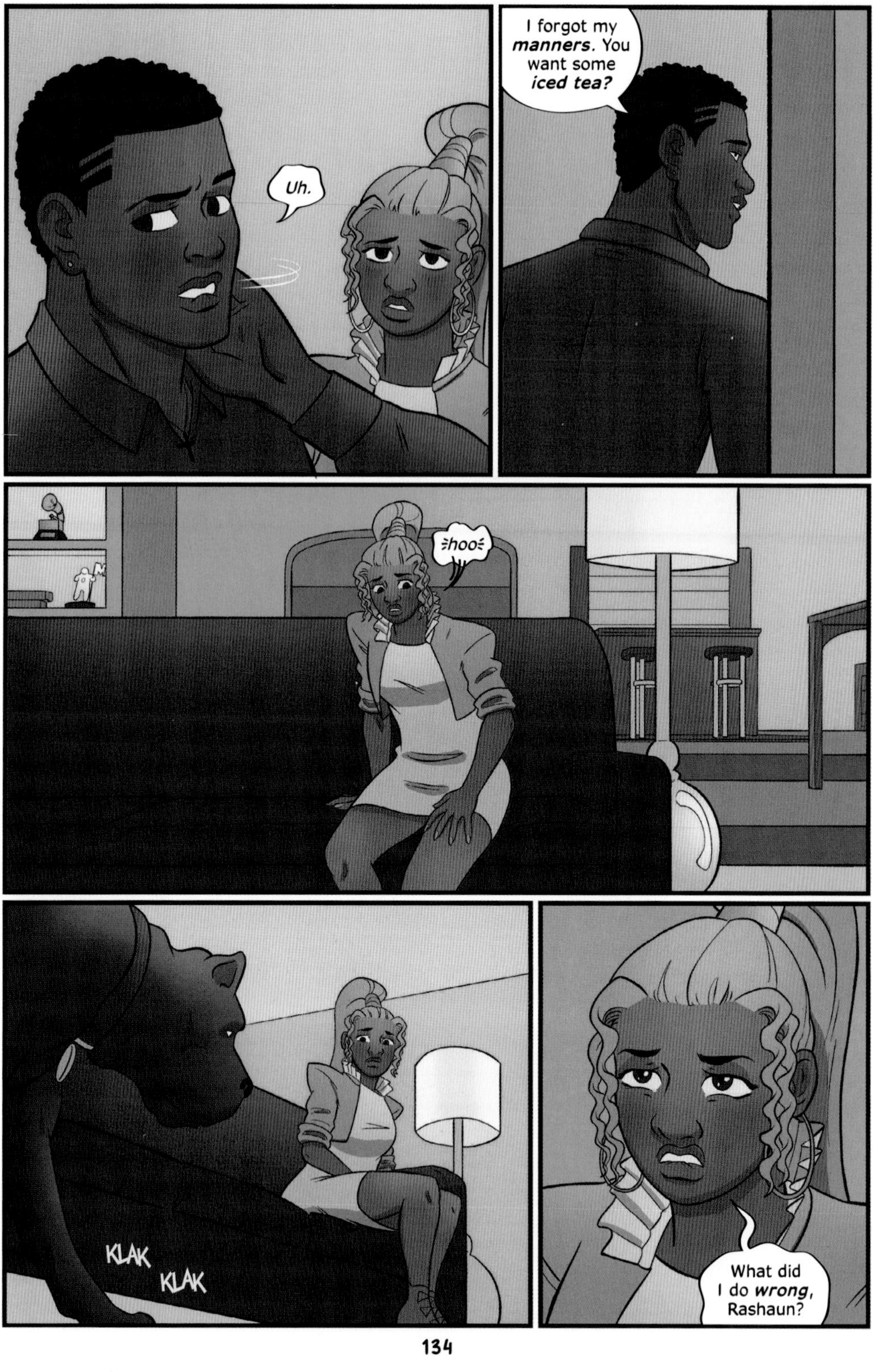
Uh.
I forgot my *manners.* You want some *iced tea?*
hoo
KLAK
KLAK
What did I do *wrong,* Rashaun?

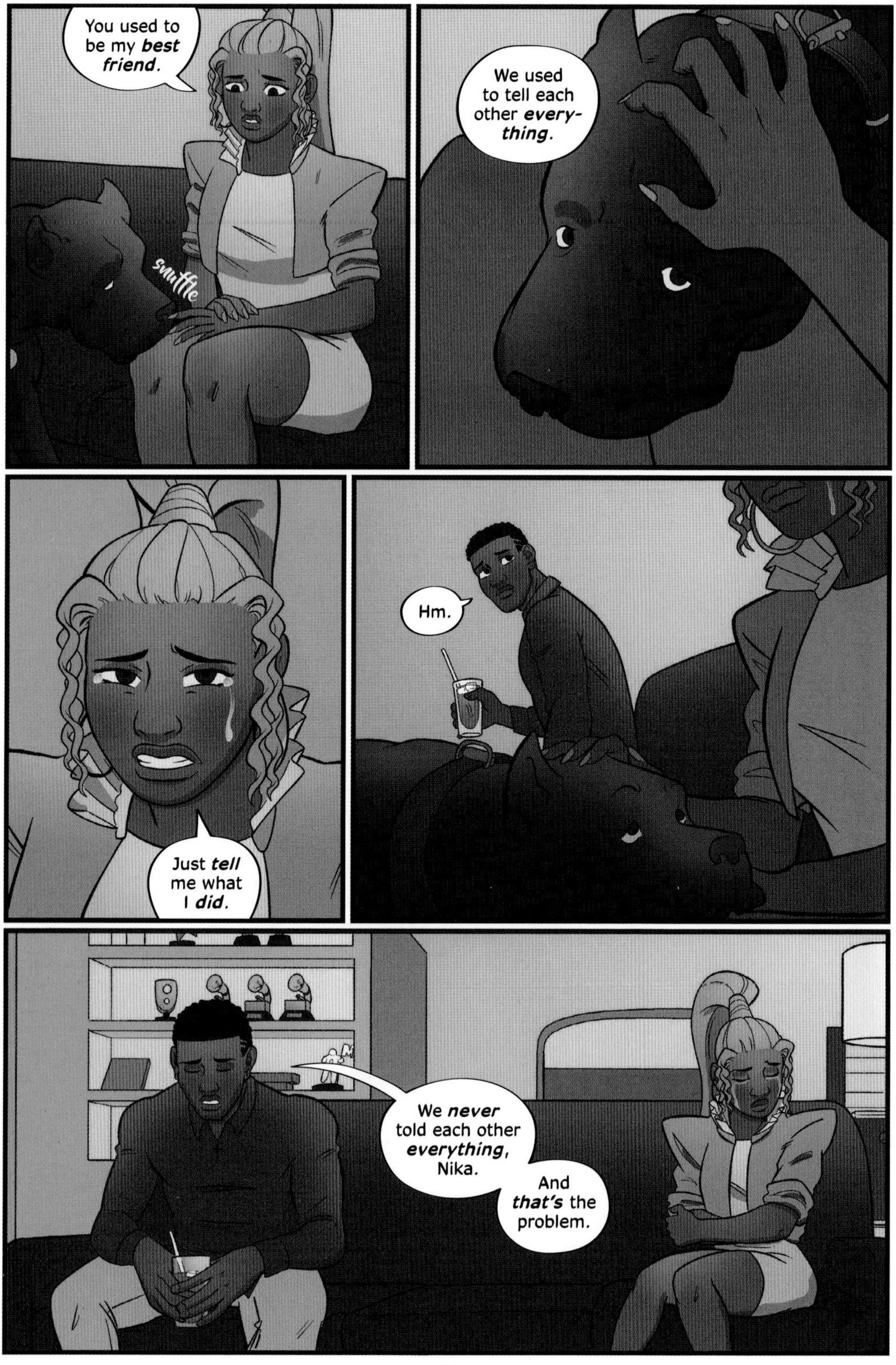
You used to be my *best* *friend*.
snuffle
We used to tell each other *every-thing*.
Just *tell* me what I *did*.
Hm.
We *never* told each other *everything*, Nika.
And *that's* the problem.

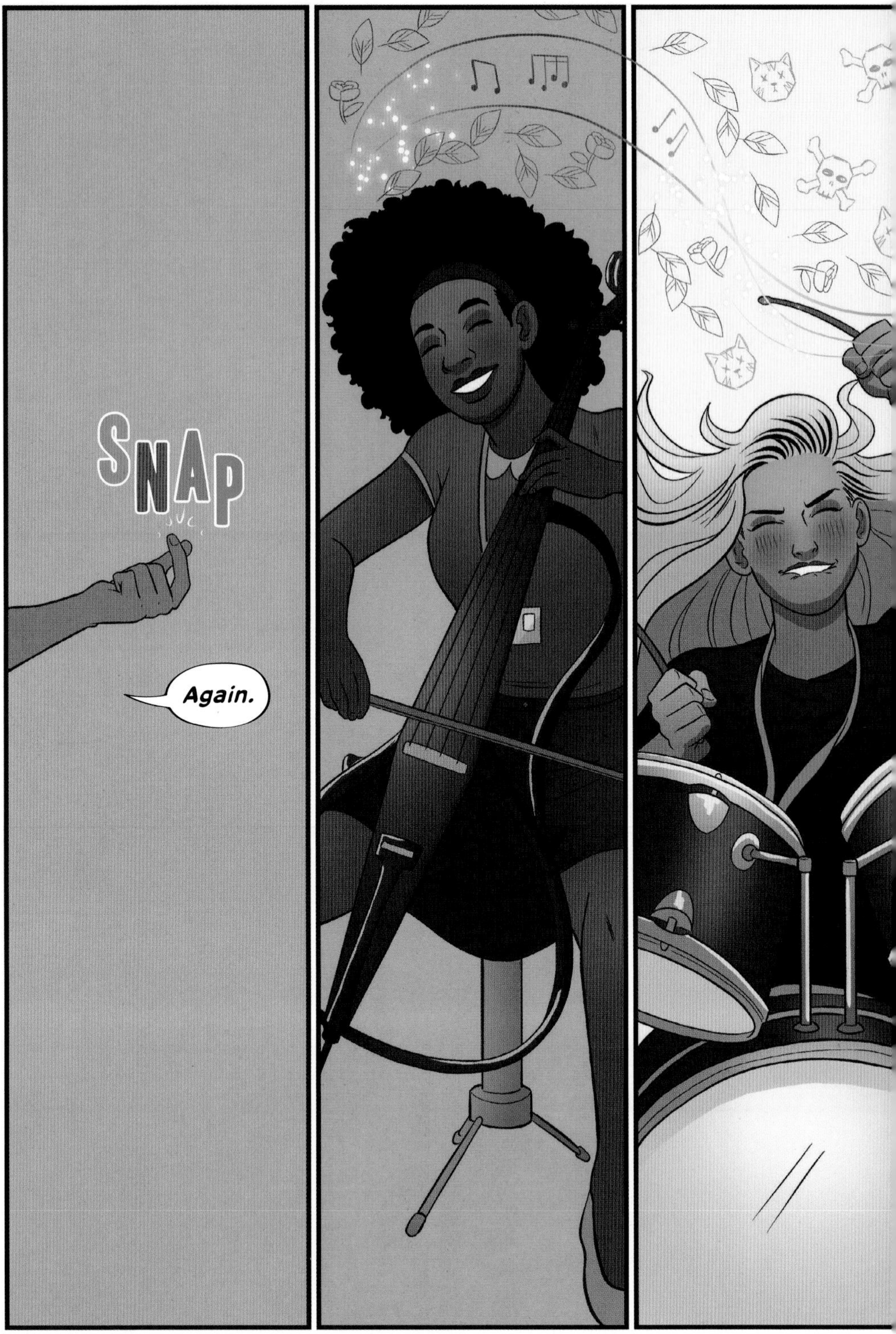
SNAP
Again.

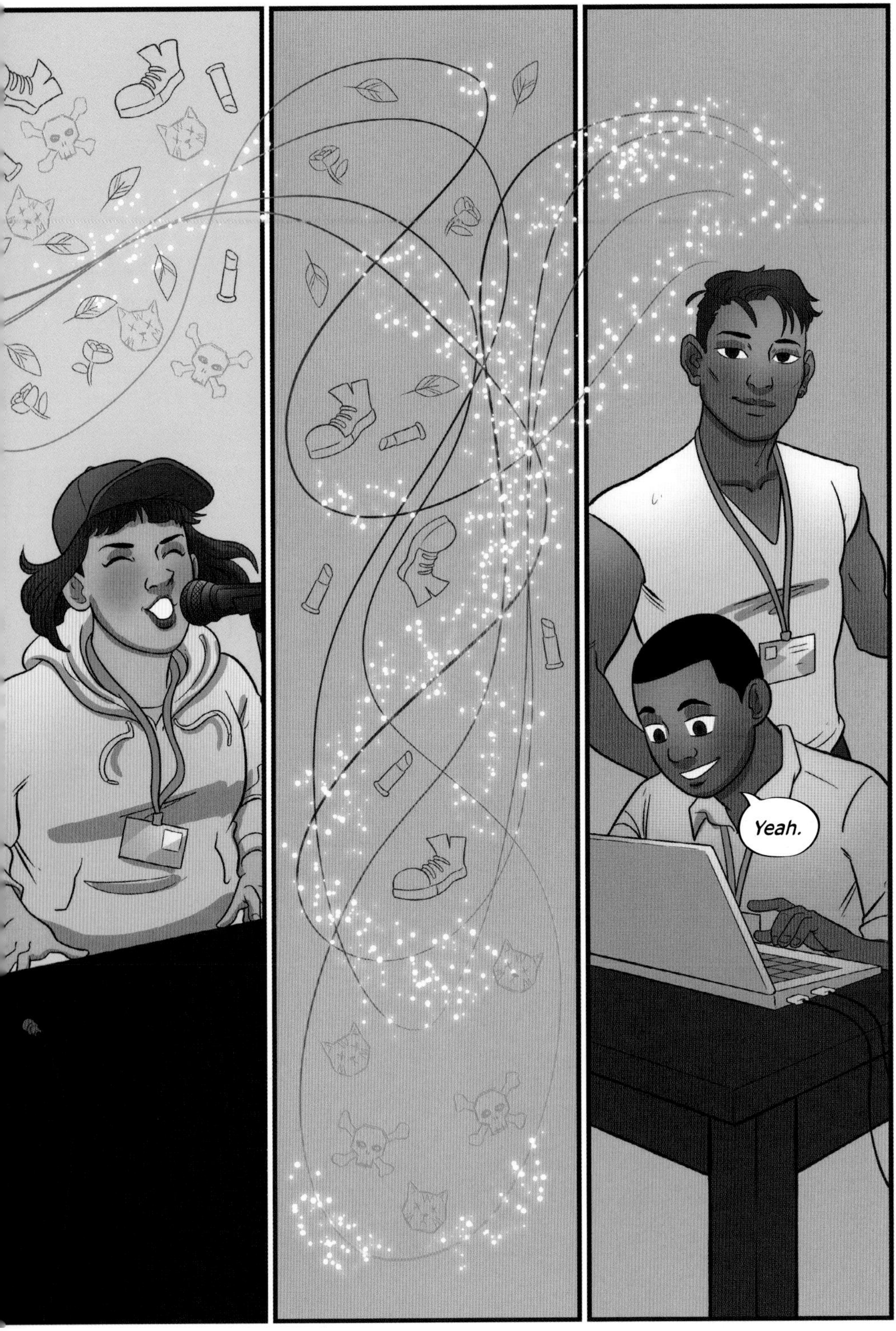
Yeah.

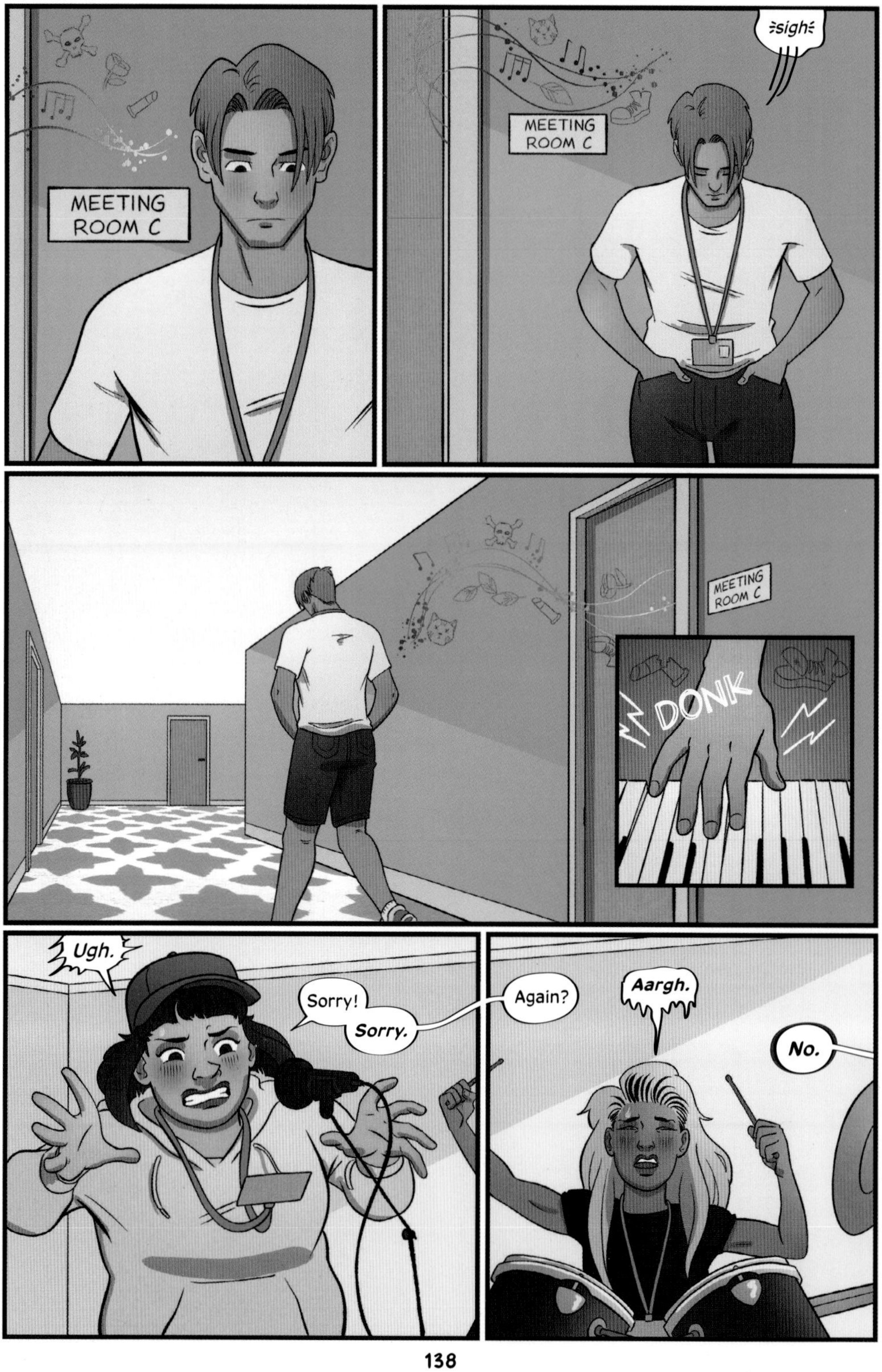
MEETING ROOM C
MEETING ROOM C
≈sigh≈
MEETING ROOM C
DONK
Ugh.
Sorry!
Sorry.
Again?
Aargh.
No.

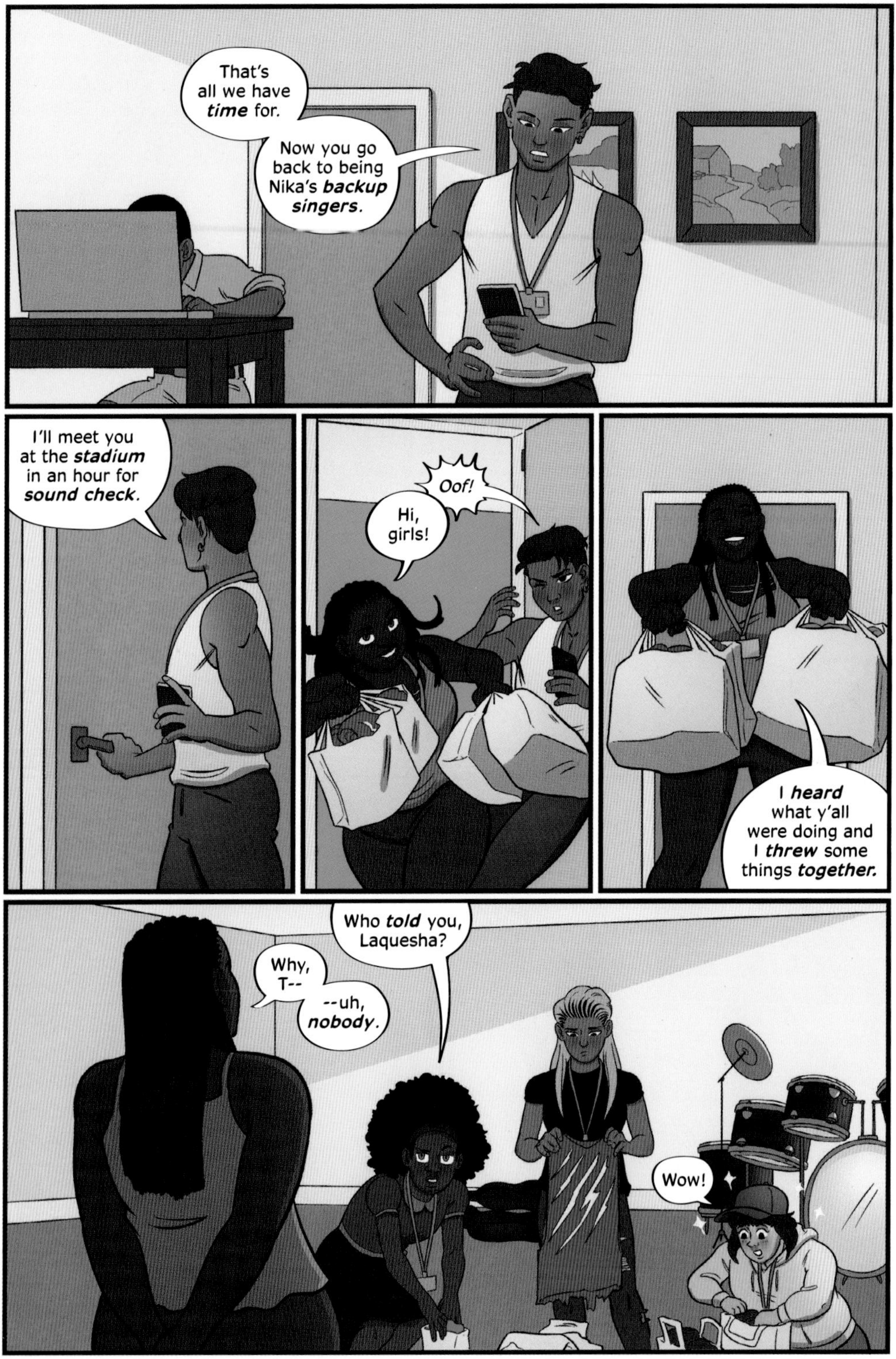
That's all we have *time* for.
Now you go back to being Nika's *backup singers*.
I'll meet you at the *stadium* in an hour for *sound check*.
Oof!
Hi, girls!
I *heard* what y'all were doing and I *threw* some things *together.*
Who *told* you, Laquesha?
Why, T--
--uh, *nobody*.
Wow!

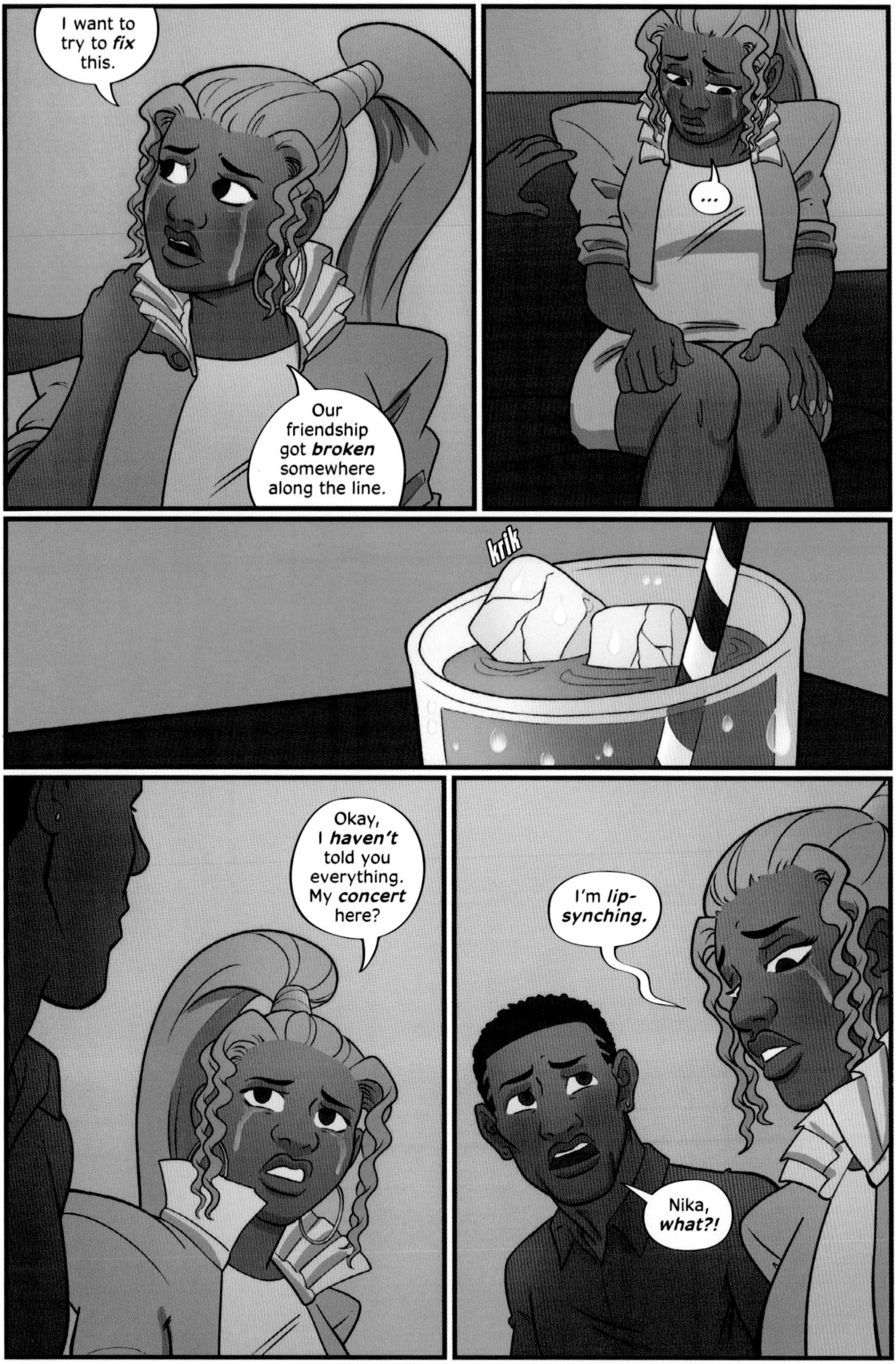
I want to try to *fix* this.
Our friendship got ***broken*** somewhere along the line.
...
krik
Okay, I ***haven't*** told you everything. My ***concert*** here?
I'm *lip-synching.*
Nika, ***what?!***

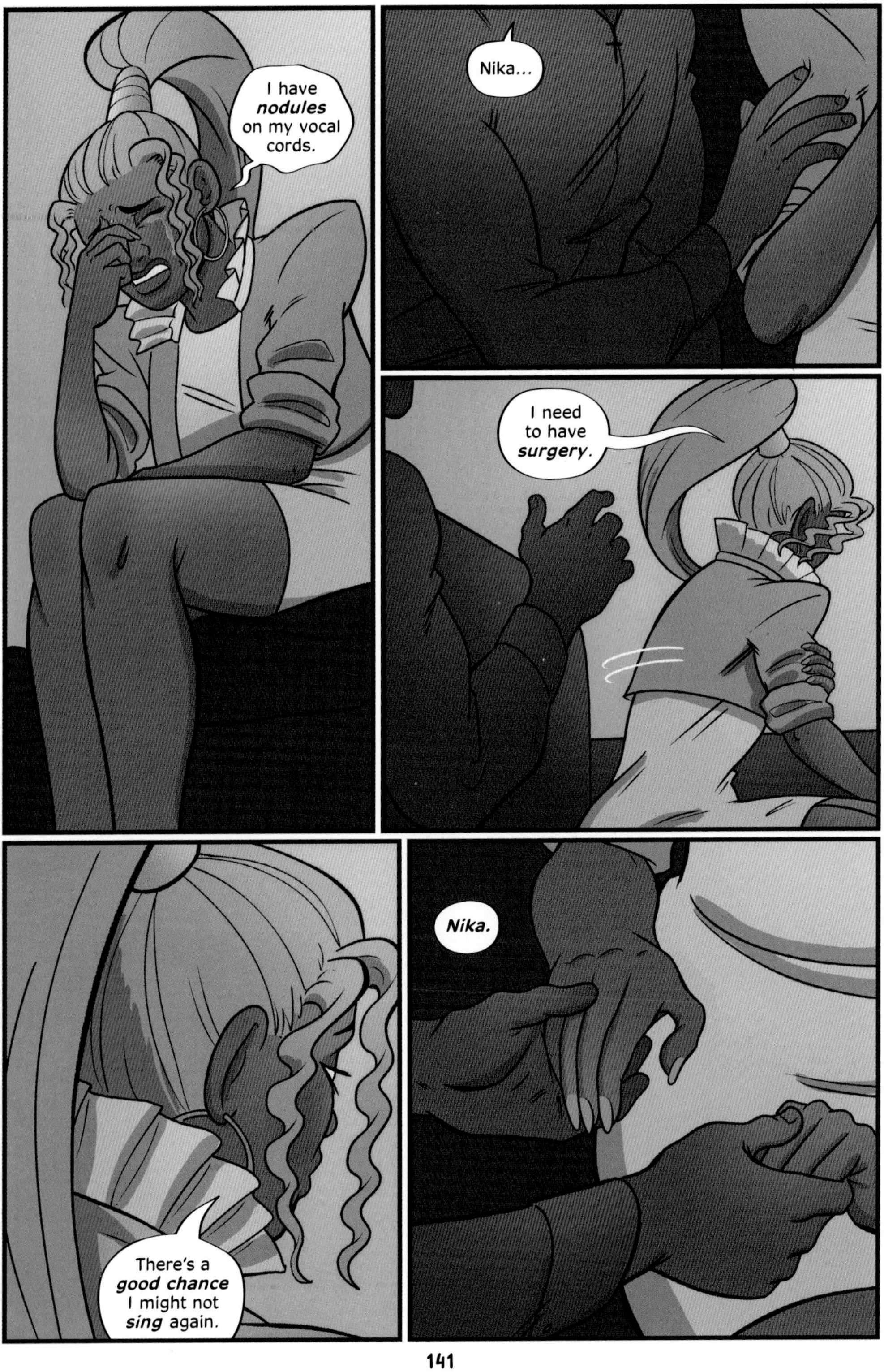
I have *nodules* on my vocal cords.
Nika...
I need to have *surgery*.
There's a *good chance* I might not *sing* again.
Nika.

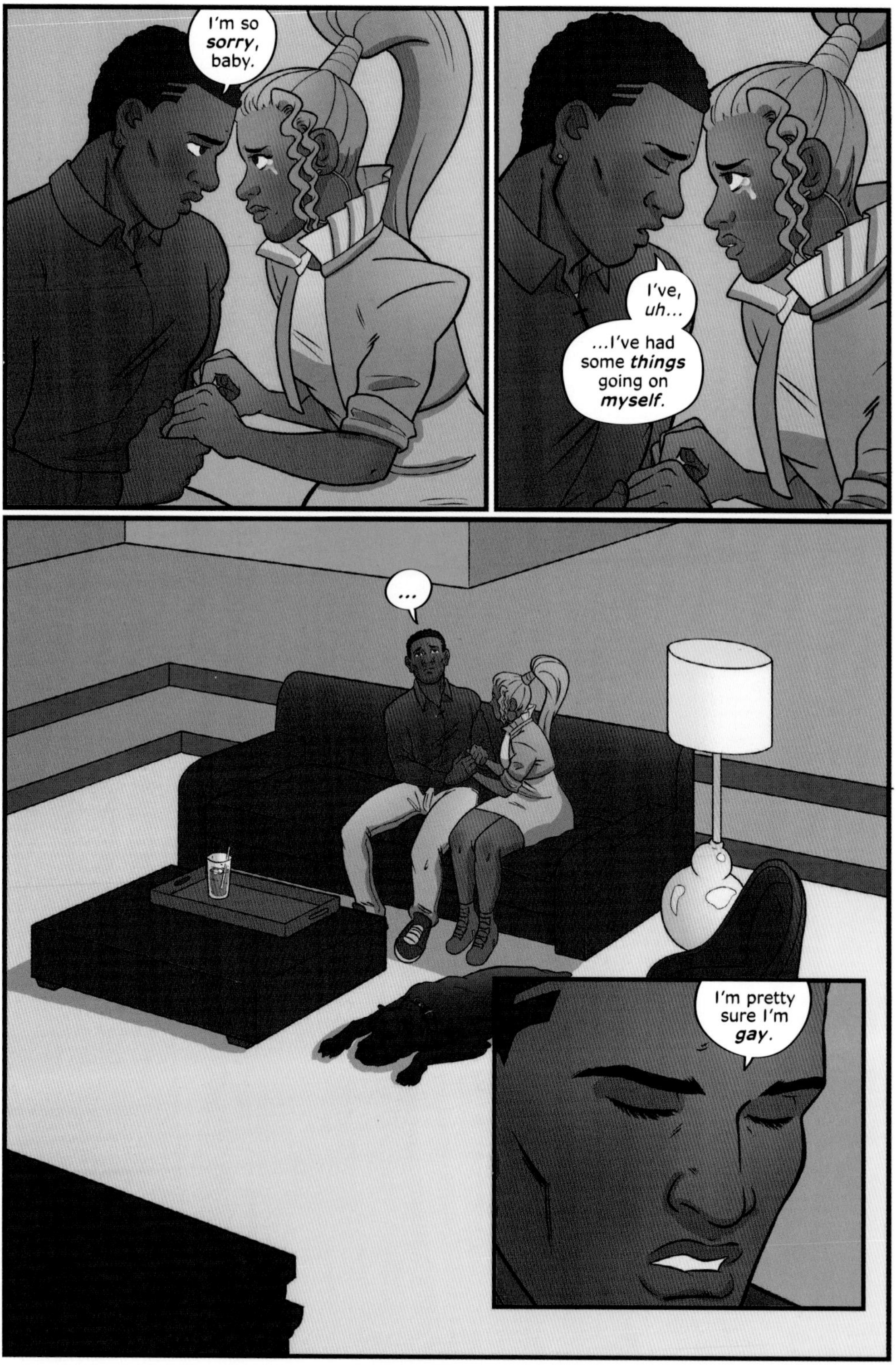
I'm so *sorry*, baby.
I've, *uh*...
...I've had some *things* going on *myself*.
...
I'm pretty sure I'm *gay*.

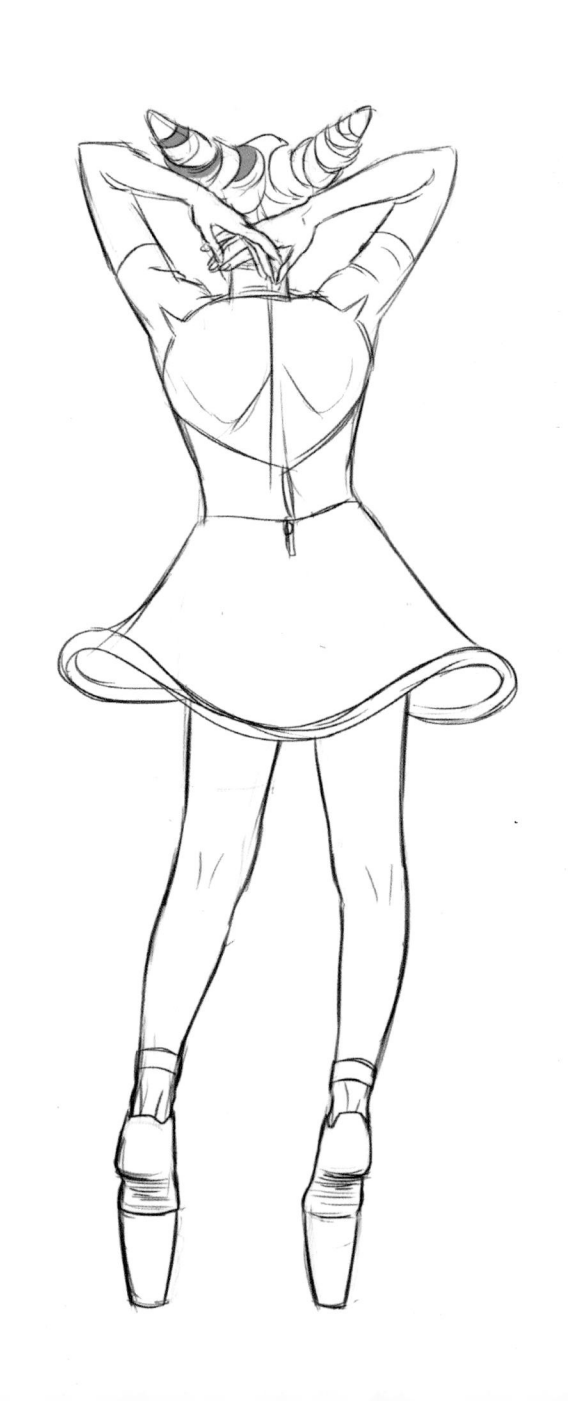

CHAPTER 5

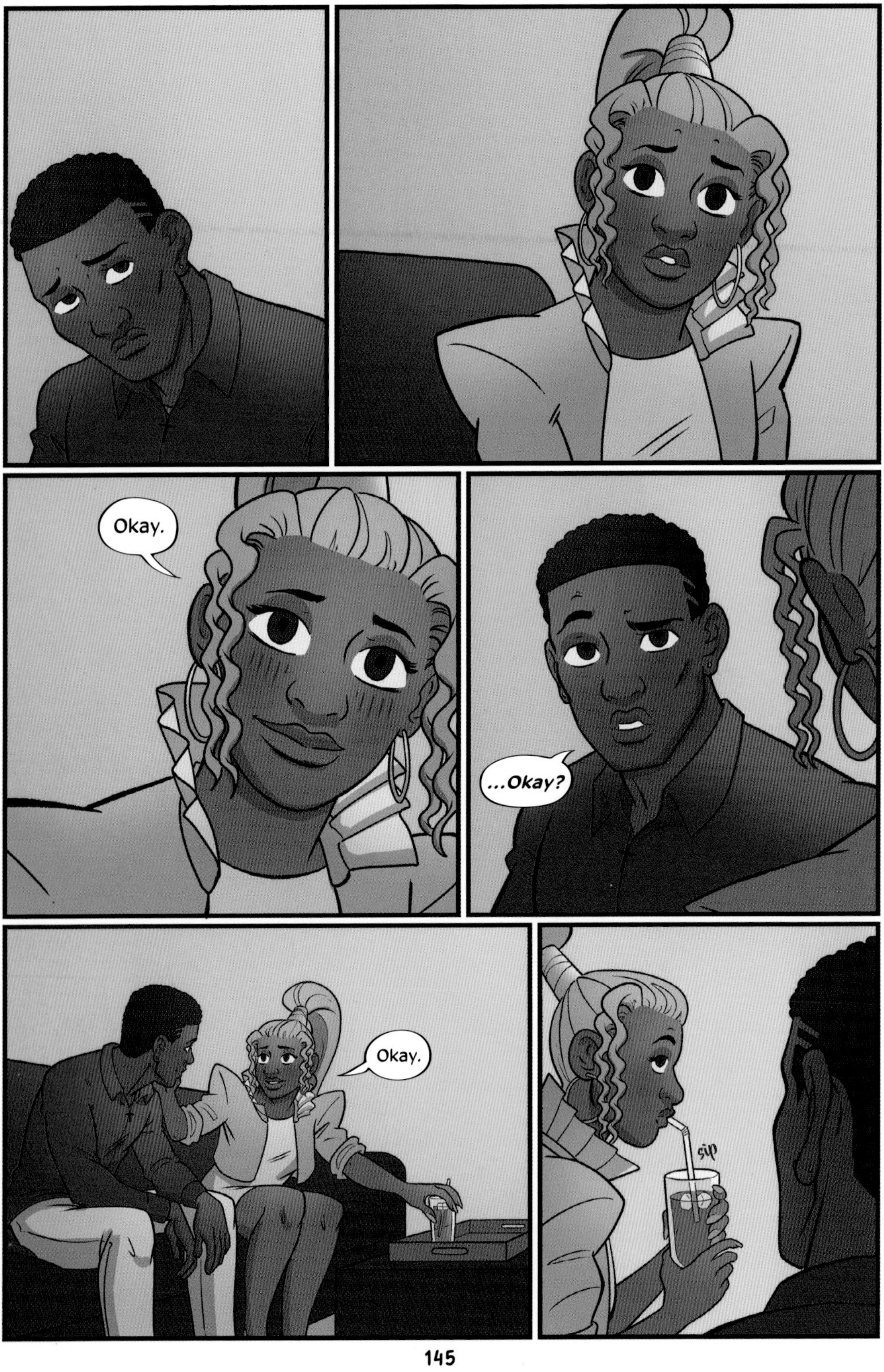
Okay.
...Okay?
Okay.
sip

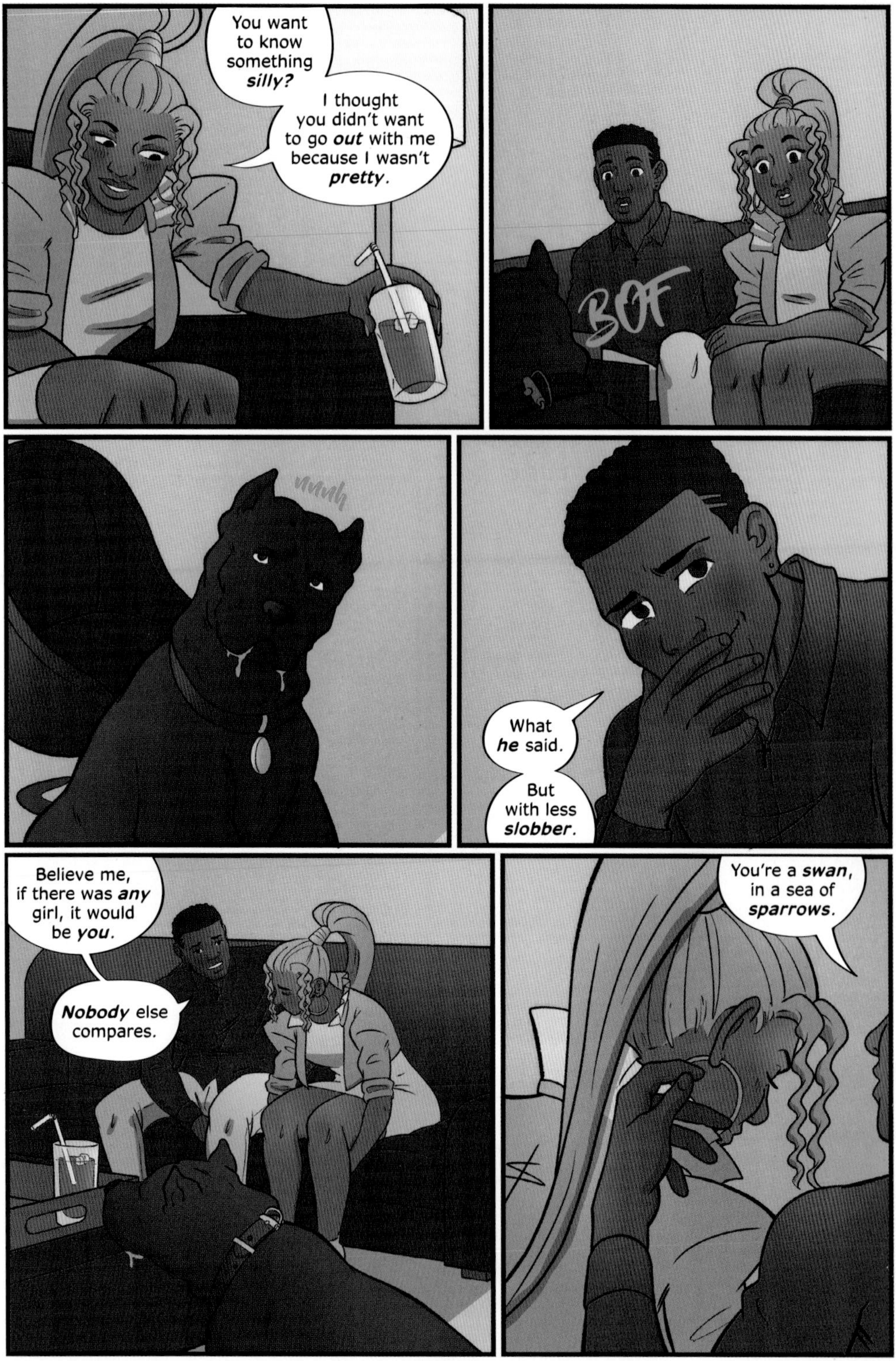
You want to know something *silly?*
I thought you didn't want to go *out* with me because I wasn't *pretty*.
BOF
nnnh
What *he* said.
But with less *slobber*.
Believe me, if there was *any* girl, it would be *you*.
Nobody else compares.
You're a *swan*, in a sea of *sparrows*.

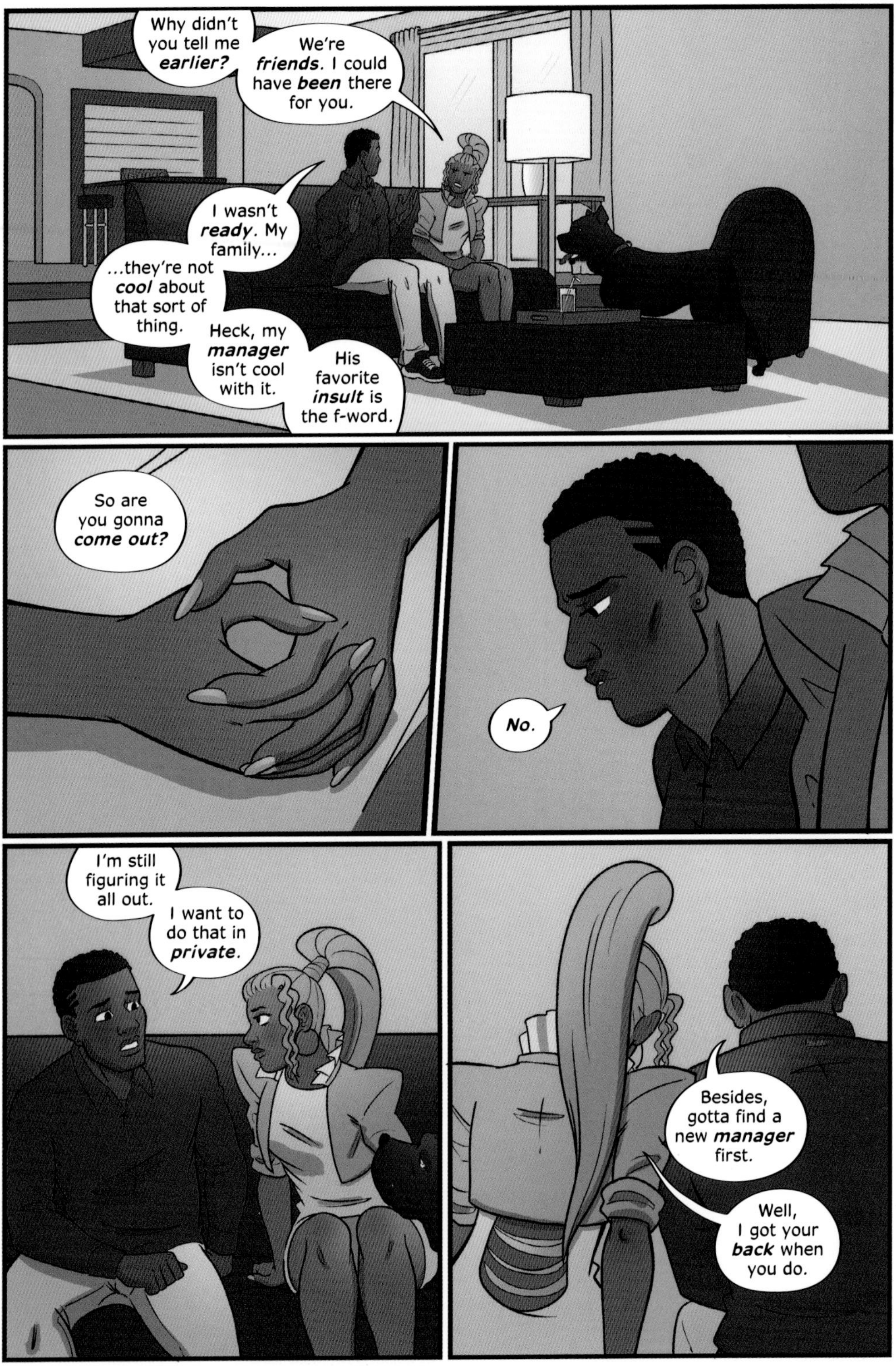
Why didn't you tell me *earlier?*
We're *friends*. I could have *been* there for you.
I wasn't *ready*. My family...
...they're not *cool* about that sort of thing.
Heck, my *manager* isn't cool with it.
His favorite *insult* is the f-word.
So are you gonna *come out?*
No.
I'm still figuring it all out.
I want to do that in *private*.
Besides, gotta find a new *manager* first.
Well, I got your *back* when you do.

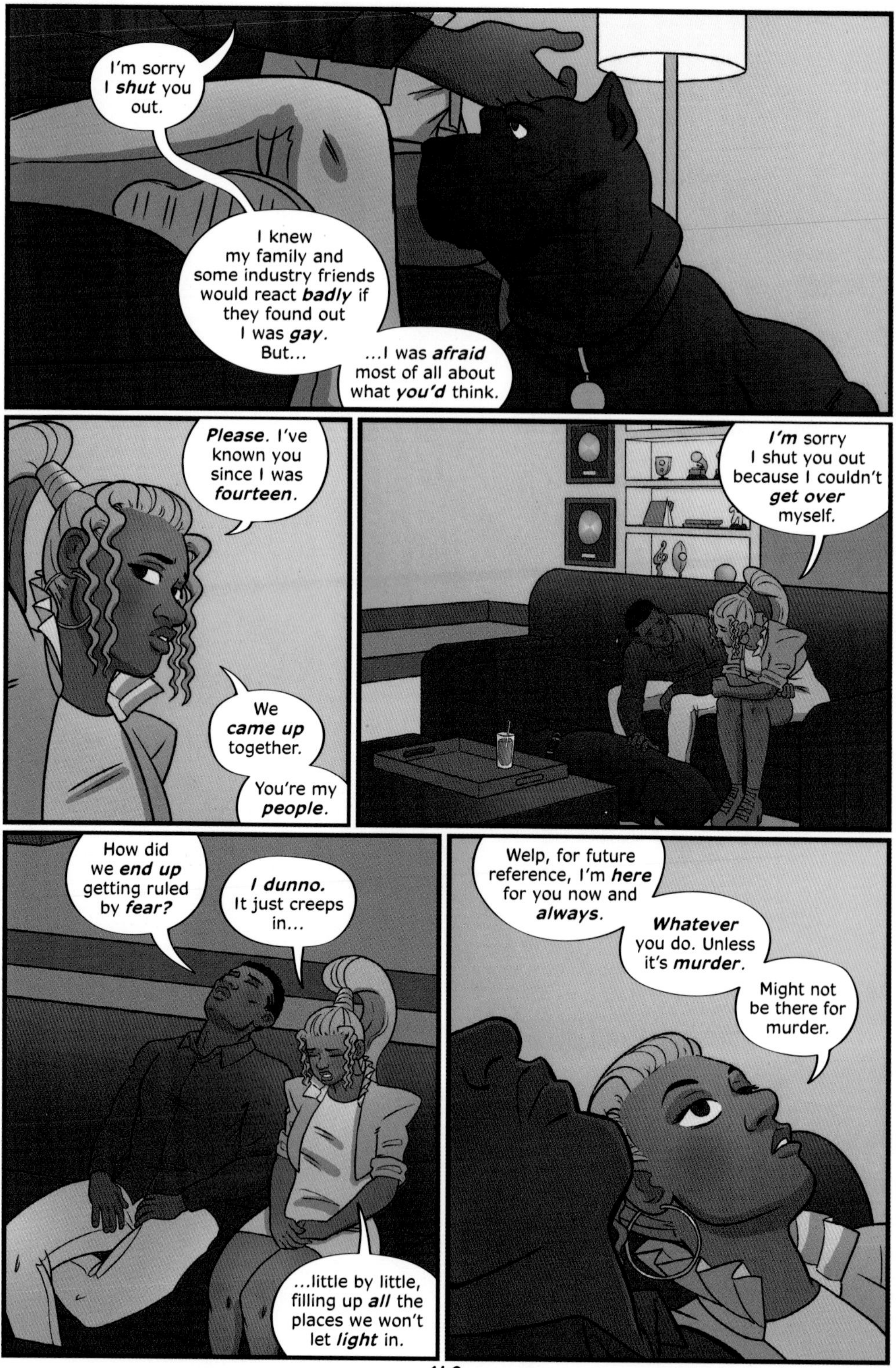
I'm sorry I ***shut*** you out.
I knew my family and some industry friends would react ***badly*** if they found out I was ***gay***. But...
...I was ***afraid*** most of all about what ***you'd*** think.
Please. I've known you since I was ***fourteen***.
We ***came up*** together.
You're my ***people***.
I'm sorry I shut you out because I couldn't ***get over*** myself.
How did we ***end up*** getting ruled by ***fear?***
I dunno. It just creeps in...
...little by little, filling up ***all*** the places we won't let ***light*** in.
Welp, for future reference, I'm ***here*** for you now and ***always***.
Whatever you do. Unless it's ***murder***.
Might not be there for murder.

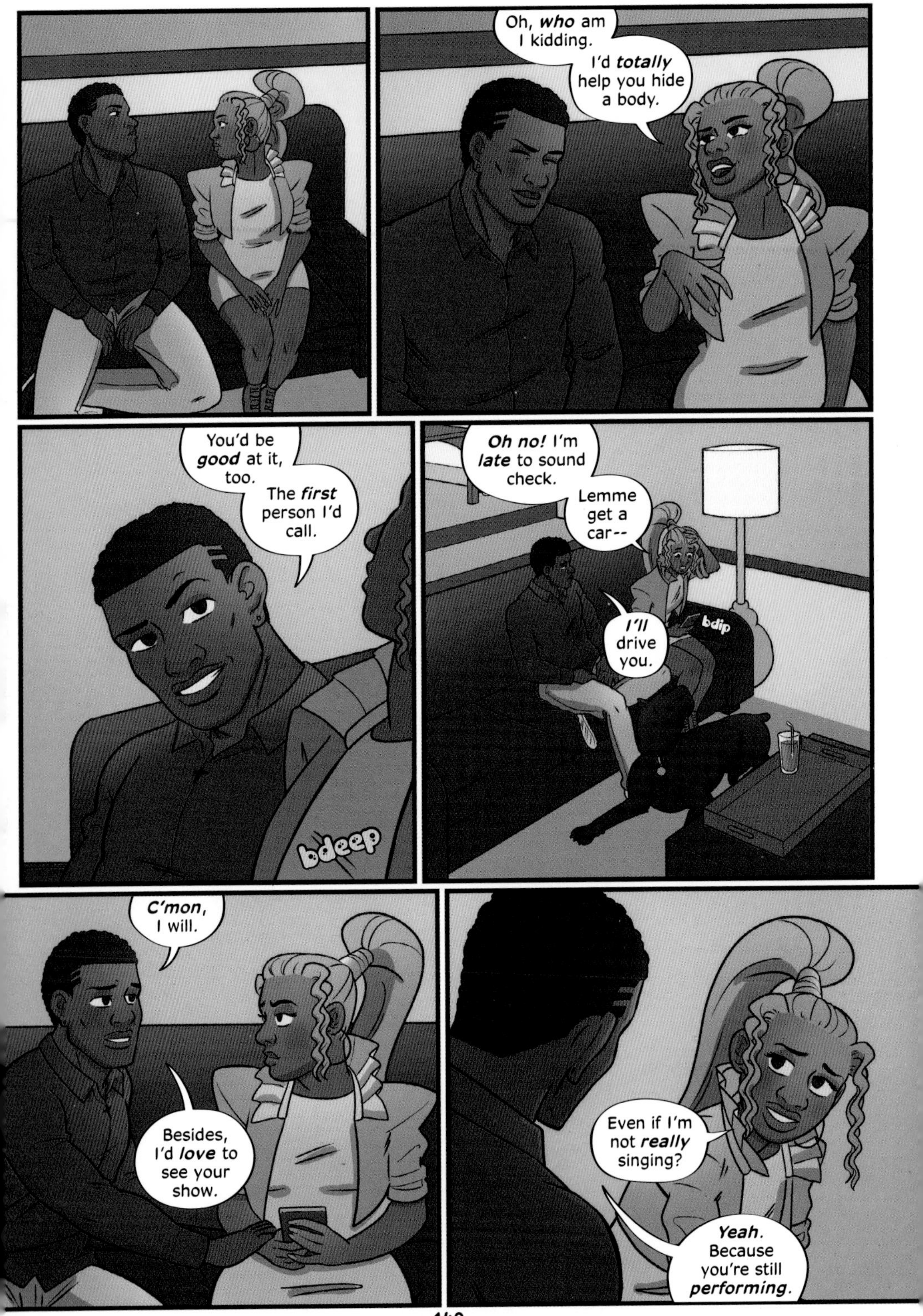
Oh, *who* am I kidding.
I'd *totally* help you hide a body.
You'd be *good* at it, too.
The *first* person I'd call.
bdeep
Oh no! I'm *late* to sound check.
Lemme get a car--
bdip
I'll drive you.
C'mon, I will.
Besides, I'd *love* to see your show.
Even if I'm not *really* singing?
Yeah. Because you're still *performing*.

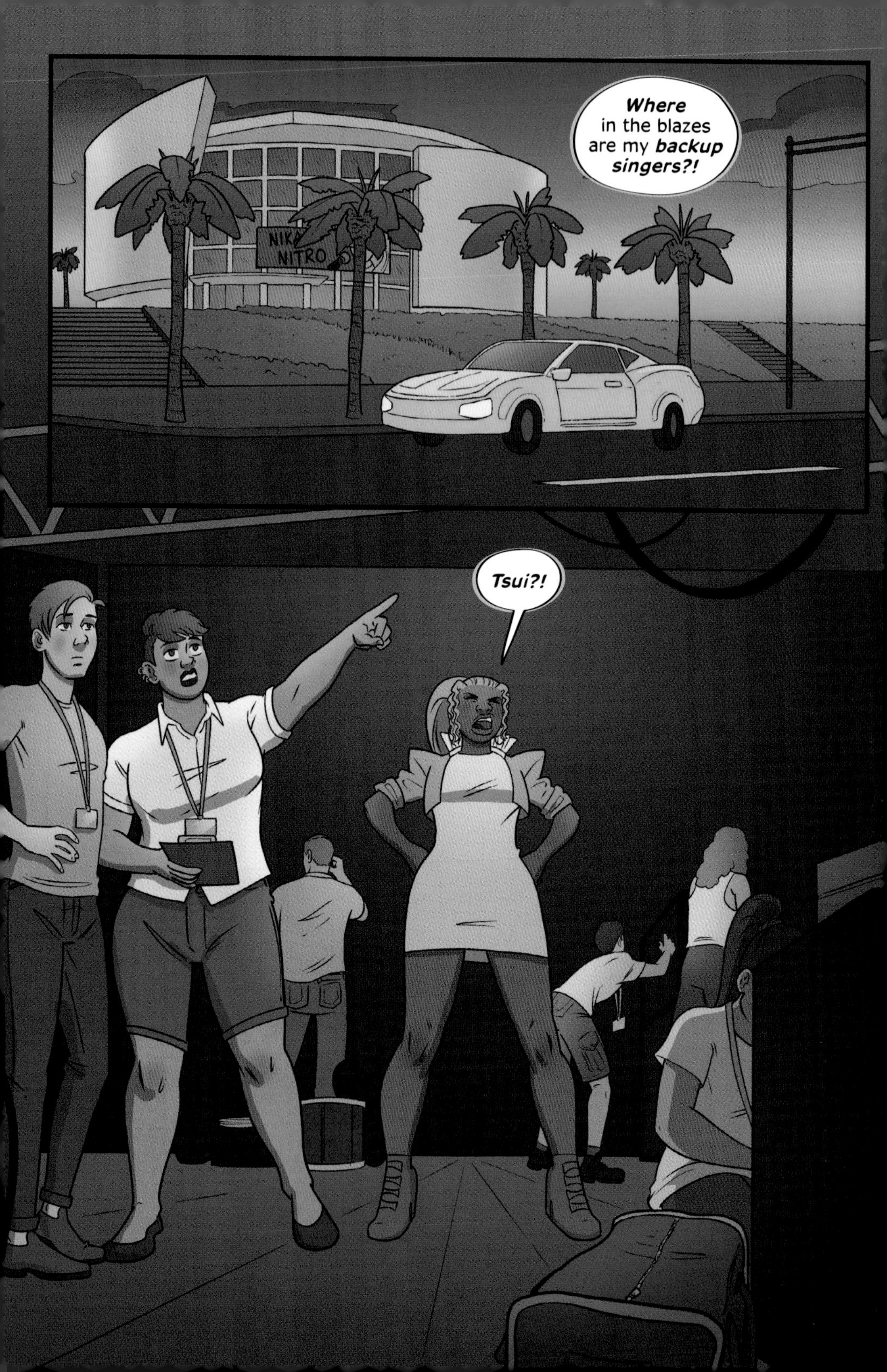
NIKA NITRO
Where in the blazes are my ***backup*** ***singers?!***
Tsui?!

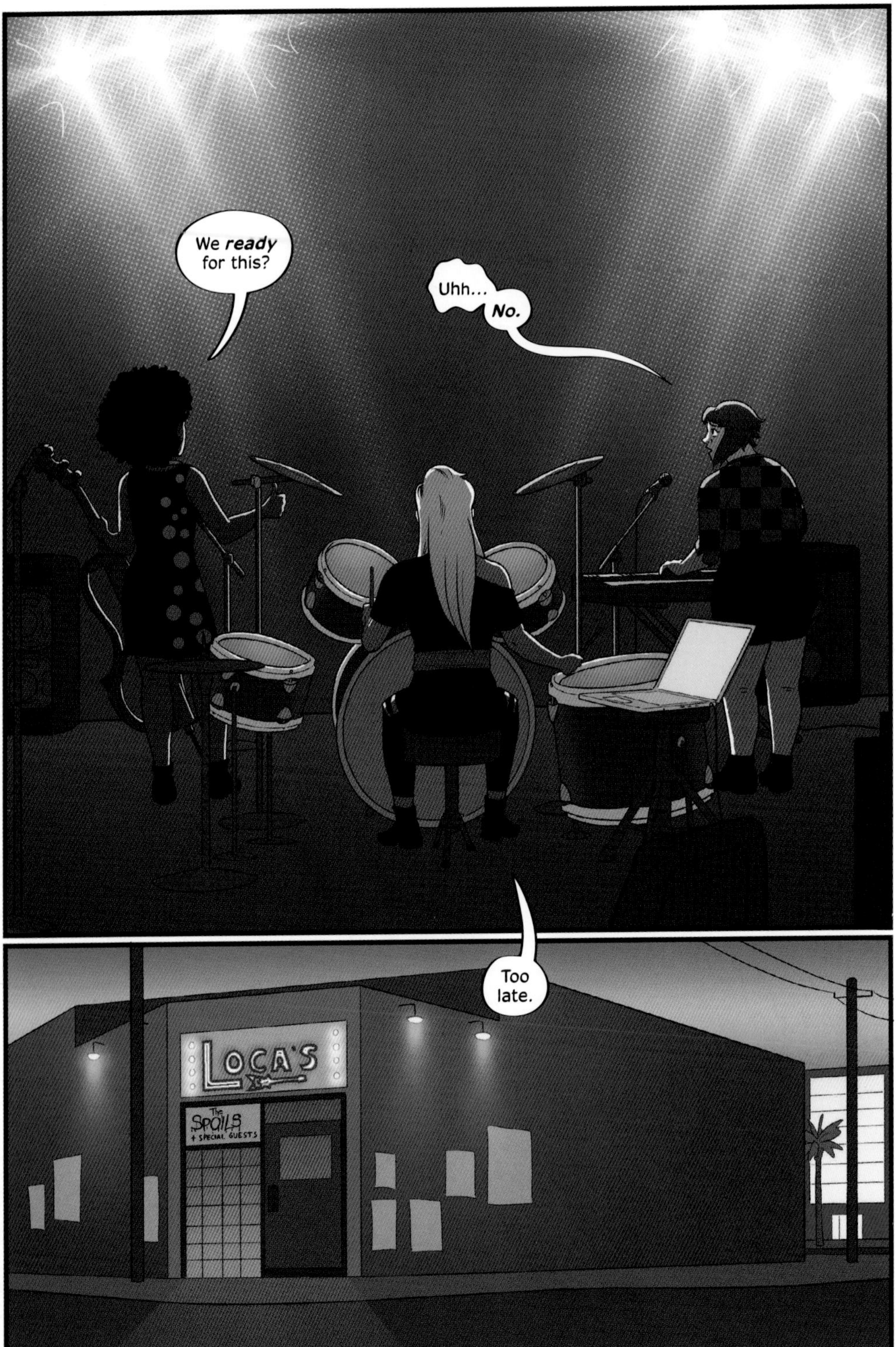
We *ready* for this?
Uhh... **No.**
Too late.
LOCA'S
The SPOILS + SPECIAL GUESTS

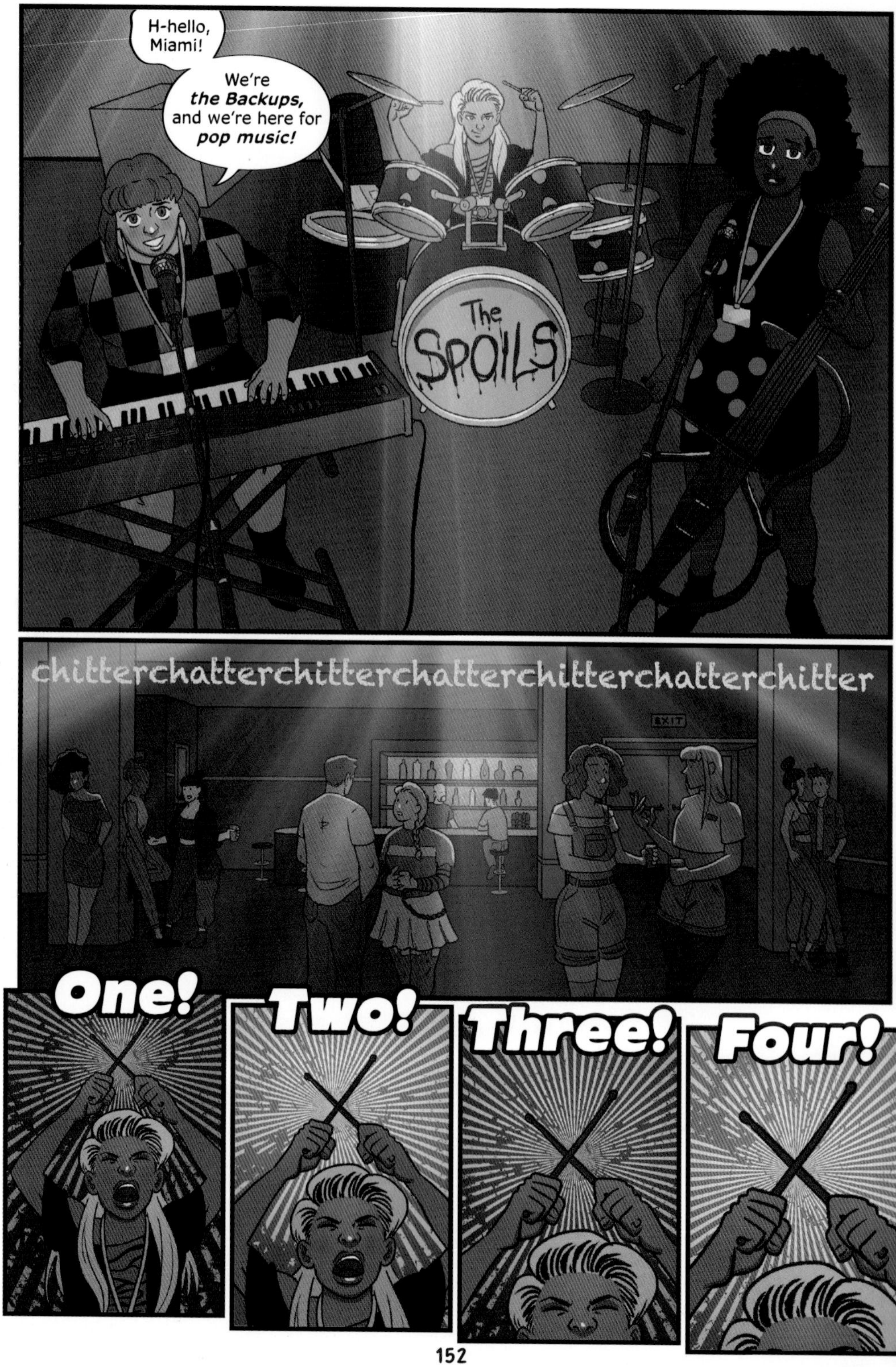

H-hello, Miami!
We're *the Backups,* and we're here for *pop music!*
The SPOILS
chitterchatterchitterchatterchitterchatterchitter
EXIT
One!
Two!
Three!
Four!

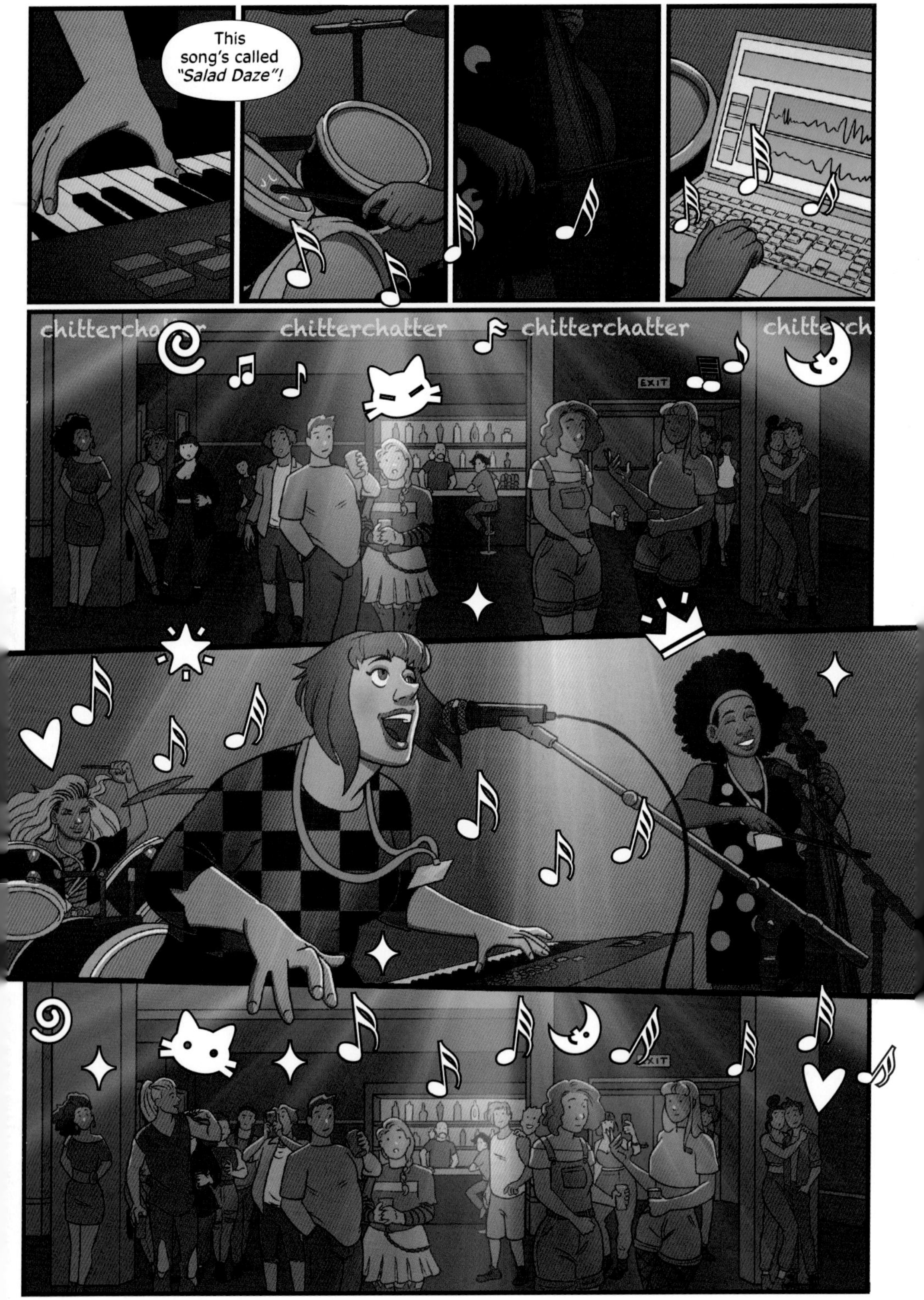
This song's called *"Salad Daze"*!
chitterchatter
chitterchatter
chitterchatter

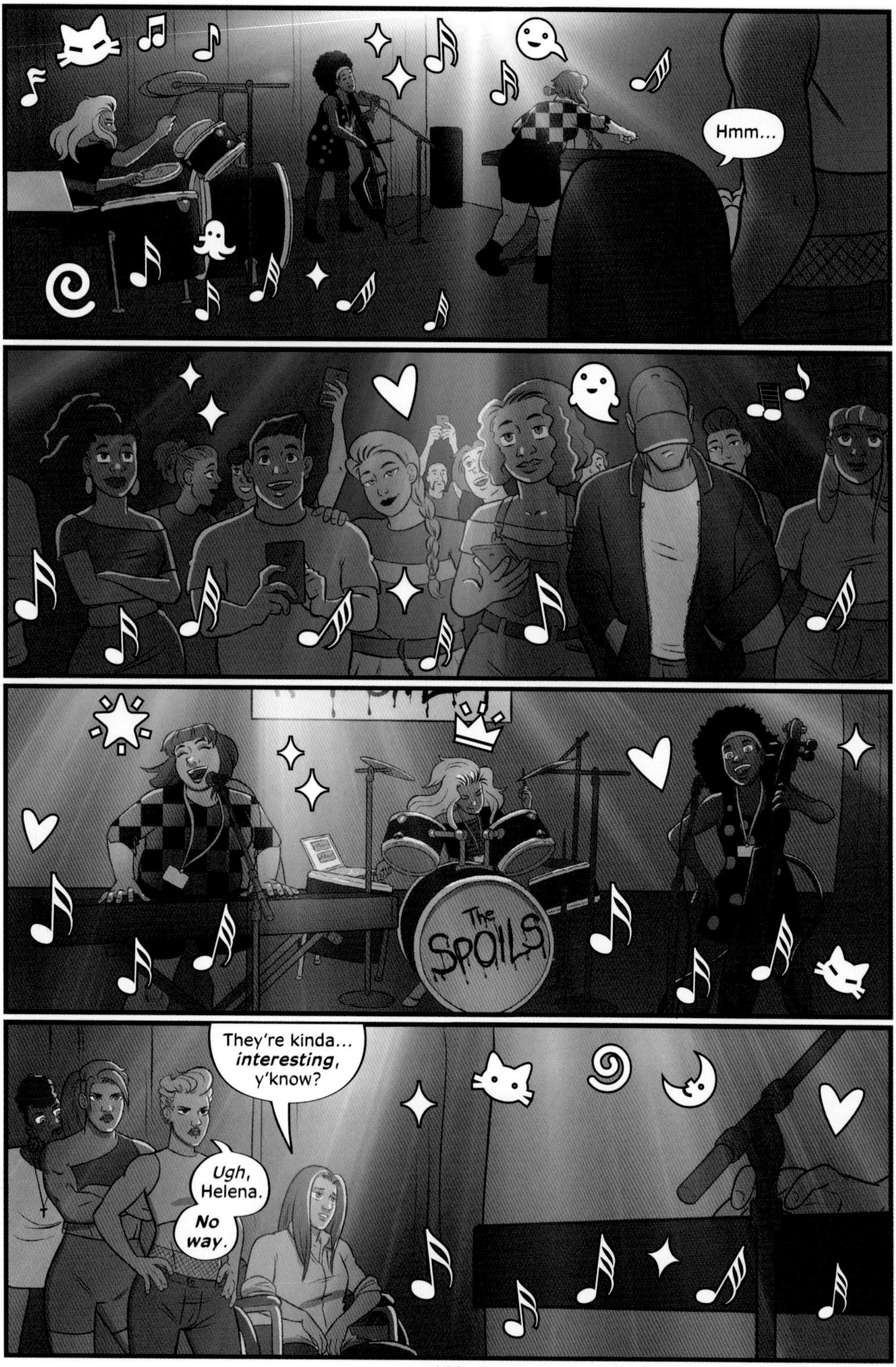

Hmm...
The Spoils
They're kinda... *interesting*, y'know?
Ugh, Helena. ***No way***.

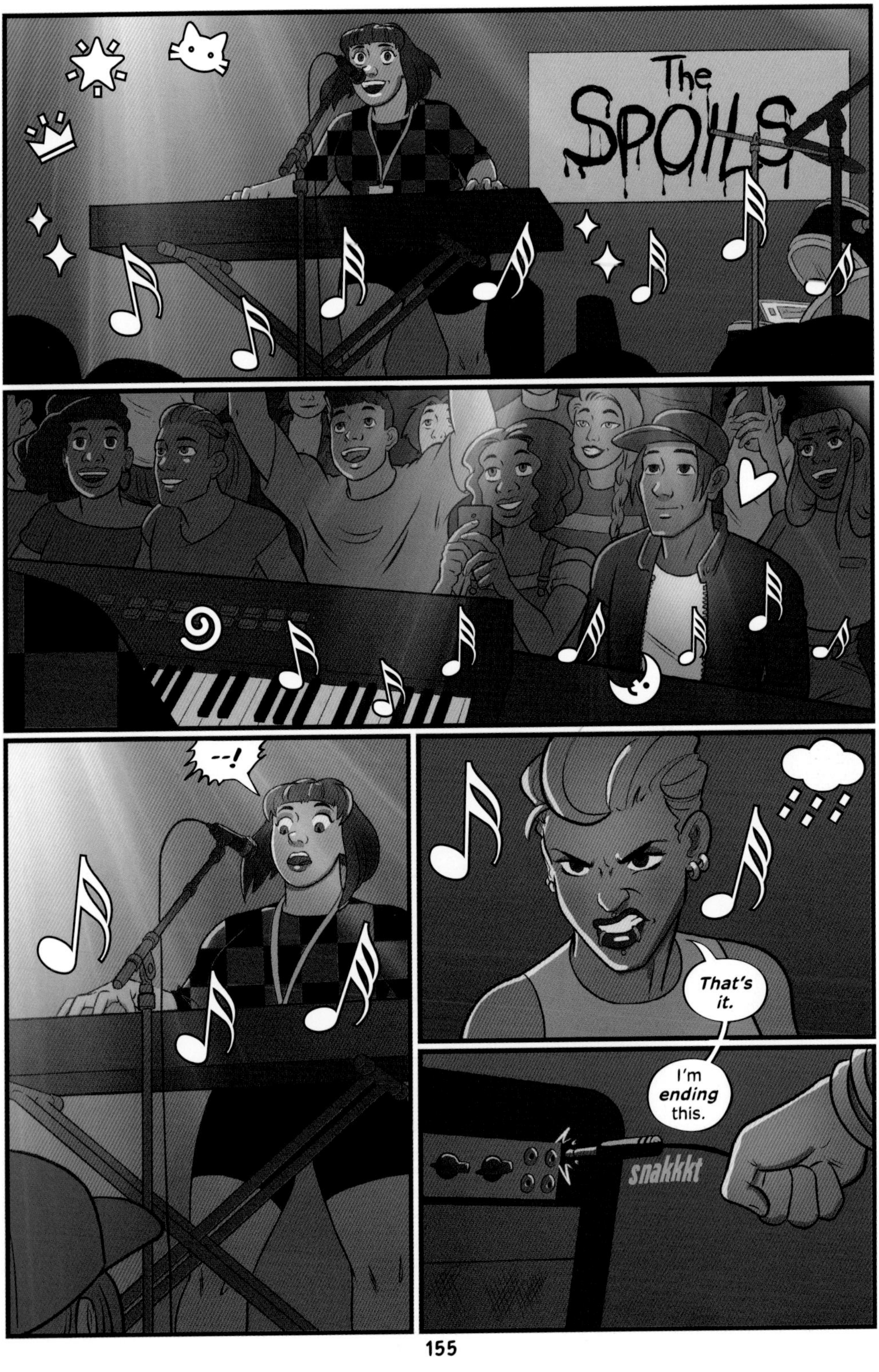
The SPOILS
--!
That's it.
I'm ending this.
snakkkt

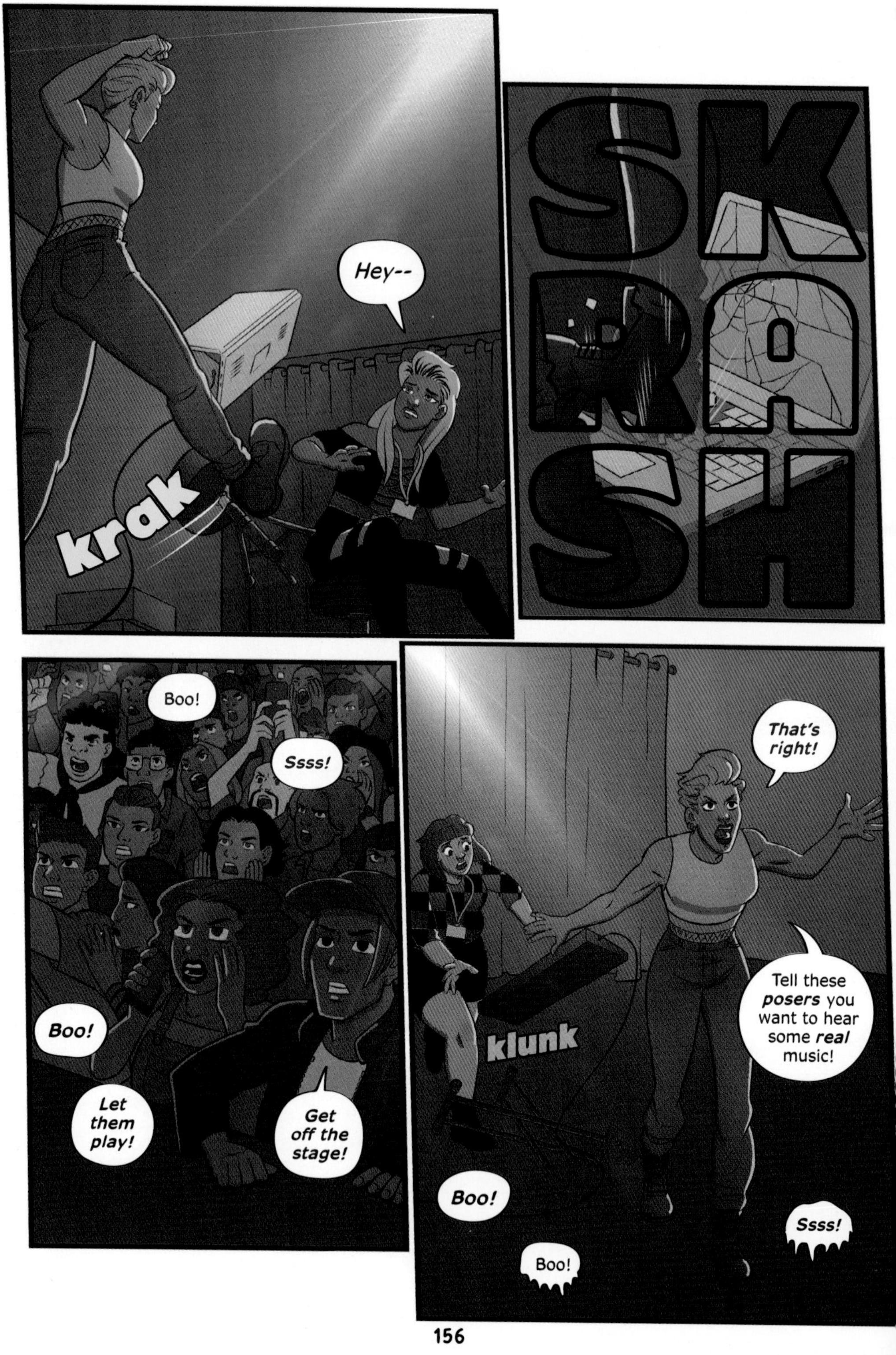
Hey--
krak
SKRASH
Boo!
Ssss!
Boo!
Let them play!
Get off the stage!
That's right!
Tell these *posers* you want to hear some *real* music!
klunk
Boo!
Boo!
Ssss!

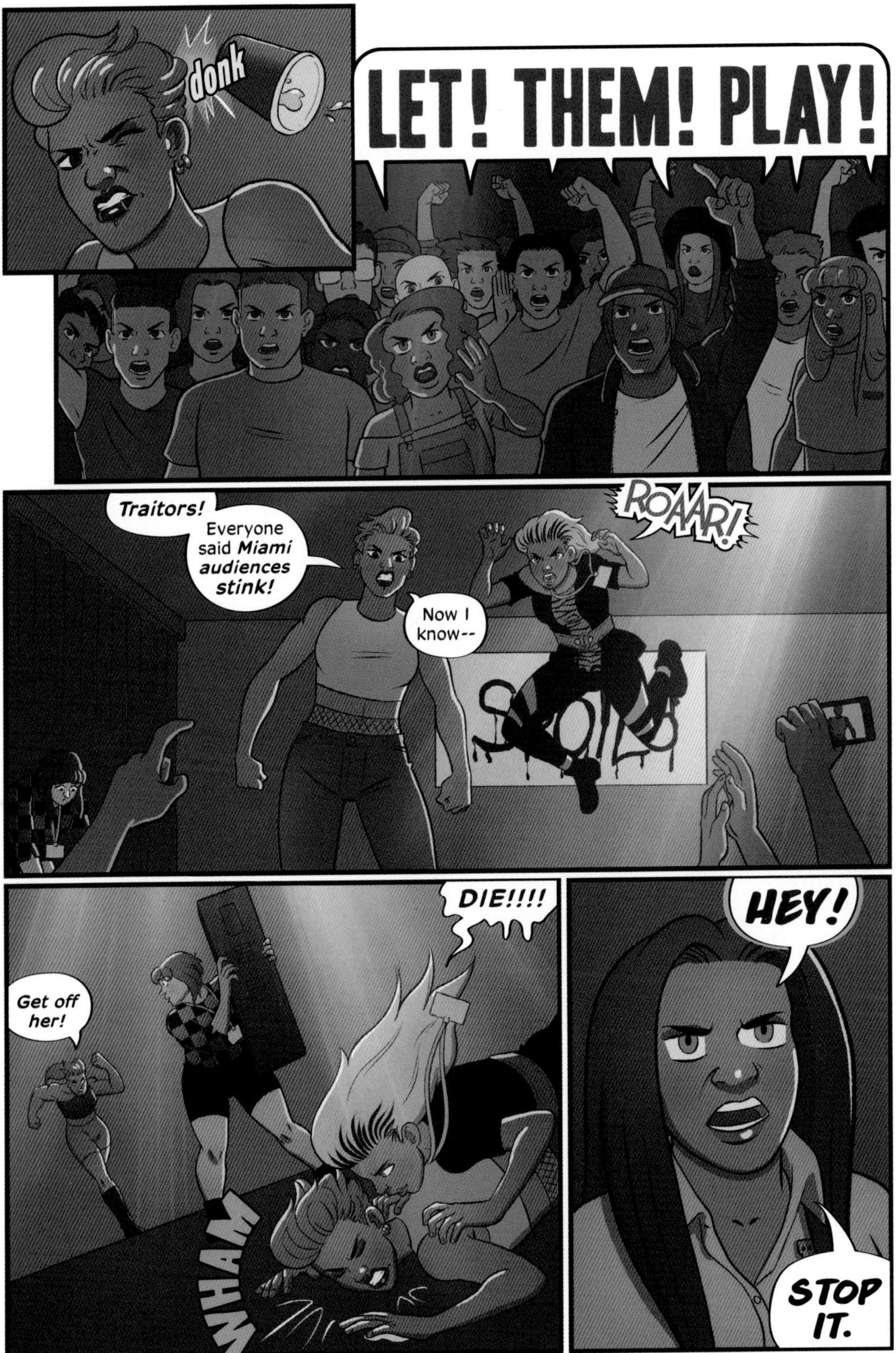
donk
LET! THEM! PLAY!
Traitors!
Everyone said *Miami audiences* *stink!*
ROAAR!
Now I know--
SPOILS
DIE!!!!
Get off her!
WHAM
HEY!
STOP IT.

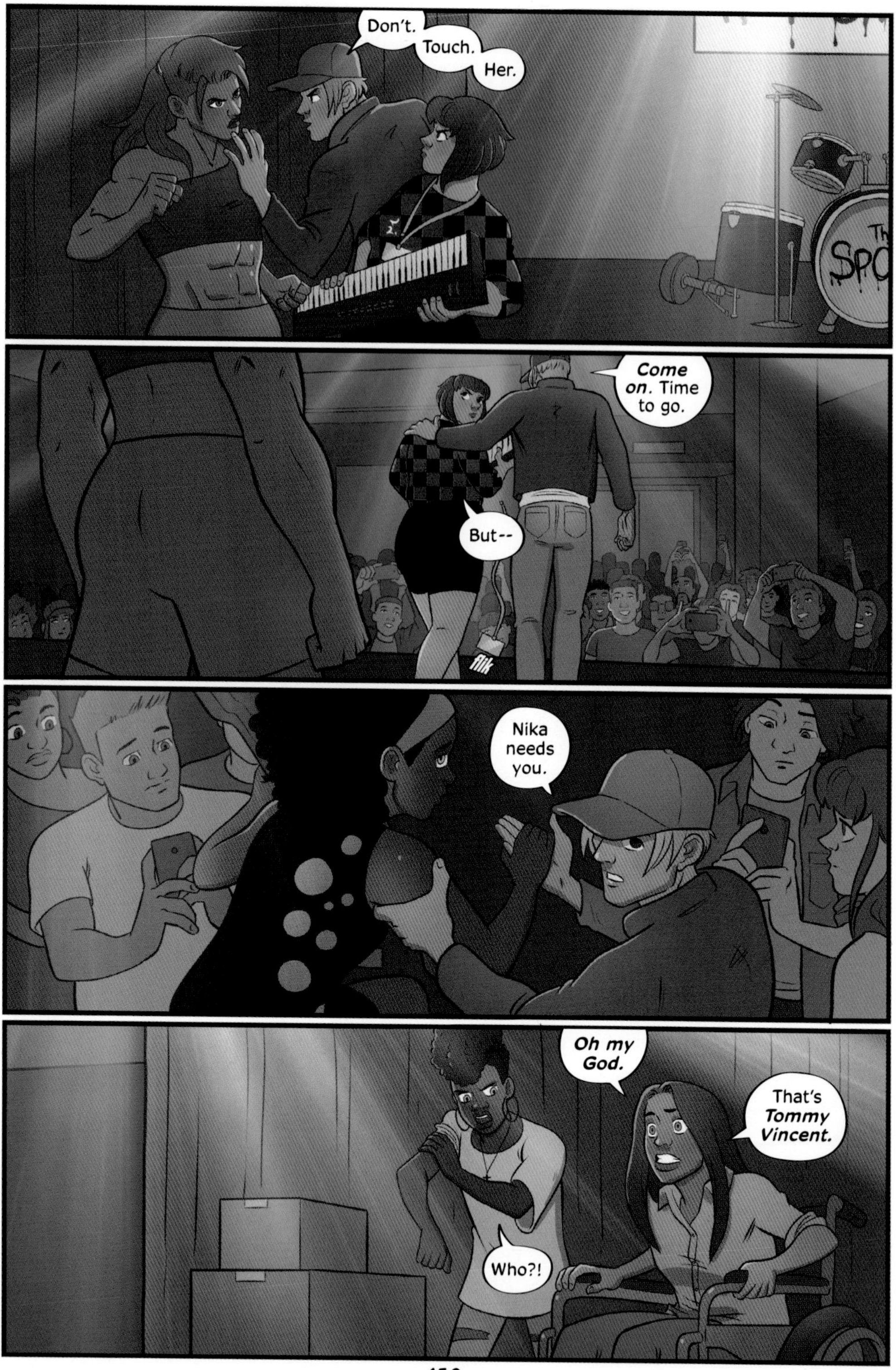
Don't.
Touch.
Her.
Come on. Time to go.
But--
Nika needs you.
Oh my God.
That's *Tommy Vincent.*
Who?!

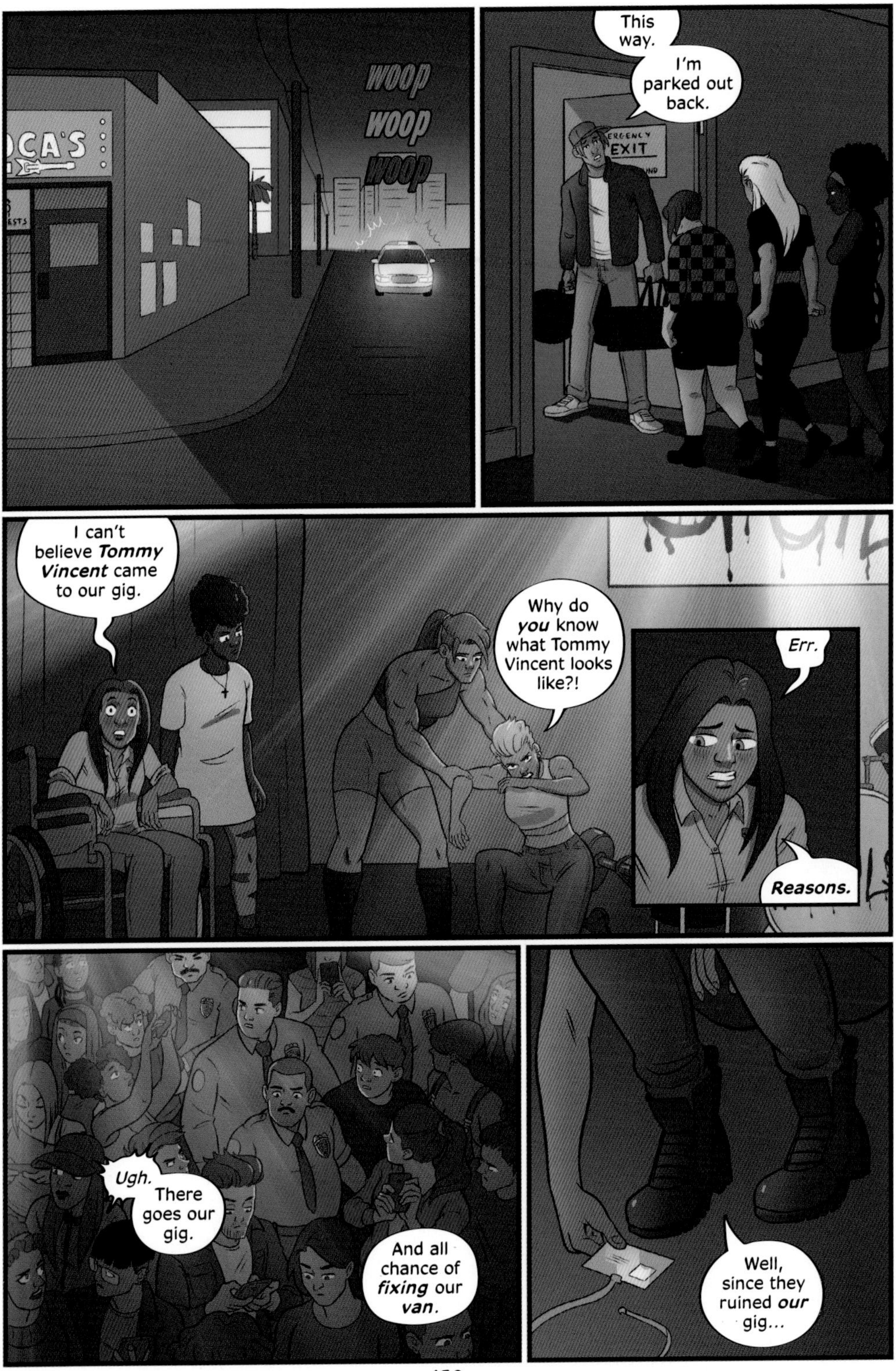
woop
woop
woop
OCA'S
EXIT
This way.
I'm parked out back.
I can't believe *Tommy Vincent* came to our gig.
Why do *you* know what Tommy Vincent looks like?!
Err.
Reasons.
Ugh.
There goes our gig.
And all chance of ***fixing*** our ***van***.
Well, since they ruined ***our*** gig...

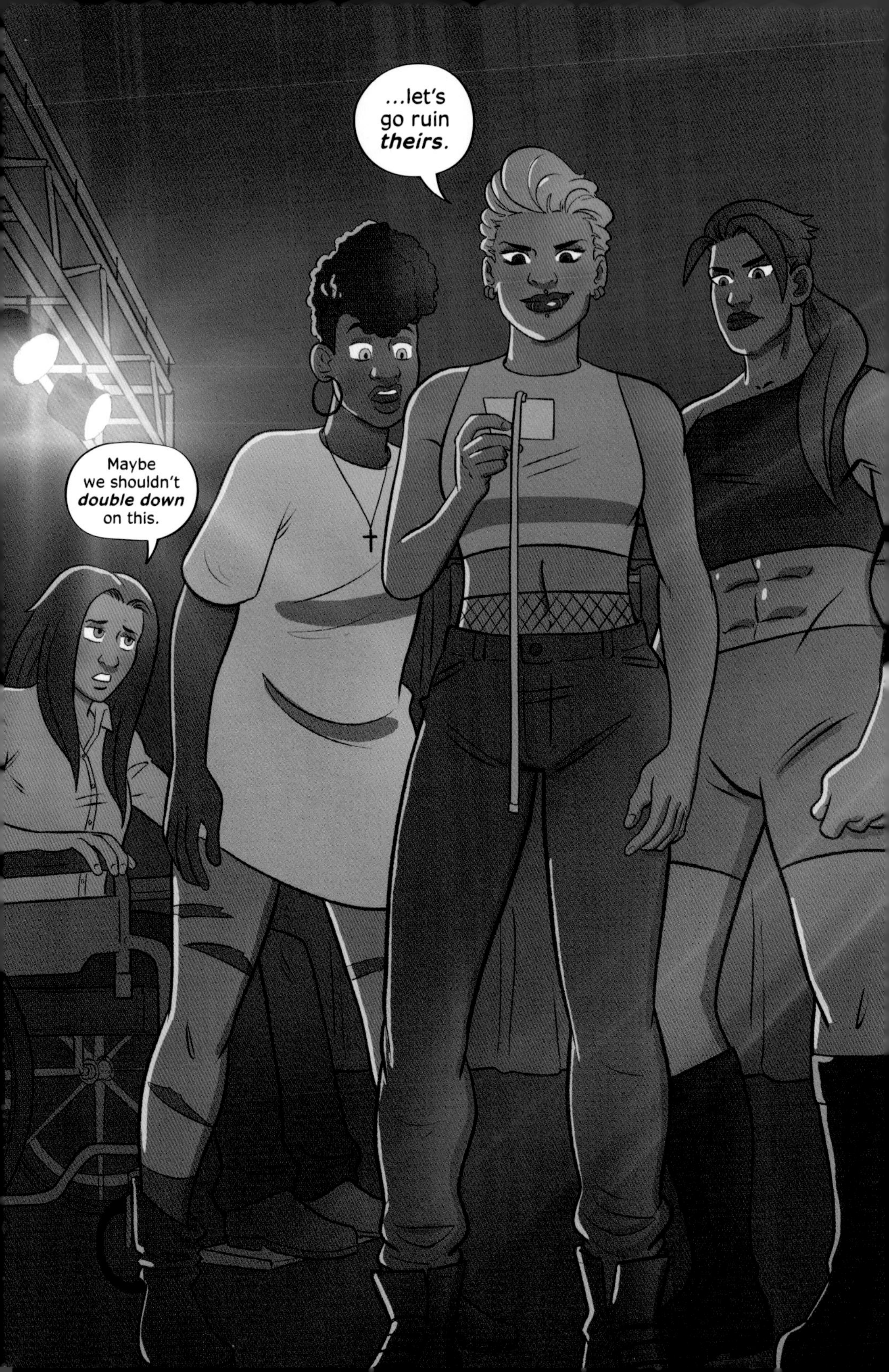
...let's go ruin ***theirs.***
Maybe we shouldn't ***double down*** on this.

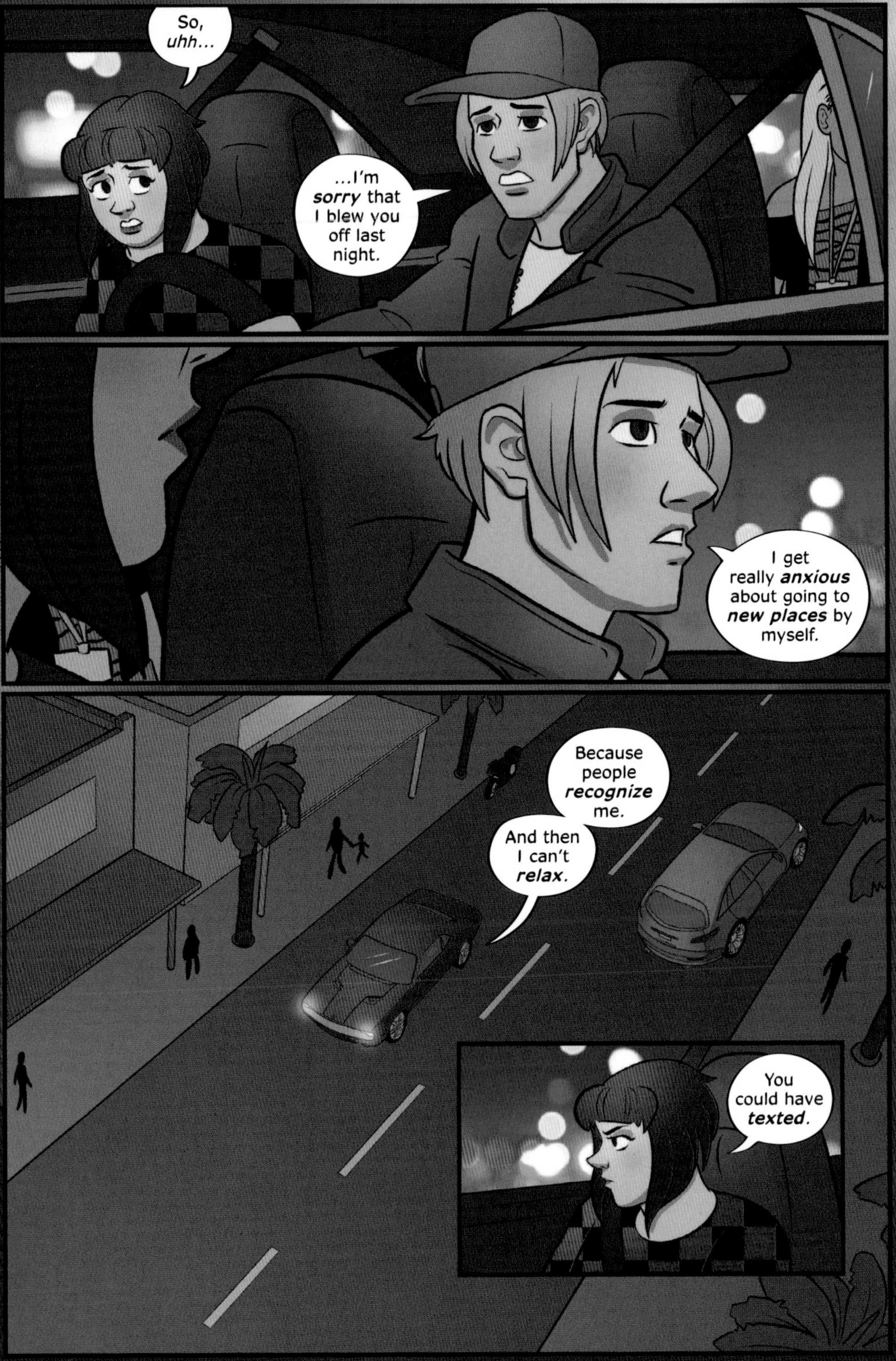
So, *uhh*...
...I'm *sorry* that I blew you off last night.
I get really *anxious* about going to *new places* by myself.
Because people *recognize* me.
And then I can't *relax*.
You could have *texted*.

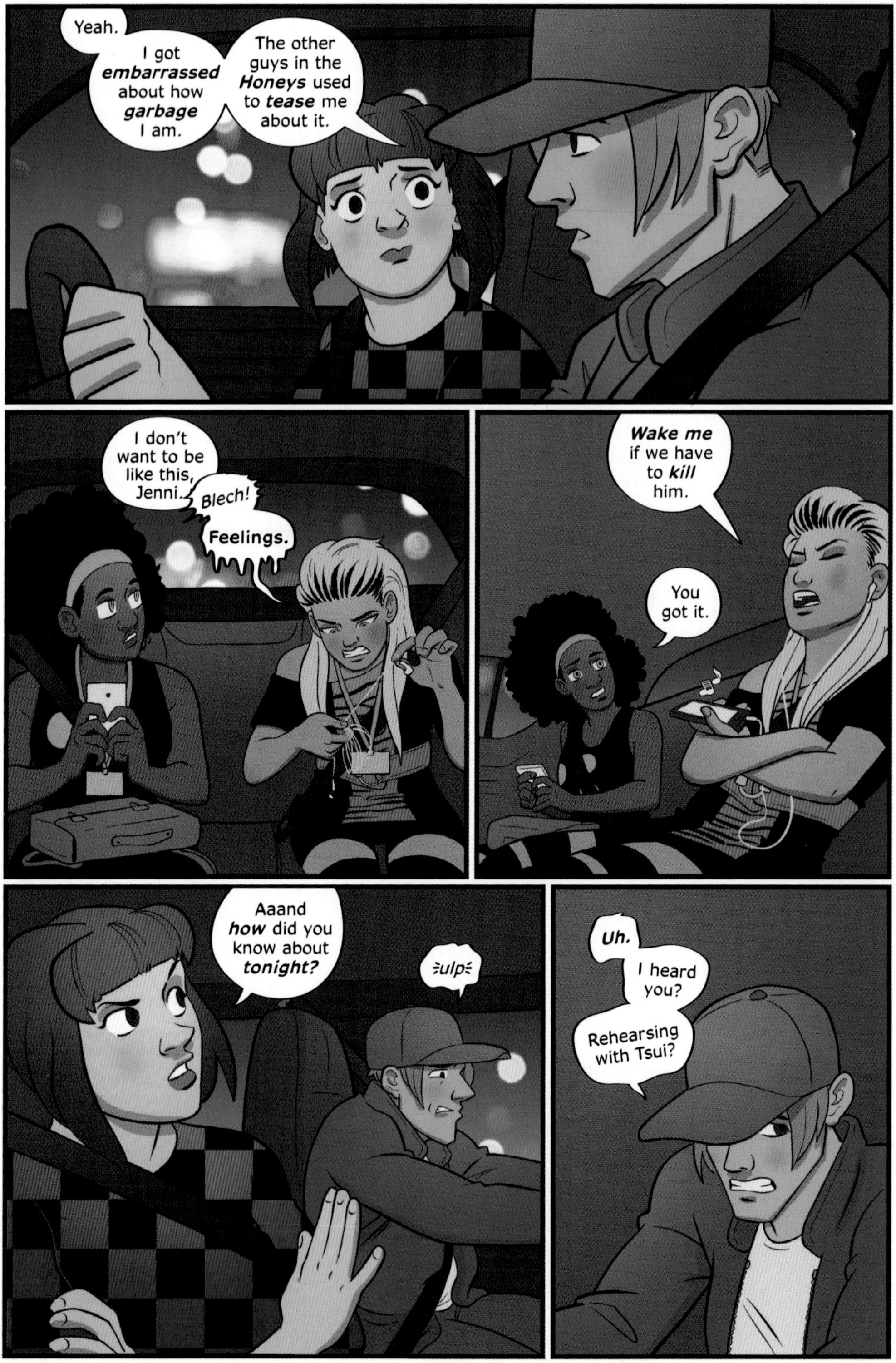
Yeah.
I got ***embarrassed*** about how ***garbage*** I am.
The other guys in the ***Honeys*** used to ***tease*** me about it.
I don't want to be like this, Jenni.
Blech!
Feelings.
Wake me if we have to ***kill*** him.
You got it.
Aaand ***how*** did you know about ***tonight?***
ulp
Uh.
I heard you?
Rehearsing with Tsui?

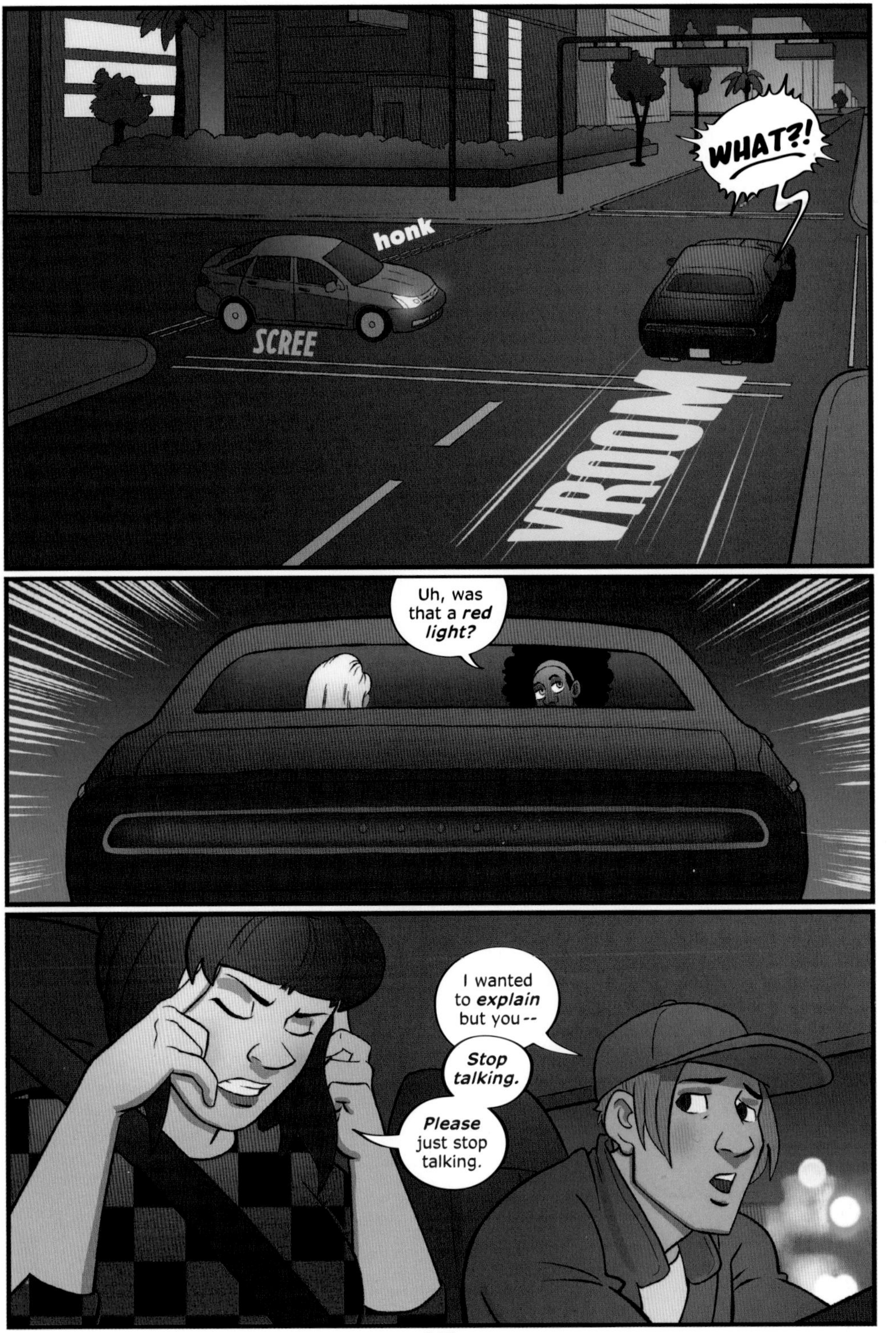
WHAT?!
honk
SCREE
VROOM
Uh, was that a *red light?*
I wanted to *explain* but you --
Stop talking.
Please just stop talking.

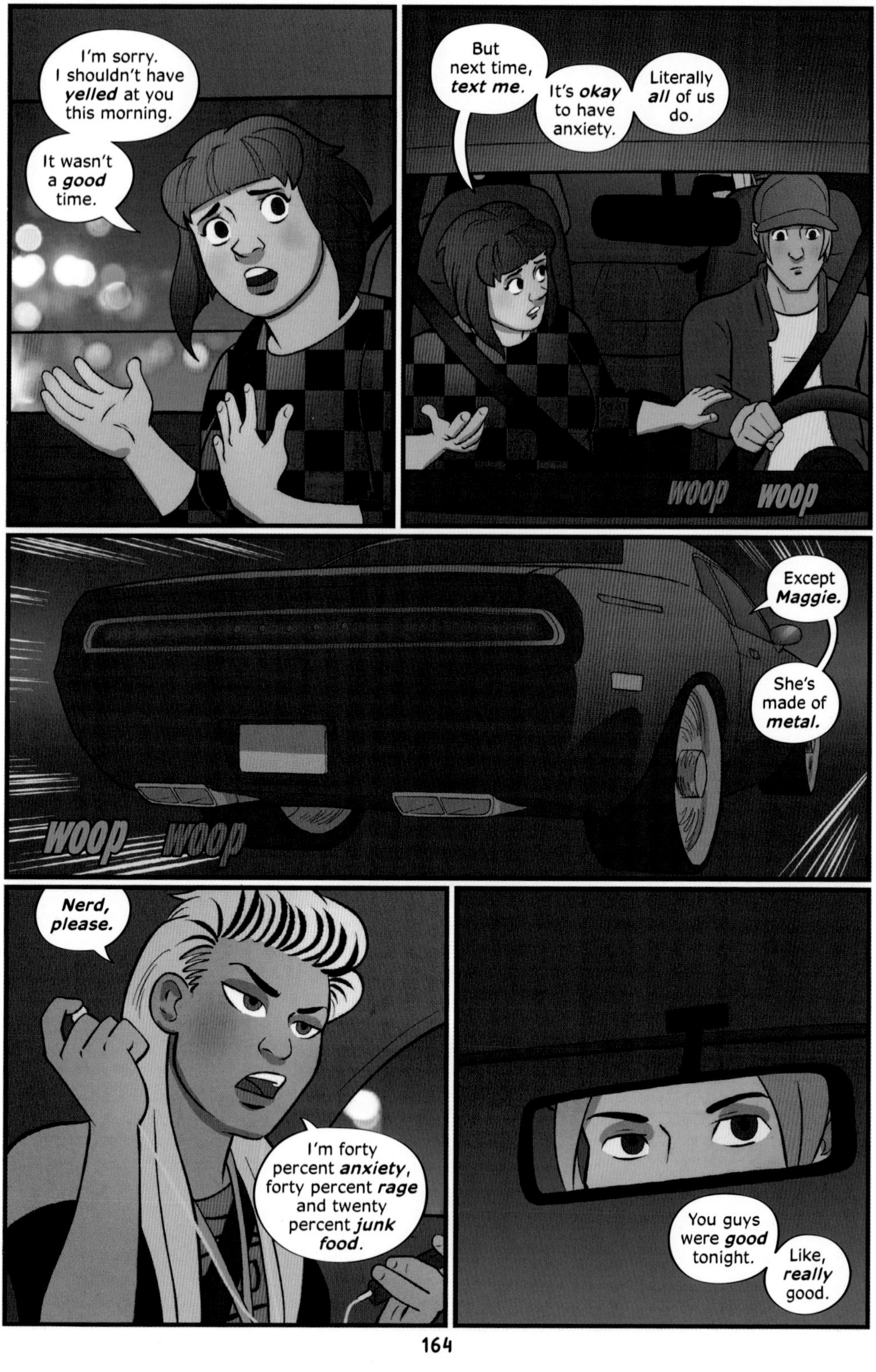

I'm sorry. I shouldn't have *yelled* at you this morning.
It wasn't a *good* time.
But next time, *text me*.
It's *okay* to have anxiety.
Literally *all* of us do.
WOOP WOOP
Except *Maggie*.
She's made of *metal*.
WOOP WOOP
Nerd, please.
I'm forty percent *anxiety*, forty percent *rage* and twenty percent *junk food*.
You guys were *good* tonight.
Like, *really* good.

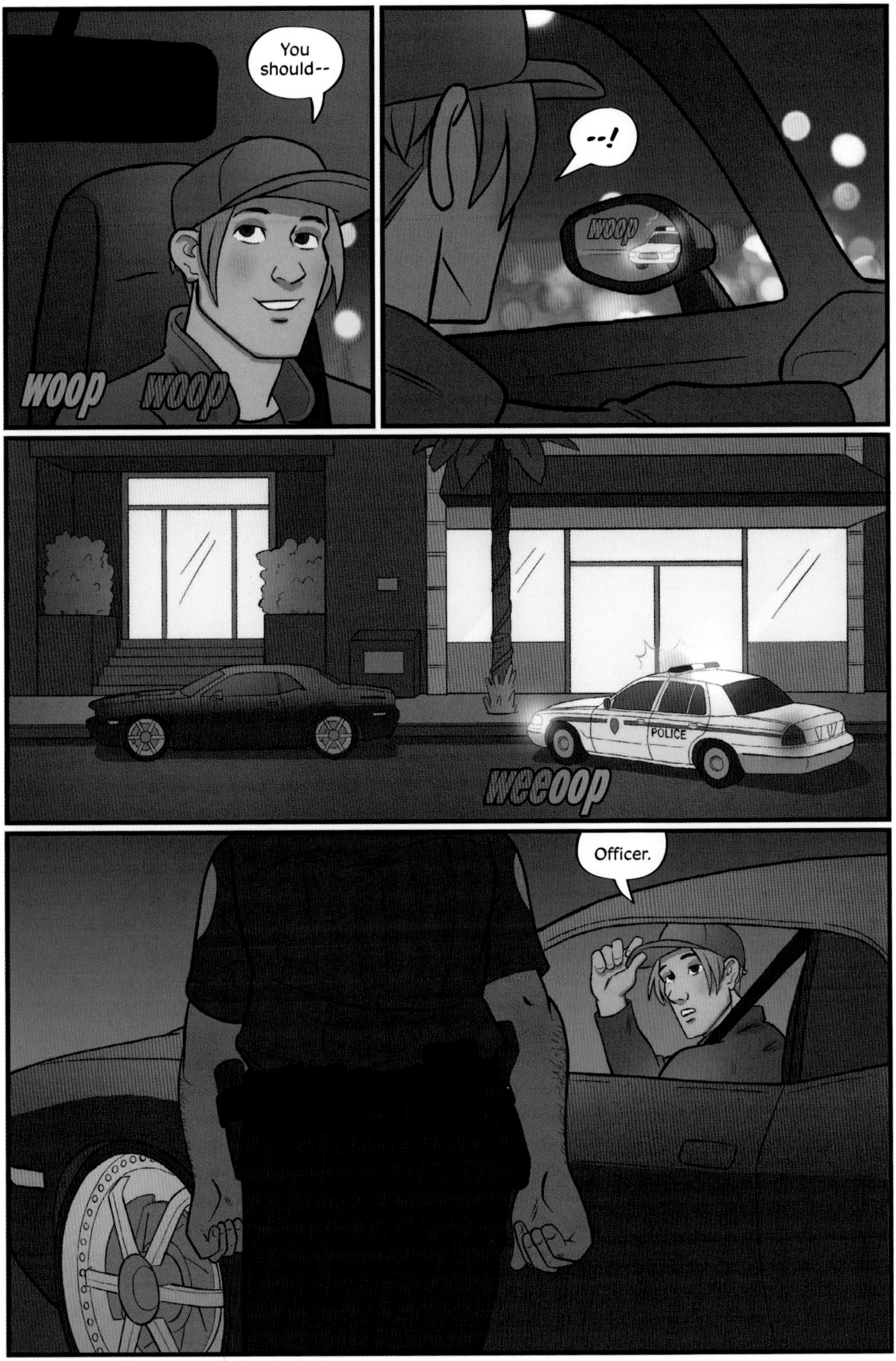
You should--
woop
woop
--!
woop
POLICE
weeoop
Officer.

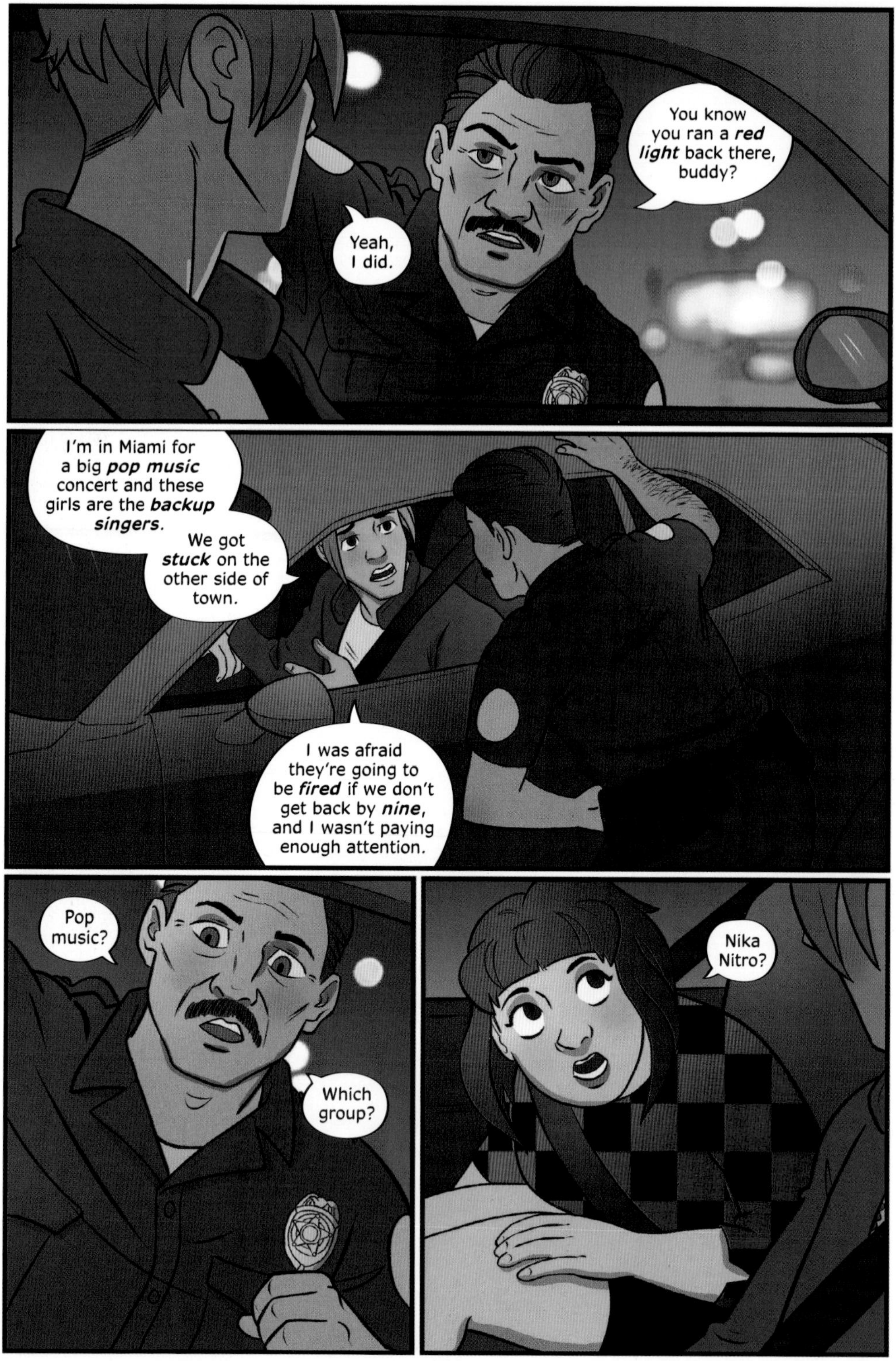
You know you ran a ***red light*** back there, buddy?
Yeah, I did.
I'm in Miami for a big ***pop music*** concert and these girls are the ***backup singers***.
We got ***stuck*** on the other side of town.
I was afraid they're going to be ***fired*** if we don't get back by ***nine***, and I wasn't paying enough attention.
Pop music?
Which group?
Nika Nitro?

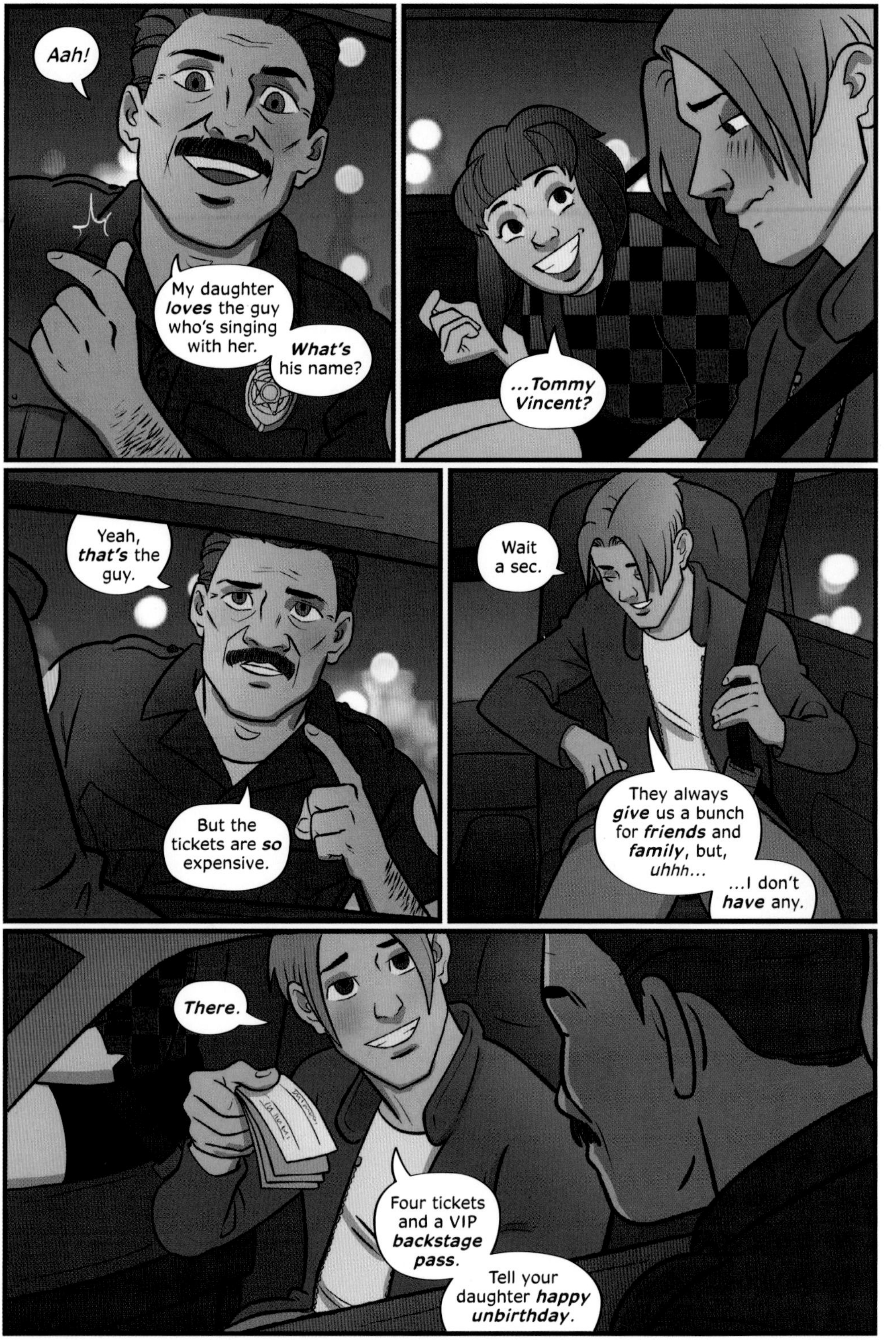
Aah!
My daughter *loves* the guy who's singing with her.
What's his name?
...Tommy Vincent?
Yeah, *that's* the guy.
But the tickets are *so* expensive.
Wait a sec.
They always *give* us a bunch for *friends* and *family*, but, *uhhh...*
...I don't *have* any.
There.
Four tickets and a VIP *backstage pass*.
Tell your daughter *happy unbirthday*.

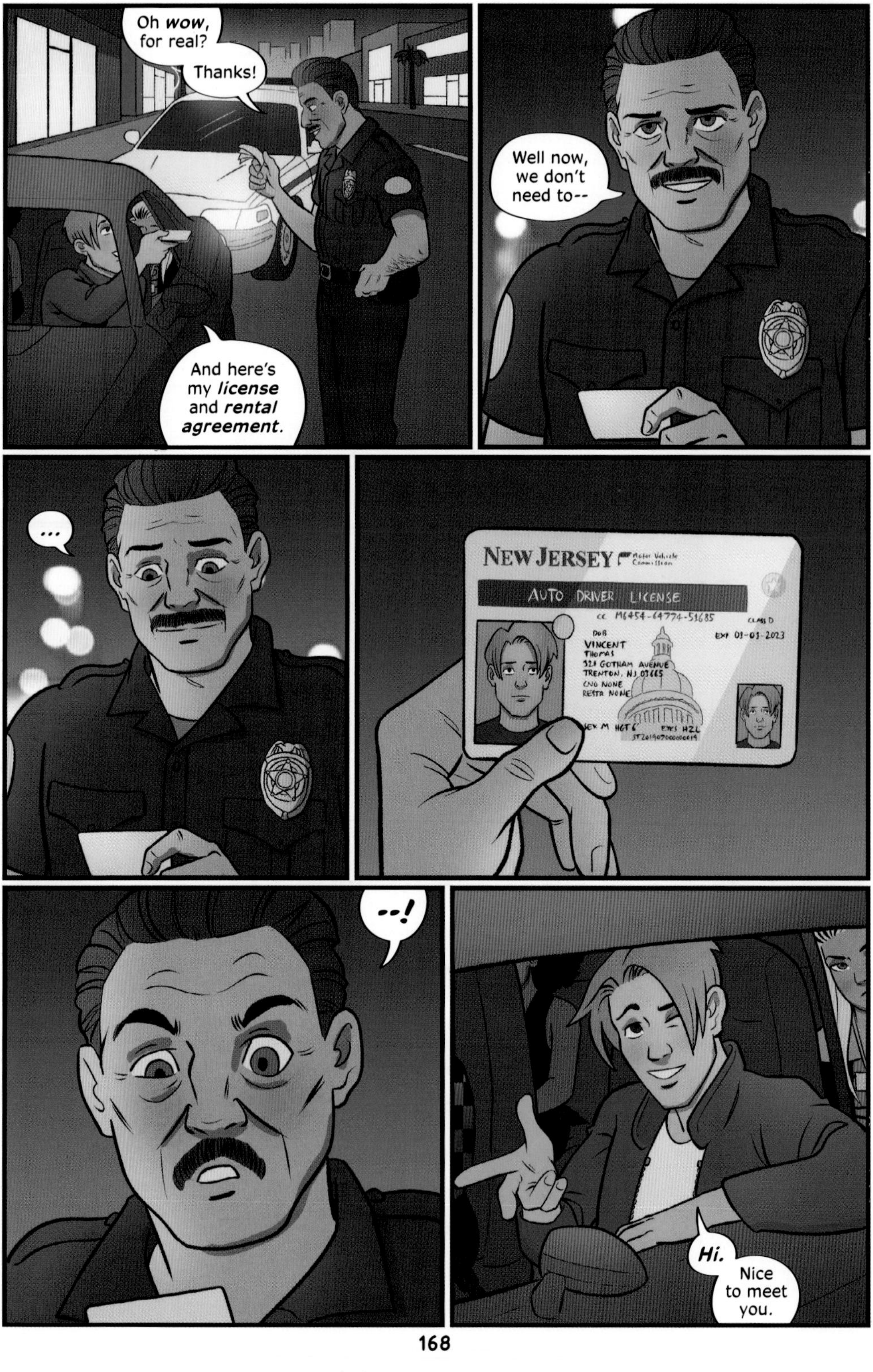
Oh *wow*, for real?
Thanks!
And here's my ***license*** and ***rental agreement.***
Well now, we don't need to--
...
NEW JERSEY Motor Vehicle Commission
AUTO DRIVER LICENSE
CC M6454-64774-51685
CLASS D
DOB
EXP 01-01-2023
VINCENT
THOMAS
321 GOTHAM AVENUE
TRENTON, NJ 03665
--!
Hi.
Nice to meet you.

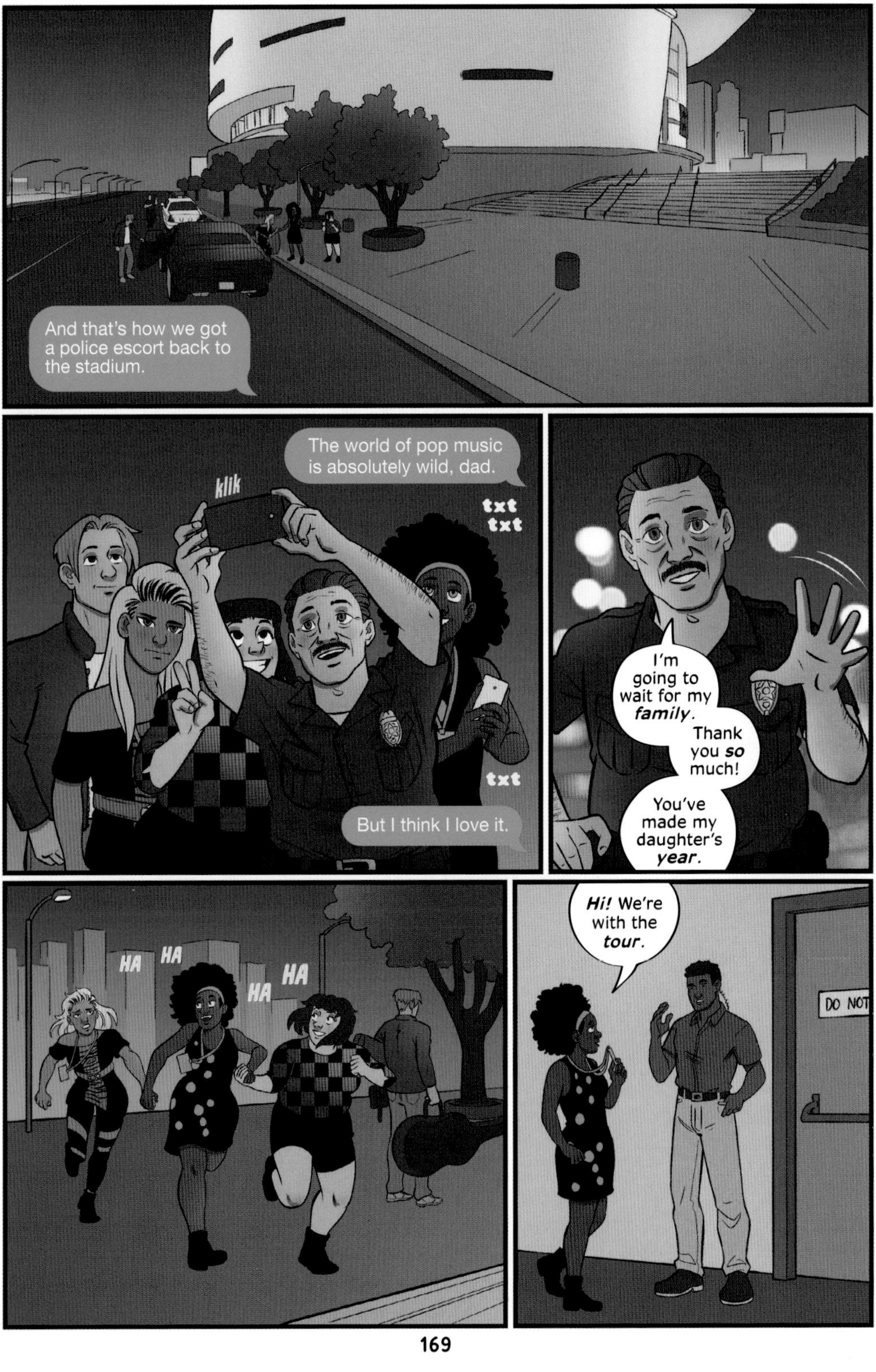
And that's how we got a police escort back to the stadium.
The world of pop music is absolutely wild, dad.
klik
txt
txt
txt
But I think I love it.
I'm going to wait for my *family*.
Thank you ***so*** much!
You've made my daughter's ***year***.
HA
HA
HA
HA
Hi! We're with the ***tour***.
DO NOT

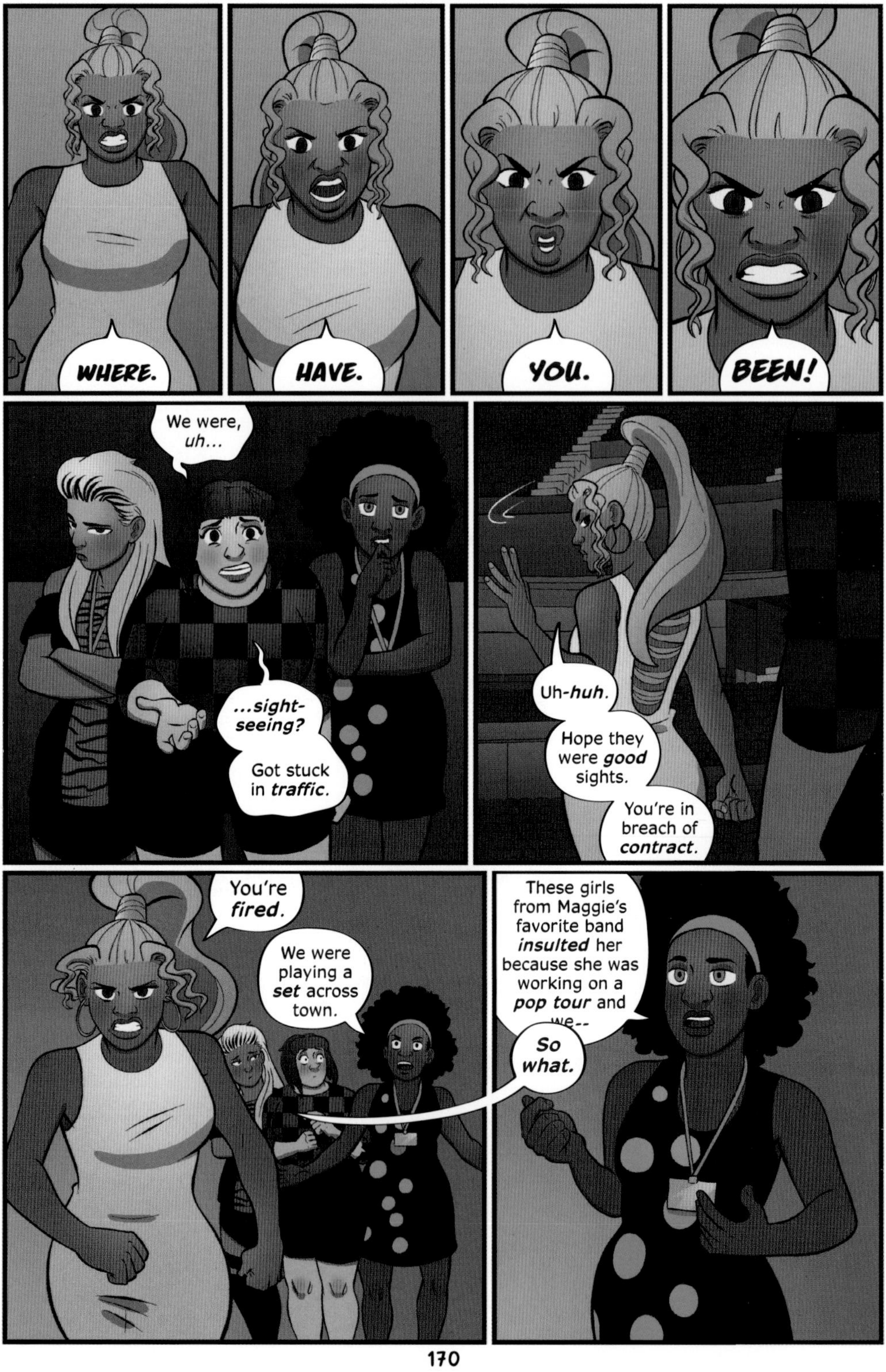
WHERE.
HAVE.
YOU.
BEEN!
We were, *uh*...
...sight-seeing?
Got stuck in *traffic*.
Uh-*huh*.
Hope they were *good* sights.
You're in breach of *contract*.
You're *fired*.
We were playing a *set* across town.
These girls from Maggie's favorite band *insulted* her because she was working on a *pop tour* and we--
So what.

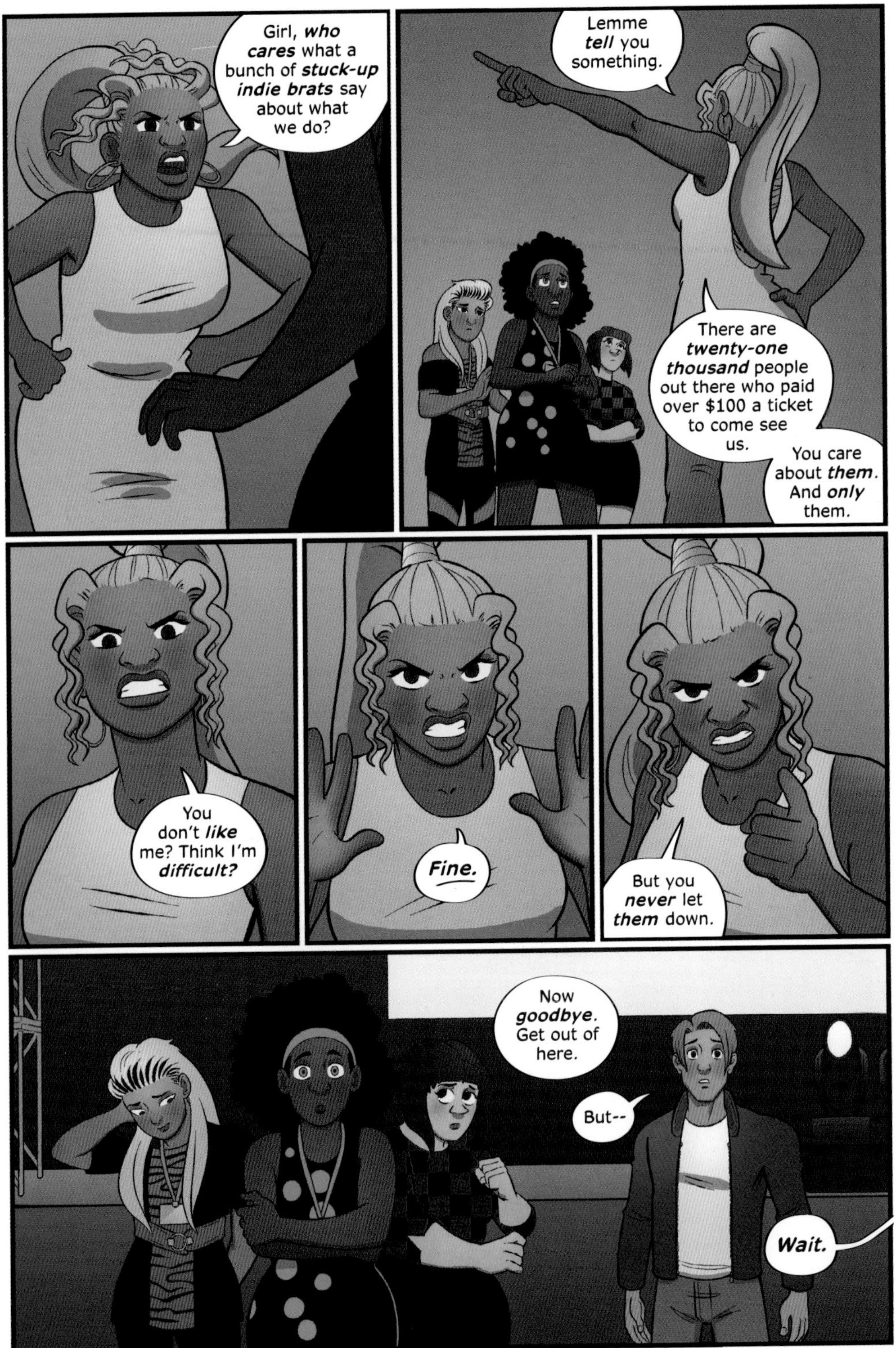
Girl, ***who cares*** what a bunch of ***stuck-up indie brats*** say about what we do?
Lemme ***tell*** you something.
There are ***twenty-one thousand*** people out there who paid over $100 a ticket to come see us.
You care about ***them***. And ***only*** them.
You don't ***like*** me? Think I'm ***difficult?***
Fine.
But you ***never*** let ***them*** down.
Now ***goodbye***. Get out of here.
But--
Wait.

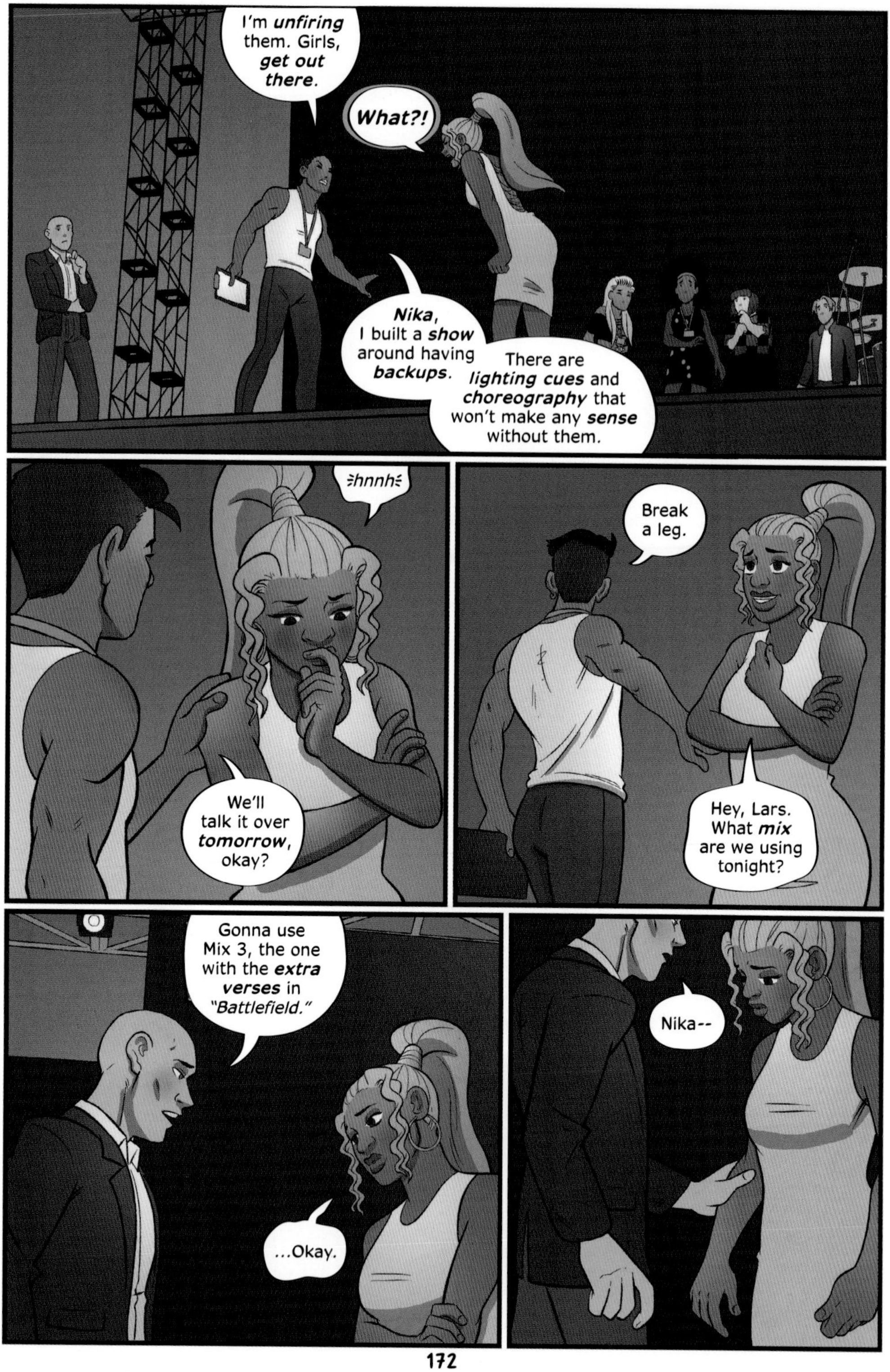
I'm *unfiring* them. Girls, *get out there*.
What?!
Nika, I built a *show* around having *backups*.
There are *lighting cues* and *choreography* that won't make any *sense* without them.
hnnh
We'll talk it over *tomorrow*, okay?
Break a leg.
Hey, Lars. What *mix* are we using tonight?
Gonna use Mix 3, the one with the *extra verses* in *"Battlefield."*
...Okay.
Nika--

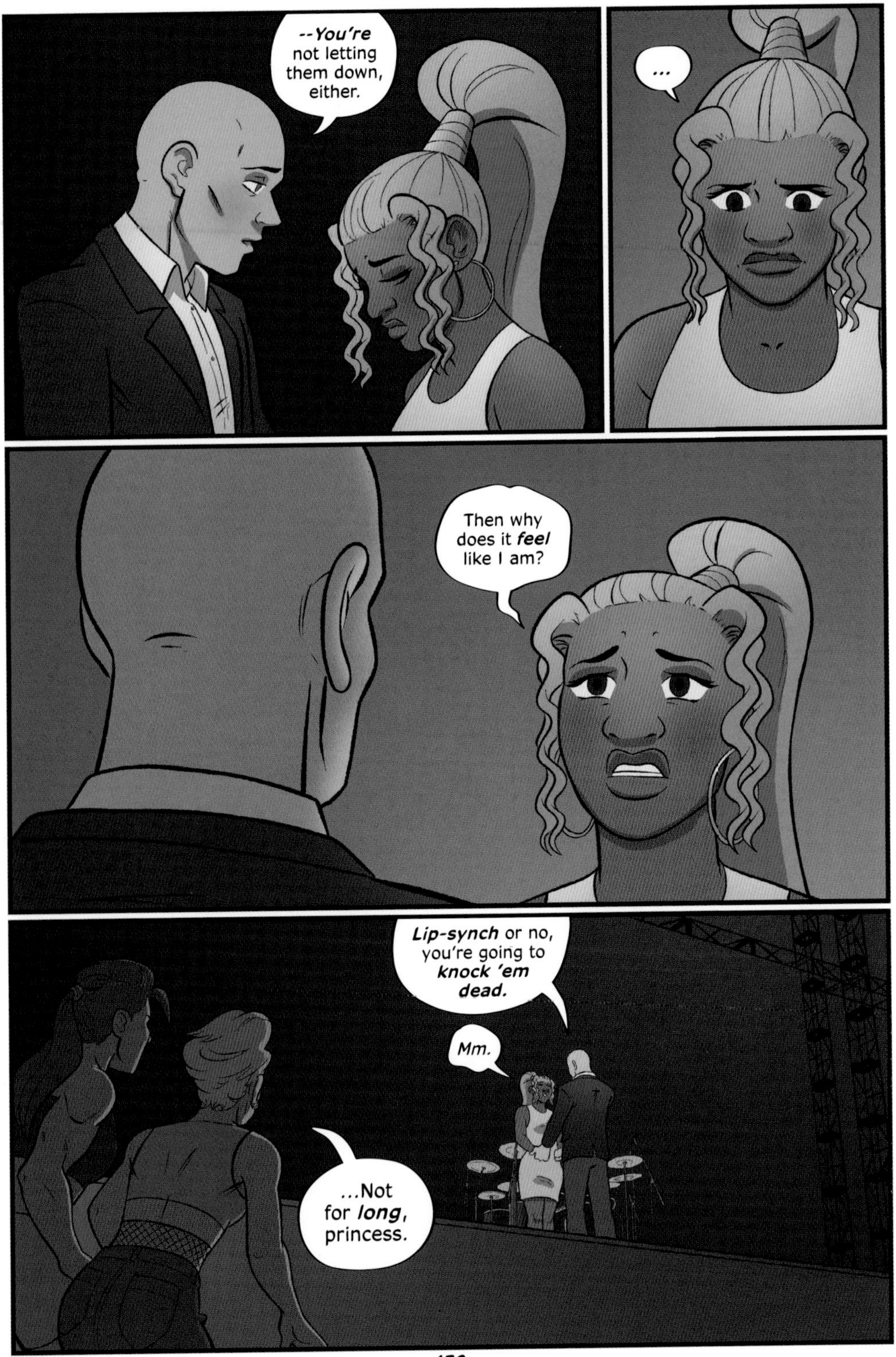
--*You're* not letting them down, either.
...
Then why does it *feel* like I am?
Lip-synch or no, you're going to ***knock 'em dead.***
Mm.
...Not for ***long,*** princess.

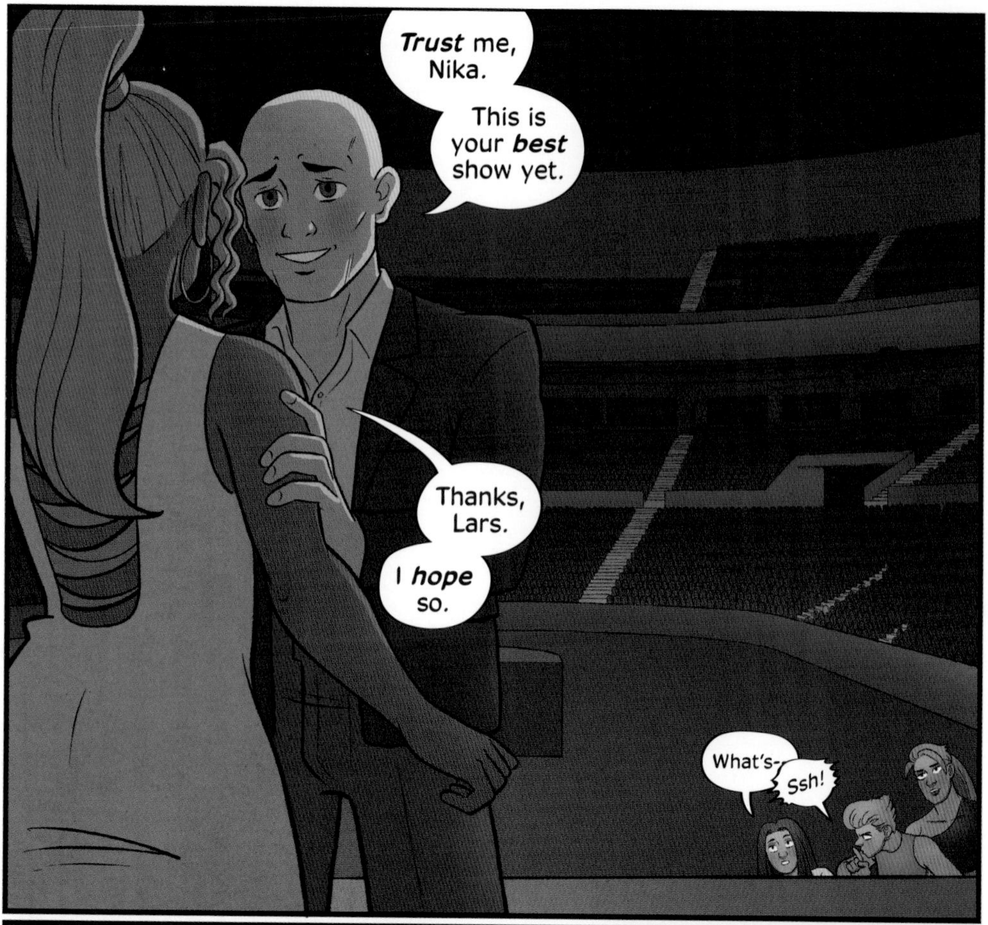
Trust me, Nika.
This is your ***best*** show yet.
Thanks, Lars.
I ***hope*** so.
What's-
Ssh!

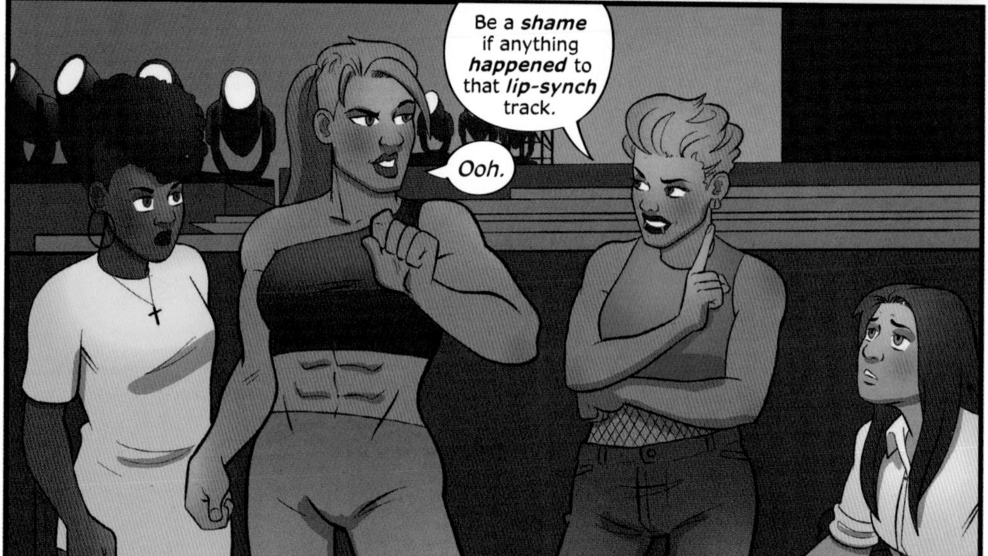
Be a ***shame*** if anything ***happened*** to that ***lip-synch*** track.
Ooh.

CHAPTER
6

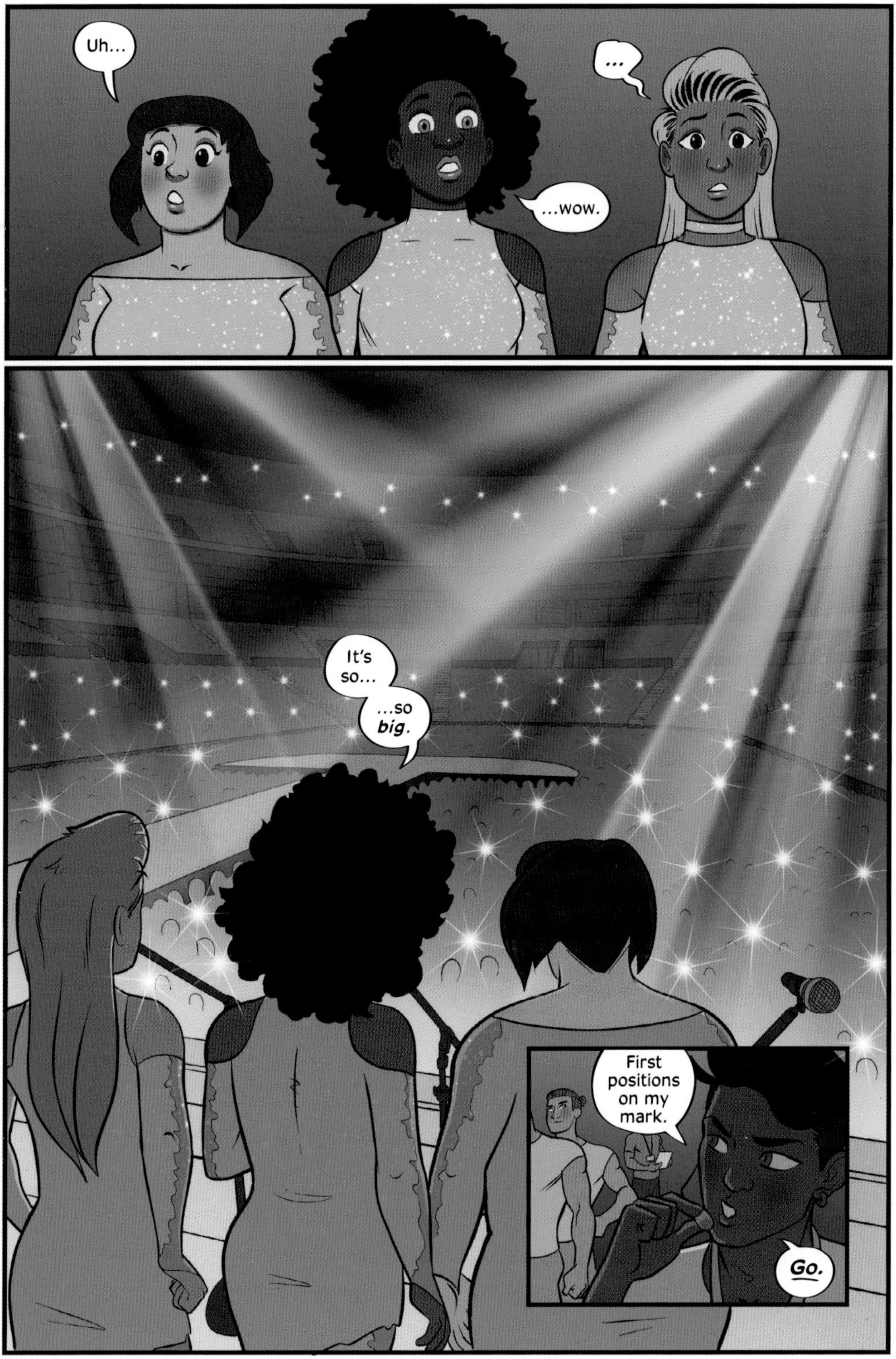
Uh...
...wow.
...
It's so...
...so *big*.
First positions on my mark.
Go.

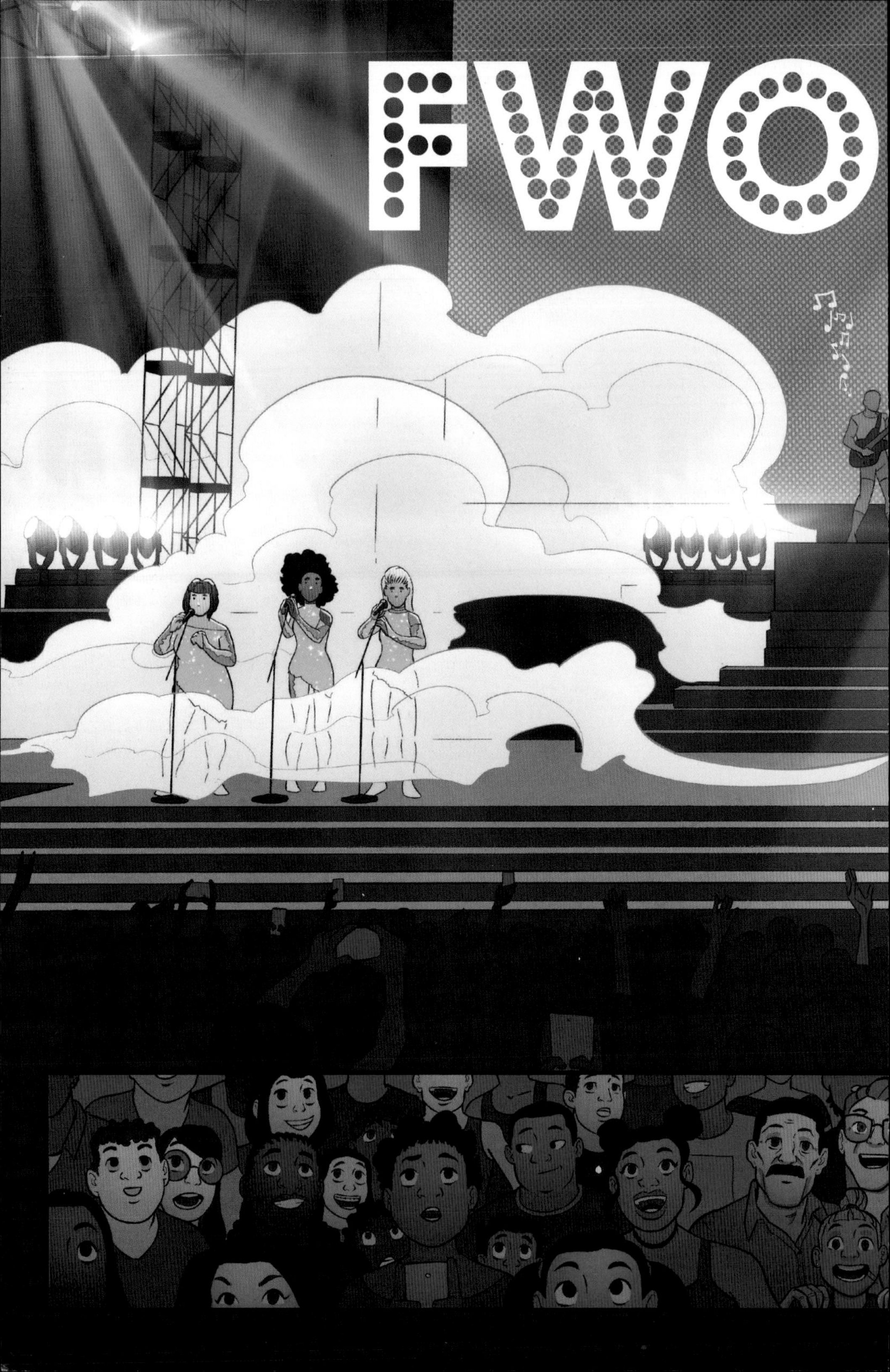
FWO

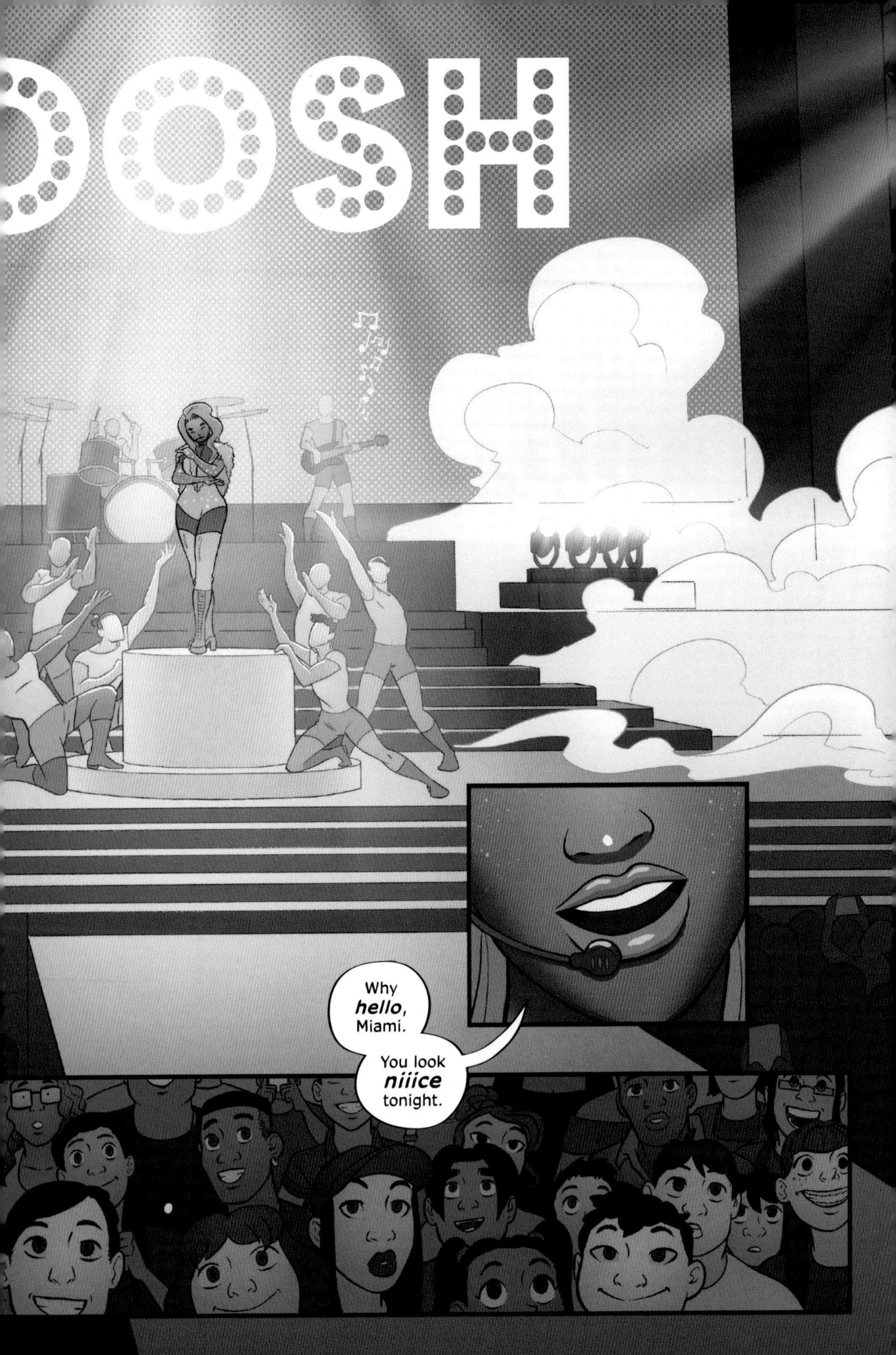
OOSH
Why *hello*, Miami.
You look ***niiice*** tonight.

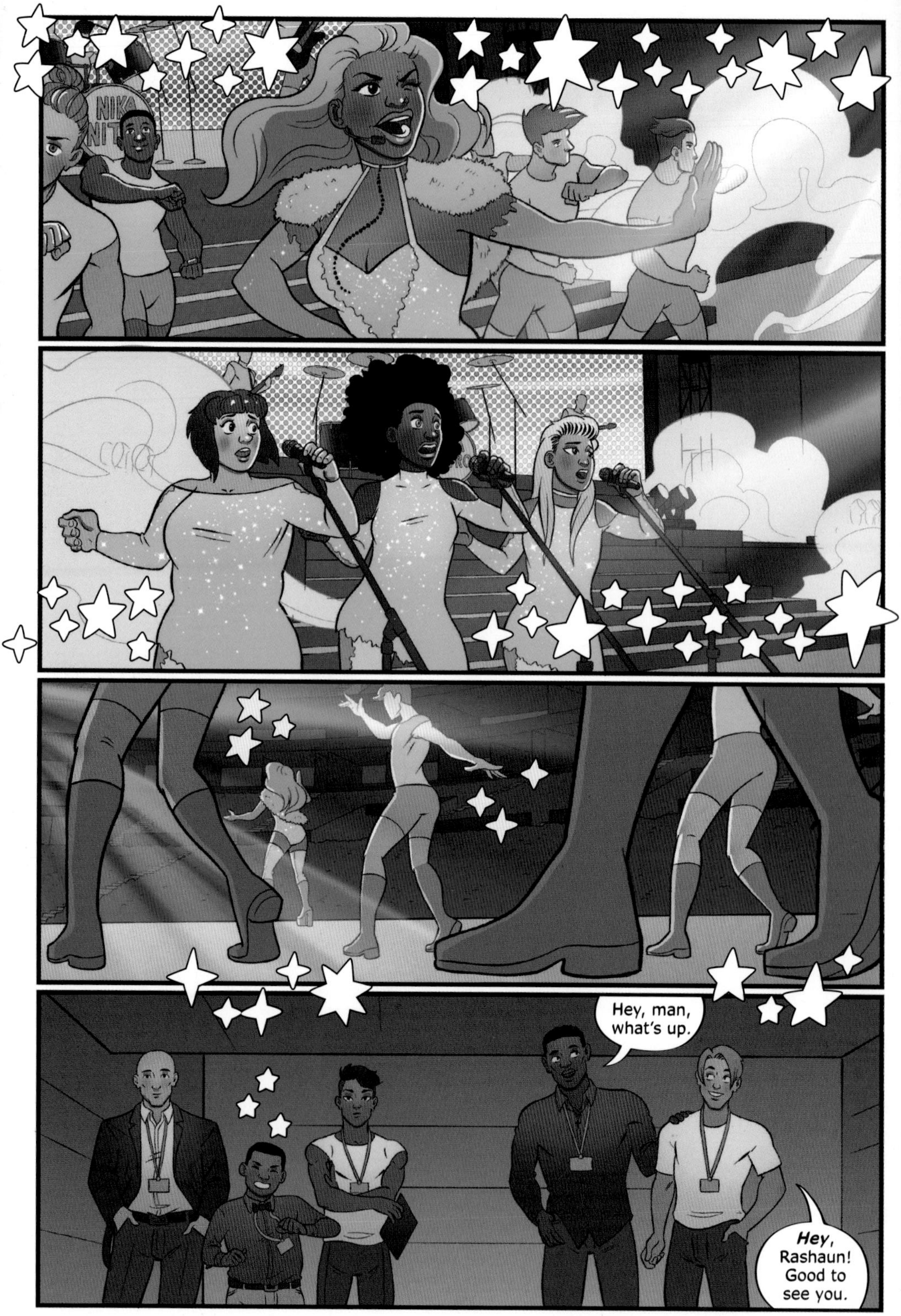
NIKA NITE
Hey, man, what's up.
Hey, Rashaun! Good to see you.

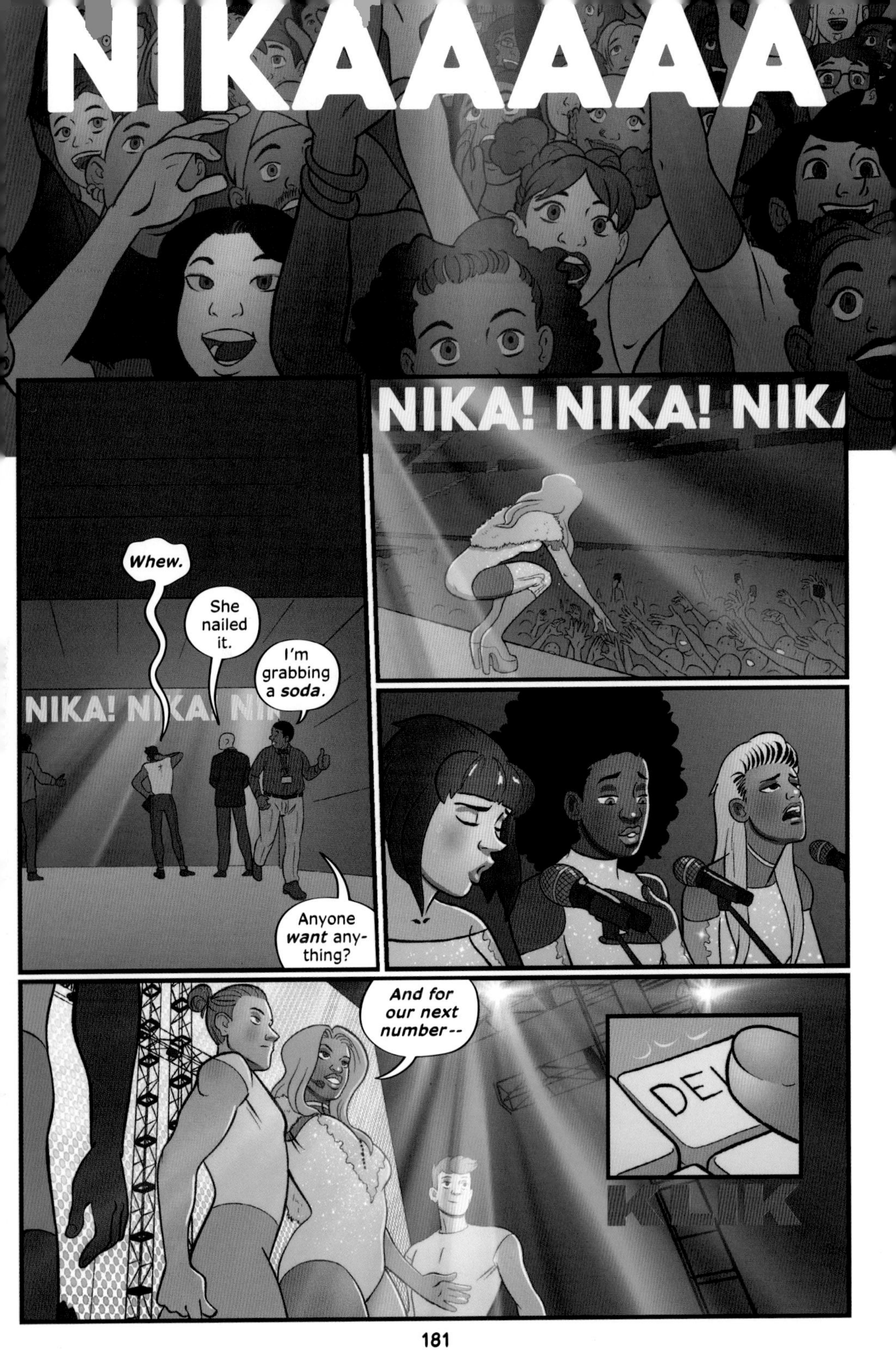
NIKAAAAA
NIKA! NIKA! NIKA
Whew.
She nailed it.
I'm grabbing a *soda*.
NIKA! NIKA! NIK
Anyone *want* anything?
And for our next number--
DE
KLIK

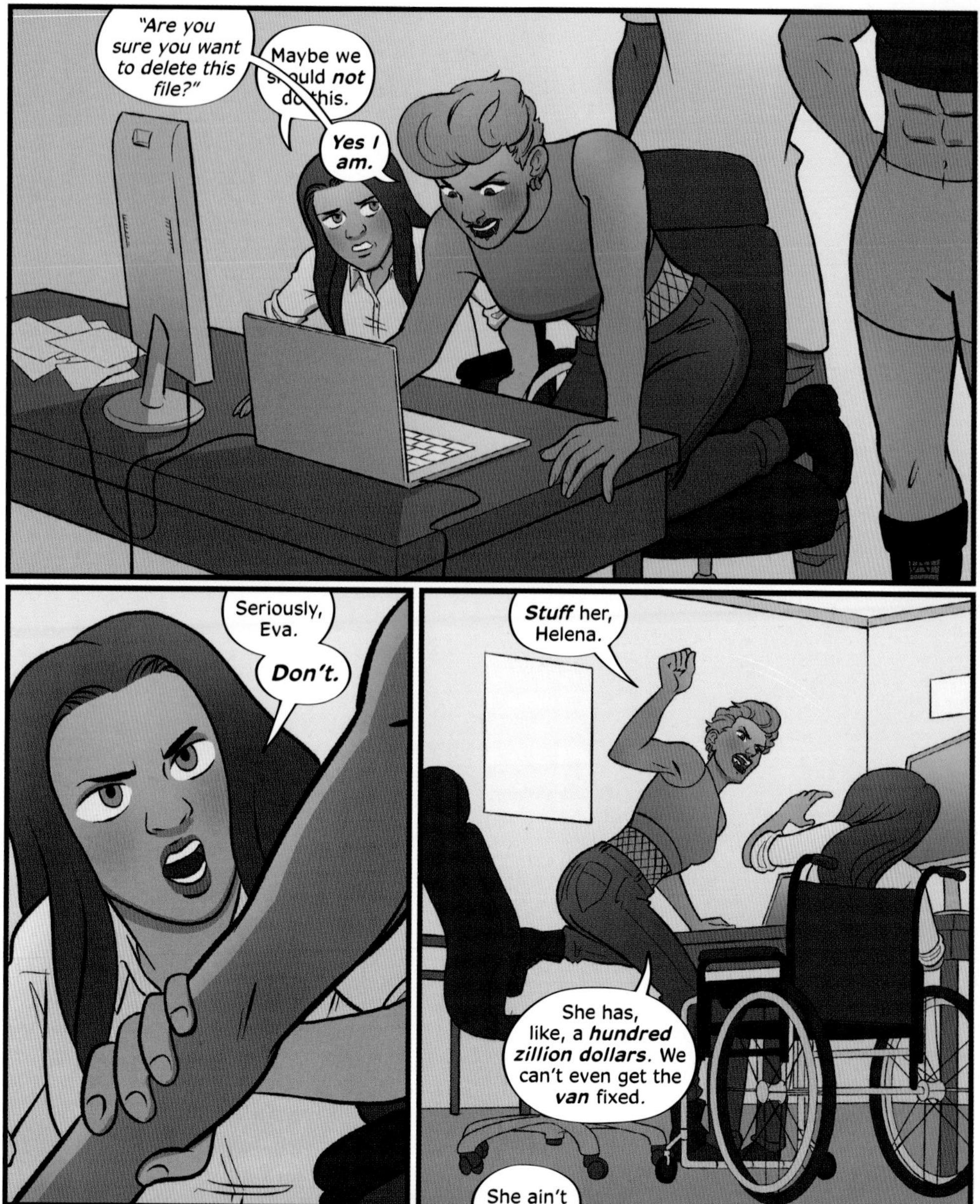
"Are you sure you want to delete this file?"
Maybe we should not do this.
Yes I am.
Seriously, Eva.
Don't.
Stuff her, Helena.
She has, like, a hundred zillion dollars. We can't even get the van fixed.
She ain't hurtin'.
KLIK
SKKKT

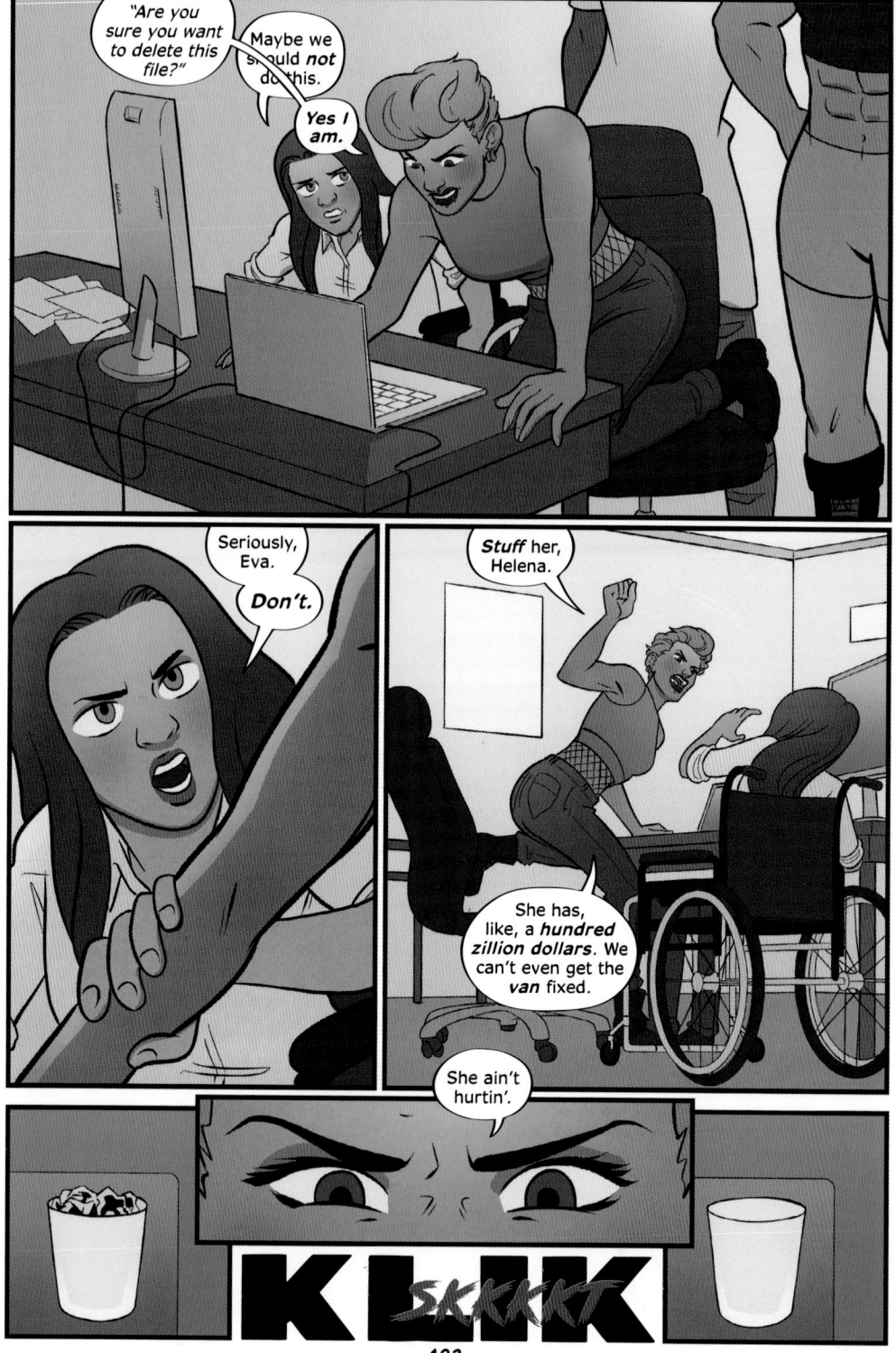

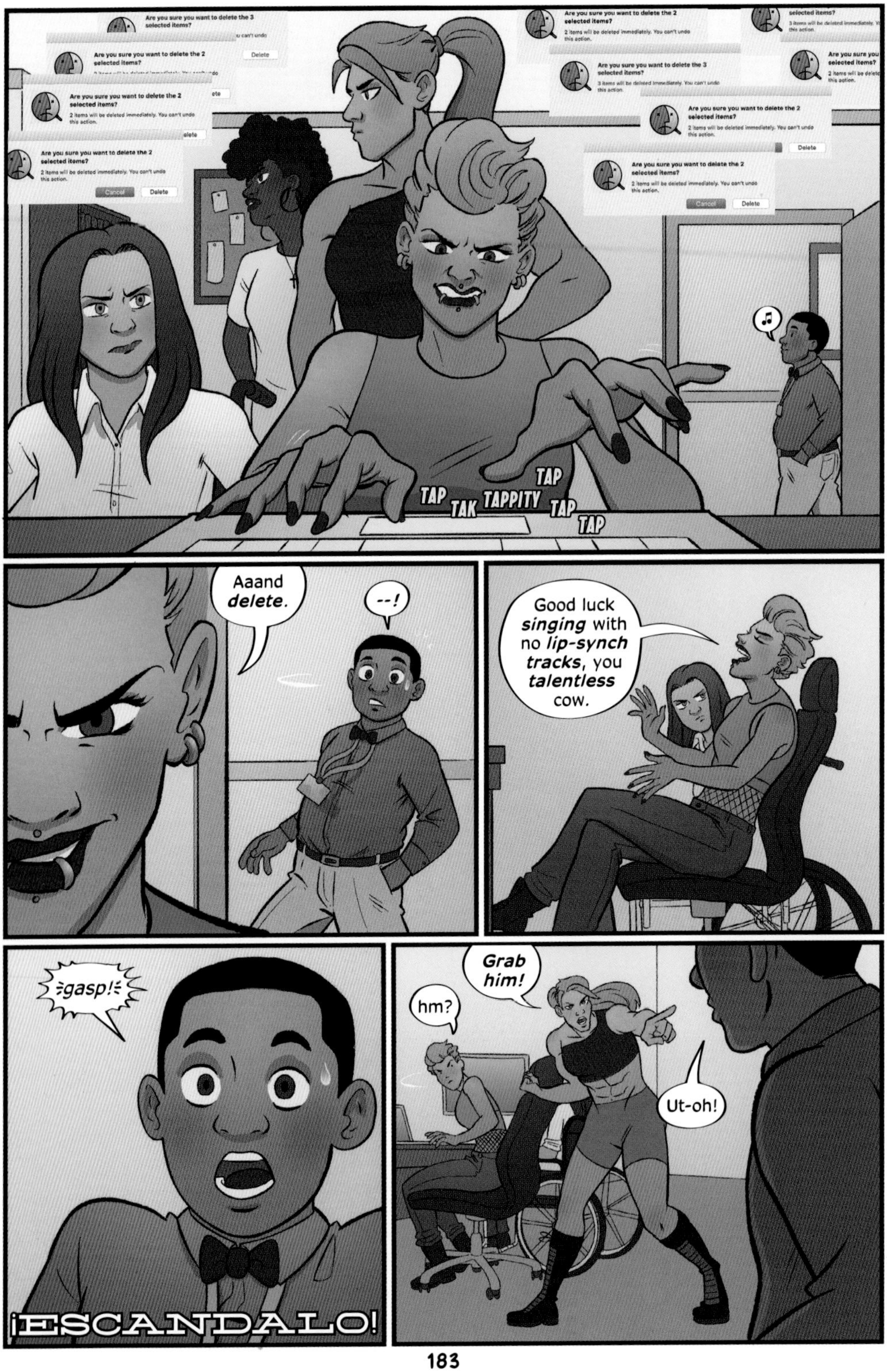
Are you sure you want to delete the 2 selected items?
2 items will be deleted immediately. You can't undo this action.
Cancel
Delete
Are you sure you want to delete the 3 selected items?
3 items will be deleted immediately. You can't undo this action.
TAP
TAK
TAPPITY
TAP
TAP
TAP
Aaand *delete*.
--!
Good luck *singing* with no *lip-synch tracks*, you *talentless* cow.
gasp!
¡ESCANDALO!
Grab him!
hm?
Ut-oh!

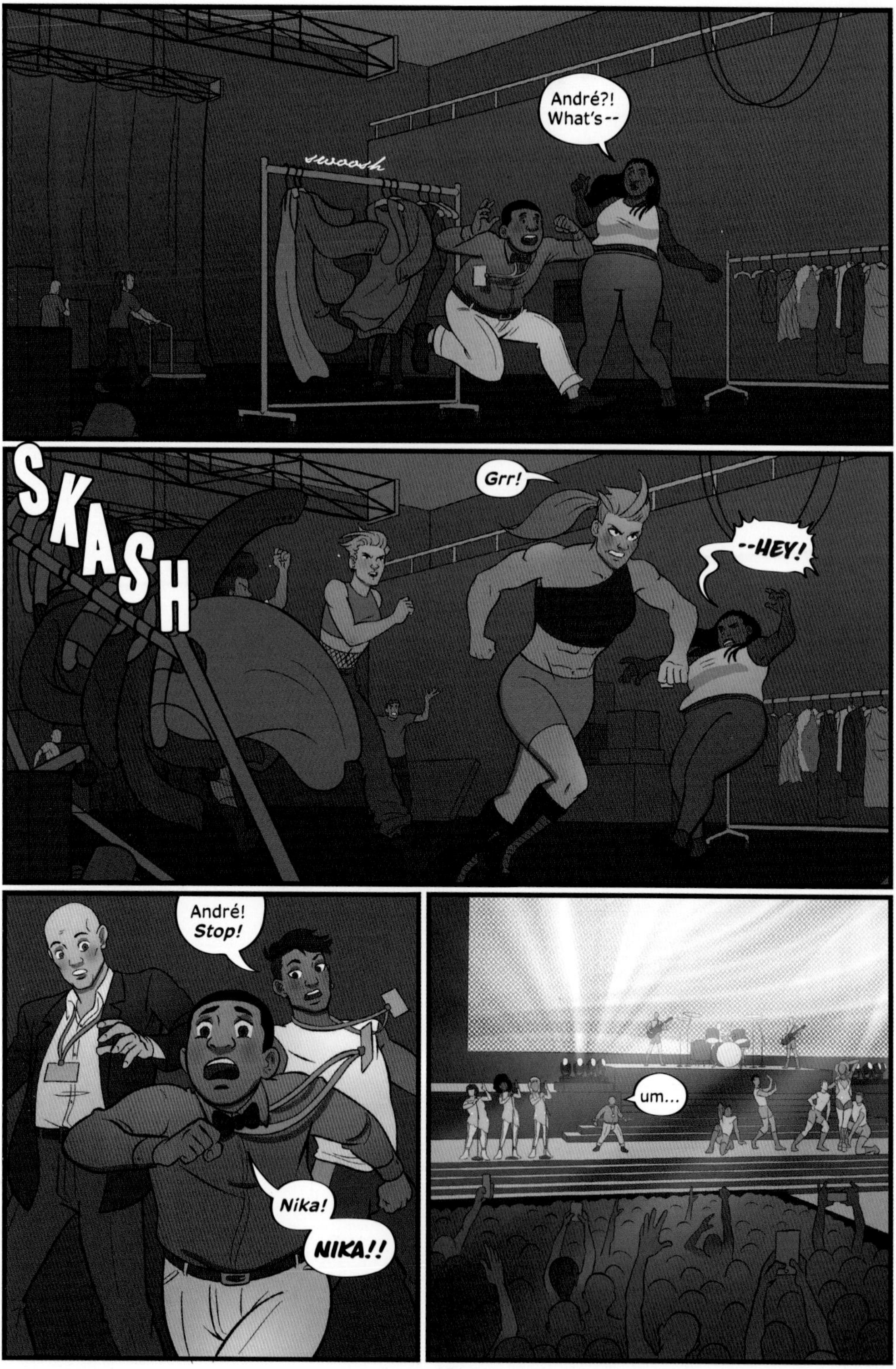
swoosh
André?! What's--
SKASH
Grr!
--HEY!
André! Stop!
Nika!
NIKA!!
um...

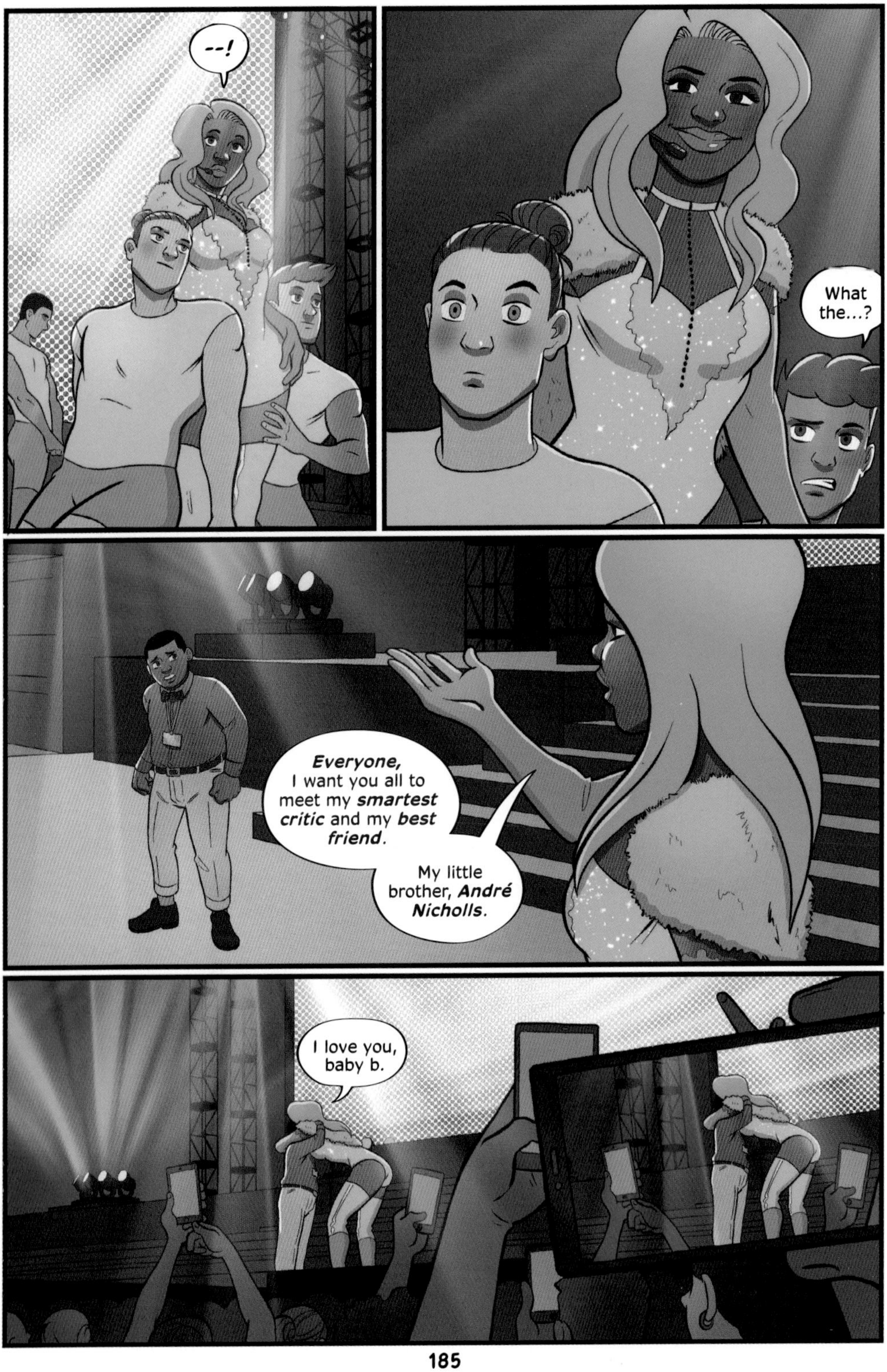
--!
What the...?
Everyone, I want you all to meet my ***smartest critic*** and my ***best friend***.
My little brother, ***André Nicholls***.
I love you, baby b.

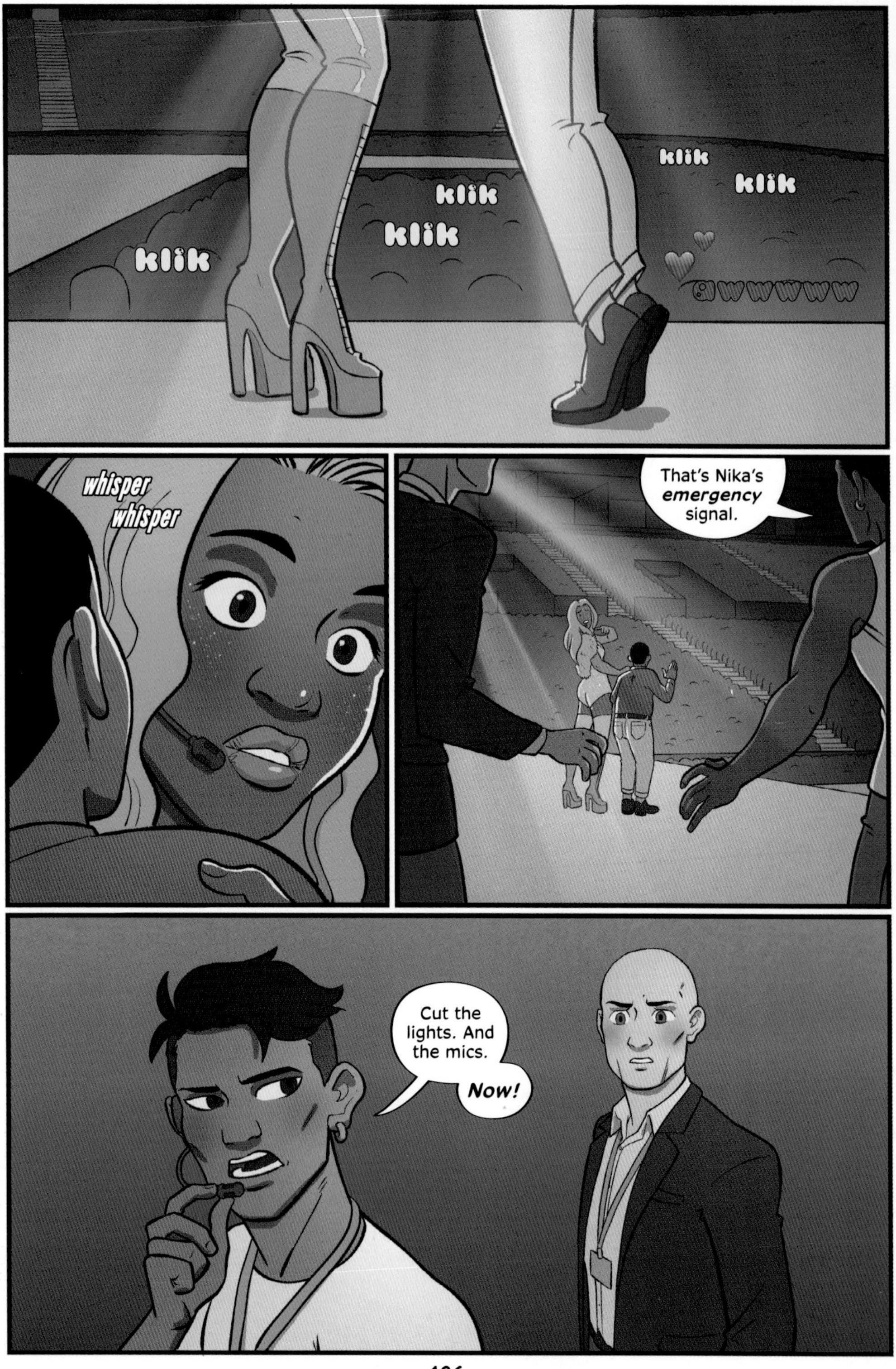
klik
klik
klik
klik
klik
awwwww
whisper
whisper
That's Nika's *emergency* signal.
Cut the lights. And the mics.
Now!

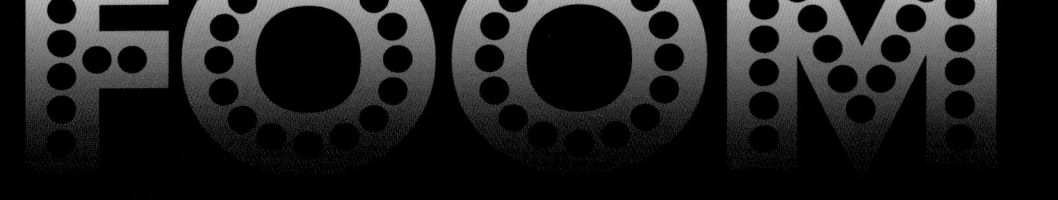

Why are the lights out?

Is this part of the show?

What's happening?

I don't understand.

What is it, Nika?

Some girls *broke in* and trashed the *vocal tracks* for lip-synch.

I have *backups* on my other laptop, but it's at the *hotel*.

W-we can't go on.

We'll have to *cancel* tonight.

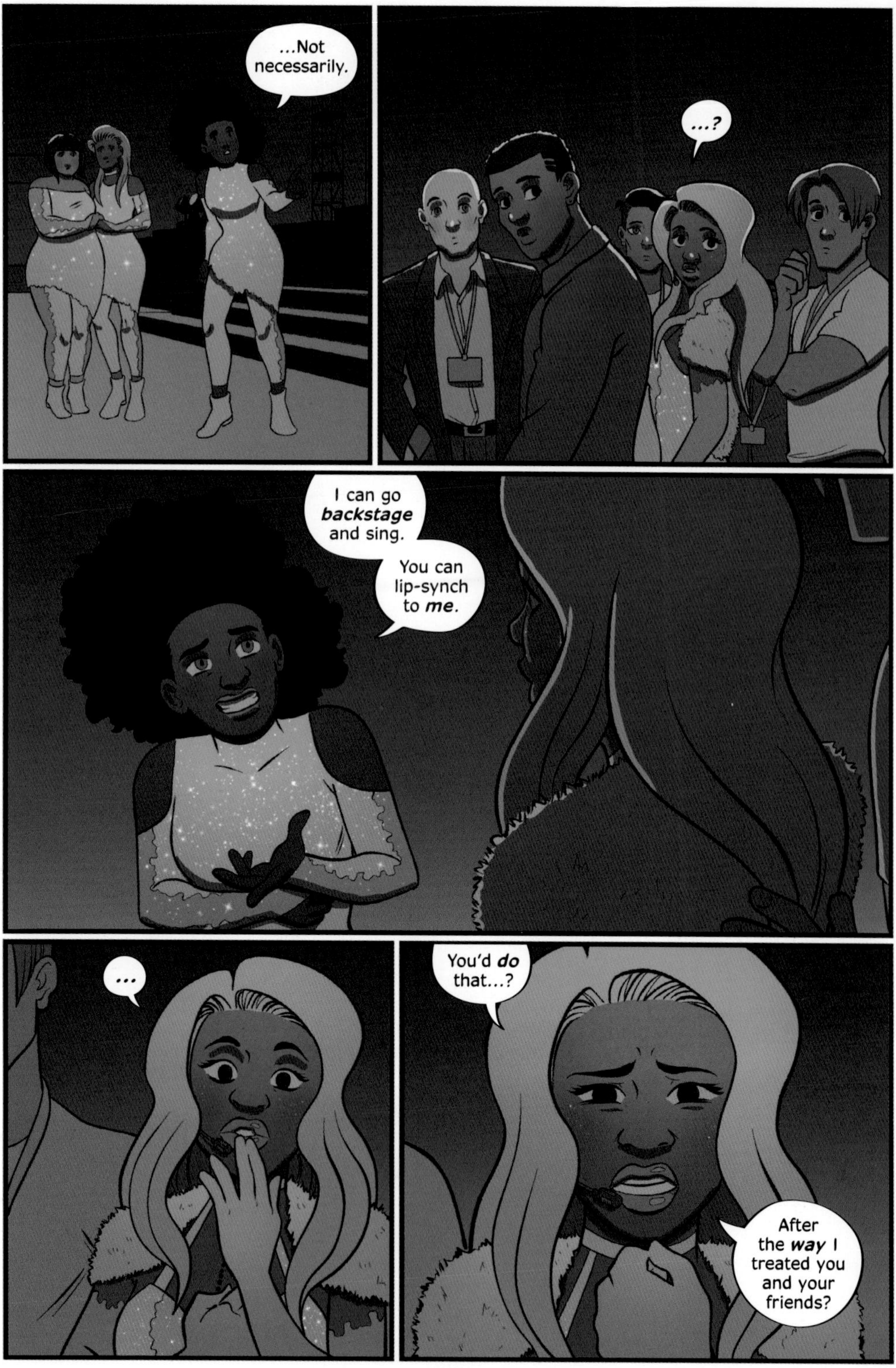
...Not necessarily.
...?
I can go *backstage* and sing.
You can lip-synch to *me*.
...
You'd *do* that...?
After the *way* I treated you and your friends?

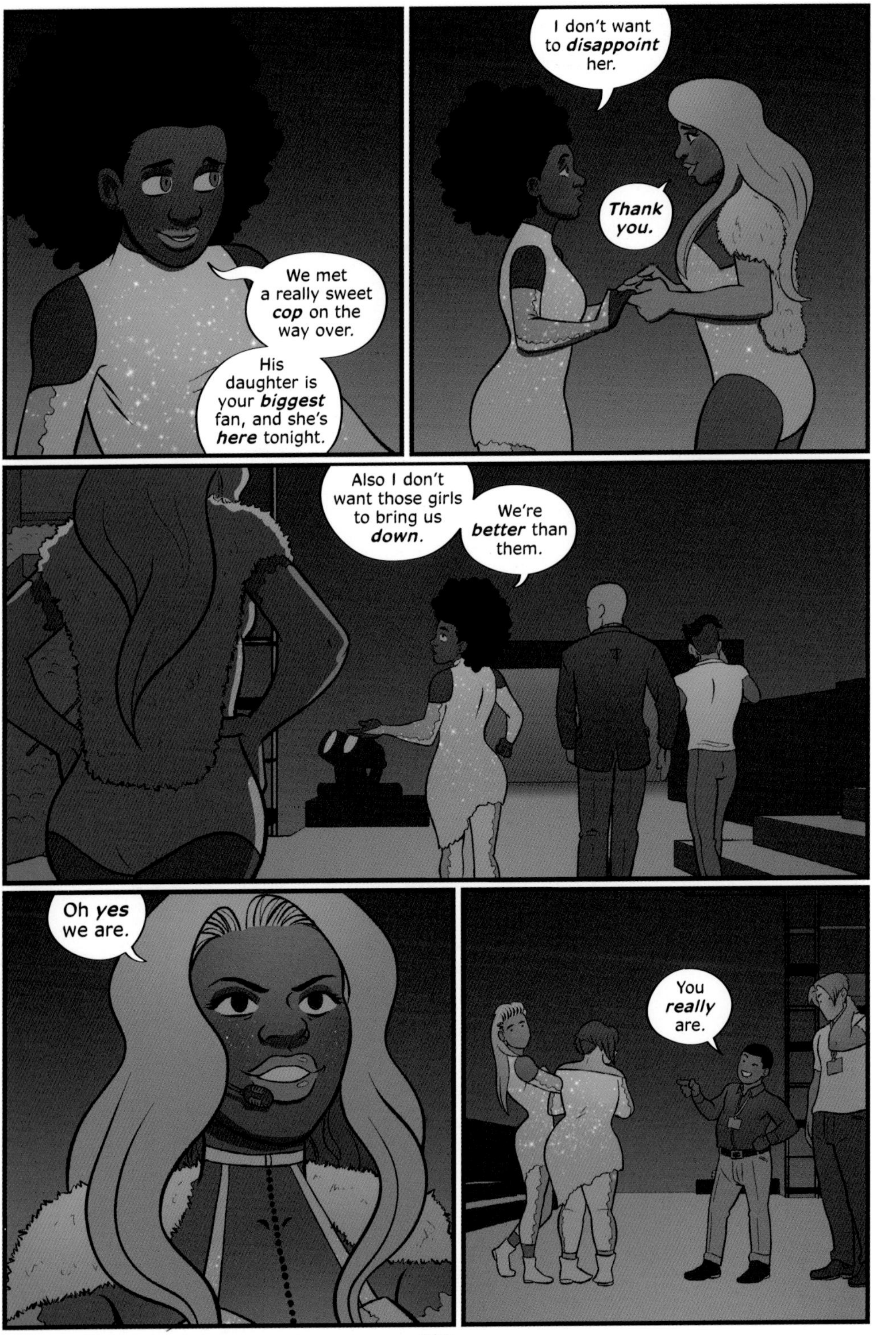
We met a really sweet *cop* on the way over.
His daughter is your ***biggest*** fan, and she's ***here*** tonight.
I don't want to ***disappoint*** her.
Thank you.
Also I don't want those girls to bring us ***down***.
We're ***better*** than them.
Oh ***yes*** we are.
You ***really*** are.

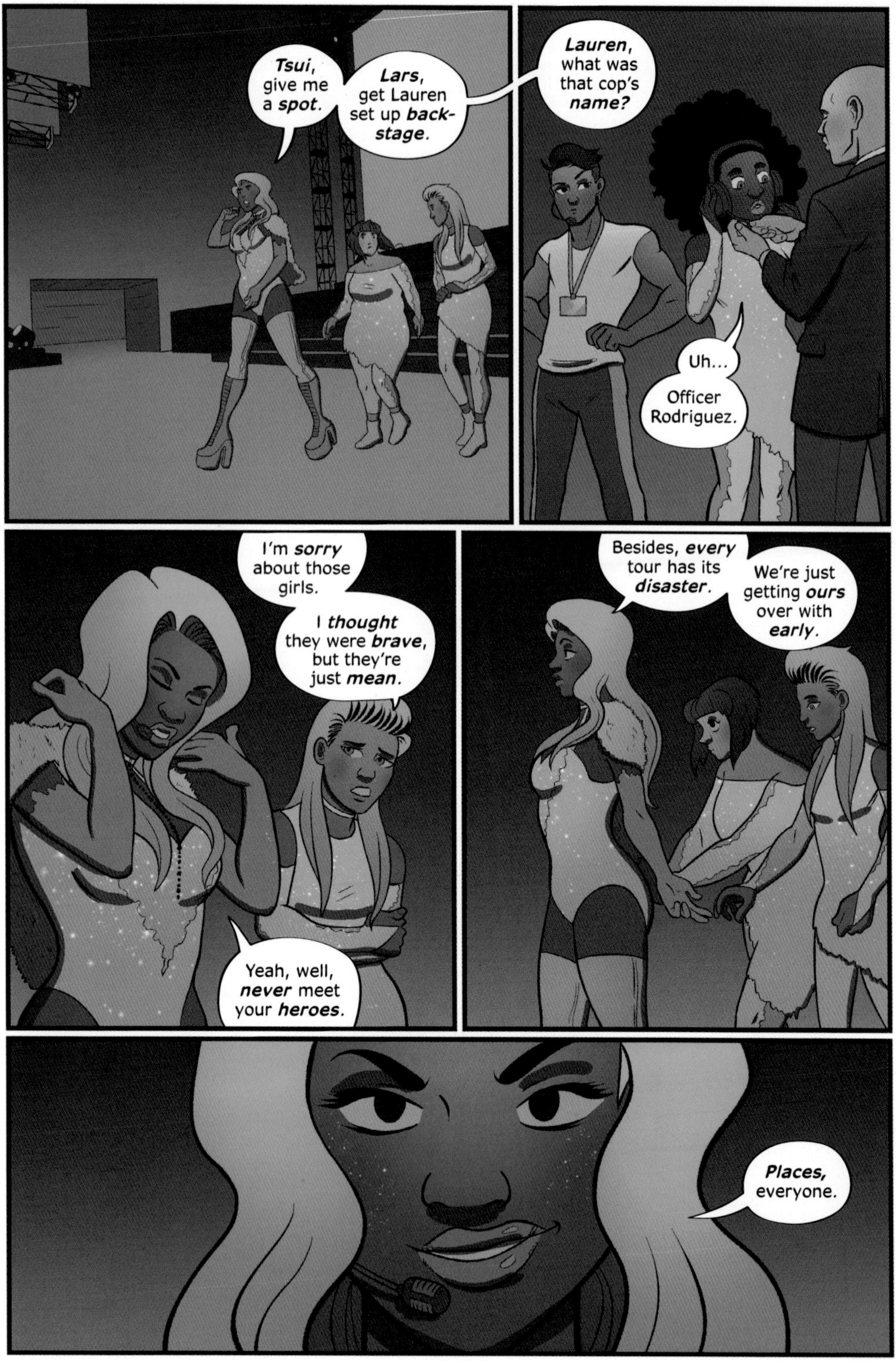

Tsui, give me a ***spot***.
Lars, get Lauren set up ***back-stage***.
Lauren, what was that cop's ***name?***
Uh...
Officer Rodriguez.
I'm ***sorry*** about those girls.
I ***thought*** they were ***brave***, but they're just ***mean***.
Yeah, well, ***never*** meet your ***heroes***.
Besides, ***every*** tour has its ***disaster***.
We're just getting ***ours*** over with ***early***.
Places, everyone.

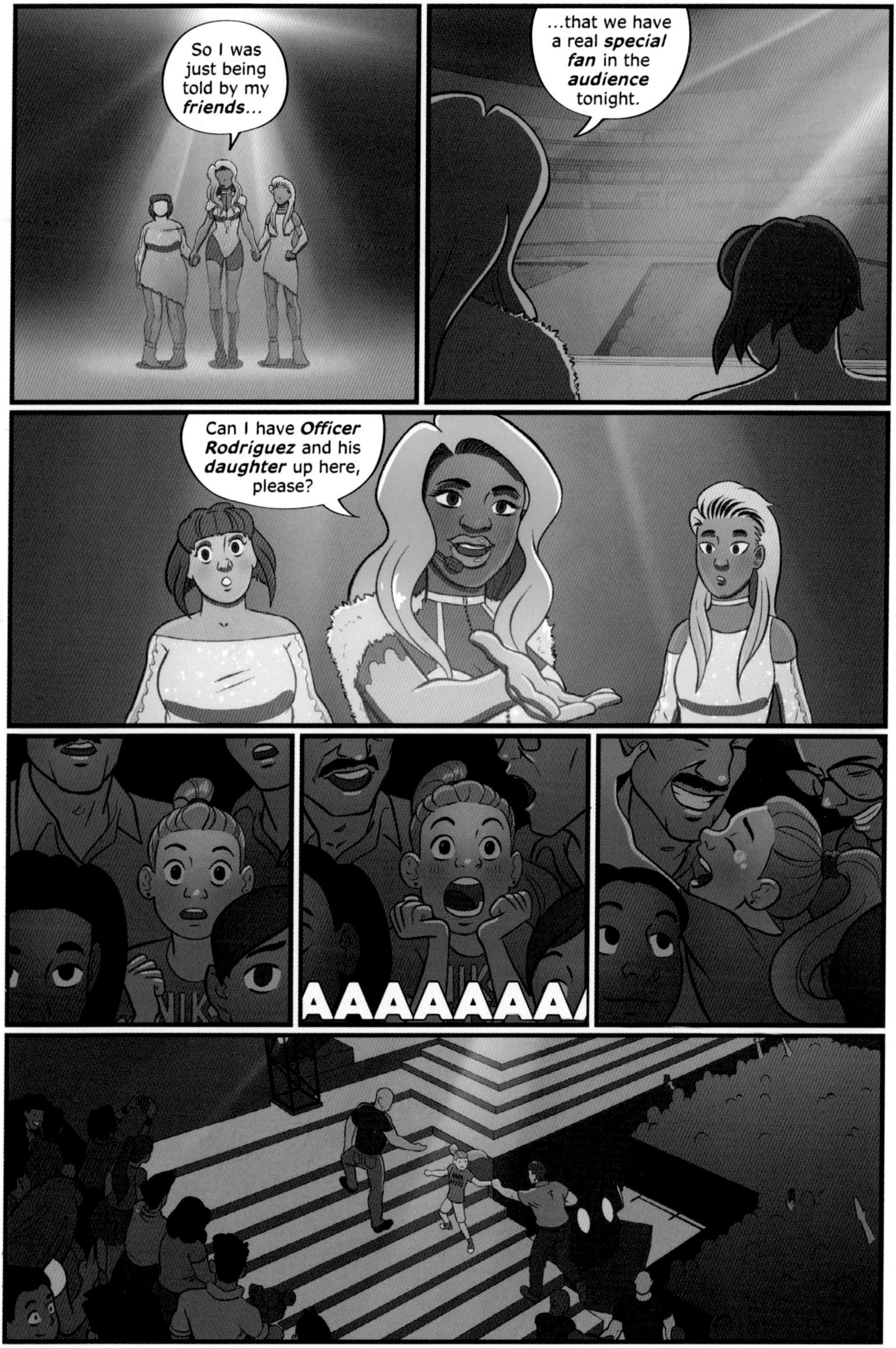
So I was just being told by my *friends*...
...that we have a real *special* *fan* in the *audience* tonight.
Can I have *Officer* *Rodriguez* and his *daughter* up here, please?
AAAAAAAA

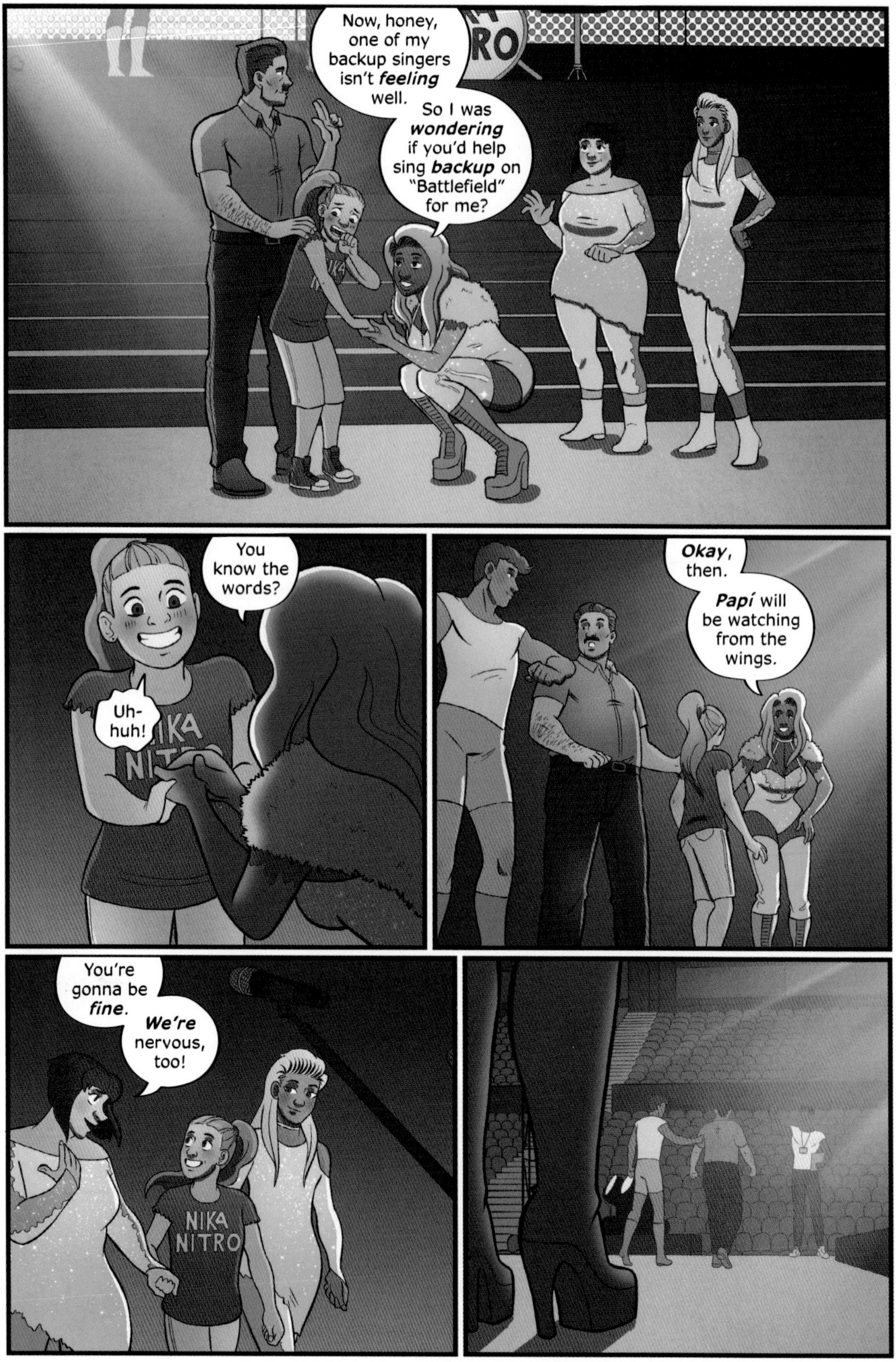
Now, honey, one of my backup singers isn't *feeling* well.
So I was *wondering* if you'd help sing *backup* on "Battlefield" for me?
You know the words?
Uh-huh!
NIKA NITRO
Okay, then.
Papí will be watching from the wings.
You're gonna be *fine*.
We're nervous, too!
NIKA NITRO

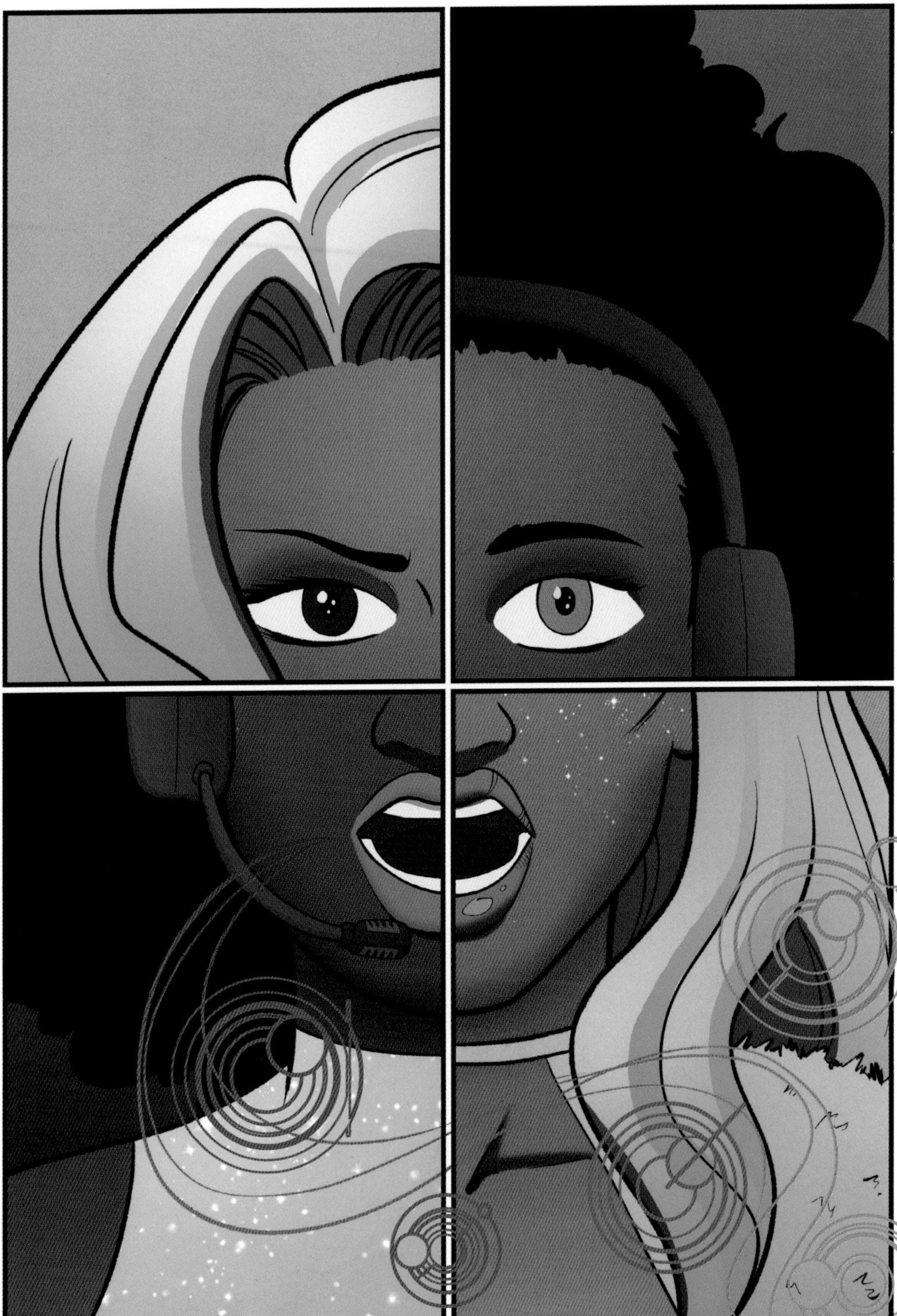

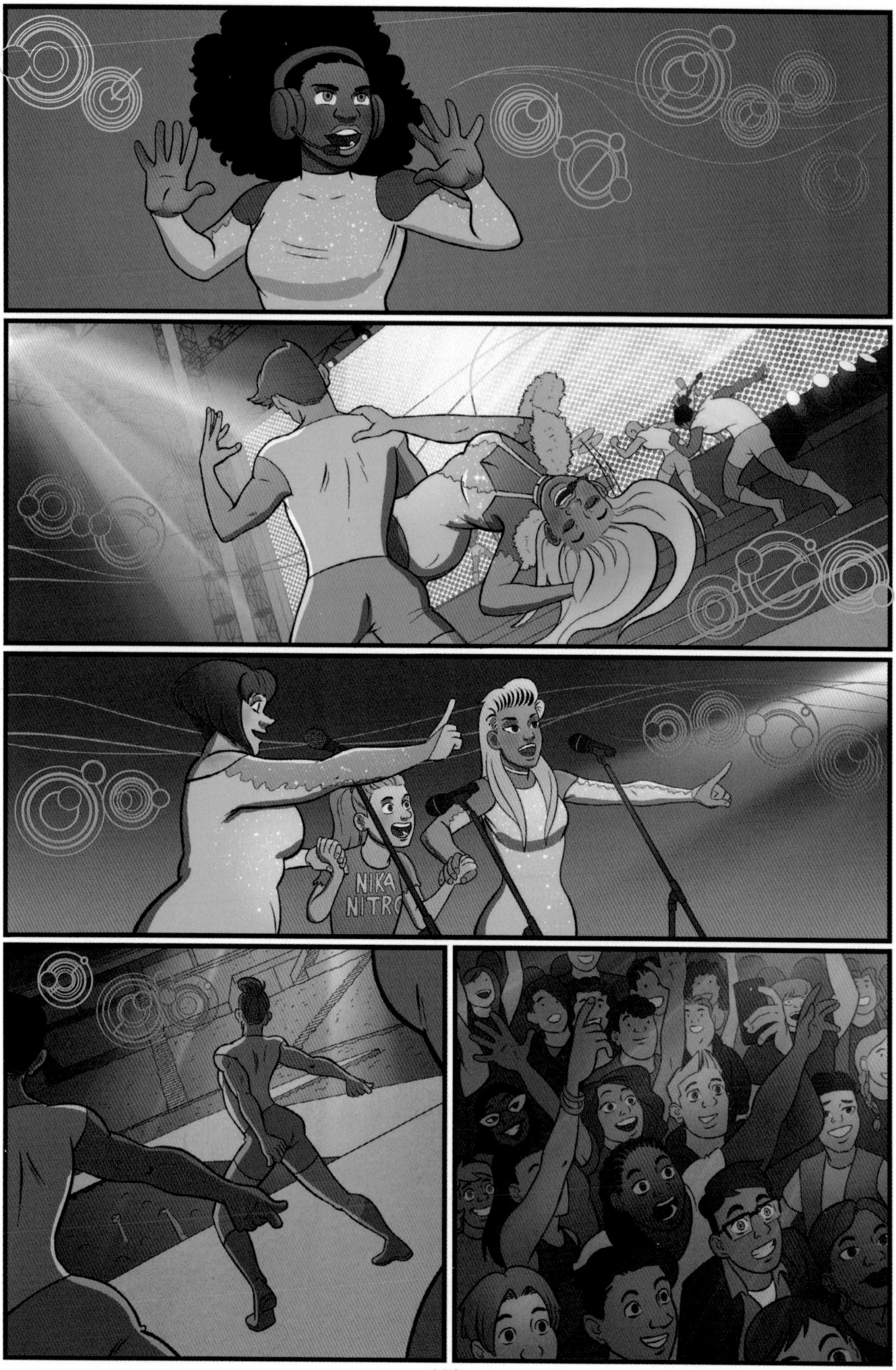
NIKA
NITRO

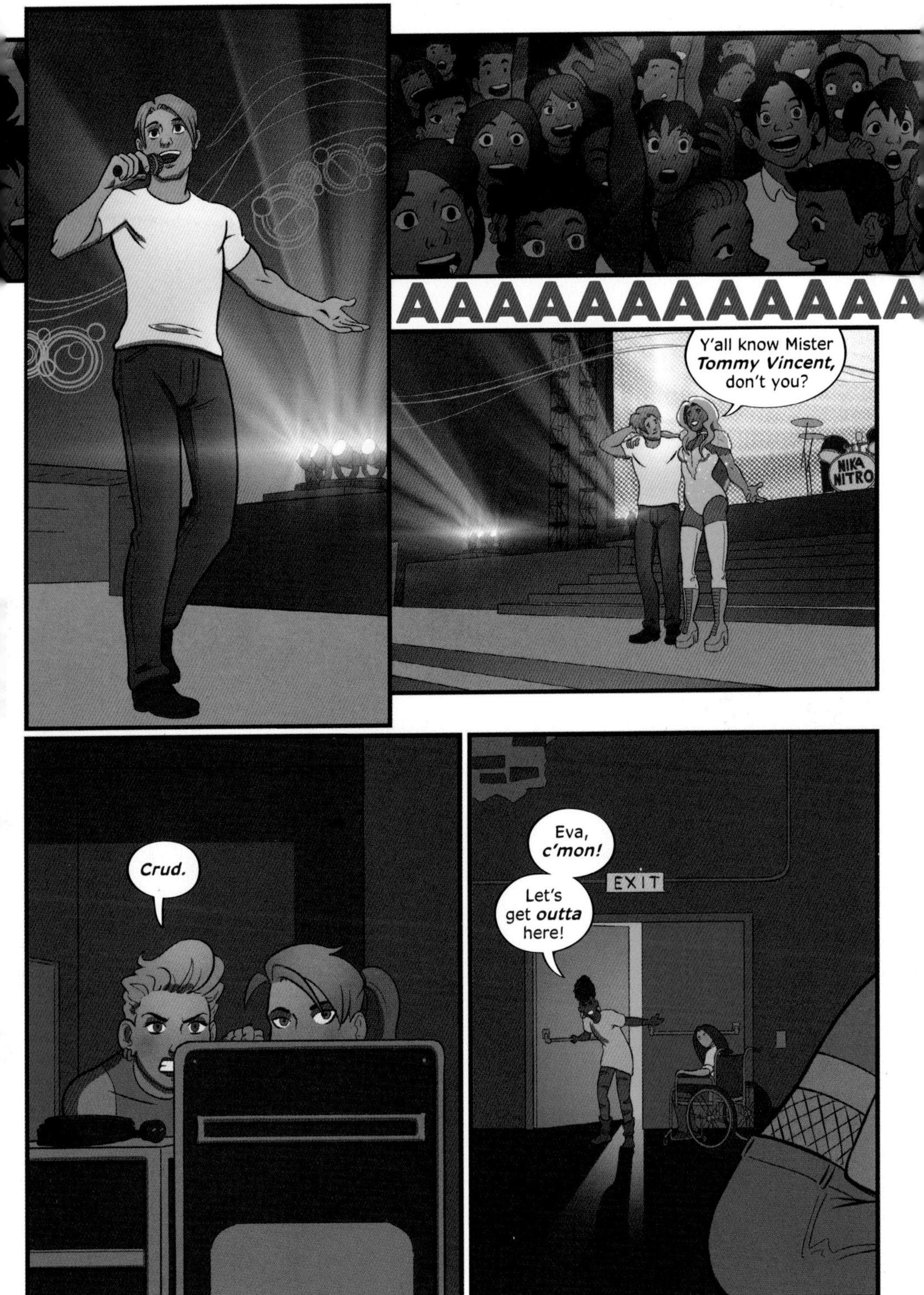
AAAAAAAAAAAAA
Y'all know Mister *Tommy Vincent,* don't you?
NIKA NITRO
Crud.
Eva, *c'mon!*
EXIT
Let's get *outta* here!

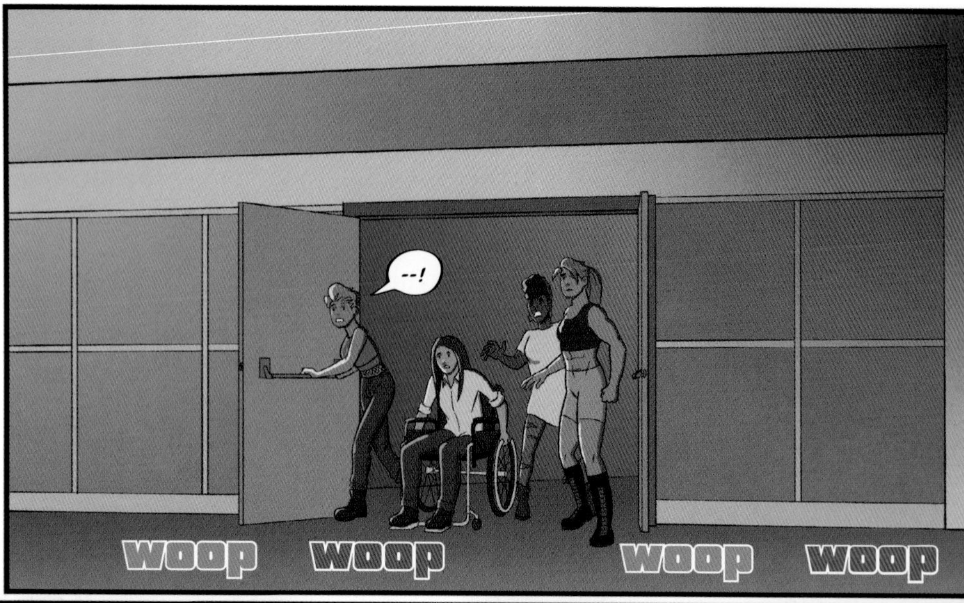
--!
woop woop woop woop

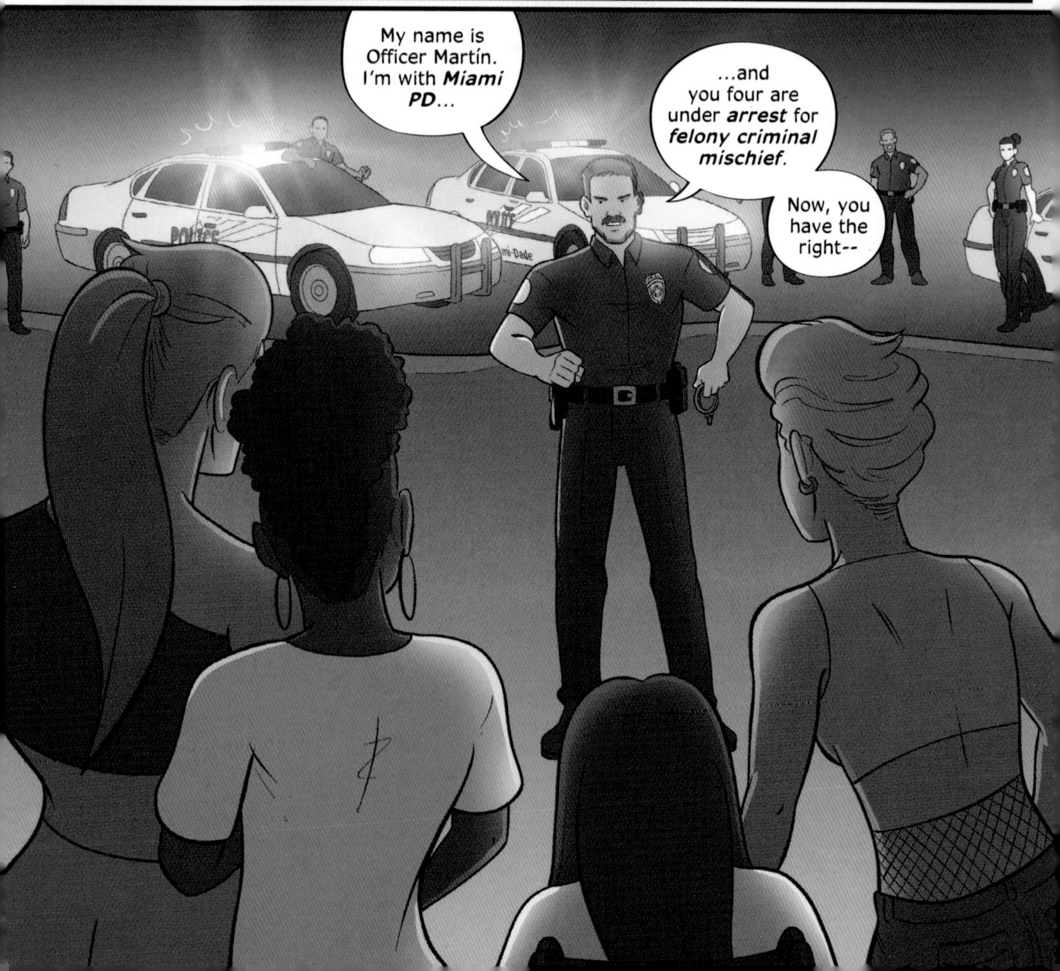
My name is Officer Martín. I'm with *Miami PD*...
...and you four are under ***arrest*** for ***felony criminal mischief***.
Now, you have the right--
POLICE
POLICE

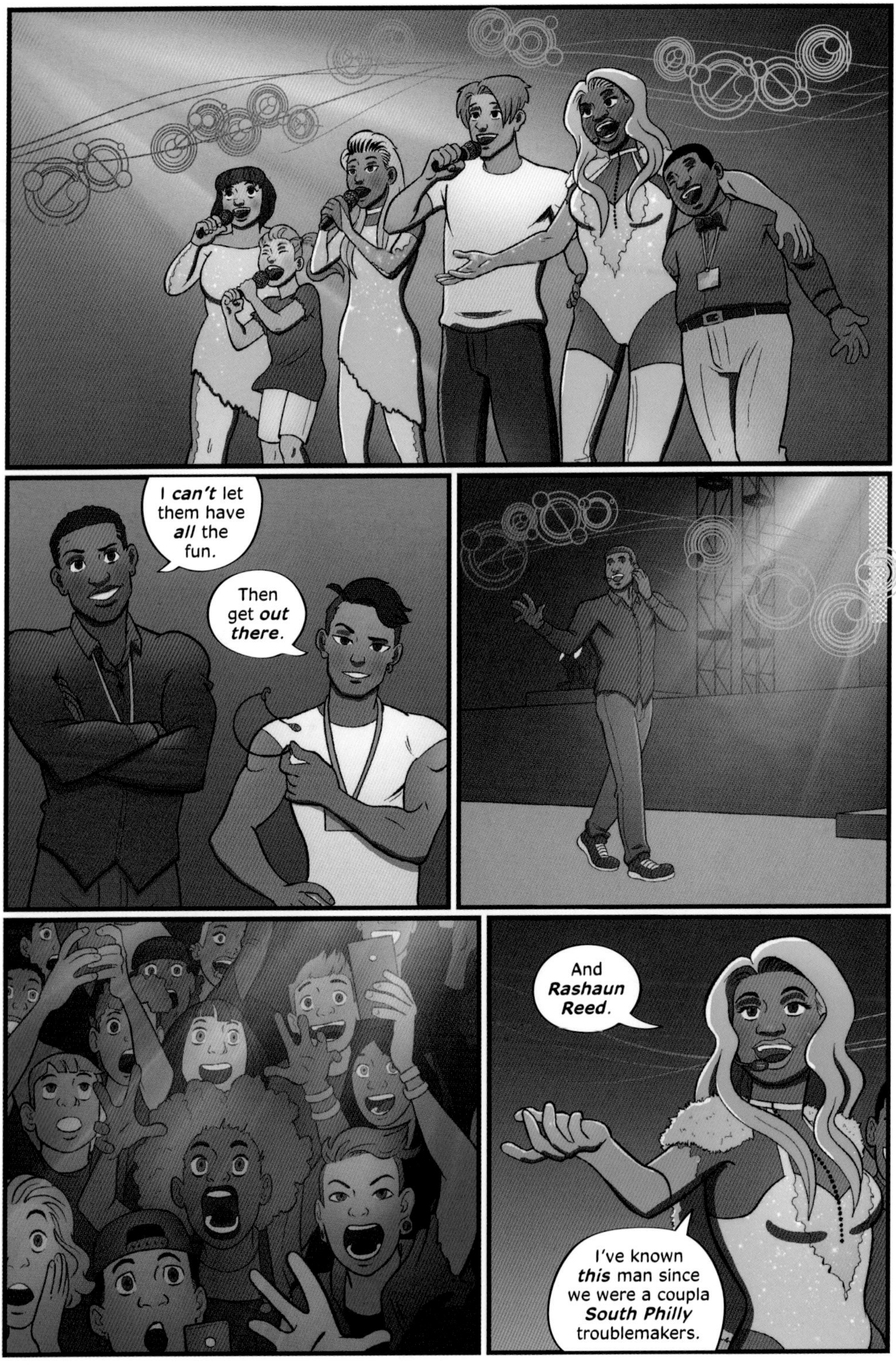
I *can't* let them have *all* the fun.
Then get *out there*.
And *Rashaun Reed*.
I've known *this* man since we were a coupla *South Philly* troublemakers.

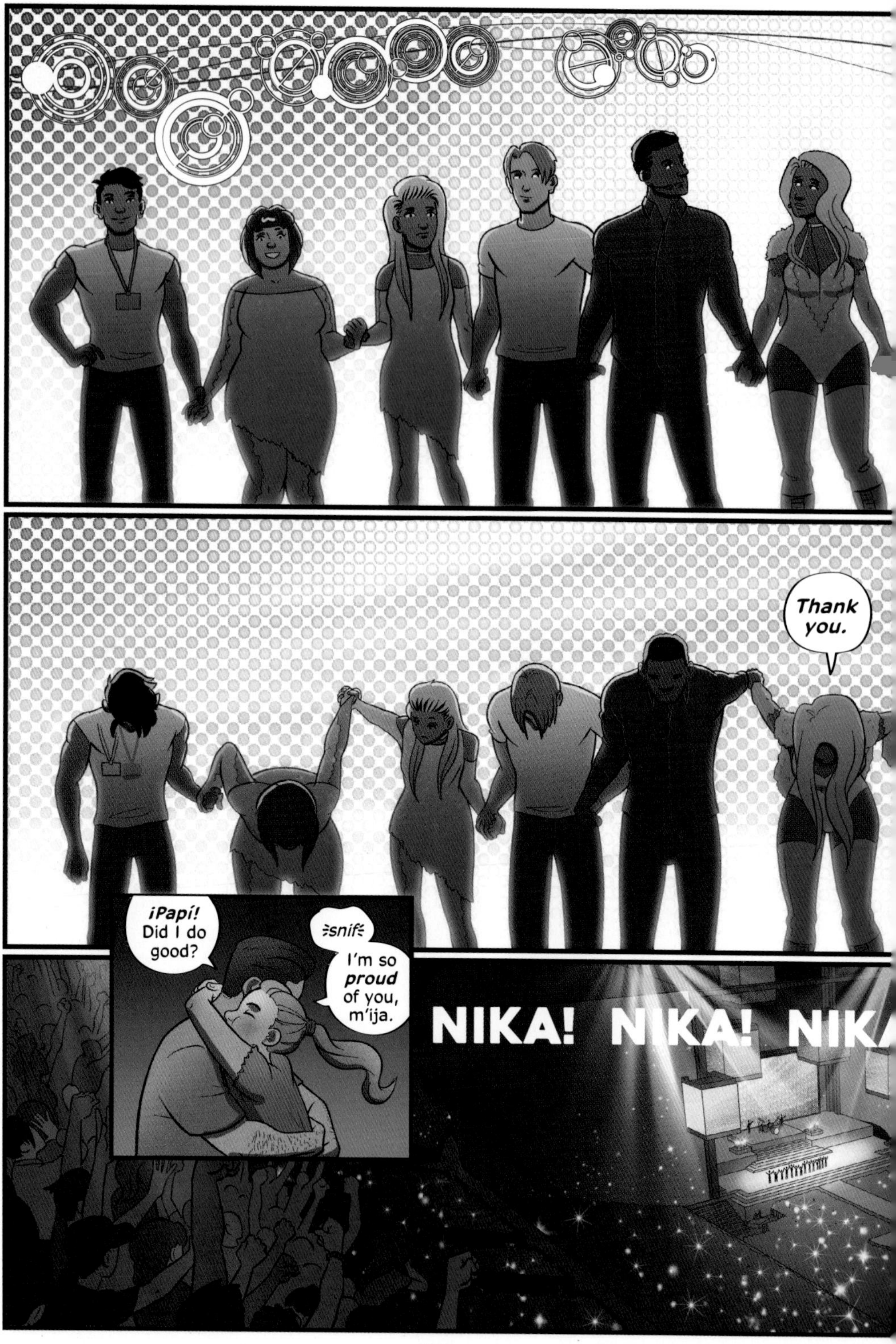
Thank you.
¡Papí! Did I do good?
≑snif≑
I'm so *proud* of you, m'ija.
NIKA! NIKA! NIKA

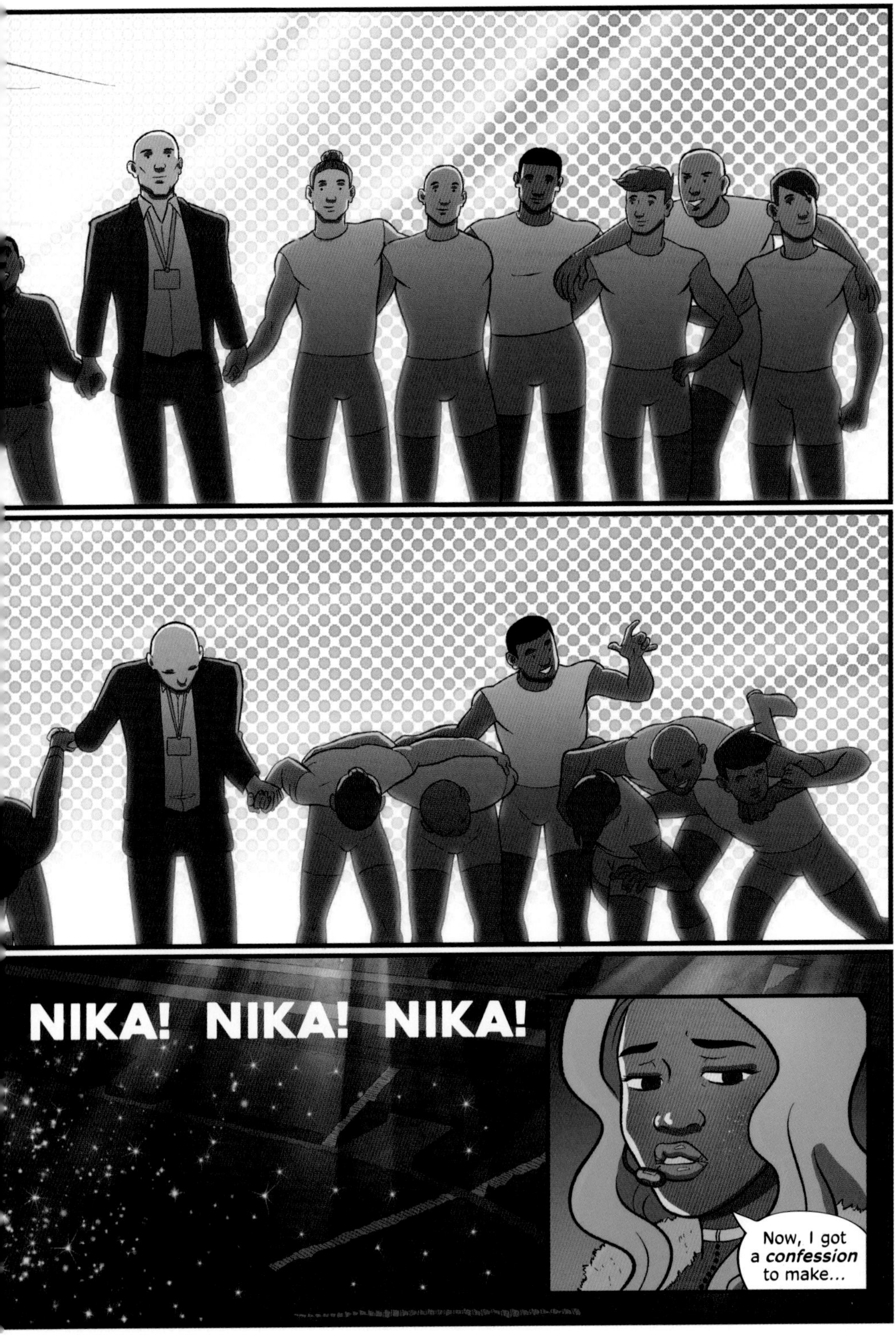
NIKA! NIKA! NIKA!
Now, I got a *confession* to make...

I didn't sing *one note* of that song.

Gnn!

Oh dear.

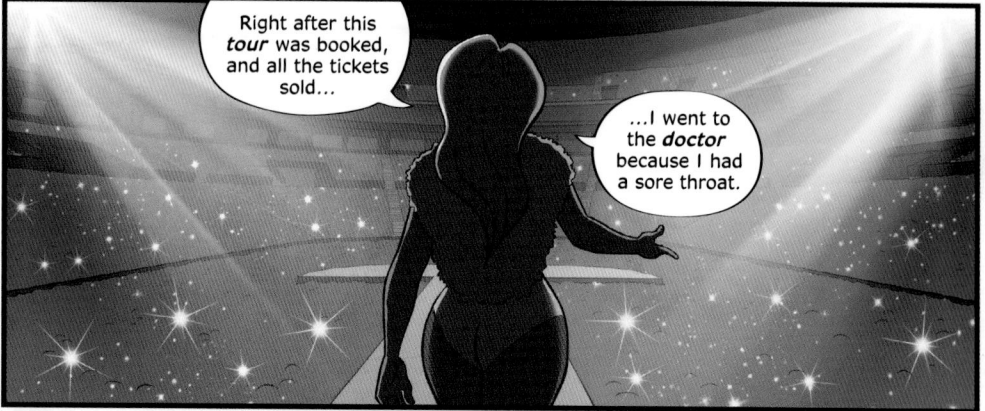

Right after this *tour* was booked, and all the tickets sold...

...I went to the *doctor* because I had a sore throat.

Th-they *found*...

They said I had *nodules* on my throat.

They said if I sang even *some* of these *fifty shows*, I'd probably *never* sing *again*.

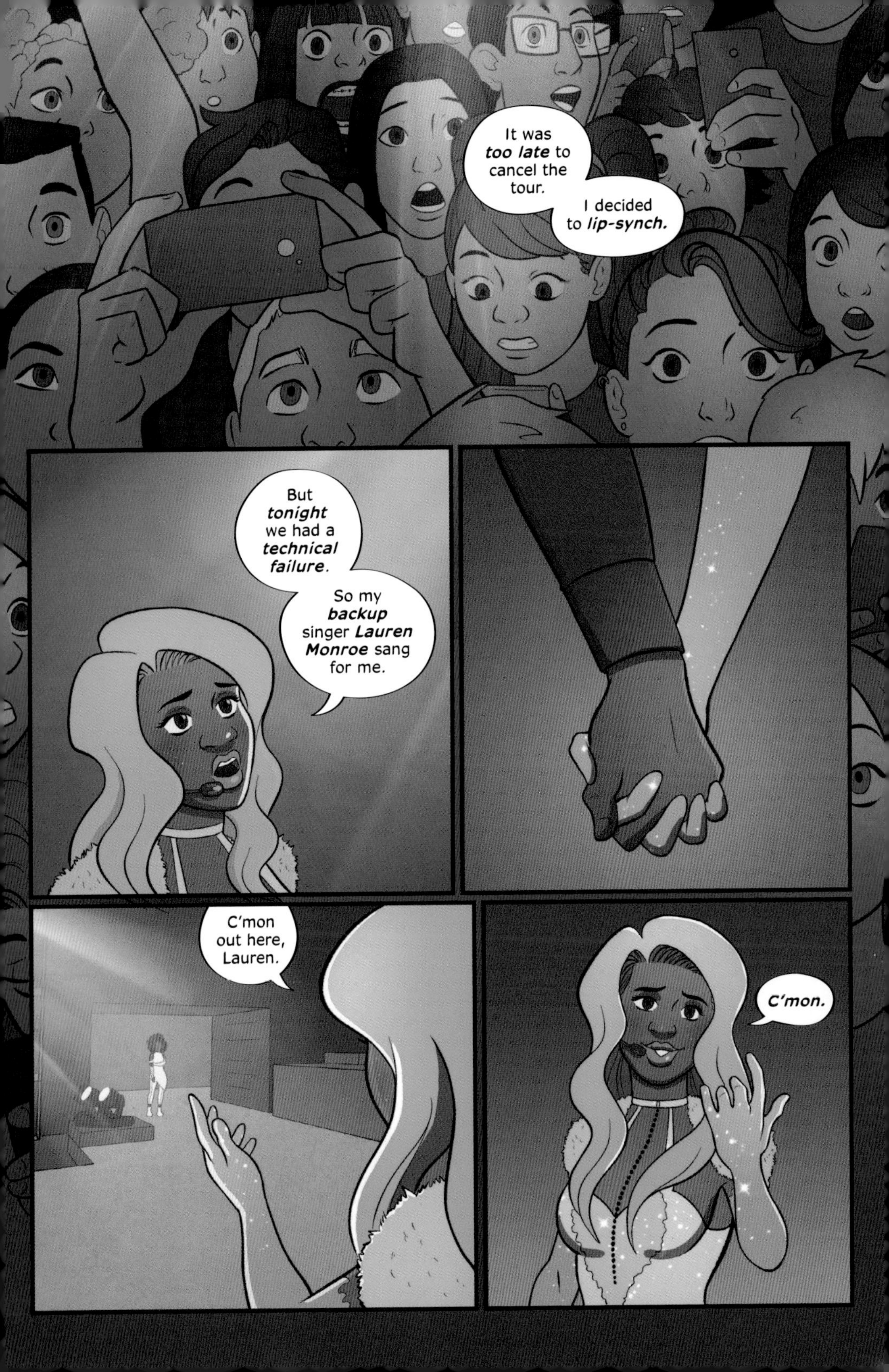
It was *too late* to cancel the tour.
I decided to *lip-synch.*
But *tonight* we had a *technical failure*.
So my *backup* singer *Lauren Monroe* sang for me.
C'mon out here, Lauren.
C'mon.

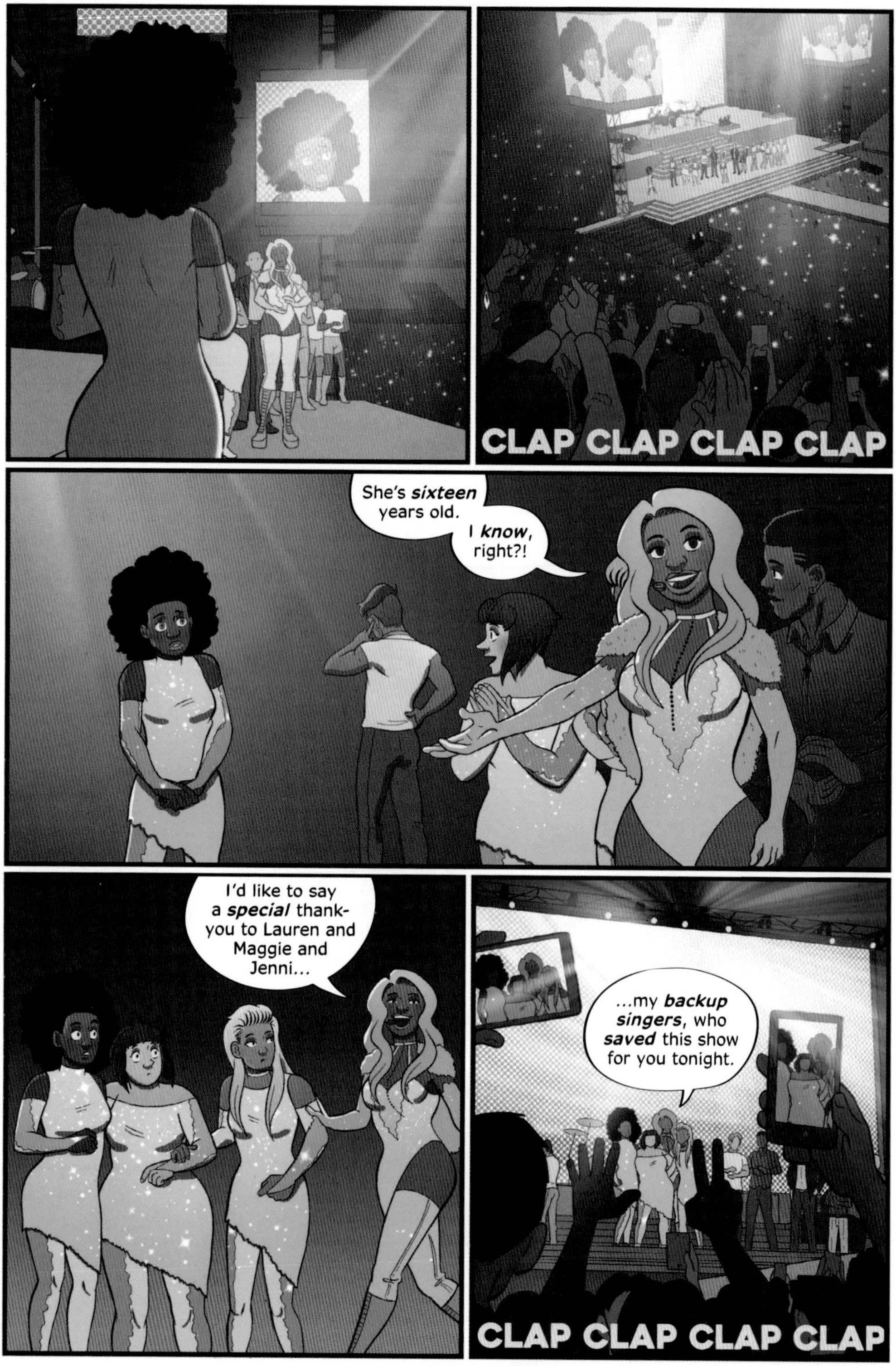
CLAP CLAP CLAP CLAP
She's *sixteen* years old.
I *know*, right?!
I'd like to say a *special* thank-you to Lauren and Maggie and Jenni...
...my *backup singers*, who *saved* this show for you tonight.
CLAP CLAP CLAP CLAP

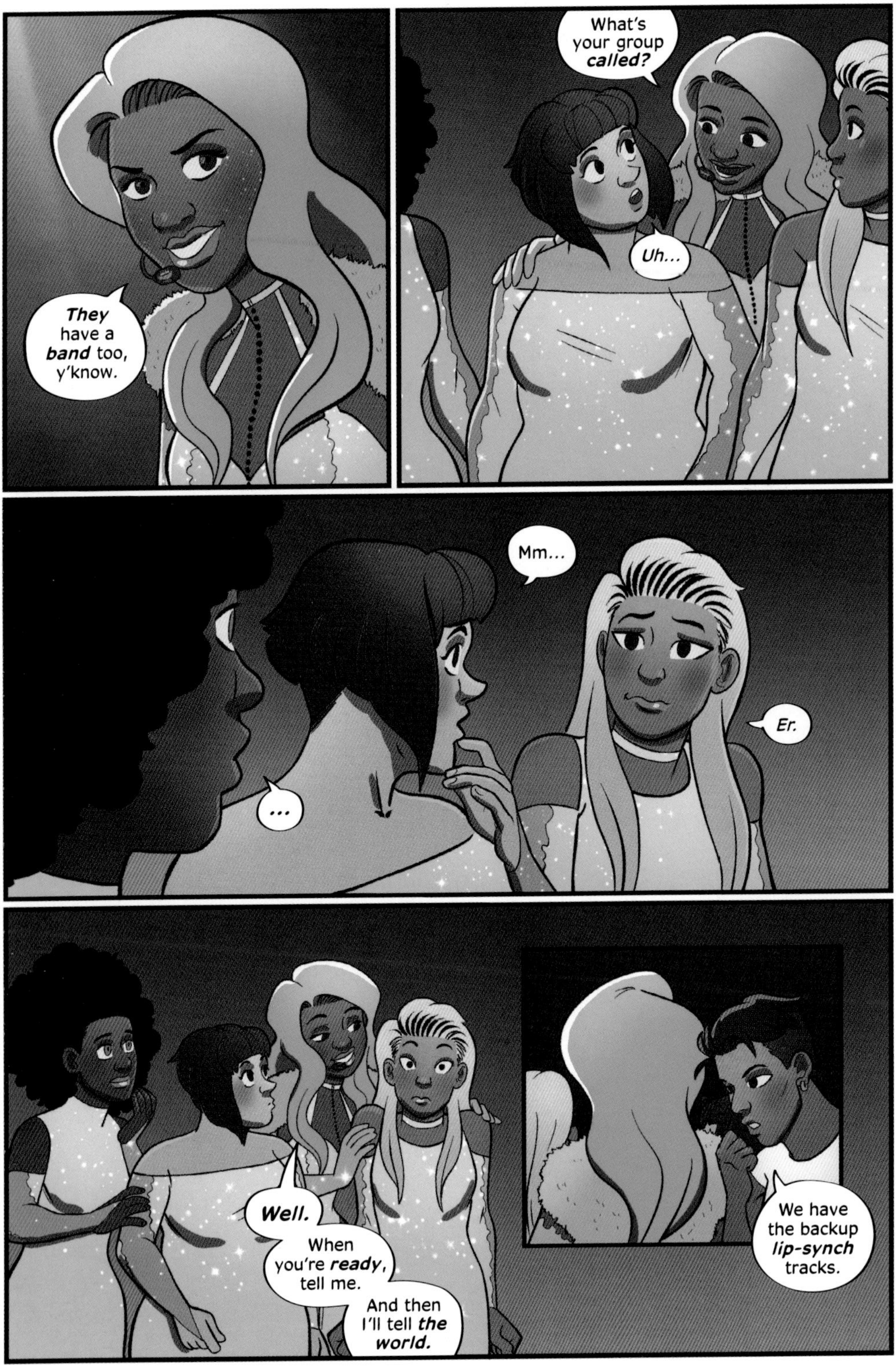

They have a *band* too, y'know.
What's your group *called?*
Uh...
Mm...
Er.
...
Well.
When you're *ready*, tell me.
And then I'll tell *the world.*
We have the backup *lip-synch* tracks.

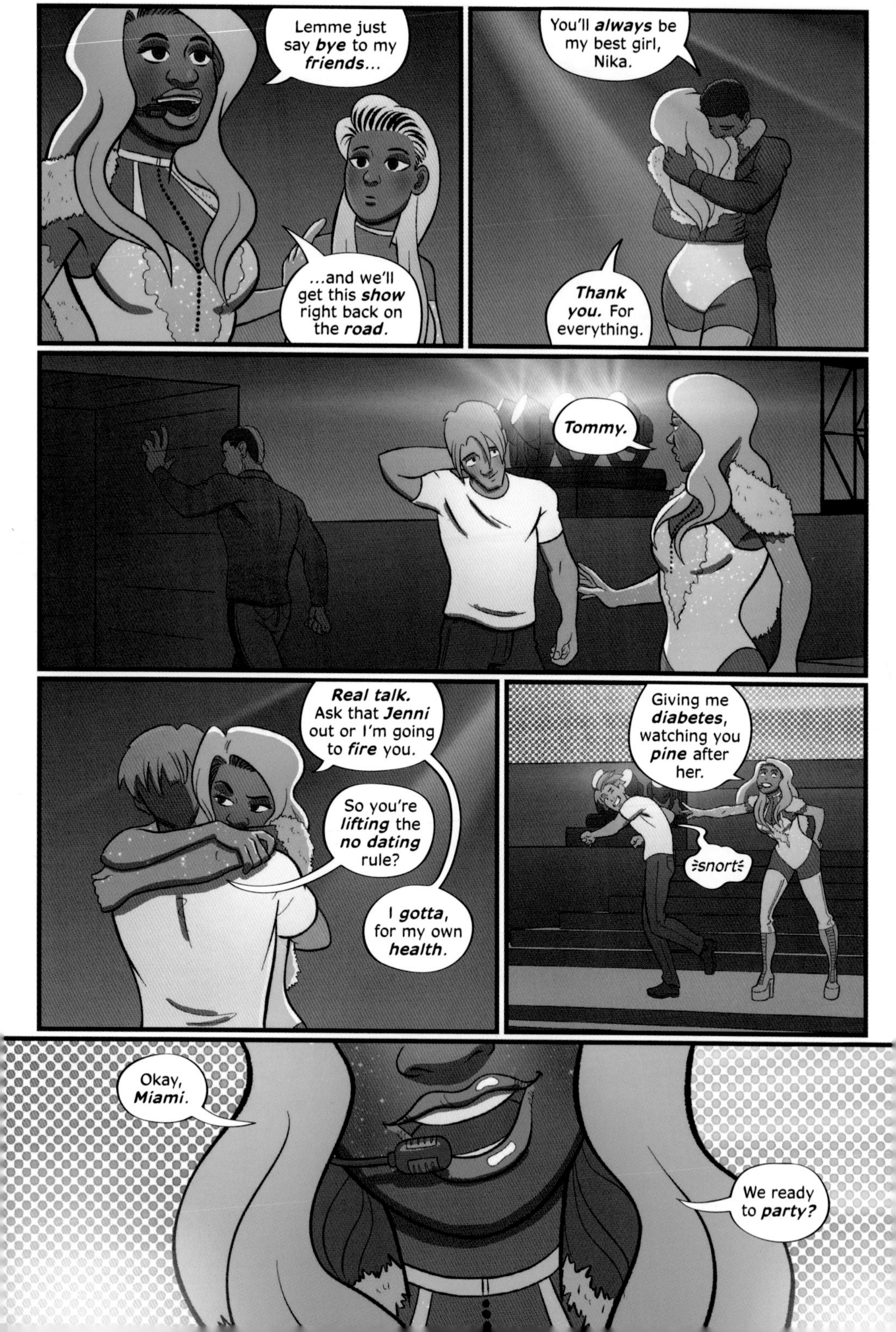
Lemme just say *bye* to my *friends*...
...and we'll get this *show* right back on the *road*.
You'll *always* be my best girl, Nika.
Thank you. For everything.
Tommy.
Real talk. Ask that *Jenni* out or I'm going to *fire* you.
So you're *lifting* the *no dating* rule?
I *gotta*, for my own *health*.
Giving me *diabetes*, watching you *pine* after her.
snort
Okay, *Miami*.
We ready to *party?*

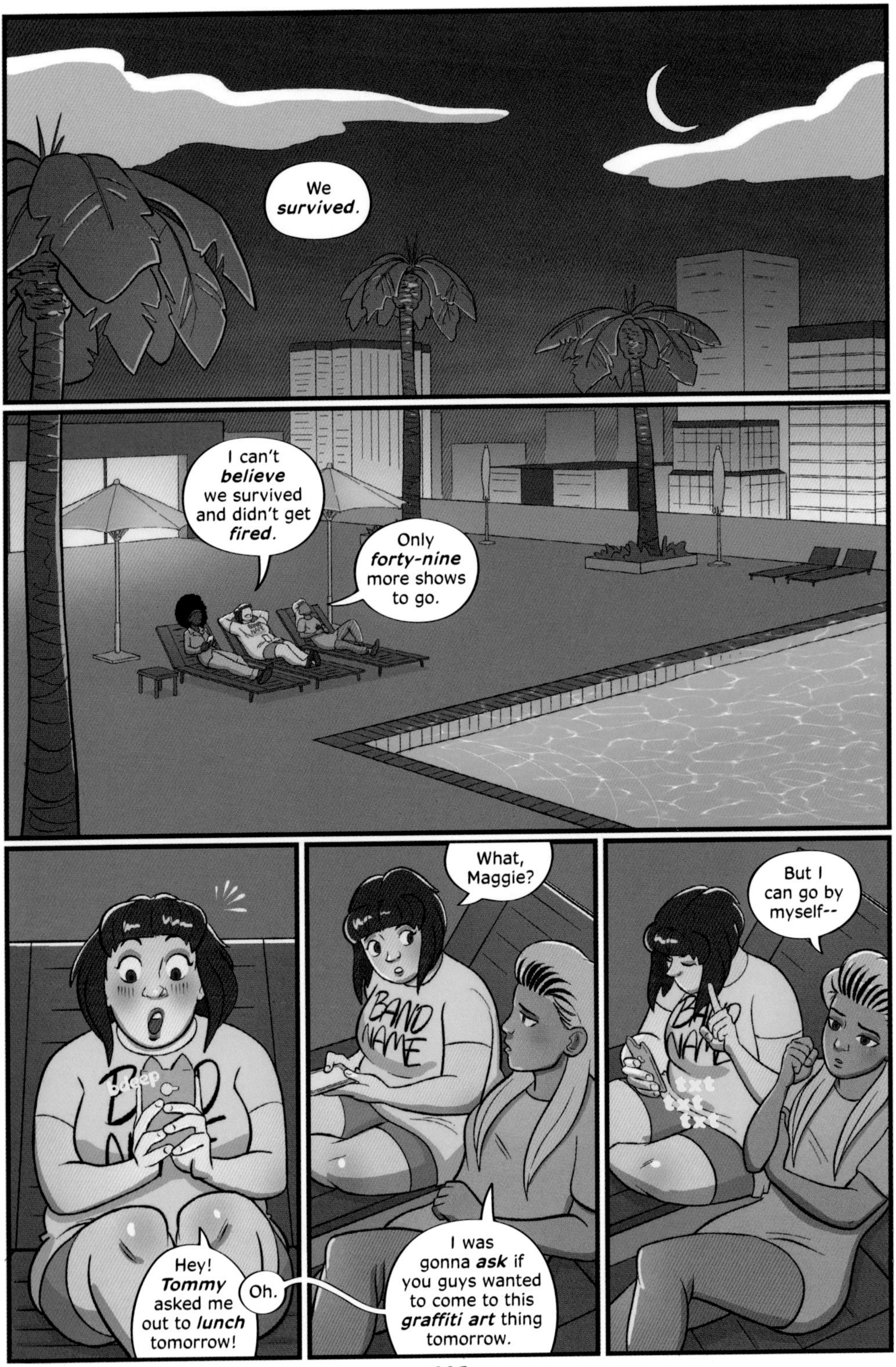
We *survived*.
I can't *believe* we survived and didn't get *fired*.
Only *forty-nine* more shows to go.
BAND NAME
bdeep
Hey! *Tommy* asked me out to *lunch* tomorrow!
What, Maggie?
BAND NAME
Oh.
I was gonna *ask* if you guys wanted to come to this *graffiti art* thing tomorrow.
But I can go by myself--
txt txt txt

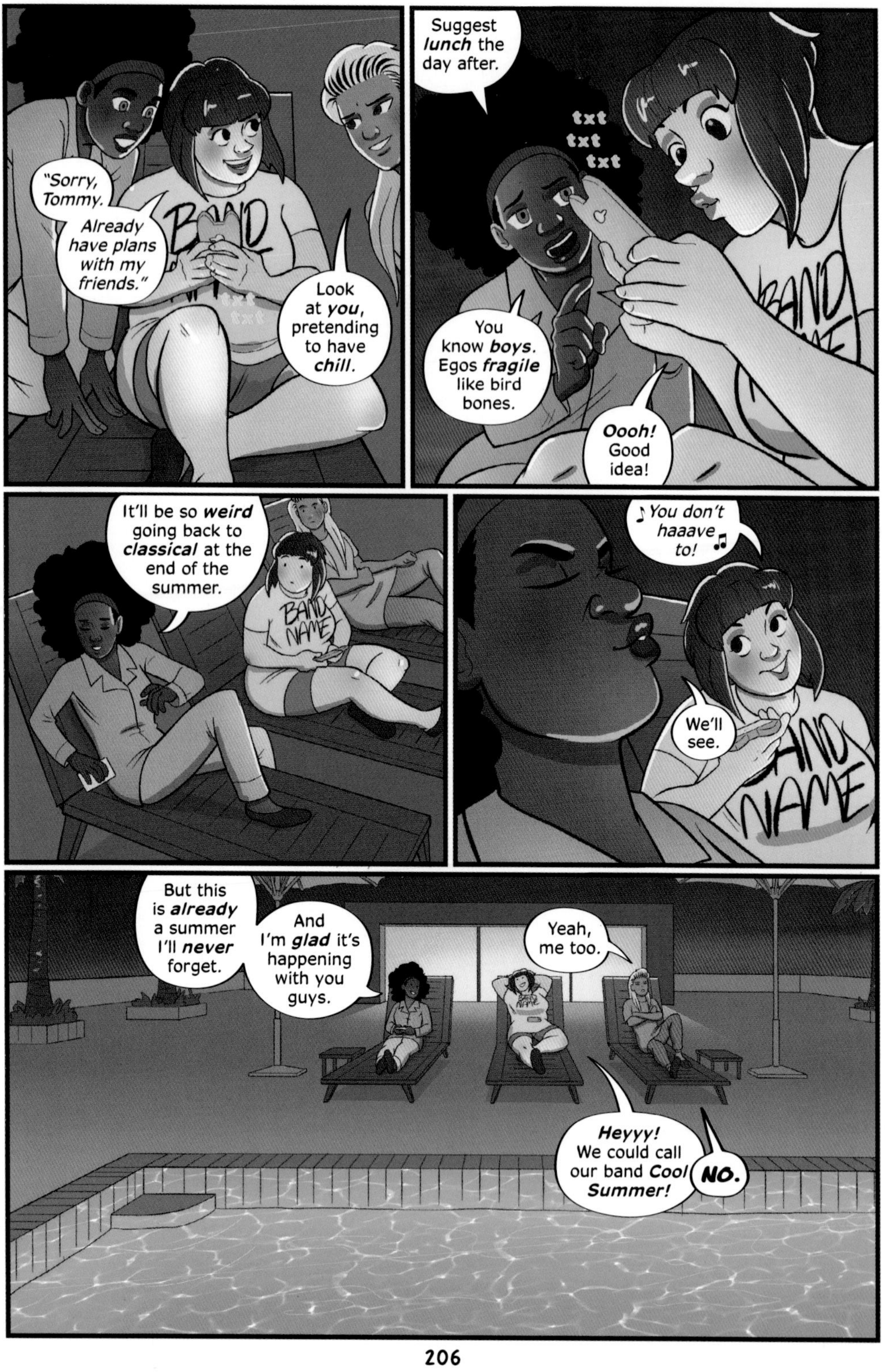
"Sorry, Tommy. Already have plans with my friends."
Look at *you*, pretending to have *chill*.
BAND
txt txt
Suggest *lunch* the day after.
txt txt txt
You know ***boys***. Egos ***fragile*** like bird bones.
Oooh! Good idea!
BAND NAME
It'll be so ***weird*** going back to ***classical*** at the end of the summer.
BAND NAME
♪ *You don't haaave to!* ♫
We'll see.
BAND NAME
But this is ***already*** a summer I'll ***never*** forget.
And I'm ***glad*** it's happening with you guys.
Yeah, me too.
Heyyy! We could call our band ***Cool Summer!***
NO.

THE END

PAPER DOLLS by Ashe Samuels

LAUREN

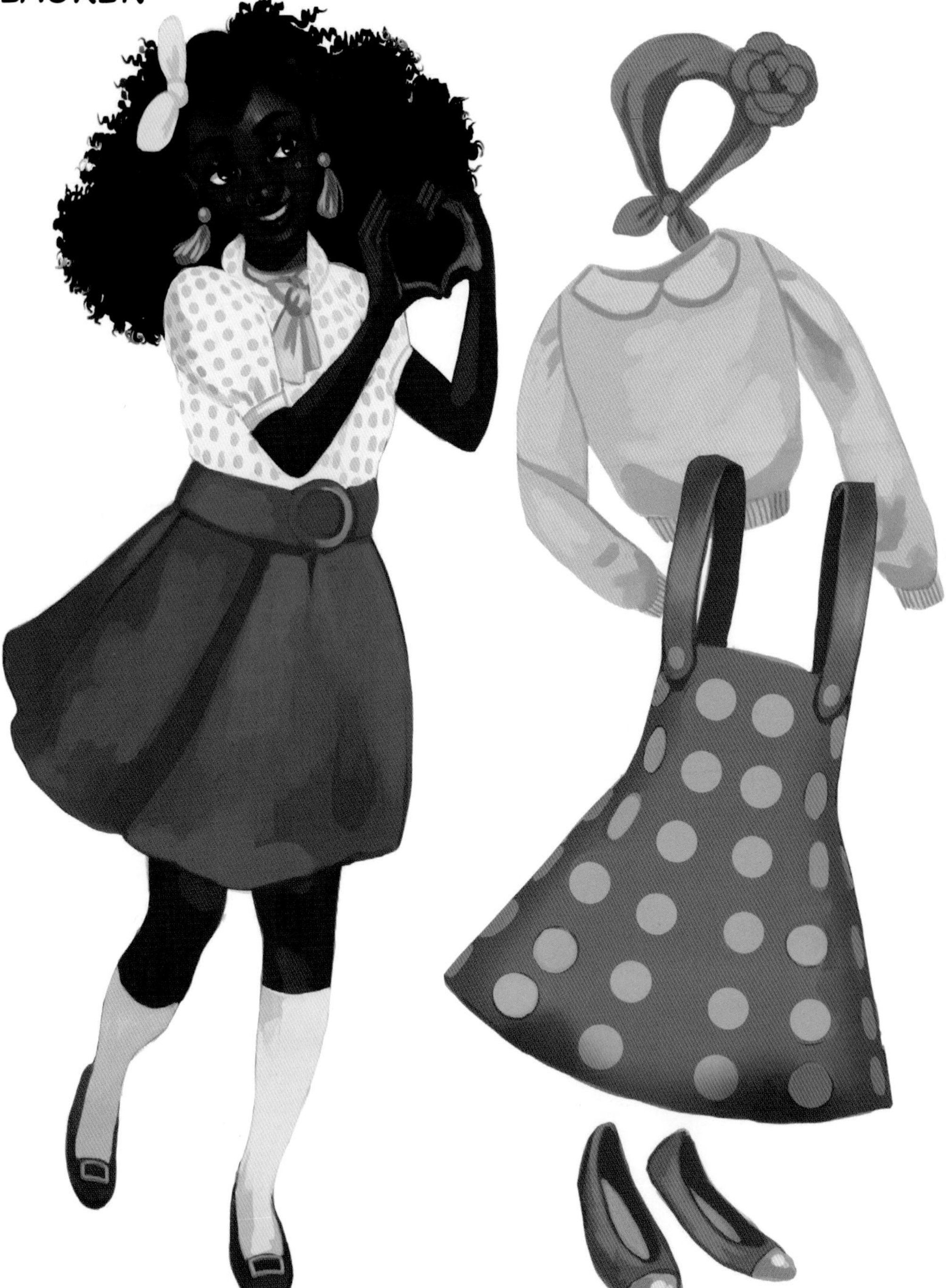

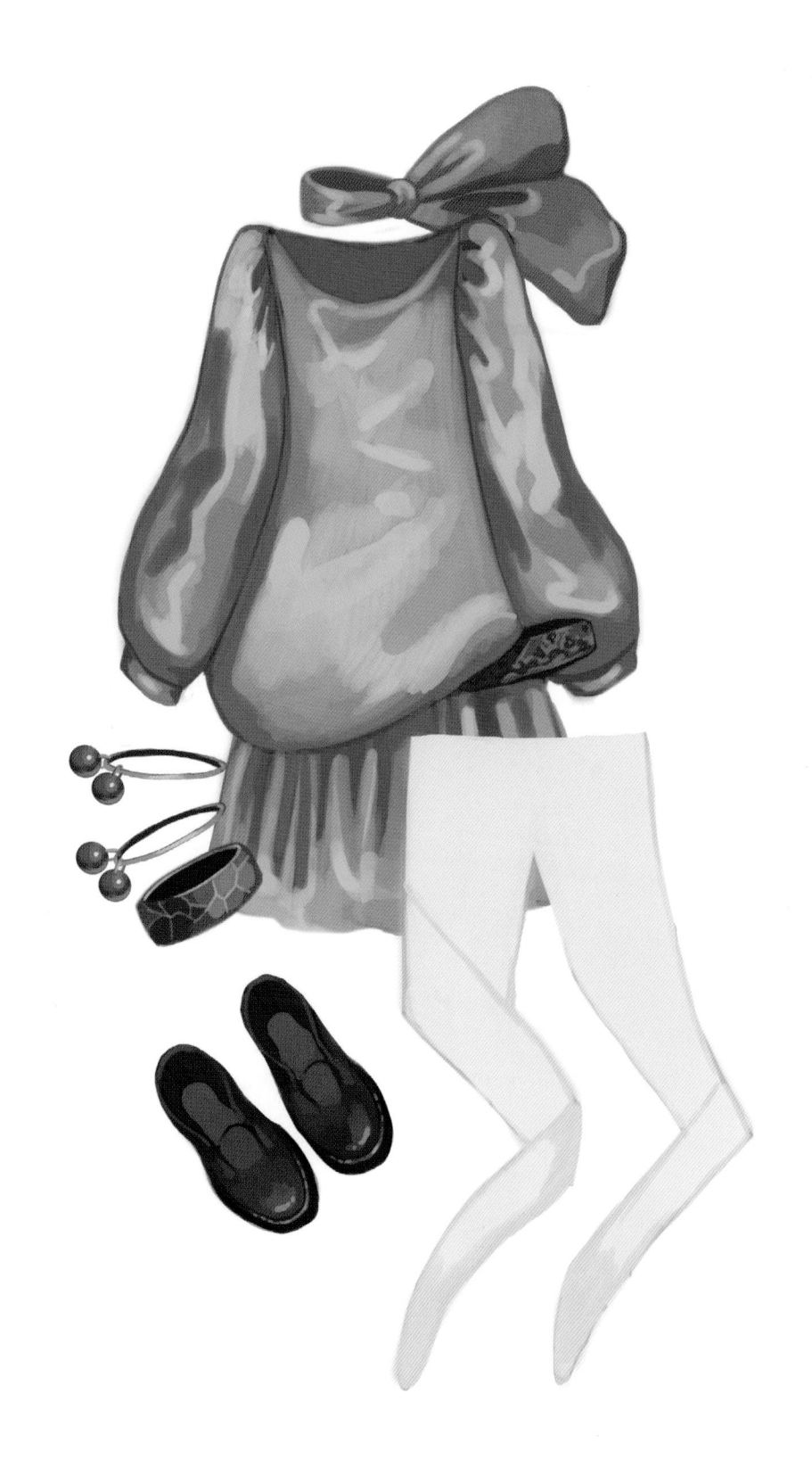

MAGGIE

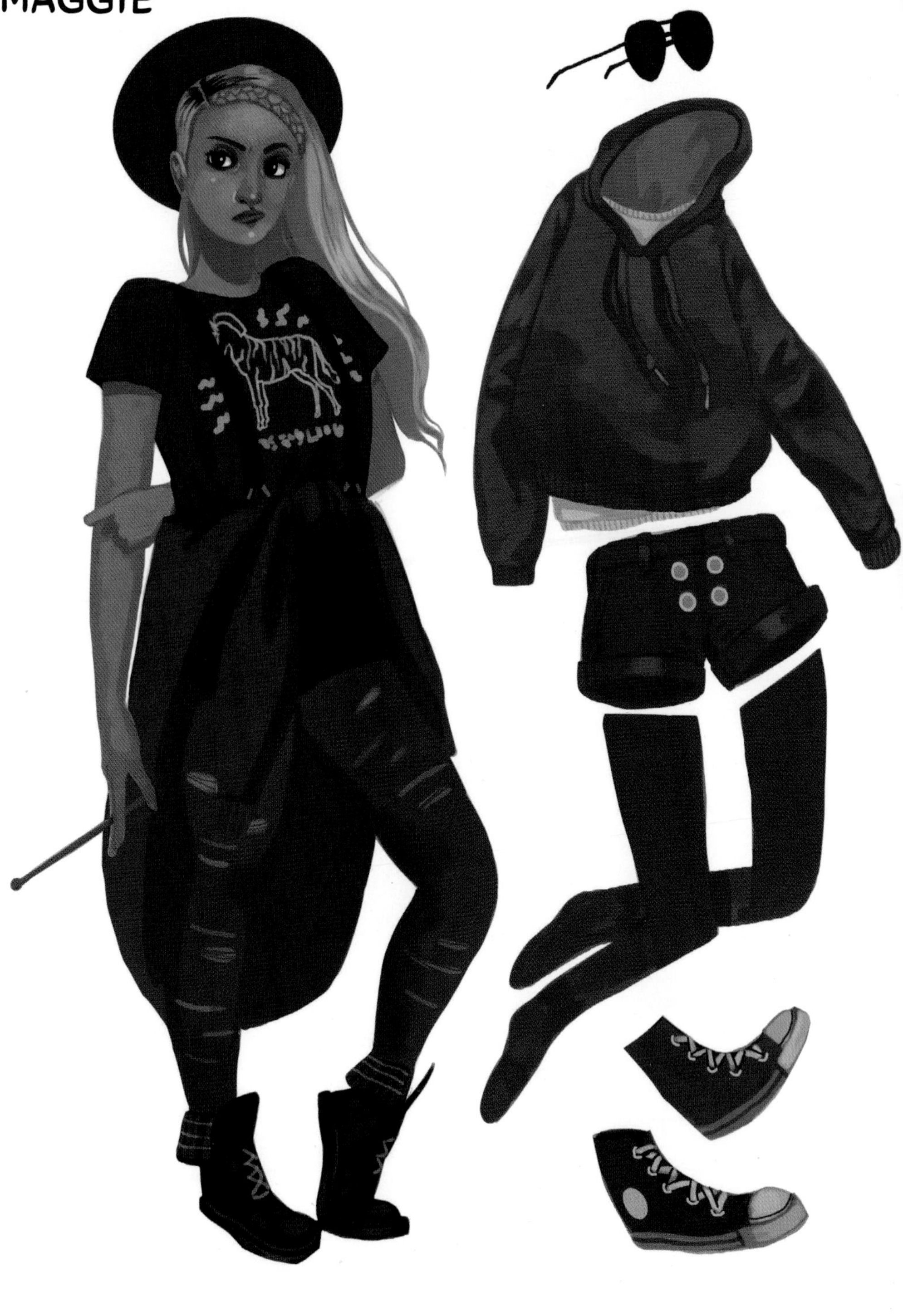

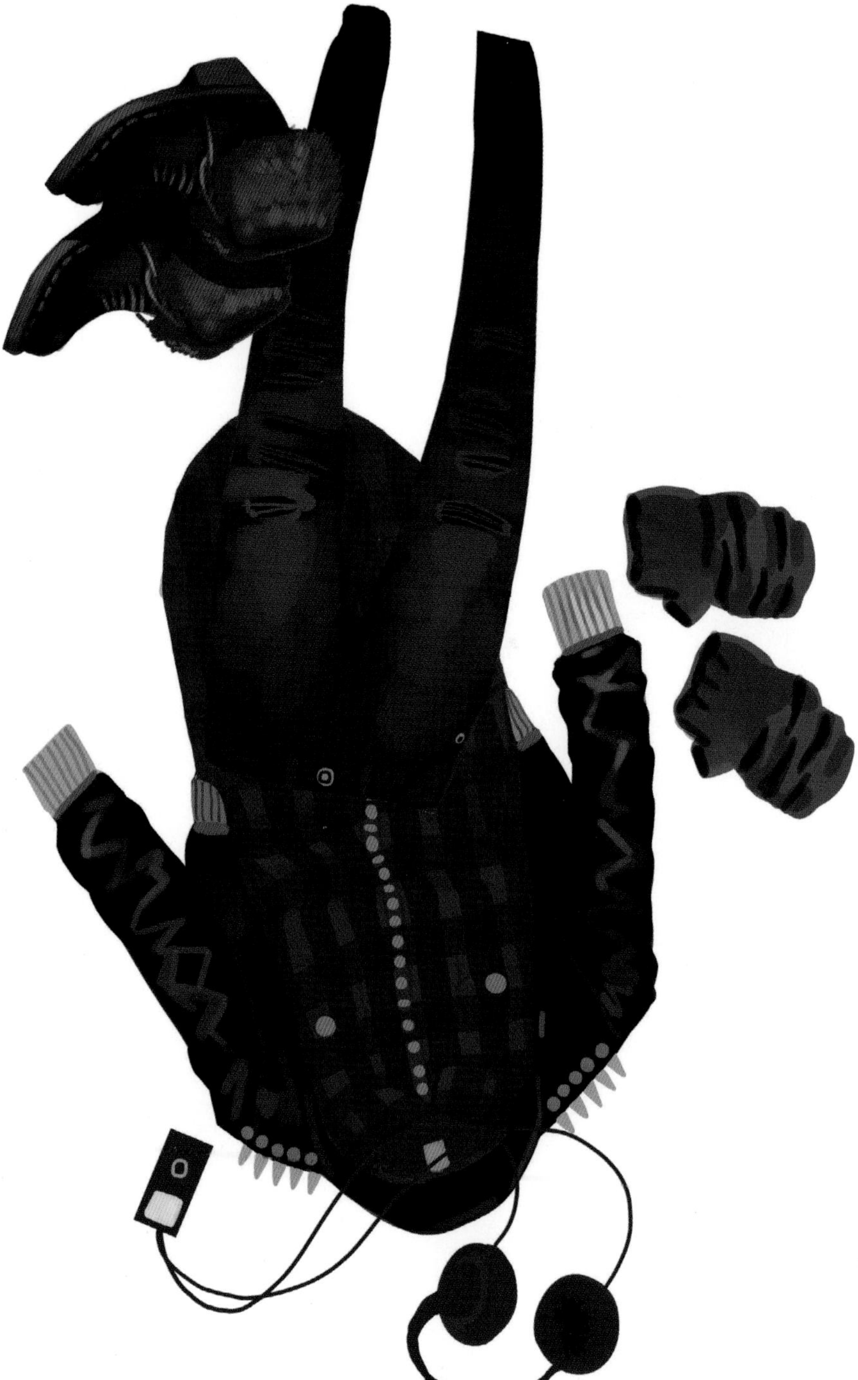

JENNI

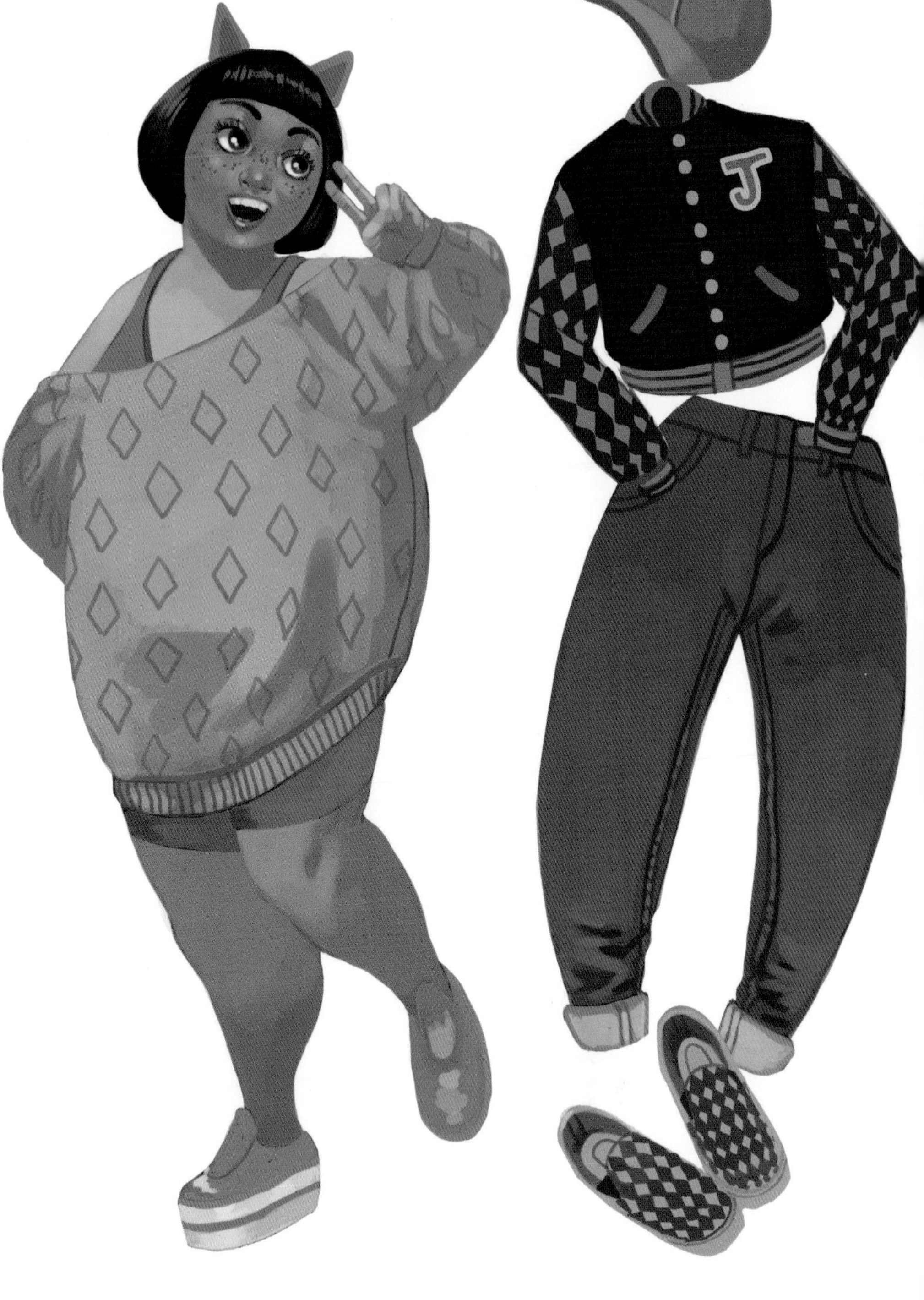
J

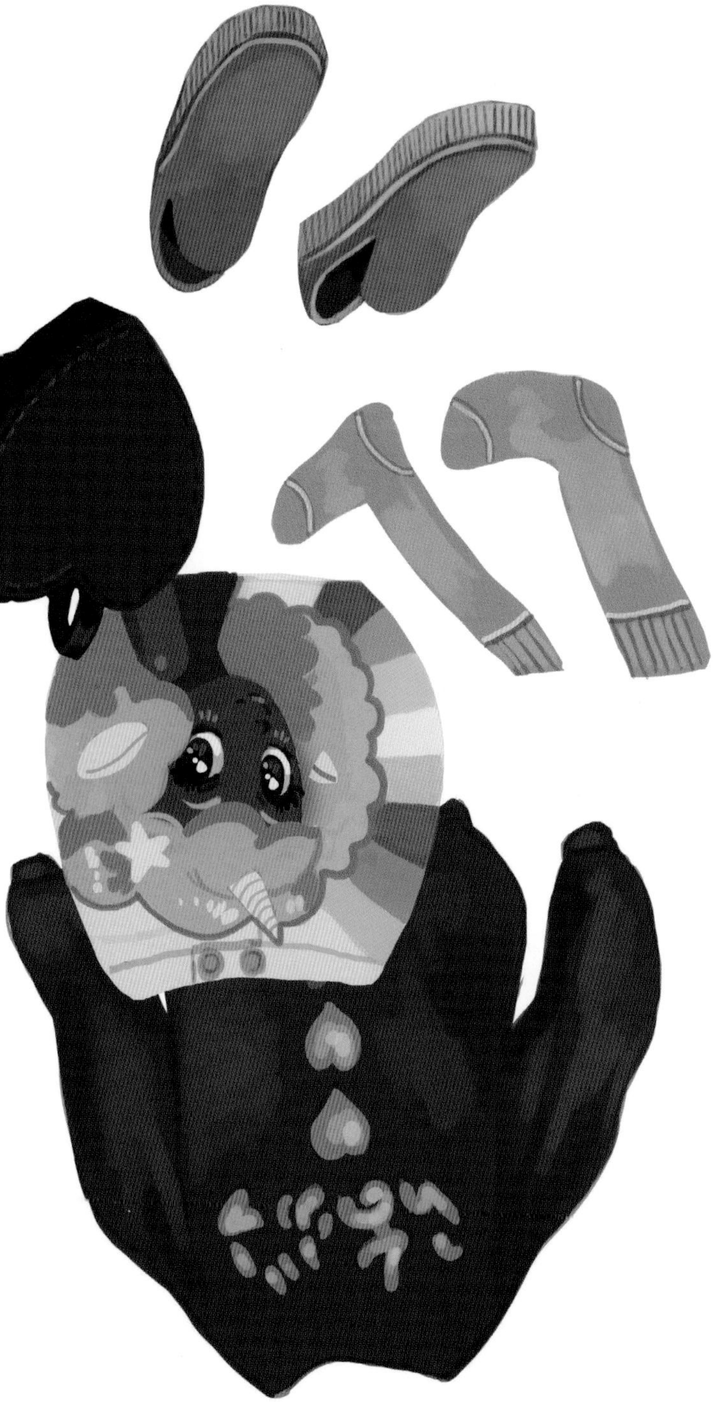

NIKA

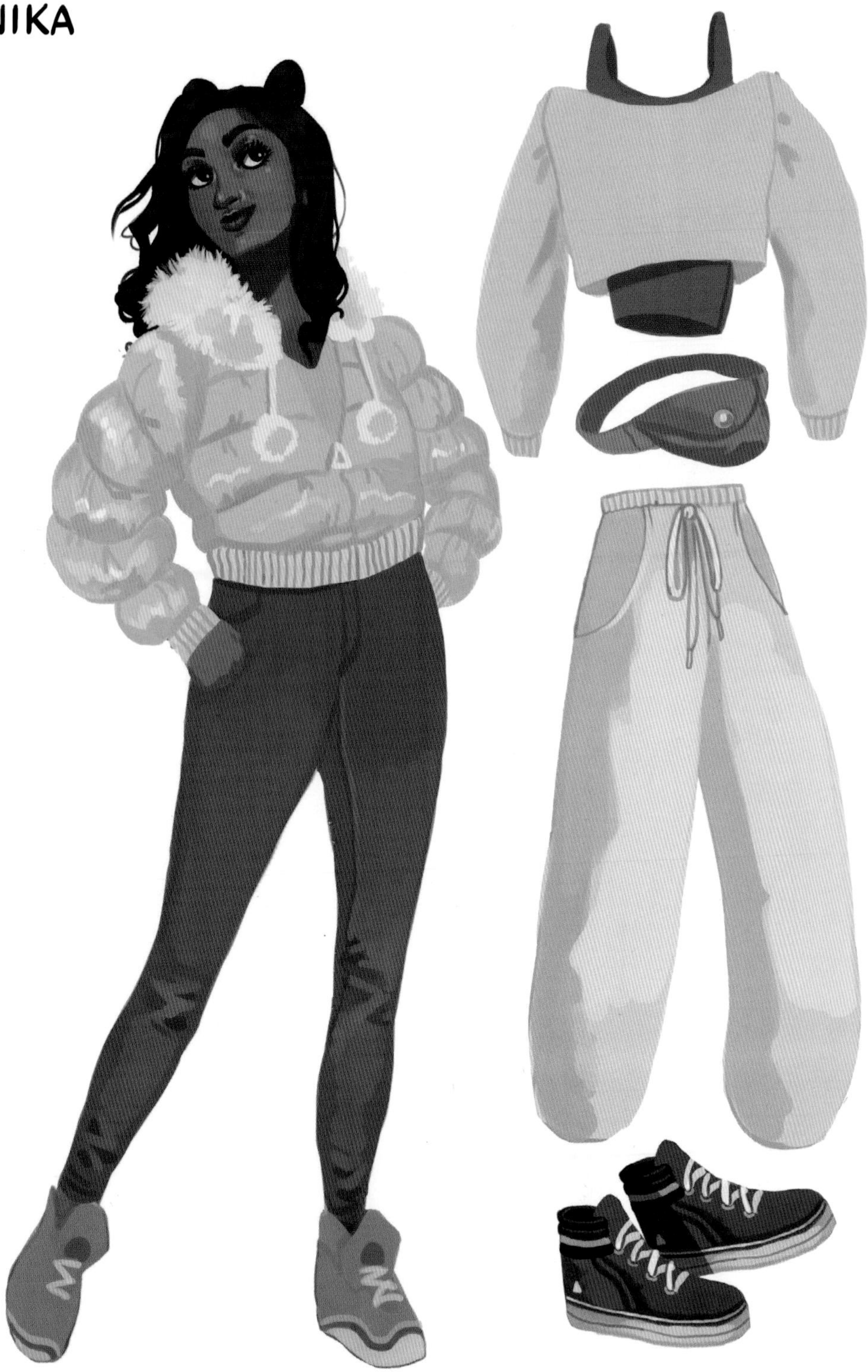

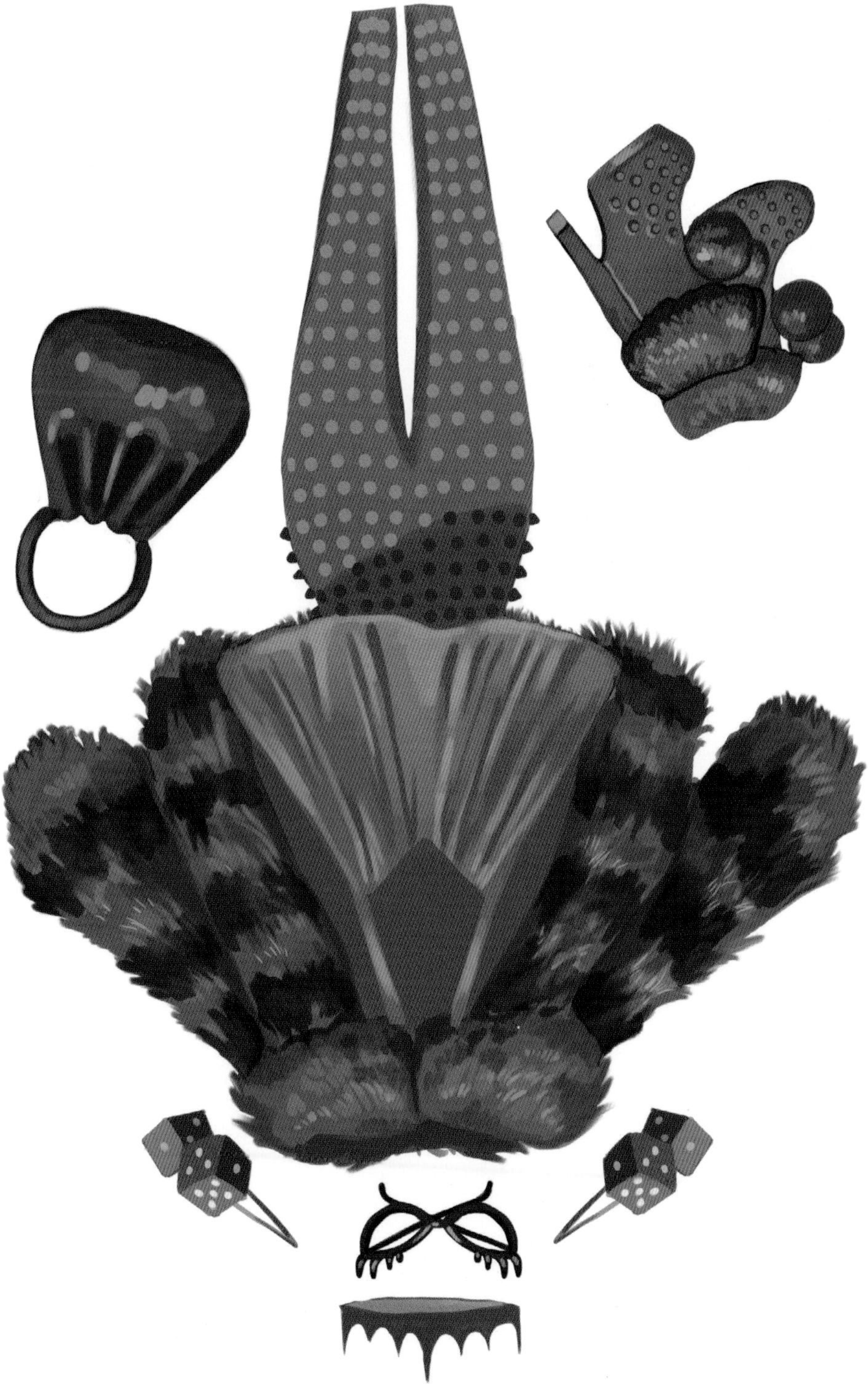

ABOUT THE CREATORS

Alex de Campi is a New York–based writer with an extensive backlist of critically acclaimed graphic novels including Eisner-nominated heist noir *Bad Girls* (Simon & Schuster) and *Twisted Romance* (Image Comics). Her most recent book was her debut prose novel *The Scottish Boy* (Unbound). Catch her YA adventure *Reversal* on her Patreon, and action-thriller *Bad Karma* serialized on Panel Syndicate. She is on most social media as @alexdecampi. She lives with her daughter, their cat, and a Deafblind pit bull named Tango.

Lara Kane is a freelance artist for animation and comics. Her career started with her participation in the short animated film *The Snowman and the Snowdog*, followed by various contributions as a storyboard artist for British animation studios such as Tandem Films, HIT Entertainment and Brown Bag Films. In comics she has worked with Dynamite, as well as collaborated with Alex de Campi on a short story for her *Semiautomagic* book. You can find her portfolio at larak.pb.gallery.

Dee Cunniffe is an award-winning Irish designer who worked for over a decade in publishing and advertising. He gave it all up to pursue his love of comics. He has colored *The Dregs* and *Eternal* at Black Mask, *The Paybacks* and *Interceptor* at Heavy Metal, *Her Infernal Descent*, *The Replacer* and *Stronghold* at Aftershock, Marvel's *Runaways*, DC's *Lucifer*, and *Redneck* at Skybound.

Cunniffe is an award-winning Irish designer who
...ed for over a decade in publishing and advertising.
... gave it all up to pursue his love of comics. He has
...ored *The Dregs* and *Eternal* at Black Mask, *The Paybacks*
...nd *Interceptor* at Heavy Metal, *Her Infernal Descent*, *The
Replacer* and *Stronghold* at Aftershock, Marvel's *Runaways*,
DC's *Lucifer*, and *Redneck* at Skybound.

Ted Brandt is a UK-based inker, though he works mostly
in the American market. He has worked for Action Lab on
the acclaimed *Raven: The Pirate Princess*, as well as Marvel's
Mighty Captain Marvel and *Steve Rogers: Captain America*. His
most known work is the Eisner- and GLAAD-nominated series
Crowded, from Image Comics.

Ashe Samuels is a commercial illustrator with a heavy
leaning toward fantasy, sci-fi, and magical realism. She also
has a perfectly healthy obsession with fashion and yearns for
the good ol' days of thrift shopping. In between projects she's
either working on a novel or playing with her roommate's cats
in an effort to "stay productive, but not really."

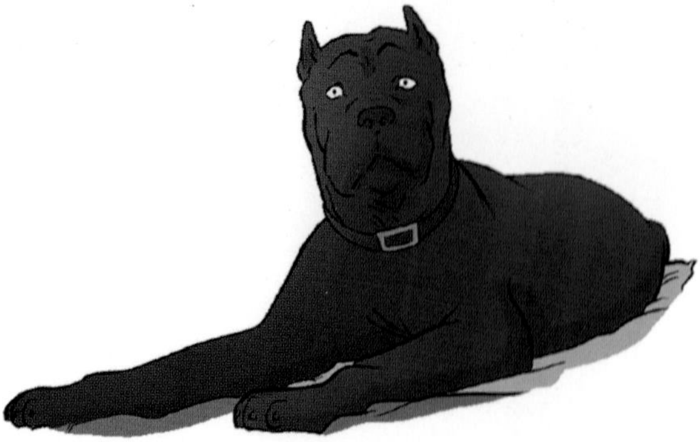

Dee
work
He
co
a

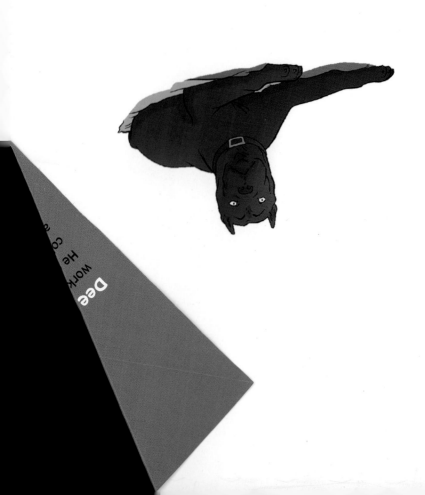